C70098100.

KT-150-897

COME THIS WAY HOME

www.rbooks.co.uk

Also by Liz Lyons

Barefoot Over Stones

COME THIS WAY HOME

Liz Lyons

TRANSWORLD IRELAND

TRANSWORLD IRELAND
an imprint of The Random House Group Limited
20 Vauxhall Bridge Road, London SW1V 2SA
www.rbooks.co.uk

First published in 2010 by Transworld Ireland
an imprint of Transworld Publishers

Copyright © Liz Lyons 2010

Liz Lyons has asserted her right under the Copyright, Designs and
Patents Act 1988 to be identified as the author of this work.

This book is a work of fiction and, except in the case of historical fact, any
resemblance to actual persons, living or dead, is purely coincidental.

A CIP catalogue record for this book
is available from the British Library.

ISBN 9781848270558

This book is sold subject to the condition that it shall not,
by way of trade or otherwise, be lent, resold, hired out,
or otherwise circulated without the publisher's prior
consent in any form of binding or cover other than that
in which it is published and without a similar condition,
including this condition, being imposed on the
subsequent purchaser.

Addresses for Random House Group Ltd companies outside the UK
can be found at: www.randomhouse.co.uk
The Random House Group Ltd Reg. No. 954009

The Random House Group Limited supports The Forest Stewardship
Council (FSC), the leading international forest-certification organization.
All our titles that are printed on Greenpeace-approved FSC-certified
paper carry the FSC logo. Our paper procurement policy can be
found at www.rbooks.co.uk/environment

Typeset in 11½/15pt Sabon by
Kestrel Data, Exeter, Devon.
Printed and bound in the UK by
Clays Ltd, Bungay, Suffolk.

2 4 6 8 10 9 7 5 3 1

Mixed Sources
Product group from well-managed
forests and other controlled sources
www.fsc.org Cert no. TT-COC-2139
© 1996 Forest Stewardship Council
FSC

For Mary and Michael Lyons

South Lanarkshire Library Service	
LN	
C70098100.	
Askews & Holts	
G	£11.99
3402308	

PART ONE

GATHERING

Home is a name, a word, it is a strong
one; stronger than magician ever spoke,
or spirit ever answered to, in the strongest
conjuration.

(Charles Dickens)

PROLOGUE

I hereby declare that this is the last will and testament of Nicholas Redmond Miller of Tobar Lodge, Tobarnaree, Co. Cork, dated this 22nd day of May, 2001. To my daughters Charlotte Miller of 3 Beacon Lofts, Gaslight Lane, Dublin 8 and Rachel Miller Jacob of Shreve Court, Old Fort Road, Dublin 9 I bequeath the sum of fifty thousand euro each along with some personal effects of mine and their mother, Sarah May Miller, deceased. Such effects are listed separately in correspondence with the offices of my solicitor Peter Dempsey & Son, Quay Street, Tobarnaree. To my daughter Regina Miller of 36 Melbourne Terrace, Tobarnaree, Co. Cork I leave the balance of my estate in its entirety comprising the primary dwelling Tobar Lodge and its contents (other than those which I have specifically set out for her sisters Rachel and Charlotte), the four holiday cottages trading as Tobar Rock Cottages, all outbuildings and their contents and the Tobar Lake fields totalling 3.92 acres. (Maps and folio details with my solicitor.) It is my sincere wish that the private fishing rights to the lake waters should be held in trust for the sole use of the residents of Tobar Lodge and Tobar Rock Cottages and not sold or otherwise leased to any club or individual. Residual monies in two accounts held in my name at the Bank of Ireland, Quay Street and Allied Irish Bank, McCauley Street, Tobarnaree are to be used to cover funeral expenses. I wish to be buried alongside my wife Sarah May in the Miller family plot in St Augustine's graveyard.

Every now and then Gina Miller took out her father's will and read it through. She knew almost by heart how the sentences flowed one into the next. The previous seven years had been ordained by her father's specific wishes, which absolved Gina of some of the responsibility for the way her life had shaped itself. It wasn't that she was unhappy with her lot as such. In fact there were parts of it she considered charmed, and chief amongst those charms were her cherished daughter and the home place they shared. However, something about holding the pages of the document in her hands gave her comfort, reminding her that she had no choice but to be here. Her finger traced the generous arc of her father's signature, its elegant lines a reflection of the fastidious man she remembered.

She and her sisters had lost count of the occasions that their father had told them that should anything happen to him three copies of his sealed will were tucked into the slimline map drawer of the writing bureau in the lodge's vast living room. They were under strict and frequent instruction to read it before they proceeded to finalize a solitary strand of his affairs. 'Yes, Dad,' they would wearily reply in the same way as if he had reminded them to drive carefully, or save tasty scraps for Crosby, his loyal cattle dog, or indeed carry out any one of the numerous instructions he felt compelled to give them at every juncture of their lives.

When the time came his daughters found their three names in order of age written out with a black pen on the ridged thickness of a milk-white envelope. *Charlotte, Regina, Rachel*. Their father had never given in to pressure from other people who used casual abbreviations of the first names that he and Sarah had chosen with deliberate care for their daughters. He clung stubbornly to the formality he favoured and when someone asked after Lottie and Gina he would answer patiently, as if to a forgetful or inattentive child, that Charlotte and Regina were absolutely fine, thank you very much. At least Rachel had never been able to tolerate anyone shortening her name and so in his youngest daughter he found an ally in the battle to keep things in just the order they should be.

His middle daughter had known the bare bones of his intentions for the lodge and Tobar Rock Cottages while he was alive, but they had seemed to Gina like a wild notion that might never come to pass and upon which it would be reckless to depend. Anything could happen in the interim, she felt, and a small part of her hoped that some change in her own circumstances might make his plan unworkable and he would have to think again. Neither she nor her sisters thought they would have to implement his wishes so soon because he had been in such fine health and always in such control, yet the will had been barely a year old when they had unlocked the bureau with the brass key from the neat bunch he always kept in the inside breast pocket of his jacket. The keys had been handed back to them along with all the small, random belongings left behind in a hospital room when their owner leaves unexpectedly: a life reduced to the jumbled contents of a clear plastic bag marked by a name and a date of death. *Miller, Nicholas Redmond, 3rd June 2002*. His worn wallet containing bank and library cards and a modest sum of cash in neat folds was stored by Gina on the top shelf of the kitchen dresser behind the fern-patterned serving platter, a wedding gift so treasured by Sarah Miller that her daughter was always nervous on the rare occasion she took it down to use.

Gina felt it would be wrong to interfere with the personal belongings of such a private man even if he was in no position to be appalled by such wilful intrusion. Her reluctance on that point remained a helpful barometer of her finances. As yet they had not fallen into such shaky repair that she needed to break her promise to herself and seek short-lived solace in the proceeds of his abandoned wallet.

Nicholas Miller's final wishes had been faithfully adhered to; the straightforward set of instructions invited no demurral from any of his daughters, although Gina didn't doubt that, when her back was turned, there had been more than a hint of a raised eyebrow or shrugged shoulder from the other two at her father's implied favouritism. But she had never asked him for anything and consequently she refused to feel guilty for what she had received.

Together she and her sisters had managed to share a wry smile when they read the details of where their father wanted to be buried. It was Lottie who articulated what her two younger sisters were also thinking but wouldn't dream of saying aloud. 'Good God, he didn't even trust us to bury him in the right place, girls! Where exactly did he think we were about to shove him? I'll tell you this much, we'd better cancel that slot in the crematorium or we'll have a bull of a ghost on our hands with revenge on his mind.'

Rachel and Gina had shushed Lottie, thinking that it was terrible to speak so irreverently about their dead father. In the silence that followed they all wondered if he would have felt the need to give a son such specific instructions or would he have trusted that a man might instinctively know the right thing to do? They suspected that in their father's eyes they had never quite grown up or at least not according to the careful way he had plotted out for them. In their many colourful clashes, after which her younger sisters had both envied her courage and dreaded the next outburst in almost equal measure, Lottie had challenged their father that a trio of daughters had left him feeling short-changed in the family stakes. She would brazenly argue that all he really wanted was a single son to carry his name and mirror his ambitions into the future.

Faced with her considerable fury Nicholas Miller would offer a sanguine smile, as if he could not even get his head around the foolishness of what his eldest daughter had the repeated cheek to suggest. Over time her father would conclude that his denial had been wasted on his headstrong daughter. Lottie remained steadfast in her belief that she and the sisters that followed her had been nothing more than an accumulated and irreversible disappointment; a gaggle of girls when all he had really wanted was a boy to call his own. A bewildered Nicholas was left to wonder exactly when and where he had gone wrong. He had loved his daughters intensely, protecting them against anything that could possibly harm them and pointing them back to the right track when he felt they were straying.

Although shocked by the suddenness of his death Gina remembered how they had felt a tangible peace saying goodbye to their father because he was either with their mother or alternatively in a place where such far-fetched aspirations had no bearing whatsoever. Neither she nor her sisters could, hand on heart, swear that they believed in any afterlife, but both parents being gone felt like a closed circle of sorts. Widowed and alone their father had seemed far from happy and his death relieved them of the pressure of feeling responsible for his despondency yet more or less powerless to solve it.

Looking at her copy of the document so long after her father composed its precise and irrefutable wording Gina noticed how the print had faded in the intervening years and the delicate pages had grown shabby with age. She refolded the sheets along the creases that had become set with time and placed it back in the leather folder in her desk that contained all the important documents life had given her reason to store. Their father's imposing oak bureau remained in the living room, having been brightened up in no small way by the addition on top of silver framed photographs showing the smiling faces of her daughter and of Rachel's children. Yet Gina remained happier at her informal perch in the alcove shadowed by the lodge's impressive staircase: the workspace she had assigned to herself close to the central hub of the house suited her modest needs perfectly.

She had new guests arriving to the Tobar Rock Cottages that afternoon for whom she needed to complete preparations. Taking shortcuts was never an option because the cottages were in the middle of nowhere and so had to build a reputation for excellence that would compensate for their remote location. Kind word of mouth and good online reviews would, she hoped, continue to maintain a resilient business over time. She set about getting everything ready at an efficient pace. Stripped beds had to be remade and all the laundry sitting waiting in unruly mounds in the lodge's back kitchen needed to be sorted, washed and hung out to dry. By mid morning on every summer Monday the cottages' flagstone floors had been scrubbed and, weather permitting, the windows opened wide inviting the freshening lake breeze in to air the cosy rooms. Gina liked to add fresh flowers and greenery in wide-necked pottery vases to the deep downstairs window sills, nothing fancy or bought but whatever hardy flowering plants thrived among the fruit trees and shrubbery in the somewhat neglected borders of the garden. It bothered her a little that she hadn't inherited either of her parents' natural skill with plants. With stubborn persistence she managed to keep most of what had been left to her alive but the garden had never regained the sense of well-managed bounty that they had both achieved so easily. The cottages were painted white throughout and furnished with mismatched but sympathetic pieces that Nicholas Miller had collected with considerable dedication at auction rooms throughout the country once the plan for the self-catering enterprise had taken root in his thinking.

Far too many tasks and not enough time for any of them had become the pattern of Gina's life. Yet she never felt more at ease than when she had a list of jobs to complete; the need to achieve always seemed to outweigh any pleasure derived from tasks already accomplished. As she crossed the courtyard that led to the cottages at a brisk pace, carrying a hamper brimming with clean sheets and fresh towels, Gina wondered if her father would have been happy with the way she was running the business he had created. She didn't have to try hard to hear his probable commentary as she set about putting every small detail in order. It was ridiculous that she should still crave his approval but she did; she had long been resigned to the fact. She unfurled the fresh sheets in Sycamore Cottage and watched with satisfaction as any niggling creases disappeared when she tucked the corners tightly under the mattress. Falling into a rhythm of work that soothed she turned her thoughts to her summer guests, hoping they would quickly settle in.

Chapter One

The stretch of houses on Lighthouse Road appeared to lean toward the sea as if they might whisper their treasured secrets at any moment. Emmet Kinsella loved the spot where he had found their home tucked into one of the quieter stretches of the north Dublin coastline. Previous owners had christened it Watershine Cottage and even though Emmet had extended it boldly and well beyond the intimate dimensions implied by that name it hadn't seemed right to change it. After all, it was the evocative name that first caught his attention in an auctioneer's window and the house had woven its own private magic on him and Jill when they came to the viewing a decade before. In the intervening years his construction business had prospered and they could have easily afforded something grander but neither could summon any real enthusiasm to move from where they had settled so happily. The character of the house was something both knew might not be easily recreated elsewhere.

The sight of their house as he spun his car into the gateway each evening still reminded him how expectant and proud they had been to call it home. It was a fulfilment of a dream for Emmet to end up as far away as he could from the landlocked place he had come from. Jill had contentedly fallen in with his plan, charmed by the house's potential and her husband's passion for a place looking out to the sea and all the freedom for mind and body he imagined that might mean. Jill had moved about the country so much as a child that she was surprised at how ready she was to love their house; she soon developed a fierce sense of possessive pride toward it.

A shaft of mid-morning sunshine cut through an otherwise overcast sky. Standing on the weather-bleached deck, Emmet traced the tumbles of unruly sea water. There were one or two working boats to be seen but no one had taken to the water to sail for pleasure. Emmet wasn't surprised. It was early in the week and slacking off work seemed in bad taste when imminent job losses threatened so many. By Friday morning, however, good manners might start to wane and the small, privately owned craft would begin to emerge, marking the beginning of a leisurely countdown to the weekend. He hadn't taken out his own boat since the previous year and he thought it unlikely that he would feel like sailing any time soon. Selling it rather than letting it sit idle might be the wisest option, except he couldn't think of anyone who might want to buy it with the way things were. He had taught his son the rudiments of sailing over several lazy weekends in previous summers and it had given him enormous pleasure that Fionn was a natural at something he himself had tried long and hard to master. The biggest joy of being a parent had come from seeing his young son cut his teeth at something new and realize that he was capable of learning much more than his father could ever hope to teach him. Pride had mixed with humility as he saw that his child was both of him and, at the same time, far more than him.

Even without recourse to his diary, which was a good deal less thronged these days, Emmet knew he had a meeting scheduled for eleven in the Wheatley Hotel. It was about a construction job that he wasn't sure would ever materialize but he felt it better to market the case for his firm's involvement in the project should it happen. It appeared that future expansion of Cedar Build would have to be put on indefinite hold and Emmet found it very frustrating to have limits put on the considerable ambitions he had for his company. The excess money that had made even the wildly improbable seem possible in previous years had slipped stealthily away from the scene the way a startled child might, having accidentally broken a much-loved ornament.

Warming his hands against a mug of hot sugary coffee (the thought of anything more substantial for breakfast persisted in making his stomach turn), he tried hard to think of an escape from the situation in which he and Jill found themselves. Everyone Emmet knew and trusted had said that time would heal the wound of losing Fionn. Those friends, compelled to say more to counteract his edgy and blatantly unconvinced silence, had added that things might well get worse before they got any better. On that miserable point he would readily concur. He had found the past months unbearable, each one more painful than the last.

This week was going to be tougher than all the others because it was the week that their son would have celebrated his eleventh birthday and Emmet couldn't think of a single thing that he might say to Jill. Or at least anything that he imagined she would linger in his company long enough to hear. Pain had trampled on their ability to connect with one another. Before it had been so easy; he'd thought that link could never be severed. But now words passed warily between them, serving to sting rather than salve their common wound. Emmet had always thought of them as utterly solid but Fionn's death had taken the legs from under them and the scale of shared grief mocked their shortcomings as a couple.

He had been mulling over the idea of booking them a holiday

in Tobarnaree, one of the places where Jill had lived as a child, but he feared that the depression that had wrapped itself around his wife might make her dismiss his plan out of hand. He had become accustomed to her rejection of him but he didn't want to invite further upset when they were coping so poorly already. What was left of their marriage resembled the fragmented rooms of a deserted house steadily surrendering to dereliction.

Less than a month before she had angrily rejected his suggestion that they go away to their Majorcan holiday home for a break, arguing that memories of past times there would make such a trip totally impossible. 'Why don't you just go on your own and leave me alone?' she had snapped, before bluntly adding that she wasn't sure if she would ever return to the island. Though he understood the grief that prompted her to say this, he couldn't accept the finality of it. Perhaps he'd pushed the issue before she was ready but the prospect of never going there again was far too bleak for Emmet to contemplate.

Yet Jill was adamant. Everywhere she would have to witness the gleeful faces of children at pavement tables outside restaurants scooping melting ice cream into greedy mouths or splashing in sun-warmed water while carefree parents kept them within the safe harbour of eyeline and earshot. What would she and Emmet do every day with no work to occupy them except try miserably to avoid mentioning Fionn's name? They could do that much more easily at home where they could each withdraw from one another to different quarters of the house and avoid any conversation more intimate than the relaying of a phone message or a reminder to pay a bill.

Emmet knew that there was a risk their marriage could fall apart from the strain of losing their child, but he was adamant that was not going to be their story – not if there was anything he could do to prevent it. In his heart he felt he would be lost without his wife. The strength of her obvious desire to move away from their shared space was matched only by his determination to keep her by his side where he felt she truly belonged. That was why he'd had the idea of returning to Tobarnaree. Of all the places her family had lived Jill had frequently said that the small and insignificant scrap of a town in the southwest was where she had been the happiest.

She had told him how she had threatened never to forgive her parents for uprooting her at thirteen from the friends and the home she loved. But her father had been offered a transfer for work and they were moving and that was most definitely that. You never considered refusing when the bosses of the bank told you to take your family and your life by the scruff of the neck and pack them without delay in luggage crates bound for somewhere new. Besides, it was a promotion that Jim Cassidy had craved for a long time: a bigger branch, a new house and a strange town at the other side of the country beckoned for himself and his family. Sentimentality didn't get a look beyond the door of his future plans.

A much bigger bedroom (its garish decor inherited from a previous, obviously more daring occupant) and a garden to lounge in did little to compensate the barely teenage Jill for the tentative sense of belonging she had left behind her in Tobarnaree. As she watched her parents unload the last of their belongings from the car in front of the new house she fought back tears she knew were pointless to shed. Instead she bit down hard on her lower lip; so hard that a trickle of blood filled her mouth with its salt taste. She swallowed it together with her disappointment at losing her friends and her home when she needed them most but could admit it least.

Even years later Jill would argue that thirteen was a most unsuitable age at which to move a child beset by new and awkward shyness and expect any sort of a smooth outcome. Emmet wouldn't doubt that she had meant every word of her adolescent threat never to forgive her parents because from his experience of being married to her he knew that once her mind was made up she settled with stubborn ease into her chosen decision. It was just that she had never taken against him before and he found her cruel exclusion of him damning.

Her outspoken nature was one of the things that had attracted him to her from the first moment he had experienced her considerable temper. Along with a few others he was on a train returning from a hugely enjoyable but heavy stag weekend. Lost in their own conversation and laughter they were oblivious to an elderly couple who, having failed to secure a seat, stood stranded and a bit bewildered next to their holdall at the end of the carriage. Jill interrupted their nonsense talk to ask sarcastically if their thirty-something padded backsides were quite comfortable on their seats while pensioners stood ignored at the end of the train. Emmet could still recall the furious energy with which his future wife had spat the words in their direction. Equal parts ashamed and smitten he rose immediately to surrender his seat while deciding there and then that this was a woman whom he would definitely have to get to know better. One of the other men in his party who had also vacated his seat winked at him to signal that he was well aware what Emmet had in mind, but much to Emmet's relief, his massive hangover meant he didn't have the energy to take advantage of a perfect opportunity for embarrassing his friend.

Alone with his thoughts, and without the teasing he would have doubtlessly endured if his company was in full sober health, Emmet contemplated how best to approach the formidable woman sitting half a carriage away from him. Adrenaline lifted his hangover with astonishing speed, his mind filling with the far more urgent question of what he could say to capture her attention and how she was likely to react.

It took the length of journey from Portlaoise to Heuston before he judged Jill had cooled down sufficiently to chance asking her for her phone number. The interim had given him plenty of time to commit to memory the look of her while she read her newspaper and did him the favour of pretending not to notice that he was watching her every move for clues. Her honey-coloured hair was pulled back casually from a face almost free of make-up. Cobalt-blue eyes scanned the morning headlines soaking in their news while not betraying a discernible reaction to any of it. She was dressed smartly in grey trousers and a crisp white shirt. A loose silver bracelet watch lay visible against the fair skin of her wrist. She wore a blue jewelled costume ring on one hand but nothing on her wedding finger, much to Emmet's satisfaction. He was overawed by his compulsion to keep his eyes on her at all costs. A businesswoman, he decided, because he was certain that the impressive streak of bossiness displayed had benefited from a good deal of practice. She flashed a warm smile at the elderly couple whose seats she had arranged with such efficiency and her future husband was pathetically jealous that they had, however briefly, monopolized her attention. He could still recall now the power of that envious feeling and how he had wanted no one, not even a day-tripping pair in their seventies, to stand between him and his chance to gaze in her direction.

He followed her along the platform at Heuston Station eager to catch her attention but still wondering what in the world he might say. She spun around when he tapped her on the shoulder. He began by apologizing for the incident on the train and she made his task easier by admitting that she might have overreacted. A touch. She scribbled her phone number on a scrap of paper torn from the back page of her *Irish Times* and told him to ask for the top-floor flat when he rang. She flashed an indulgent smile at him before dashing toward the cluster of green buses whose engines droned at the station's Liffey exit.

Emmet worked like a demon for the rest of the day, smiling even when things went catastrophically wrong, as they were more or less bound to when his workmates were all in the horrors of drink, barely able to grasp the simplest details of the job at hand while their heads pounded. He liked the simple prettiness of her name written with a black biro on the torn shred of newspaper. Jill Cassidy. He had never thought about the name before but now it sounded perfect for such an attractive girl. Surrounded by oblivious company he allowed the sound of it to make him smile as he repeated it silently to himself. Failing to return to Dublin on the last train the night before and giving in to another unplanned bout of heavy drinking suddenly seemed like the brightest slip-up he had ever made.

After their first phone call he found out that she worked in administration at the Raglan Hotel just a couple of streets away from the small building project he was working on. He wasn't sure if he had fate or chance to thank for putting them on the same train that morning but he was grateful if either of the two had conspired in his favour. It all seemed like a lifetime ago but the memory of their first meeting still had the power to sustain him.

Buoyed by the comfort of reminiscing, he decided he would go ahead and book somewhere in Tobarnaree that very day but he would keep the destination a surprise until the last minute so Jill had no opportunity to refuse to go. He knew that in her estimation he hadn't had a good idea in a very long time but he had to keep trying to repair what had been broken by a moment's misfortune. He refused to admit that he couldn't salvage something from a mess of his own making.

They had lost a son and it hurt him that in everyone's mind his right to sympathy and understanding seemed to come a very poor second to that of the grieving mother. Unlike Jill, Emmet had returned to work quickly after the accident because he knew that immersing himself in the job was the best chance he had for avoiding total collapse. His prompt return to his normal life had made people assume he had at least partially recovered, but the truth was that he was afraid if he stopped he would fall apart completely. He'd found that it was possible to function well at work while their home life slowly disintegrated but even the power work had to distract him had begun to diminish in recent weeks.

In his sunlit office at the top of the house Emmet logged on to Tobarnaree's tourist website and found links to accommodation in and around the town. He knew that the Cassidy family had no relatives remaining there who could suggest somewhere pleasant for them to stay. They had passed through half a lifetime ago and would have left only fleeting and scattered memories in the minds of those who once had called them friends. Undeterred, Emmet was confident that he could rely on his instinct to choose somewhere perfect for them as he had done so many times before. The three of them had had some great holidays together before they had lost Fionn. Suppressing the tears that began to well in his eyes he got on with the job of planning a summer break. It always felt like a victory of sorts when he managed to keep distress and its toxicity sealed away. Getting on with things when under the most dreadful strain had become one of the talents that Emmet Kinsella had regretful reason to practise.

There was a hotel and a handful of guesthouses which all looked pleasant enough but he felt it was vital they had their own space where they could talk or shout things through, if Jill proved willing. He followed the self-catering link to Tobar Rock Cottages. He couldn't explain why but immediately something about them suggested the type of place that might hatch a little miracle. The four homely-looking cottages named Alder, Rowan, Sycamore and Beech had their backs set to the edge of Tobar Lake and close to the craggy-looking lodge where the owner of the cottage complex lived. Tobar Rock Cottages traded as a family-run enterprise and that detail appealed to him, as if the warmth and intimacy of a family welcome might make a difference to the outcome of their holiday. In the past he and Jill had been such a tight and happy unit; having their own space but within a family setting might remind Jill of what she risked losing.

Emmet scanned the webpage that outlined the folklore attached to the cottages' tranquil lake setting. Apparently the lake's deep waters, sheltered by the imposing shadow of Tobar Rock, were lucky and each new local chieftain would come to swim there to celebrate his accession. His followers would then drink the icy water from their chieftain's cupped hands to give them tenacity and courage in future battles. Emmet grinned to himself as he read the neatly packaged site history; the country was rife with this type of dubious local legend. But the cottages looked cosy and not at all flashy and crucially they were a million miles away from the type of exotic places they had holidayed in recent years.

He raised his eyes to a framed photograph of his son hanging on the wall above the desk taken in a Phnom Penh market the summer before. Emmet had captured his white-haired and cheeky boy making faces at a tray of ugly-looking catfish on a fish stall. He could still remember the foul smell and the deeply unimpressed local woman, legs astride a wooden bench, wielding a gutting knife in the direction of the strangers who she knew had no intention of buying any of her exotic catch. He knew it was irrational, but a part of Emmet persisted in feeling that if he could somehow return to Cambodia and the safe distance of a year before he might find his inquisitive son still wandering the smelly and noisy market eager for adventure and memories to bring back home. He forced his sad eyes back to the computer screen and tried to focus on the more mundane attractions of Tobarnaree. If change was what they needed surely here was as good a place as any other to begin.

Emmet read how the cottages attached to Tobar Lodge had been painstakingly restored in the late nineties by a retired farmer named Nicholas Miller, father of the current owner, who had made them available to let as holiday homes. There had been an extensive tract of farm land attached to the lodge but most of it had been split from the house and sold off during difficult years when farmers struggled along with everyone else in the country to make anything approaching a comfortable living. The lake and the surrounding fields still belonged to Tobar Lodge and use of that amenity was available to the cottage guests.

Reading the background information, Emmet was overcome by powerful memories of his own father working at his farm week after miserable week and yet at the end of the year having nothing to show for ever more calloused hands other than a barn of hay and that only if the Mayo summer had surrendered enough of its sunshine. As a disillusioned teenager Emmet had sworn to himself that he would grasp with both hands whatever opportunities life might offer apart from treading the path of drudgery worn by his father.

He left school at sixteen and Paddy Kinsella's house when he'd earned enough to rent a damp one-roomed flat at the end of a narrow Castlebar lane. While there he battled with regular outbreaks of loneliness; looking back he might call it depression, but at the time depression had seemed like something that happened only to other people. Yet he knew in his heart that the house he had left possessed no antidote for any of life's afflictions. He would have company of sorts in his father but that was company he was reluctant to keep.

From Castlebar he went back and forth between Dublin and a handful of English cities where there were building contracts on offer. Short bouts in London, Birmingham and Manchester followed, finding work and leaving just as quickly when a better opportunity presented itself somewhere new. Once the habit of moving established itself he realized that it was a learned skill like any other. The more he practised moving on and cutting ties the easier it inevitably became. Had he not met Jill Cassidy he would most likely have stayed like that; content to hover at the edge without ever properly belonging anywhere or to anyone. Certainly no other woman had managed to hold his interest for long.

When he returned to his home place for Paddy Kinsella's funeral more than a decade later he didn't have a single misgiving in arranging for a sale hoarding from an auctioneer's firm in Westport to be nailed to a wooden stake at the farmyard's shabby entrance gate. By then he had the tentative promise of a future with Jill and a home in Dublin to get back to and he was in a hurry to do just that.

The new owners of Paddy Kinsella's farm fell in helpless love with the heather-clad hills visible from his mother's kitchen windows, which were then cobwebbed and dusty. He didn't doubt that the lush violet haze of the hills glowing in the forgiving light of early evening played a part in securing the deal. While their inquisitive boys explored the ramshackle garden, a sum a little below the asking price was settled on because Emmet had no interest in delaying or indeed risking the deal by insisting on the last penny. His bank accounts were thriving without having to pluck more money from a young couple who could probably ill afford the added outlay. It satisfied him that what he considered a minor flaw of the deal would cause immense annoyance to Paddy Kinsella. If it was possible for someone to feel cheated from beyond the grave then Emmet hoped that his father was suffering that helpless fate. Being different from his father in every manner possible was the guiding principle of his life.

He wished the young couple luck with their dream of owning a self-sufficient rural idyll, wagering they would need it in spades. He hoped the couple's children, then busily playing hide and seek, might have a happier time there than he ever had. Remembering how his mother loved the view from her kitchen, he hoped too that the heathery hills might shelter a family more at ease in one another's company than his own had ever been.

All the old neighbours said he could have held on to the home place for sentiment's sake because it wasn't as if he was short of a few pounds. They were right of course because Emmet Kinsella had indeed done better for himself than he had dared imagine. What the neighbours certainly must have suspected was that he would have given away the house for nothing if it meant he could erase his memories of living there. Etched into his mind were the painful procession of days and weeks returning from school to a house that was far worse than just empty. Touching traces of his absent mother were everywhere at first but the rough and careless attitude of his father meant that the house soon began to show evidence of neglect and abuse. Julia Kinsella had died on the thirteenth day of May almost thirty years before. On the day her husband and son came home from her funeral the cherry tree outside the living-room window began to shed its blossom shower encouraged by a vigorous summer breeze. Julia had always regretted that its mesmerizing display didn't last for a few weeks longer. Emmet had heard her say that she spent all of springtime waiting for it to flower, then dreading the day it would be too frail to withstand the wind blowing westward from the mountains clearing all before it.

What had begun as a persistent pain in Julia's abdomen the year before, which she had tried hard to live with, finally grew severe enough to overwhelm her. Emmet's father had chastised his wife for carrying far too much weight and told her that was the simple reason she suffered aches that incapacitated her. 'You don't need any sort of doctor to tell you that being as fat as a farrowing sow is asking for trouble,' he taunted with a voice lacking any inflection of kindness. When her difficult and wiry husband spoke to her like that Julia would just throw her eyes to heaven and put on a bright smile for her listening son, pretending they were only cruel words and therefore had no lasting power to harm her. If Emmet didn't look straight into the black pools of her sorrowful eyes he might believe she'd learned not to be hurt by anything her husband said.

In those moments, cast in the role of his mother's shy but steadfast ally, Emmet added to the ever-increasing store of reasons to hate his father. 'Take no notice of him, Mam. You're grand and if Dad had a brain worth talking about he could see that you've lost a good bit of weight in the last while. Your clothes are definitely looser.' He would speak to her light-heartedly in an effort to bring a real smile to her tired face. When Paddy Kinsella wasn't looking, Emmet would slip her a favourite bar of Fry's peppermint chocolate that he bought from Flynn's sweet shop out of squirrelled lunch money.

At her son's insistence Julia finally paid a visit to a new doctor's surgery in the squat red-brick bungalow on the edge of Westport, hating above all to make a needless fuss but desperate for some explanation or small respite from the pain. By the time Dr Driscoll had sent her for enough tests to elicit a diagnosis, no amount of medicine, much less dieting – to her husband's irritation – could halt the steady progression of a tumour that had burrowed into her stomach wall. Emmet concluded that his father must have been upset by his wife's illness and death but he would be hard pressed to tell as much from anything Paddy said or did in the miserable weeks during which she had unwillingly slipped away from her life and theirs.

Work on his precious farm continued as usual as if it remained the most important thing in the world. On the evening Julia died his father insisted on milking the cows himself despite offers of help from neighbours and friends. The poor man needed to keep himself busy, relatives said in well-intentioned explanation, but Emmet could not find it anywhere within his angry self to agree. Was it too much to ask for him to sit and witness her leaving them? He was glad that before she faded away entirely his mother had slipped to a place where she might not have realized that her husband had chosen to stand in solidarity with his pampered livestock rather than with his ever-weakening wife.

At first neighbours had come laden down with reviving pots of stew and soup or bread just out of hot ovens crying out for smears of softened butter, anxious to offer whatever small but sure comfort that food could bring. The newly widowed husband and his teenaged son were a misfortunate pair and they could not but be pitied. But the interfering swell of sympathy was one thing that Paddy Kinsella found he could not abide and when the first traumatic days had passed he made it clear that he was capable of adequately providing for himself and his son and wouldn't be availing himself of the well-meant charity of others again. Provide he did, in a small and limited fashion, until Emmet left for good, yet he never seemed to miss his wife. Even the increasingly shabby house Julia Kinsella had left behind appeared more aware than her husband of the loving pair of caretaking hands it had lost.

Emmet, helped by his only aunt, Julia's younger sister Kathleen, tidied away his mother's belongings from his parents' bedroom in the weeks after she died. Everything was to be cleared out on his father's specific and gruff instructions. There was no point in falling over her possessions if the woman herself was not there to keep them in order and he made it plain that he didn't want any mementoes other than the wedding photograph that was hanging at a careless angle on the living-room wall. She had looked her best then before she let herself go, he would say to anyone close enough to listen to his harsh conclusions. If he had ever admired his wife at all this was as much as he was willing to admit. Losing her had not softened his harsh judgement of her one whit.

A furious Emmet made sure not to save Paddy anything of his mother's in the unlikely event that his father would come to regret the coldness of his decision. For himself he kept some small pieces of jewellery in a blue and gold tea caddy, thinking that one day he might have a girlfriend or a wife who would be happy to wear them. As he grew older he recognized them for the cheap and mostly worthless trinkets they were. But if anything, their limited value made him treasure them more because, worthless or not, they were the finest things his mother had owned.

In the well of his mother's almost empty wardrobe Emmet found a stash of peppermint chocolate bars bought by him that nausea or lack of appetite had prevented her from eating. With tears welling in his eyes he carried the bulging plastic carrier bag to the bin and daydreamed of a time not far away when he could escape and never set foot in the house again.

Turning his back on where he had come from was the best move he had ever made. He had chosen to move ever forward and not be hampered by the past and things he might wish to change but never could.

Looking at the website of Tobar Rock Cottages it seemed as if their owner had made a similar break with the past, choosing a new venture when his old business had lost either its attraction or usefulness. It signalled an open mind, which Emmet saw as a sign that he had found the ideal place. Surely somewhere new but with ties to a happy childhood for Jill would be a place they could begin teasing out their difficulties? He felt optimistic that she would appreciate his thoughtfulness and good memory for the details of her family's scattered history. A fresh approach was needed to unlock the gentleness toward him she had once possessed.

He sent a brisk email to Tobar Rock Cottages enquiring about availability for any weeks in July. He was the boss of Cedar Build and he could take his holidays whenever he felt like doing so. He murmured a silent prayer of gratitude that he had got out of a number of big projects in the last year with his financial skin intact, if a little bruised. He had held his nerve when others had bottled under pressure and consequently had guaranteed the firm's survival; temporarily at least. He felt it was an achievement not to be taken lightly in the current difficult climate.

Jill would once have been proud of Emmet's wily ducking and diving and hungry for details of his clever stunts. But not any more. When he came home at night, on the rare occasion that she was not already in bed asleep, or pretending to be, she could not stand to look at her husband. Consequently he had no natural opportunity to tell her they would be fine or that she need not worry because he was taking care of everything.

The sudden slump in trade gave him the mixed blessing of adequate time to observe how his marriage was unravelling itself and to feel the pain of that disintegration. Time away from the house on Lighthouse Road, so full of memories, might well be their last hope as a couple. He had always thought the best part of a holiday was the feeling of turning the key in the front door when the trip home had been negotiated successfully. He hoped it wasn't too much to ask that in mourning what they had lost they could come to appreciate something of the precious fragility of what remained.

Chapter Two

At Tobar Lodge Gina Miller had spent an uneasy week putting off telling either of her sisters that they were going to have a good deal of unexpected company on their holidays that year. For the past seven summers Rachel and Lottie had considered the month of July at Tobar Rock sacrosanct family time, arriving at the cottages early on the first Monday of the month and leaving reluctantly and late on the last day quite inconsolable to think it would be another year before they would all be in the same place for a decent stretch of time.

The Miller sisters purported to enjoy each other's adult company almost as much as they had insisted that they loathed the sight of each other whilst growing up. But even good things had their cut-off point and a month in close quarters seemed to be the upper limit of their sisterly tolerance for one another. Their raw edges would fray quite significantly in the last days as the prospect of escape to their own worlds beckoned; whereupon they began to assert their substantial differences, as if that might ease the transition away from the family unit to their separate lives, in which being one of the Miller girls was just a fragment of their story. For her part Gina did her best to keep the peace but even she breathed a sigh of relief when sister-free August loomed for herself and her daughter Sadie. Yet by the time another summer rolled around they had all resolved in advance to forgive the small but trying tensions of the previous year and dwell only on the good times in broad nostalgic brushstrokes.

Since she now lived in their childhood home Gina suspected that her sisters considered July at the cottages as part of an inheritance from which they had foregone their fair share. They had each made good use of their father's financial bequest. Lottie had rented a small premises to start her own gallery and Rachel had ploughed her share into her husband's fledgling architect practice. Gina was fairly certain that on some level they held it against her that she had been left Tobar Lodge and the restored cottages. Her sisters had never expressed any resentment but she felt a palpable undercurrent in any conversation about the house in which they had grown up. They knew their father felt sympathy for Gina because she was raising her daughter alone and could do with the income that the cottages might realize if they were well managed. He had selfish reasons too; he'd told Gina that it would make all the work he had put into the redevelopment of the cottages worthwhile if he could be sure that a Miller would come back to live in Tobar Lodge. She knew that he had decided that Lottie and Rachel's lives away from Tobarnaree meant that they were unlikely to settle there permanently and the house might well pass out of the family and into the hands of strangers or, worse still, to a covetous local. He had lost Tobar land to the worst of those opportunists and he was adamant that the same fate would not befall his and Sarah's beloved lodge.

His middle daughter accepted that the time might well have come and gone for her to leave her home town so she graciously accepted the generous offer that secured her future. By the end of their first year back at Tobar Rock she and her daughter had almost settled in despite Sadie's sporadic but nevertheless impressive teenage tantrums that she would never forgive her mother for uprooting them from their perfectly cosy flat in town and bringing them to live in the middle of nowhere with only the murmuring water of the lake and an ignorant lump of rock for company.

The kernel of Sadie's argument bothered Gina more than she cared to admit; yet there was no point in adding further fuel to her daughter's fire. On wet winter evenings, when darkness had fallen long before six o'clock, loneliness and isolation threatened to undo all Gina's well-meant plans for them. It took months before she could truthfully say that she felt completely at home at the lodge and it only happened when she had stopped expecting it to be anything like the full and noisy house she remembered as a child. Slowly but surely she began to make the house her own and she settled into the peaceful rhythm of life, learning to make do without the surrounding noise of town which had become so familiar.

She would never have been able to afford to buy a place herself on the meagre wages she earned and it was a relief not to have to worry about making the rent every month. Without that strain it was going to be possible for Sadie to choose the course that she really wanted to do the following autumn and not automatically plump for something in a local college because they couldn't afford her first choice. Looking back Gina knew for certain that it had been the right move for her daughter and herself and she couldn't now imagine them living anywhere else. Not that she would expect Sadie to admit as much. Her teenage identity depended in substantial part on Gina always getting things spectacularly wrong. Having no interest in being engaged in constant warfare her mother mostly let her think this was the case. Choosing peace and letting go of the need to be right, despite the fact that her daughter sometimes didn't deserve such gentle patience, had been one of the slow-burn lessons of parenthood but was perhaps the one that Gina valued most.

CHAPTER THREE

Jill Kinsella's mobile phone beeped in the roomy leather hand-bag that lay tossed at her feet. She had selected the phone's subtle tone specifically so that only she and none of the gallery of intent faces that sat close by her desk might detect its telltale sound. Loud and aggressive ring tones were just one of a list of things that could drive a person to distraction working in the office of McCartan & Sheils Accountants, but the alternative for Jill was to sit at home and mull over things that would only ever cause her heartbreak. It's not as if she could have returned to work in the office of Cedar Build where she had spent much of the previous decade expertly handling the payroll and keeping the company accounts in prim order.

She hadn't entertained the possibility even for a split second, despite Emmet's almost daily pleas to have a spark of sense and do just that. There was no way she could go back there and slot right in as if nothing of any consequence had happened; or at least nothing that couldn't be successfully erased with the passing of time and the resumption of habit. If life insisted on going on after her son's death then she could see to it that the weight of familiarity didn't add to the pain involved. Change was imperative if she was going to endure the relentless and repetitive days that stretched ahead of her. Somewhere new on the other side of the city where no one would know much about her or care less had proved an easier prospect. Commuting to work by Emmet's side was yet another discomfort that a new job allowed her to avoid. The amount of money she earned was pitiful in comparison to before but that hardly mattered since her need for money had more or less evaporated. She once adored the personal space that shopping allowed her and was happy to spend hours trawling through favourite haunts seeking out an ideal gift or the perfect shoes to finish an outfit. Ferrying the bags afterward to a secluded corner of a café to sip from generous mugs of coffee and scan a glossy magazine added another layer of luxury to the relished treat of time alone. Now the mere thought of the noise and glare of the city exhausted her before she had even begun but more to the point she could not countenance the frivolous waste of time and energy on something so futile. She shopped now only when she absolutely needed something and with time she'd found it was possible to need very little indeed. The generous amount of money lodged by Emmet into her account every fortnight (her salary deposited religiously on the second and fourth Friday of the month whether she turned up to work with him or not) remained there untouched; a symbol of an ever-widening chasm between them. She would not spend a cent of it and its steady and speedy accumulation served to make her even more determined to achieve independence and isolation; although she wasn't entirely sure which of the two she desired more.

The fancy trappings of life that she had assembled around her as vital to ensure comfort and success didn't matter an iota now. She had shed the skin of the Jill Kinsella that everyone knew. The question was not if that woman might ever come back but whether she would even recognize her if she did. Her reflection in the mirror continually surprised her. It was proof, if proof were needed, of a life and the face it was known by fading out one day at a time. The offices of McCartan & Sheils seemed like a harmless world where she might exist quietly and unnoticed, her anonymity a fine accomplice to a grief running out of control. In a place where no one knew her or expected anything of her other than competent repetition of tasks, she felt free to give in to every miserable feeling that rose within her.

Sheer pride meant she wouldn't allow herself to cry while she was ploughing her way through a relentless array of accountancy spreadsheets on her computer screen. The office was busy with companies and individuals anxious to file early tax returns in the hope that a revenue rebate might ease cash-flow difficulties in hard-pressed times. Jill worked hard and long hours and if anyone noticed that her heart broke a little bit more each day then no one had yet summoned the courage to mention it. The most personal thing anyone approached her about was what type of pastry she might want delivered from the bakery that bookended their building on Bowen Parade.

She reached down and plucked the mobile phone out of her bag. Even before she looked at it she guessed that it was Emmet sending yet another text message.

If so it would make it the third text that day and the clock was still an hour shy of lunchtime. Grief mingled with guilt – though not nearly enough of the latter, Jill felt – had turned Emmet Kinsella into a persistent if well-meaning nag. His wife would not have thought it possible but she missed her husband's slightly casual approach, which had characterized the earlier part of their marriage. She had never doubted that he loved her but he was mostly content to let those words remain unsaid.

He was a man who thought – once he had successfully pursued her – he shouldn't have to make an elaborate song and dance about his feelings. He adored his wife but his sincerity and devotion was in his opinion obvious from the fact that he had committed to and enjoyed getting into bed with the same woman every night for the previous dozen years. Back then Jill used to think that their lives would be a good deal simpler if Emmet would express his feelings a little more but all she truly craved now was to have their happy if imperfect life back exactly as it had been when there had been three of them together. She was appalled to think that it had taken such a devastating event for her to appreciate what she had had. What remained of her family now was an ill-fitting pair bruised by blame, haunted by memories and more comfortable looking anywhere except directly at one other.

Jill put her mobile on the desk next to her computer. She was grateful that her husband hadn't made a phone call to the office expecting her to engage in conversation. Emmet's voice sounded strange to her now just like everything else but if she left the phone deliberately to ring out she just looked heedless or crazy or both. When pressed on her evasion of his calls she always used the excuse of being far too busy with work. Curiosity outweighed her avowed disinterest this time and she read his message. He had booked a holiday for them down the country and she was to ask Rory McCartan for leave of absence for the first two weeks of July. The destination Emmet was keeping as a surprise but he hoped she would be really pleased.

Did he now? She could not remember the last time she had been pleased about anything he had said or done. He finished the message with *Love you, E x*. She swallowed hard, unwilling to bear witness to the searing expression of his feelings. The intimacy of the sentiment embarrassed rather than comforted her. Those words were never welcome if you felt you would be lying if you forced yourself to say them back. And why would a holiday solve what nothing else had? Her son was gone and she and Emmet were completely out of step. She didn't know if they would ever manage to regain the rhythm of their relationship and fall back into being the couple they once were.

She ran her thumbs against the rough edge of her desk until they were marked from the coarseness of the wood. The resulting indentations pleased her. She watched as the flesh scurried back to resume its natural outline showing little more than a hint of redness. An irrational temptation to bruise it more next time took compulsive hold within her.

Switching her phone to silent she tossed it back in her hand-bag without any plan to reply. A rough kick shunted the bag along the claret-coloured carpet under her desk and garnered a quizzical look from the rugby-shouldered accounts assistant crouched over his desk opposite her. He grinned at her as if he knew how she felt, as if one action allowed him to see right through her. Her face colouring at being examined by her other-wise bored colleague, Jill promised herself she would leave her phone in her jacket pocket in future. She had no intention of contributing to an episode of any office soap opera. They could look for their entertainment elsewhere.

She turned her attention to the endless rows and columns of figures on the screen in front of her. Stark light from an over-head fitting illuminated the worksheet but its glare made her dizzy. Her eyes swam from the strain of repressing the budding shoots of a headache. As she struggled to regain her concentra-tion she was overwhelmed by the repeatedly imagined memory of her crumpled ten-year-old boy lying on damp winter concrete with a seemingly insignificant trickle of blood pooling where his smile used to be.

Reluctantly Gina went to the phone in the hallway of Tobar Lodge to make the long postponed phone calls to her sisters in Dublin. She would try Lottie first because diving in at the deep end of her sister's interrogation seemed like the brave thing to do. With any luck her elder sister would be in the middle of making a sale in her art gallery on Gaslight Lane and wouldn't have time to haul Gina over the coals for allowing their precious weeks at Tobar Rock to be ruined by the presence of a few people they didn't know.

Unluckily for Gina her sister was alone and getting steadily more frustrated in the gallery's smaller-than-phone-booth-sized office as she failed to pin down what had happened to an errant fifty euro of petty cash. She welcomed the diversion of her sister's phone call and was only too willing to talk about anything if it meant she could set aside the cursed cash box. She didn't like much of what her sister explained to her and as always her opinion was outspoken.

'What do you mean?' she bleated in a petulant tone. 'It's nearly always been just ourselves during July. I thought you tried to arrange it that way on purpose because you liked having your holidays while we're all around to keep you company. Sure you wouldn't know what to do with yourself otherwise.'

Gina took a deep breath before trying to justify this year's change of plan in the face of her sister's undisguised irritation. She felt grateful that they were close neighbours for only a few weeks at a time. She wouldn't be able to stick Lottie's endless appetite for going through the small print of every decision if they lived closer to one another. She had long come to the conclusion that a family was not so much a neat and harmonious unit but more a stray bunch of individuals frequently startled by how differently they thought about anything that really mattered. How Gina saw fit to run Tobar Rock Cottages was hardly Lottie's concern but she could bet that her sister would never agree to see things that way.

'Bookings for the start of the season were quiet enough and my hours cooking at the Lime Tree have been cut. Trade is in rag order and Louis Corrigan has decided to just open for lunch now and dinner only at the weekends. All those changes mean I work about half the hours I worked this time last year. I just couldn't turn down two high-season bookings after a rather shaky start. Besides, it makes no sense, when you and Rachel only need a cottage each, to leave the other two to sit there gathering dust when they could be making some extra money for myself and Sadie.'

'If the cottage enterprise is heading for disaster too I suppose you will be asking myself and Rachel to cough up more cash this year for the pleasure of spending a month at home? Or I guess we could all move in with you and Sadie in the lodge if you want to let out our cottages at a knock-down rate. It'd be a bit of a squeeze but sure you're spoiled there with too much space to yourselves. Mind you, it would be like old times, wouldn't it, with us all there together?'

'I never said the business was heading for disaster. It's just that much money would make a big difference to us and you and Rachel will still get your month in Tobar Rock as usual. And no I don't want you all staying in the house with us, thanks very much. I know my limitations and I fancy having a tiny fraction of sanity and good humour left by the end of your holidays if at all possible.' It suited Gina much better when her sisters got over their hangovers in the privacy of their own cottages and came to the lodge only when they had thoroughly bolstered their stocks of good humour and were ready for another attempt at a sociable day.

Succumbing to a belated bolt of conscience Lottie decided to let her sister off the hook. Sadie was due to start college in the autumn and she knew that her sister was going to find that responsibility a considerable strain on what she could only imagine were rather paltry finances. She chided herself for being a selfish little git. 'OK then I suppose if it can't be helped. I bag Rowan and Alder for myself and Rachel. Let the blow-ins duel with each other from opposite ends of the courtyard. They can listen to the concert of ghosts that howl around our little lake at night. A few unexplained clatters, a well-timed whistle or a high-pitched screech outside their windows at nightfall might get rid of them in a flash and normal July occupation at Tobar Rock can be restored.' As much as some of her sister's visitors to Tobar Rock loved to think they were in a land thronged with the spirits of past heroes Lottie was certain they wanted those ghosts to keep firmly to themselves.

Gina was not impressed by her sister's plan to amuse herself at the expense of the paying residents. 'I'm glad I didn't get you to write the content for the webpage or I'd have no business at all. Less of the ghost talk now when you meet the families that are spending July with us, OK? I would quite like a bit of repeat business from this year if possible. It's brilliant when people book for the following year before they drive out the gate. Takes the worry out of things for me if I know that at least a few bookings are guaranteed before the year kicks off.'

'Go on then, hit me with the array of lunatics I'll be sharing my home place with,' Lottie said, her resistance to the idea melting somewhat and being replaced by rampant curiosity. Strangers meant stories. There might be a man, she thought, and then just as quickly she decided not a chance. Some crowd of do-gooders on retreat, knowing Lottie Miller's dodgy luck. Well, they could keep their good intentions to themselves. There would be no meditation sessions at the rock or early morning hikes around Corrallis Woods. The shooting bolt secured on the cottage door and the lovely curtains that Gina had fitted drawn across could keep out all manner of undesirables if the worst came to the worst.

'Did you say lunatics, Lottie? Pot calling kettle black there now, don't you think, Sis? The Millers are not exactly all balanced in the head department, wouldn't you agree? So we'll be in good company.'

'I beg your pardon. Don't be cheeky to your elders. Go on, spit it out. What team of misfits have you lined up to ruin my precious month at Tobar? I live for this break all year, you know, and I can't bear to think that it's going to be spoiled by having to be polite to strangers and pretend they are not inconveniencing me.'

Gina picked up the email printouts that she had brought with her to the phone and scanned the booking details again. 'Emmet Kinsella's one of them and he's booked for the first two weeks of the month. He's from north county Dublin – in construction, I think, which probably explains why he has a bit of time on his hands at the moment. Not a lot of building going on, I'd imagine, if around here is anything to go by.' The half-built houses that lined every road were stark evidence of how everything had changed so quickly and served to make Gina feel all the more lucky to have a house to call her own.

'So who else are we playing host to besides this Emmet creature with the bales of discounted breeze blocks tucked beneath his muscular wings?' Lottie demanded, her appetite for all the details satisfied only for a split second before more information was required to feed her insatiability. Gina felt a mixture of despair and comfort that some things never change. 'The other reservation is for an American writer Ellen Carter, her two children and maybe the husband. She doesn't seem entirely sure that he will actually show up. Separated maybe, although it's none of my business. None of yours either, for that matter, so don't go prying when you meet her because I know what you're like. You can never manage to keep your nose on your face when you spot an opportunity to dip it in where it's not wanted.' Gina had often been mortified listening to Lottie interrogate an unsuspecting visitor, never pausing to consider the possibility of fragile or bruised feelings.

'I don't *pry*, as you so uncouthly put it. It's called taking a friendly interest in the plight of other human beings. It's what we are all put on the planet for, if you ask me. If we all minded our own business as well as you, no one would know the first thing about anyone and where would we be then? Daddy was right about some things and he always said knowledge was power.'

Their parents had run a very gregarious and open house at Tobar Lodge with neighbours and friends forever coming and rarely going without taking a mug of tea or a tumbler of something stronger at the kitchen table. It was a tradition that Gina felt she was keeping up but bearing in mind that these people were not personal friends but paying guests she felt that they deserved the privacy for which she had accepted their cash. Lottie on the other hand couldn't help feeling that they had cheekily pitched a tent on her home turf and therefore shouldn't mind having to explain themselves or the varied but usually regrettably mundane reasons why they had chosen to come to Tobar Rock. Disappointingly enough no one had ever (that they were willing to admit anyway) come to Tobarnaree to flee a Mafia contract on their life. The amazing scenery and a sense of peace were the most commonly avowed factors in their decision. That same stillness was what had driven Lottie away; she had been sure anything happening elsewhere would be more interesting. Dublin was home now but, with the passing of time, Tobarnaree had become her place of escape.

Gina was not for turning on the matter of guarding her guests' privacy. 'All I'm saying is that she's probably coming here for some quiet time out so we should leave her and her family to their own devices. Same with this Kinsella man. He rang after he made the booking online to make me promise that the place was peaceful. I stopped short of saying that a car coming up the road is regarded as the supreme highlight of our day in case he thought the place abysmally quiet and decided to cancel on me. Wasn't about to lose a fortnight's booking by being strictly honest about Tobarnaree's ever so slight drawbacks. If Sadie had got the phone before me she would have told him she'd checked for a pulse and the place had been declared stone dead. I wonder where my daughter gets her brand of tact from?' she enquired playfully of her sister. But the point was lost as Lottie veered off on a spectacular tangent.

'He might be on the run!'

Gina was quick to deflate that theory. 'Well, it sounded to me like he might be bringing someone on a romantic break because he insisted the place had to be just perfect. But I don't know that for sure because I didn't ask. As long as they pay me what I'm owed I'm quite happy to leave them all to their own devices. That's why people like Tobar Rock so I don't want you channelling Oprah Winfrey and interrogating anyone about their deepest darkest secrets while my back is turned. Do you understand?' She would have to make Lottie realize that Tobar Rock was a holiday destination and not just a fascinating case study for her sister.

Lottie did her level best to sound offended at her sister's implication. 'Relax. I'm not going to force anyone to sit on my comfy couch to have a chat against their will. It's true that people in trouble gravitate towards me but I can throw shapes at diplomacy and discretion as good as the rest of you if that's what's called for. Besides, it looks like I will be the childless and manless stray in the middle of all your pleasant domesticity and probably won't have a screed to say to anyone. I'll have to pick up a couple of starving and mange-ridden cats from the animal shelter on the way down and strew the pair of them around my neck, an anti daisy chain if you will. They'd be the perfect props to complete my sad spinster vignette. Thanks a heap in advance for showing up the shortcomings of my lonesome crock of a life.'

'Well, that's just bloody typical! You think the whole world revolves around you. Besides, didn't you tell me you were going to ask the love god Joe along for a few days this year so we could all have a good swoon in the man's mighty presence?'

Lottie had talked incessantly about her new man, Joe King, over the previous few months until her sisters' faces ached from the forced smiles that seemed necessary to convey adequate amounts of enthusiasm. Who would have guessed that Lottie

Miller's stellar destiny might ever go by the unspectacular name of Joe? The way he had just shown up at her workplace and not when she had been actively out on the town intent on snaring a man proved to Lottie that the ideal partner could be right there under your nose without you realizing. She had lectured her sisters about the ease of finding love at any age at the Easter Sunday dinner she'd hosted in her uncomfortably crowded apartment on Gaslight Lane, confident that the days of calling its fairly modest dimensions her home were numbered. She eyeballed an unconvinced Gina as if being single was an unfortunate and undesirable condition she could easily avoid if she would just open her mind to what was possible. Joe was away on business over Easter, otherwise they might have met him in full and glorious colour; it was a considerable disappointment, for Lottie with all her girly excitement had whetted her sisters' appetite for a meeting.

In their phone calls to each other Rachel and Gina had nick-named him Elvis – nothing else seemed flamboyant enough to capture the force of nature that had turned Lottie's carefully controlled world upside down. Sadie had taken to doing very poor hip-swivelling Elvis impersonations in the background when her loved-up aunt rang Tobar Lodge, willing her mother to crack up laughing in the middle of another highly intense conversation.

Joe was a lavish-spending customer of the Gaslight Gallery and had swept Lottie off her feet with flowers, tickets to the concert hall, the Abbey and the Gate and hints of a future together that had their experience-chastened sister, in spite of her better judgement, totally mesmerized. She had always said that financial means didn't matter in her pursuit of a man; personality and appreciation of the arts and her work won every time. Yet suddenly her conversation was peppered with evidence of what Joe had bought or was planning to buy. Gina and Rachel sincerely hoped that in person he would live up to their sister's glowing report even if he was beginning to sound like the human incarnation of an itemized credit card bill.

Lottie desperately deserved a bit of luck in the love department but she was quick to correct her sister now. 'The little wanker went back to his wife two weeks ago. I suppose suddenly remembering you have a wife is a rather pressing – if not very original – reason to go home, when you come to think about it.' She blurted out her revelation with the last scrap of good humour she could round up.

Gina spluttered the coffee from the oversized mug she always filled when she had a couple of what she feared might be lengthy and exhausting phone calls to make. 'I didn't know he was even married!' she managed as she took a damp tea towel to her shirt and rubbed in vain at the ugly stain creeping across the delicate blue cotton print.

'Neither did I, Gina. Neither did I. Actually to be quite honest I couldn't be quite sure he ever properly left the darling spouse in the first place. Certainly going back to her didn't seem to rattle his world order that much. Just left me reeling, that's all. Spun me some story that he had his brother who was down on his luck living with him and he would not upset my appreciation of fine things with a visit to the pigsty he reluctantly had to call home. It was an unsatisfactory but temporary arrangement that could be corrected with time, he said, and I was dunce enough to believe him. In the meantime he made himself thoroughly at home in my place planning our future bliss. We spent ages poring over the property supplements looking for *our house*. He said he would know it the minute he saw it. Guess what? The little plonker had such high standards for me that he never saw a house worthy of me turning the key in the front door or hanging all my lovely paintings on the wall. More fool me for believing him and forgetting my golden rule that if it sounds too good to be true it's probably out and out codswallop. I suspended all my good judgement so what the hell else can I expect but disaster delivered in massive consignments?'

'Oh God, Lot, I'm sorry. He did sound pretty close to perfect from all you told us. You shouldn't have had to go through all that on your own. Why didn't you ring myself or Rachel and let us know?' Gina was genuinely saddened for her sister and immediately felt guilty for all the jokes she and Rachel had shared at her expense.

Lottie cleared her throat, becoming animated about the extent of her own bad judgement. 'Well, that's one question I know the answer to anyway. I didn't ring because I felt like a prize gobshite. I built him up to be *the One*. Bet I bored you both senseless but you've been charitable not mentioning how sickening I was. Anyway I'm finding it very hard to admit that the fecking joke is on me yet again.'

Gina spared her sister's feelings by not agreeing with her but instead offered her wholehearted support. 'Rachel and myself would have tried to help, you know, if you had said something. Sisters mind each other so you should allow us to do what we can to make you feel better. I know you think that you're braver than the whole rest of the world put together but you should know better than try to cope with this on your own.'

'I must admit I had a bit of a wobble a few nights ago. I made it as far as Rachel's house but the place was in pitch blackness. They must have all been gone to bed early. Didn't want to chance getting Ciaran down the stairs to answer the door in his jocks or worse still without any at all so I just turned on my heel and left. To be honest I'm glad because Rachel seems to me to be a bit stressed at the moment, not really herself. So we'll have to take her in hand too when we all get together in Tobar. It's obvious that she's hiding something from us. Have you not noticed her sounding a bit distant in herself when you're talking to her?'

'Can't say that I've noticed anything too different about her but Rachel's always so busy with Orla and Billy, ferrying them here there and everywhere, that it seems only normal when she is preoccupied. I guess that admission makes me a most inattentive and heartless sister, does it?'

'Well, I think that on balance I am the most intuitive and perceptive of the Miller girls but I've always believed that it's in the poorest of taste to blow your own trumpet and risk upsetting others who probably mean well but fall short in their efforts.'

Never stopped you before, Gina felt like saying but she bit her tongue. Being heartbroken had not increased her sister's humility an ounce. Lottie could be insufferable when she became excessively in tune with her know-it-all goddess within. Too many self-help books read to the exclusion of pretty much everything else, and their shaky philosophies taken far too seriously, but Gina thought it better not to invite a rant by provoking her on that score.

Lottie continued, oblivious to her sister's strangled silence: 'Anyway, the last thing Rachel needs is me blubbing about another one of my romantic disasters, whereas you asked a straight question, Gina, so you get to hear the unpalatable details in all their messed-up glory. I'll tell Rachel when we get as far as home ground next month. By then I hope to be well and truly over the dipstick. I plan to rally from this shite and get back on the only two feet I've ever been able to depend on. No other choice really, have I?' she asked, her voice threatening to tremble a little.

'No, I guess not, but stop being funny and brave and tell me how you're really feeling? It's such a shitty disappointment when you were sure he was a good sort.'

'I feel a whole host of lousy things and listing them all out again will probably make me feel a shade worse, if that's possible.'

'Well, I promise we'll all mind you when you get home to Tobar Rock. You deserve better than a waster like him.'

The one bright side of her sister being let down by Joe was that Lottie was usually much better fun when she was on her own than when she was escorted by a new man. In the company of someone she was working hard to impress Lottie appeared to mislay her considerable array of charm. She had never seemed to get the knack of just relaxing and being herself, although presumably her compounded negative experiences with men were partly to blame.

Selfishly, Gina was glad that she would not be the only Miller sister to be without a man at her side this summer, though she hated herself for the unbecoming pettiness of the feeling. She hadn't had a man in her life for a few years and it annoyed her that the issue could still rankle as it did. Although as she came to think of it could she truthfully call any of them men? She could say for certain that there were none she was sorry after apart from Matthew Gordon but that was all so long ago it might as well·have happened to somebody else. She wondered if there might come a time when the shape of her perfectly adequate life would satisfy her or at least a time when she would stop imagining a different existence and if that moment might bring with it peace or only a sad sense of resignation. She listened as Lottie complained bitterly about yet another letdown and scooted her own niggling unhappiness to the back of her mind where, despite her best and brave attempts to pretend otherwise, it always lingered.

Lottie was on a roll but then again there was nothing she liked quite as much as talking. The topic varied but her energetic delivery never flagged for a moment. 'Joe was a pure chancer. He's still ringing my home phone pleading into the answering machine for a chance to explain. Thankfully the beep always cuts him off midstream so there's a strict ninety-second limit to the nightly torture. A saner woman would just delete the lot of his meanderings without listening or do the brainy thing and change her phone number, but you know me: I always like to go that extra mile and a quarter for pain. Nobody could accuse me of lacking dedication. What was it Dad used to say about me?' She could hear the words clearly as if it had been just yesterday and her father was appraising a fresh disaster for further evidence of her carelessness. ' "Charlotte Miller, you are a disciple to your own undoing." I think he got some kind of pleasure each time I fecked up because it made him feel that his pronouncements about me were spot on.'

Gina knew what Lottie was talking about. 'In fairness I think that Daddy thought all his daughters were prone to deviating from his plans for us so I wouldn't take it personally if I were you. None of us followed his advice strictly enough for his liking. Except maybe for Rachel. There was no one he approved of more than Ciaran Jacob and he approved of the way she got her hands on him without hardly even trying. As for us two, he had everything worked out for us and couldn't see why we just wouldn't do things his way.' Determined not to get maudlin, she decided to let Lottie rant on about Joe a little further by asking what excuses he had made for his unreasonable behaviour. Gina was glad she had never met him and hadn't wasted time being courteous to someone who so clearly didn't deserve it.

'Nothing he says any night is worthy of repetition. As if he could ever come up with a satisfactory explanation for being such an asshole. I have my two girls here at the gallery on high alert in case he tries to get his smug phiz in the door. I won't do public humiliation, not when I have had to endure too much of the private sort.'

'Look, you just weren't to know he was lying, Lottie. It could happen to anyone and does all the time, I'm sure.'

'Just can't credit that I fell for his sort of bunkum. It's not like I haven't been around the block, is it?' Before Gina had a chance to agree Lottie continued: 'I should have the words "will never learn" tattooed on my deficient little forehead.'

Gina murmured something about there being plenty more fish in the sea but Lottie was having none of her sister's line of consolation. 'I've snapped my poxy little fishing rod in two. That's me finished with men. Such a procession of absolute wasters I have brought into my life. I wrote all their names down last week on a piece of paper. My squillion-euro-an-hour therapist suggested it as a way of taking genuine ownership of my mistakes, as if I might be considering the possibility of inviting a bidding war for them on eBay. She supplied a pen and a distressingly large sheet of paper. I suppose I should be grateful that her exorbitant fee included the stationery necessary to fully outline my disaster-prone nature.' Lottie laughed at herself.

'Did it help?' Gina asked, wondering when her big sister had seen fit to start seeing a therapist. It seemed like such an outlandish suggestion for anyone brought up around Tobarnaree. People in their home place generally pretended that their hearts weren't of the breaking sort and they steeled themselves against the reality of pain with eyes that looked resolutely straight ahead. For the most part their future survival depended on the least amount of people knowing they were in any distress whatsoever; denial was their default position.

Lottie snorted at the question. 'Shag all help, to be honest with you. Made me want to curl up into a small ball of shame. Someone would pay money to see such a list of transgressions against hope and faith in mankind. I'm seriously thinking of knocking the counselling sessions on the head too. God knows, no matter how much you analyse failure at the end of the day it's still just that – and all the while the therapist gets to live off the proceeds of my misery,' she added sharply.

'I take it you'll not be docking in to Tobarnaree spotting for the likely swell of local talent, so.' Gina felt if she could tap Lottie's well of sarcasm it might help her cheer up a little and the paucity of even vaguely attractive male company in their home town was always a good way to get her started on the road to humour.

'Oh please! I exhausted that well at thirteen when Theo Corrigan dumped me for Jill Cassidy, that lanky bank rat with the big saucer eyes and her sad Rapunzel hairdo. Besides, if there's a decent unattached man within an ass's roar of that town you would surely have tracked him down and reeled him in by now. Or have you got your eyes permanently shut these days in case a man with a dram of hope or love in his heart might have the temerity to cross your path?'

Gina was not about to let Lottie repeat her theories about how her sister avoided relationships in order to dodge getting hurt. She felt much more comfortable when the spotlight was trained on someone else. 'Now that you mention him, Theo Corrigan is back home after a stint in New York. He's taken over his father's farm; well, at least the bit of the Corrigan ranch that used to belong to Daddy and to Tobar Lodge. It seems that he's intent on doing up the home place to live in it. It'll be some job. I think the roof has all but fallen in. Another Tobarnaree winter would have finished it entirely so he's swept in like Superman to do battle with the elements.'

'I thought Louis was the farmer in that family? Didn't think Theo would dirty his delicate hands with livestock, silage and the like. It's a bit of a sorrowful leap from managing hedge funds on Wall Street to clipping hedgerows in the tail end of nowhere.'

Lottie let her mind wander at the possibilities that might flesh out her sister's sketchy revelations. Theo Corrigan back in town? She would certainly take an exploratory look during July, she decided. Maybe even pay the run-down Corrigan homestead a flying visit and give young Theo a hint of what he'd turned his back on. She tried but failed to rein in her impulse to be juvenile. Maturity was for her grown-up life in Dublin and she felt she was allowed to be silly in the place she had grown up.

After all, what were holidays for if you couldn't have a bit of a laugh? She listened as Gina outlined, as only a local could, how the Corrigans had divided up the acres of land that they had been left by their father.

'I'm glad Daddy's not alive to see it. He took it bad enough when Bill Corrigan bought Tobar land but it would kill him to see the sons mess around with his farm when up to a few months ago at least one of them couldn't tell the prosperous end of a cow from the other.'

Lottie knew that Gina was right about their father. He could not have abided the notion of the young Corrigans running what he still thought of as his land right up until his death. All the financial difficulties that the farm had run into had left him with no option but to sell. The absolute clarity of the decision did nothing to make it easier to bear. The entire process was heartbreaking for him and it compounded the misfortune that Bill Corrigan was the first in the queue with swathes of cash in his greedy hands. As neighbours they had never liked each other. It was just one of those things, Sarah May Miller had maintained, two very different men living far too close to each other for comfort. There had been no falling out as such yet everything about his neighbour seemed to annoy Nicholas Miller profoundly. Lottie for one could relate to that. There were plenty of people she had no good reason to hate but detest them she did and with considerable energy and enthusiasm. High standards inherited from her father most likely, she thought as she listened to Gina give a rundown on the teenage boyfriend who had the cheek to dump her.

'I think you will find that New York and age have definitely improved Theo. Not that you and I could ever agree on such a thing as a good-looking or a decent man.'

Lottie couldn't agree with her sister more. 'True. If there's a roll call of dismal partners that could possibly rival my own it would have to be yours. All your choices were hamstrung from the outset, except maybe for Matthew. He wasn't bad, I suppose, if you discount his lack of staying power once things got tough – a serious flaw, you'd have to admit? Never had the spirit for a bit of a scrap and sure that's what makes a man a man. Gumption, backbone, balls: call it what you will. That's what your selection box of soft-centred men never had.'

'Well, thank you kindly for that tirade. Your penance can be ringing Rachel to tell her that we have company for July and while you are at it tell her I will give her a call tomorrow when I've more time on my hands and you haven't annoyed me so damned much.'

Before Lottie had time to protest Gina put down the phone and pulled her shirt off over her head, pushing it through the open slot of the laundry bin in the back kitchen. She hated to listen to anyone talk badly of Matthew because he didn't deserve it and she of all people knew that. Her heart lurched at the mention of his name and she had to quickly rein her thoughts away from the night when she'd known for certain that he would never come back to them.

Gina found her eighteen-year-old daughter, still barely half awake it seemed, leaning against the kitchen counter munching toast and wiping butter-laden fingers against worn jeans. It took a supreme effort on Gina's part not to remark to her how late it was to be getting up and what a beautiful sunny morning her daughter had missed. She knew instinctively that neither issue would concern the teenager unduly but might well plunge her into a lousy mood that she would find it hard to shake for the rest of the day.

She was paying Sadie, not a lot she had to admit, but as much as she could afford, to help with the running of the cottages and so far she was lucky if Sadie emerged from her bed any time before midday. She knew that teenagers liked to sleep late, behaving as if they were some sort of hibernating creatures compelled to build up their strength in order to survive the harsh demands of winter, but she wished she had suggested Sadie get herself a proper job in one of the shops in town instead of pretending that she was working for her mother. At least she might have to force herself out of bed occasionally if someone she thought of as a real boss was waiting for her to turn up for duty. Her mother had convinced her sentimental self that it would be lovely for her and Sadie to spend the last summer before she went off to college together and so it was absolutely no one else's fault but her own. It was just as well she was used to managing the cottages herself because her sleep-walking assistant was proving to be precious little use.

Sadie watched her mother's slight figure as she busied herself around the kitchen tidying every stray household item. Gina could not bear to let anything exist for a moment outside the place she had deemed to be its proper home. Her neat breasts were contained in a girly pink bra and her stomach was lean and flat, unlike the bulging soft-as-dough belly that Sadie's too-tight jeans struggled to contain. Her father's genes were obviously a little more sluggish than her mother's, although from the hazy picture of him in her head she couldn't really swear what size he had been. Then again she couldn't remember much about Matthew. His long absence had whittled her fragile childhood recall until sometimes she doubted if she had real memories of him at all but only manufactured ones prompted by the talk of others. The empty space he had left was far more real to her than he had ever been.

She knew he had been a family friend of her Auntie Rachel's husband Ciaran. Indeed, it was through knowing Matthew that the Miller girls had met Ciaran in the first place, though she knew the two men were no longer in touch either. There had been photographs, of course, but none had hung in Tobar Lodge since they had moved in seven years before. Her mother had taken the opportunity of the move from town to stow them in the attic or maybe dump them entirely – Sadie wasn't sure because she hadn't asked. She didn't think there was much point in admiring the face of a father and a partner who had decided that anywhere else was a better bet than being at home with his family.

Matthew Gordon had gone to visit his sister in Aberdeen two weeks after Sadie's fourth birthday and she had never seen him again. Two years passed before Gina felt ready to give the charity shop on Quay Street the three coats he had left hanging in the hallway and the working boots lined in orderly pairs beside the back door. In return for her sizeable and welcome donation Mollie Gilsenan who ran the shop invited Sadie to pick out a book or a jigsaw from the brightly coloured stack of used toys that cluttered the children's corner at the rear of the store. Delighted with her luck Sadie chose a jigsaw depicting a smiling young couple in a blue rowing boat. It was far too difficult for a girl of her age but neither her mother nor Mollie Gilsenan had the heart to discourage her once she had made her choice. With her small determined fingers wrapped around the scribbled box the little girl was not about to leave without her carefully selected treasure.

Mollie had smiled at Sadie and then turned to Gina and said, 'Aren't you the lucky mammy to have this little one to call your own?'

Gina had nodded and managed to turn away before tears began to stream down her face. Yes, it was true she had Sadie and true also that she wouldn't know where she might turn without her. She felt terrible that she wasn't more grateful for that but she thought it must be like when people lectured someone who had suffered a bitter disappointment that 'at least you have your health'. Everyone knew you could only properly appreciate that health the moment you feared you might lose it. In the same way she knew that having Sadie was a blessing but it didn't make up for all that they might have had together. Was that to be the sum of her whole life? Would she always have to remind herself to take comfort from the fact that worse things had not happened? Constantly having to breathe a sigh of relief that she had evaded greater unhappiness was not what she considered a life well lived, but for that she herself was largely to blame.

Gina and Sadie had worked on the jigsaw together, kneeling on the sitting-room floor until the wooden boards made their kneecaps redden and ache. The puzzle indeed proved to be well beyond Sadie's childish ability but she patiently handed her mother the pieces, willing her to find them their correct place, watching silently as Gina tried not to be bested by the task. Long before it was finished Gina knew in her heart that there was a good chance that some pieces would be lost and she wished she could stand between her daughter and the inevitable disappointment. When they completed it a handful of pieces to make up the sea and the sky were indeed missing but an adamant Sadie insisted on it being left for weeks tucked along the edge of the fireplace on the richly knotted boards of the living-room floor. Gina would watch as her daughter repeatedly visited the almost complete puzzle, trying to imagine what comfort constantly checking back with it gave her. It was in the attic of Tobar Lodge now, its box a little more shabby and doubtlessly missing even more pieces, but Gina had never thought of throwing it out. It was a part of what had happened to them and the memory of it was something she would not dispose of lightly.

Matthew phoned from time to time at first and told a rapt Sadie that he hoped he would see her soon, though it became clear to the little girl as months and then years passed that he mustn't have been hoping all that hard. The journey from Aberdeen to Tobarnaree wouldn't have taken a massive feat of energy or indeed a lot of money to organize. Though only a couple of hundred miles away the place seemed to Sadie to represent the furthest reach of the world. How else would someone go there and never return despite protesting that was their true intention?

She remembered how her mother would balance her on one of the high kitchen stools in their old flat on Melbourne Terrace so that she could reach the phone to talk to him and how she would attempt to conceal her own upset by burying her hot teary face into the back of her daughter's dress as she held her steady and hugged her close for support.

In recent years they had rarely mentioned him at all and Sadie felt fine with that, thinking it better to know how things stood and were likely to stay and not to always wish they could be different. Even if her mother missed him a little there was no reason to expect her to admit it now after all these years.

Sadie buttered another round of toast and set about a good-natured tease of her mother. 'I didn't know that bookings were so low, Mam, that you have to go topless at the gate to tout for business. That's obviously what Fáilte Ireland were talking about when they suggested offering value-added extras, and there was dopey old me thinking that they had the odd escorted river walk or a home-baked rhubarb crumble in mind.'

'Ha bloody ha. Very funny. This body of mine wouldn't tout for much, Sadie Miller.' Gina reached into the airing cupboard and pulled out a soft sweatshirt. It remained a favourite of hers though she tried not to think how many years ago she had bought it. The anonymous label was not something that anyone remotely fashion conscious would tolerate in their wardrobe. She took great care over her limited selection of clothes and so they lasted long past the span in which they could be deemed even remotely fashionable. Her unchanging slender frame meant that everything still fitted glove perfectly. Looking at her in her spotless but tired dregs drove Lottie and Rachel to distraction, but their reaction just made Gina thoroughly resistant to change in case they thought any improvements in her wardrobe might be due to their less than subtle interventions.

She might be their far from sophisticated country sister but they all came from the same place (and not very long ago, for that matter) and her siblings would do well not to act as if they were so different from her. The way they carried on, anyone would think they lived in a Manhattan penthouse or in some posh London neighbourhood and not just a few hours away in Dublin. She tried not to be too upset when every Christmas or birthday present she unwrapped revealed a new top or scarf that they hoped they might subtly persuade her to wear. Without exception their choices were perfectly lovely and while she could admire them Gina felt she didn't have occasion to wear any of them. Her life called not for style but for durability, and so the new clothes remained carefully folded in her bedroom's chest of drawers.

'I'd swap my body with yours any time, Mam,' Sadie said sadly, grabbing the midriff bloat she detested with both her hands.

Gina eyed her daughter and wished she could shake some sense into her. No matter how many times she told her that she was beautiful Sadie was consumed by feelings of her own inadequacy. It didn't help of course that her first real boyfriend had dumped her at Christmas. Leo McLean told her she was far too intense. Too intelligent by far might have been closer to the mark but Sadie put that opinion down to Gina's highly charged maternal prejudice and she wasn't having any of it. She had been rejected by someone she had admitted to loving and that proved a lot harder to stomach aged eighteen than it had been at four.

Gina disappeared into the office alcove under the staircase and returned with a copy of an email that she hoped might cheer Sadie up a little.

Ellen Carter, the Boston writer who had block-booked one of the cottages for six weeks, had enquired if Gina knew someone who would be willing to escort her family around the sights of Tobarnaree and anywhere else that might take their fancy during their stay. She handed the email printout to Sadie. 'This would be a perfect way for you to earn some extra money for college and it would mean you wouldn't be stuck here every day with me.'

Sadie reluctantly took the page, sensing that she was being walked into something and should resist it strongly for her own protection. She scanned the email suspiciously. 'The sights of Tobarnaree? My God, who's this mad woman and what exotic corner of the planet does she think she's booked a ticket to? Does she not know that a few poxy standing stones, the lonesome back wall of an abbey and a full-to-the-brim graveyard is about the size of what this town has to offer? At full tilt she could have the sights of this place covered in ten minutes flat, unless the Taj Mahal has shown up at the top of McCauley Street while I haven't been paying attention.' Sadie snorted, smacked the email down on the kitchen table and returned her attention to her breakfast, but her mother was, firmly but kindly, sticking to her guns.

'Oh Sadie, it wouldn't kill you to be obliging and I'm blue in the face from listening to you complaining that nothing ever goes on around here. This woman seems very nice from the contact I've had with her. She's traced some of her family's ancestors back to Tobarnaree and she's very excited about the trip so the least we can do is be helpful and hospitable while she's here.'

'Well, if the place was so bleak that her ancestors fled from here all those years ago maybe she should take the hint that it's not worth her while returning for a second look. Not very much has changed around here since they left, I'd imagine. When are this brigade threatening to touch down anyway?' Sadie was already dreading their arrival and she had only read their email. How much worse might they be in person?

Undeterred by her daughter's negative attitude Gina glanced

at the yellowing face of the clock that had hung for as long as she could remember above the mantel shelf of Sarah Miller's beloved Aga. 'Looks like you managed to rise yourself from your slumber pit in the nick of time because they're coming today and I told her you'd meet them in the lounge of the hotel at two and show them the way out here. She's quite nervous about finding the place even though there's a perfectly good map on the website. You wouldn't think that two miles of nearly straight road from town would prove too much for anyone but city people are different. They get completely unnerved by ditches and potholes and we've a never-ending supply of both around here, so be a pet and bring them back here smiling and in one piece?'

Sadie's face settled into a rigid sulk and her mother was left in no doubt that she was annoyed that she had been timetabled without prior consultation. 'What am I exactly? Some sort of slave?'

'No such luck but now that you mention it a slave is an excellent idea. You, my dear, are a paid employee of Tobar Rock Cottages and if you do this for me I'll overlook the fact that I have been on my own cleaning the floors and toilets of all the cottages for the past four hours while you lay in bed resting your weary bones. Now move it or you'll be late on top of everything else!'

'Mam!' Sadie pleaded but Gina was quick to dismiss the seeds of her rising sob story. 'You shouldn't take the wages every week if you don't want to do any work. You can try and find another job that might suit you better if you want and I could pay someone here that would actually help me instead of the non-stop whining I get when I ask you to do something.'

Sadie knew better than to continue this spat with her mother. From the curt tone of her voice it was obvious she would be fighting a losing battle. Gina Miller in full no-nonsense form was not to be challenged lightly; in fact complete capitulation was often the best move when her mother got this shirty. 'Yes, boss.'

'Now that's more like it. And Sadie?'

'For God's sake, Mam, what else?' Crikey, she was only just out of bed. She hoped her mother hadn't made a list of jobs to soak up what was left of the day. Had she not heard of holidays? Just because Gina Miller had a problem relaxing didn't mean that Sadie had to fall in with her punishing regime and pretend it was normal.

'Don't forget to be nice. The Carters are staying for six weeks and we'll be seeing them a lot so it'll be miles better for everyone if we all get on. So smile. You know, that facial muscle thing you were so good at before you decided approximately six months ago to appear bored by everyone and everything?'

Sadie tried not to be stung by her mother's pointed sarcasm. She had been in a desperate mood, there was no denying that, but could anyone really blame her, considering what had happened? Being dumped by Leo McLean had floored her completely. She had been incredibly happy with him and with what they had together – blindly so, she could see now from a distance, because she obviously hadn't meant a thing to him. She hadn't spotted the clues to his imminent rejection of her and she chided herself that they must have been plain for all to see, except the goon with the lovelorn eyes. Despite her friends' reassurances that his dumping of her had come out of the blue she felt stupid for being so dim and trusting. In fact she had fondly imagined that he had been working up the courage to say he loved her too when he coldly announced that he had his freedom to think about and he didn't want her clinging to him as if for her dear life. He was a young man seeking out excitement and good times and most definitely not in the market for a steady and, worse still, needy lump of a girlfriend. He hadn't actually *said* lump but that didn't stop her imagining him saying it. It had been over six months and yet Leo McLean was the first thing Sadie thought about when she woke up and invariably the last thing she thought of before she finally dropped off to sleep at night. She had a photograph of them together at the Halloween bonfire at Carty's Inch in the top drawer of her nightstand and she played a torturous game with herself every night as she lay in bed daring herself not to pull it out to feast her eyes on him. If she did weaken and take it out she tried hard to avoid looking at her own face in the photograph because the scale of her gullibility, so obvious in her deluded expression, mocked her cruelly. A good night was when she summoned enough willpower to keep the drawer firmly closed and forced herself to go to sleep without the mixed blessing of seeing what she still regarded as the unsurpassed handsomeness of his face.

She thought that her mother might manage a little more understanding of what she was going through. It was hardly as if she needed reminding of what a broken heart felt like. Sadie would never forget the nights she had heard her mother cry slow racking sobs when all was quiet and she presumably thought her young daughter was sound asleep in the adjoining room in their flat on Melbourne Terrace. Still, there was no point in dragging that up now expecting anything resembling a satisfactory explanation. Gina Miller preferred to avoid talking about her past as much as possible. She had stacks of photos and elaborately annotated memory albums of all the special days of Sadie's life and was happy to discuss the smallest detail of a birthday party or an outing but reminiscing about her own younger life always made her touchy. Sadie generally preserved the peace and her mother's mood by keeping the conversation in the here and now where her mother was a good deal more comfortable and forthcoming.

Sadie dumped her dirty plate into the sink but she thought better of leaving it there; she decided to rinse it and put it on the draining rack when she saw her mother glancing in her direction, no doubt disapproving of her sloth and the trail of crumbs that she had left on the bread board and across the kitchen counter. 'God, Mam,' she said, 'you are just nonstop hilarious today. I think all the undiluted bleach you like to scrub those cottage floors with may have gone to your head.' Then to change the subject (which she thought was probably advisable): 'Have you broken the news to my lovely aunties that they can't expect to be spoiled with the same exclusivity this year at Tobar Rock that they've become accustomed to? That they'll be fraternizing with strangers who won't know or care who the hell they are?'

'Well, I've just told Lottie and I gave her the job of spreading the word to Rachel. My sisters will have to like or lump the situation. You and I can't live on thin air and that's a fact your aunts would do well to remember before they start getting bossy with me about who can stay here and when.'

'By Jesus, Mam, that's fighting talk,' Sadie ventured and she left the kitchen before Gina got so irritated that she thought about giving her a dig in the ribs that her daughter felt on the whole she probably deserved.

CHAPTER FOUR

The trip home to Tobar Rock to spend a month in the company of her sisters was one of a list of considerable worries occupying Rachel Jacob's mind. Another horribly dishonest and irritating fight with her husband before he left for work had left her wondering quite how they would manage another week in the same house let alone a long month on holidays with her family. Ciaran had in the past likened time in the company of his family-in-law to being abandoned to the patchy mercies of a witches' coven where the lack of grown male company of any description only added to his misery.

'The three of you never stop meddling and gossiping and dobbing each other in. I don't know why you insist on holidaying together. Poor Gina has no choice since by an accident of geography and inheritance she has the misfortune of being your put-upon host. You and Lottie descend on her every year whether she likes it or not. Have you ever actually thought that maybe she'd rather if you both called for a spot of tea with a rake of sandwiches and a box of cream buns on your way around to a sweet little caravan park in Wexford somewhere and left her and Sadie in peace? I bet Gina would jump for joy at the blessed release of a summer to herself to get on with running the cottages and her job in the restaurant. She might even visit you all in Curracloe or Rosslare if you set up camp there and God forbid have a scrap of a holiday herself instead of minding us lot the whole time.'

'Don't be mad, of course she wants us there! It's our home place, for God's sake. Why would we rent somewhere in Wexford when we can go home? You're just being contrary now.'

'Have either of you ever had the guts to ask her out straight if she'd prefer if you both went and holidayed somewhere else?' Ciaran challenged, full sure of himself as always.

Of course Rachel thought that was just her husband being downright perverse. She knew for sure that Gina, not that she'd said it out straight as such, lived for July when she got to spend time with her sisters. Lottie was always saying they must never give up the holiday for all their sakes but especially for Gina's, who was bound to be lonely in the house that they had all once called home. The Miller girls should stick together and so July had come to mean time in Tobarnaree and Rachel hoped it always would. Memories of her home place acted as an anchor for her, informing the way she lived her life elsewhere. Except this year she felt her grown-up life was under so much strain that contemplating the trip back brimming with nostalgia and good memories made her nothing but maudlin. She had always felt happy (smug, she was honest enough to admit to herself now) that she had a lovely life to go back to after her holidays, except this year she wasn't at all sure what might await her in Shreve Court when August brought them home again.

As she worked through the folding of a pile of warm-as-toast laundry, stretching and pulling stubborn over-dried items into reluctant shape, she swallowed the choking sadness in her throat. At the rate Ciaran was working lately it seemed highly likely that he might only manage to come to Tobar Rock for one or two of the weekends. That's if his mood lifted enough for him to concede to join them at all. Certainly leisure time at their house had ceased to be the welcome and restful punctuation to a long day's work that it had always been. More often than not she shouldered the responsibilities of being a lone parent, feeling every inch a deserted spouse coping on her own. Time was when her husband would clink a glass against a chilled bottle of wine after they had finished putting the children to bed as if to say *our time starts now.* Rachel wondered what pressing item her husband had seen fit to replace his family with on his schedule. She felt redundant and ignored. It was as if she was living with some temperamental stranger who was refusing to fill the role of husband and father Ciaran had once relished. Her notion of herself had been thoroughly bound up in being part of a happy couple for so long now that without him she hardly knew who she was.

Their children, Orla and Billy, always loved the time spent with her sisters and big cousin Sadie in Tobarnaree and so, despite her own misgivings, she was reluctant to give up the tradition because of what she hoped was merely a bad patch in her and their father's relationship. Besides, time together in a different setting might serve to diffuse the tension that simmered between them. Certainly the coerced and stifling closeness of a bad-tempered marriage wasn't doing themselves or their children any favours. If they could manage to talk to each other long enough without fighting it might be possible to find out if he was willing to travel to Tobarnaree this year. She felt that she would probably go with the children anyway because she had sufficient practice of handling them on her own. She needed the adult company of her sisters and besides she couldn't allow Ciaran's mood to ruin the summer for Orla and Billy.

She couldn't pinpoint what exactly was the matter with Ciaran but he seemed ready to use every word they exchanged as a weapon in a potential fight or a final scuffle before he resorted to the safety of surly silence. She hoped it would turn out to be the pressure of work and nothing more than that because she couldn't bear the thought of him having an affair. The very notion of it was ridiculous. He had always been her Ciaran, the pursuer rather than the pursued, and she hoped that whatever pressure had caused him to change so drastically would soon ease and she would get her husband back and their hitherto happy life could resume.

He was rarely home before the children went to bed and it saddened her to watch them keeping their distance from an increasingly tetchy father. With Orla she knew at least some of her reluctance was an age thing. At an alarmingly adolescent seven and a quarter (the incremental fraction proving to be remarkably important as she held on to the promise of each bigger birthday with gusto), she was too cool to even show her own daddy how much she craved his attention. What really broke Rachel's heart was the way that Billy had taken his older sister's lead. He held back in his father's company, biding his time and judging the mood and possible reception before he would risk plunging headlong to claim the affection that was rightfully his. Recently Ciaran had run the gamut of disinterested to snappy with the little boy, who'd begun to show discernment well beyond his age in avoiding any interaction that might aggravate his father's crabby mood.

They had experienced one bleak weekend after another as Ciaran took to hiding out in the den with his BlackBerry, his laptop and his drawings, unwilling to communicate with any real people while he could keep in electronic contact with colleagues and clients of his architectural practice. Left alone to parent her children Rachel had struggled to cope with stroppiness that stemmed from disappointment at their father's protracted absences. Somehow she would have to pull their relationship back from the abyss towards which it appeared to be relentlessly heading. She decided that the weeks at Tobarnaree could hardly make anything worse and she clung to the glimmer of hope that time away from the city and freedom from the restrictions of her husband's routine might put them back on a happier track.

Her four-year-old son appeared at the heavily fingerprinted door of the playroom. She tried hard not to examine the chaos he had unleashed with such speed and ease behind him. Toys were doubtless strewn everywhere as one imaginative game ran randomly into another with no need for the decks to be cleared. The mere hint of the jumble was enough to make her head spin. Instead she tried to concentrate on him and wondered how he managed to look so fresh even though he had prodded her awake at five a.m. begging for toast and jam. And a glass of milk. Hot milk. Faced with his pleading expression now she could tell he was on the verge of asking for something, which apart from telling dubious tales on his older sister pretty much soaked up all of his time. It helped his chances of success enormously that he looked so damned cute in the asking. This time he wanted pancakes for lunch. Orla did too but she had bundled him through the door primed with the request and a winning smile that required no prompting at all; his beseeching look would, his sister hoped, clinch the deal when otherwise her mother might appeal to Orla's good sense that she simply didn't have time to make pancakes from scratch and would a toasted cheese sandwich or a ham roll not do instead? Orla had warned him not to say that she had put him up to it but he was unable to summon the necessary deceit; he launched into an all-out frenzy of begging completely devoid of the slightest shade of subtlety.

'Orla says you'll say yes if I ask you. Will you? Can we? Please? Pancakes, Mammy, please! Can we? You can have some too but we'll have to make hundreds because we're starving!' His big brown eyes swooned with desire to have his request met and quickly too, as his patience had already reached critically low levels.

After the dreadful morning Rachel had had, making a batch

of pancakes for a leisurely lunch featured on the list of last things she might feel like doing, but another look at her son's sweet face and she relented. She called on her scheming and eavesdropping daughter to help and soon they were engrossed in the hypnotic task of measuring and stirring. After a few short minutes the kitchen filled with the heady sweet smell of vanilla and hot butter. The batter bubbled and ran towards the edge before settling into a neat circle on the hot pan. Rachel was glad she had agreed when she had absolutely not felt like it. It calmed her to watch them together happily caught up in a joint activity. Apart from one spate of all-out war over who got to ladle the batter for the first pancake into the pan it was a peaceful and therapeutic task. Rachel encouraged Orla to flip the final few pancakes on the well-seasoned pan and when she seemed reticent and afraid of making a mistake her mother patiently took her hand in hers and promised to do the manoeuvre with her. Wonder and pride replaced worry in Orla's face as the pancake did a graceful flip before settling back golden side up.

'Next time you can have a go,' she said to Billy but he had already made a start on the food and his mouth was so full of scalding sweetness that he was unable to beg for a chance there and then.

Orla carried the stack of pancakes, varying in shade from brown to somewhat blackened, to the table with studied reverence. She moved gingerly, protecting the precious cargo that she had been entrusted with. Having squeezed juice from the bowl of oranges on the counter, Rachel brewed a plunge pot of coffee for herself with three level scoops of ground and water just off the boil. The juice was for the children but she needed the added bounce that only caffeine could provide after yet another poor and restless night's sleep. She kept the supply of maple syrup, lemon juice and sugar to manageable amounts, giving generously every time a request was made but never letting the children help themselves because from experience, with Billy at least, that would have been asking for the walls behind the kitchen table to be artlessly sprayed with all manner of stickiness. When she sensed that they were full she pulled a clean plate to herself and began to eat the single remaining pancake, doused with far too much sugar and a robust slick of juice squirted from a faded plastic lemon that had seen a few Shrove Tuesdays come and go. She washed the food down with speedy gulps of black coffee, willing it to revive her.

Before the afternoon was out she would have finished one pot and brewed another, unable to relax without the promise of a mug in her hand. She was addicted but she hadn't the energy to care. She needed something to get her through the day; on the scale of things she might be addicted to she rated coffee as next door to harmless. Sated, the children drifted off to resume a game that sounded as if the services of a gutsy referee would be called for and very shortly too.

Rachel was glad of the ringing phone in the hallway that called her away from the tedium of yet another kitchen clean-up. It was Lottie calling from the Gaslight and gagging to fill her in on her conversation with Gina. Rachel struggled to pay attention while her sister went off on one of her spectacular rants. The details of what irritated changed but the haughty and aghast delivery remained remarkably constant. No doubt *how dare they?* would pop up in her sister's monologue if it was allowed to run interrupted for a moment or two. It was a pet phrase of Lottie's when she was exasperated at others' cheeky behaviour. Rachel imagined that it must be great to be absolutely certain you were right all the time as her big sister seemed to be. She herself had no such comfort at the moment but despite her distress she had no intention of telling either of her sisters how bad things were with Ciaran. Occasionally before when she had told them about minor spats that had put her in bad form, both sisters had treated her husband like a pariah long after she herself had forgiven him or decided to forget the transgression. She hoped things would improve before they all met again. The trouble would have to be dealt with inside her own four walls because she believed that this was exactly what people meant when they said you had to work at your marriage. Relationships just didn't keep chugging along without proper care and attention and on that score Rachel was determined not to be found wanting.

Paying the minimum attention possible to her sister's spiel, Rachel considered the differences between her sisters and herself. Gina was the calm and even-tempered one, always had been, while Lottie prided herself in being a straight talker, no matter what upset that direct approach might cause. Rachel felt she fitted somewhere between the two extreme positions favoured by her sisters: tough when she had to be but laid-back when she didn't.

Unfortunately Lottie noticed that Rachel wasn't listening properly and she decided to haul her sister forcibly into the fray of conversation, not even attempting to hide her irritation at her sister's lacklustre response to Gina's plans. 'I'm surprised you're not just as pissed off as I am about Gina having all these strangers lurking around the lodge and nosing around our cottages during July. What about Orla and little Billy? They'll hate it!'

Rachel felt the time had come to put Lottie back in her box. 'The cottages are Gina's business and her and Sadie's livelihood. We've no right to interfere with the way she runs the place. We get to stay there for half nothing every summer, which she surely can't afford either. Besides, it might be nice to have some other people around the place. We might drink some more and not get so maudlin if we are in company that demands we lift our heads from our own little world and be a bit sociable with those around us.' Rachel knew in her heart that Lottie was the best in the world but when she was being this annoying she needed to be kept in check for the sanity of those around her.

'For God's sake, Rachel, if we drank any more than last year we may as well find a friendly AA meeting on the way home, unpack our bags there and be done with it. Besides, there's nothing to do in Tobarnaree except sit around having a chat with a glass of wine in one hand and the corkscrew in the other ready to uncork the next bottle. It's a holiday without the slightest scrap of pressure. Sure that's why we all adore our time there.'

'I suppose you're right, although we haven't been to France this year so we'll actually have our clothes in suitcases instead of using the fleeces and the rain jackets to cushion the car full of wine we arrived with last year.' Rachel was attempting to be light-hearted but she imagined she wasn't being at all convincing. Last July seemed like a world away, sketches of a past dream in the frame of a present nightmare. Ciaran hadn't even mentioned France this year; presumably she was to glean from his sullen silence on the matter that going would be an absolute impossibility. She could have gone herself, she supposed, but the ferry on her own with two children would have been tough and without Ciaran would have felt very strange. They had gone together every spring since they had met, missing only the year that she had been heavily pregnant with Orla and unwilling to risk getting stuck in the unforgiving door of a ferry cabin or worse still actually having her baby in the confines of its narrow berth.

At least if he didn't come to Tobarnaree this year she would still have her sisters and her niece to help with the children and for that she should be grateful. Sadie was wonderful with them and maybe their noisy carry-on might distract her from her heartbreak over losing her first proper boyfriend. She knew that Gina was hoping that her daughter's dismal mood would lift before she started college. It would be nice if she could leave her brace of shoulder chips behind her and throw herself into enjoying the freedom of a stint in college. Weighed down by the uncertainties that consumed her, Rachel thought she would give anything to be back at that stage in life, almost free of responsibility and with every tantalizing and untried possibility stretching out in front of her ready to be grasped. The truth was, of course, that everything Rachel had ever aspired to surrounded her now as if she had cunningly ordered it all in precise detail: Ciaran, the children, their lovely house and a comfortable lifestyle. Yet, although everything had turned out just as she'd planned, nothing seemed to fit properly.

Rachel tuned back in to hear Lottie rambling about the prospect of it being a parched month in Tobarnaree. 'Well, you can tell that husband of yours that it's very remiss of him to have skipped the wine-purchasing trip to France. I know he's rushed off his feet but the needs of the humble Miller wing of his family are not to be discounted while he busies himself designing homes and haunts for the great and the good of the capital. At off-licence prices in Tobarnaree we'll all be bankrupt long before anyone manages to get drunk. A girl might have to think about brewing her own to combat the enforced drought.'

'Oh come on, things aren't that desperate,' Rachel said.

'A holiday without enough drink? I'll tell you now, a few home-brew kits and a demijohn or two humming away nicely in the hot press might be just the remedy, seeing as your dearly devoted husband has left us not so high and very dry.'

'I'll tell him you're narked with him when I see him,' Rachel answered, although right at that moment a small and bitter part of her stoked by the persistent upset of too many arguments couldn't care less if she didn't lay eyes on him for a week or more. 'Oh and by the way I wouldn't chance brewing wine in one of Gina's cottages. I'd bet that she has some bye-law against that in the manifesto of Tobar Rock Cottages. She quietly attends to rules and regulations better than anyone I know.'

Lottie laughed. 'She can't bar me for anything. I'm family and with that comes the odd divine right or two. Chief amongst those rights is making myself completely at home no matter what. I'm a fixture in Tobarnaree for the month of July – unless I get a better offer, of course, and I am forever hopeful. A pampering cruise down the Nile or a beach hut in Thailand could well tempt me but as usual no one's offering anything in the way of alternatives.'

'But what about Joe? It will be nice for you to have him there won't it?' Rachel enquired, mustering as much enthusiasm as she could for her sister's love live.

'Joe won't be coming,' Lottie said as evenly as she could. 'We've had a parting of the ways, but if I go through the details again I will spend the rest of the day crying so I'll fill you in next time I see you.'

'Oh Lottie, that's desperate. I am sorry.'

'Me too, honey,' Lottie managed before delivering a rushed goodbye.

Rachel breathed a sigh of relief when she hung up without having to put words to the worst of what she was feeling. She took some comfort from the fact that she must have sounded much more relaxed than she felt or perhaps Lottie had been too busy wittering on to notice anything amiss. Rachel's marriage deserved the first call on whatever eloquence she could gather together and she trusted that her husband surely felt the same despite his hurtful behaviour of late.

It was well after nine when Ciaran finally arrived home. Rachel had cooked his favourite: salmon in sorrel cream sauce; an attempt at a peace offering maybe although she told herself as she carefully prepared the meal that she would not let him off the hook easily. His actions did not merit the benefit of the doubt. She loved him but these moods of his were unreasonable and he would have to prove willing to change. She added the neatly coiled strands of pasta to a pan of boiling water on the hob while Ciaran excused himself for a shower with a barely audible mumble. For her own sanity she needed them to talk properly because she could not allow the horrible atmosphere to run on indefinitely in the company of their children.

Ciaran remained preoccupied when he finally sat down to the table, as if the longed-for shower had failed to revive him in any way. He had exchanged the formality of a smart charcoal suit for jeans and a shirt that Rachel had bought him for Christmas or maybe a birthday; the detail escaped her memory though its subtle pattern was still pleasing to her. Although casually presented in his home clothes his thoughts were obviously still firmly locked away somewhere else. He might as well have stayed sitting at his desk at Jacob Design for all of him that was really present in their kitchen. She watched as he pushed the increasingly sticky and cold strands of pasta around the plate with his fork as if hunger could not touch him now either. After two meagre mouthfuls he pounced on his ringing mobile phone on the table near him. It was clear that he was glad of the reprieve from the duty of keeping his wife company.

Rachel's annoyance at his blatant need to escape from her made her snap despite countless promises to herself that she would try to remain calm. 'Would you just switch the fecking thing off, Ciaran? We're trying to have a meal here,' she said crossly, her voice doing significant battle with the piercing irritation of a ring tone that pleaded for his attention.

'I have to take it. It might be important,' he said sharply before he greeted the caller on the phone with an upbeat tone in his voice that she hadn't heard addressed to anyone at home for weeks. He walked out into the privacy of the hallway, pulling the kitchen door after him as if she could not be trusted to overhear what he had to say. Rachel reached for his dinner plate and with an angry and efficient slick of a knife emptied the contents into the waste bin under the sink. She dumped her own dinner too because she was far too resentful of the effort involved in preparing what had been neither needed nor appreciated. Hunger cleared a space for fury that she gave considerable vent to by flinging the dishes roughly and every which way into the dishwasher. The sauté pan and the pasta pot she had washed while Ciaran showered upstairs made a satisfying crash as she stowed them in the hollow belly of the pot drawer. Were it not for the fact that Orla and Billy were sleeping soundly in the upstairs bedrooms she would have relished finding something appropriately noisy to smash.

'I didn't realize dinner would be suddenly declared over just because I'd to nip out to take a quick work call,' Ciaran said dryly when he returned to the kitchen, motioning to the wiped-down table, empty save for the open wine bottle and his nearly drained glass. He slipped his mobile phone into his jeans pocket, afraid it seemed to let it out of convenient reach.

Rachel took a deep breath before she answered. She didn't want to make things worse but she wouldn't allow herself to be made a quiet fool of either. If Ciaran didn't know she deserved better then she was about to remind him of the point. 'Ten minutes during dinner is not a quick call and, let's be honest, it's not like you were actually going to eat it, were you? I really don't know why I bother cooking and haven't the slightest notion why you even come home any more. You can barely hide the fact that you have zero interest in what goes on in this house. Now, maybe I'd put up with that if it was just me. I'd go out with a few of my girlfriends any night I could and forget I had a dipstick of a husband at home. To be perfectly honest with you I'd quite happily leave you the way you're behaving at the moment but have you forgotten that we've two children that depend on us for their future? I'm finding every pocket of patience I can for you but our children upstairs should not have to deal with a father they barely see. Even when they do you fail to fake even the slightest bit of enthusiasm for anything about them or their lives.'

Ciaran shook his head and she detected the merest hint of a disbelieving smirk. He had a catalogue of disapproving glances that he deployed when words could not adequately cover how disappointed he was but in their years together Rachel had rarely been their target. Watching him now, so deeply unimpressed by her, was even more maddening because she was sure that she was the wronged party and that her husband didn't have a leg to stand on.

'You're overreacting now,' he retorted. 'The kids know I have to work. They understand even if you don't. I see them plenty – just not that much at the moment, I admit.'

'You missed Orla's school concert and her end-of-term prize-giving and what was all that bullshit about taking Billy to the junior football training? The session times have been pinned to the noticeboard over there since last January but you never get home in time to take him even though you know he's been dying to go. I offered but he keeps saying he wants to go with you because Odhran Kelly's daddy goes with him and he wants to fit in like everyone else. When did it get to this, Ciaran? When did you decide that nothing or scraps of nearly nothing was good enough for your family?' Rachel sat down exhausted by the overpowering swell of disappointment and anger that consumed her despite her best efforts to stay in control. She was worked up to a point that further words failed her. Did he really need his deficiencies pointed out so plainly? Did he not know how badly they had been treated?

Ciaran took a seat at the edge of the kitchen table as if he felt she might not welcome his presence any closer to her. He cleared his throat. 'Look, Rach' – cornered and nervous he'd forgotten the abbreviation made her wince – 'I'm just up to my neck in work. It's all go and I admit I've been stressed and not here with you all as much as I should. Cut me a bit of slack for another while and I swear to God I'll make it up to you and to Orla and Billy too. It's all for you guys, you know? Please don't ever doubt that. It's just this one project that's breaking my heart at the moment but I swear I am this close to clinching it.' He gestured with his thumb and index finger all but touching. 'If it comes off – I mean *when* not if, of course – we will really be in clear blue water. I need a bit more time to hammer the details out, that's all.'

'Was that what the super-secret phone call just now was about?' Rachel asked curtly, making it plain that it maddened her to feel unworthy of inclusion in her own home.

'Kind of, I guess,' he said. 'It's just that someone made a promise to me about an aspect of one of our big projects and I need to get them to keep their word. I swear I'm doing this for us. So you and Orla and Billy for that matter will never have to worry about anything. I know it's tough but just give me a little bit of scope on this and I *will* make it up to you eventually.'

'Your family want something from you beside money every month, you know, Ciaran. We need you here with us. We miss you. The four of us used to have such fun together. I can hardly remember the last time we all went out for something to eat in town or to see a crap movie with the kids. Your work can't take over the way we live in this house. There has to be something more to life or else what is all the effort for? They're growing up fast and you've already missed six months of their lives with your head stuck firmly in the sand. How much more are you prepared to lose because some shitty project at Jacob Design is going against you? Bring one of the other architects on the team to get the project out of the mire. Sure that's why you hired a slew of juniors in the first place. What's the point of the huge outlay on staff every month if you end up doing everything yourself anyway?' Rachel's tone was as even as she could make it. She wanted him to hear her point so she tried to conceal as much of her anger at his behaviour as she could manage.

Ciaran took a thirsty gulp from the glass of wine he had filled as she spoke, unable to withstand the temptation of the open wine bottle any longer. Rachel was used to its habitual presence in his hand on the rare occasions they now shared time at home. He seemed to need it to quell or to deny the stress he was under. 'Look, love, we always knew the start-up was going to be hard. The easiest thing in the world for me would have been to become a jobbing architect in someone else's firm and let them carry all the risk and worry but that's not me and that's not my style. Come on, you know Ciaran Jacob doesn't ever take the easy road. I thought that was one of the things you loved about me. You used to like my ambition and that's the only thing that will keep Jacob Design on the list of the most progressive practices in the city. Business has fallen back, of course, but we have some great new young architects coming through and if the practice rallies in a few years I can try and pull back a little.'

He was on a roll. When he started to refer to himself in the third person she knew her husband was gone, having been temporarily replaced by smooth-talking corporate Ciaran. She felt she was being treated like a disappointed client who needed his morale boosted by a bracing pep talk from the top man. Where had the man she knew disappeared to in all of this? Was he only the suit and the talk now? If he was then she knew she could not stomach the disappointment of knowing that he was so shallow and not at all the person she imagined him to be. 'You're right; I loved how ambitious you were. I admired that you wanted to take the challenging route and build something from scratch. But ambition is not half as attractive if it's a person's only discernible characteristic and that's the way you're heading. You're behaving like your wife and children must always play second fiddle to whatever is going on in the company. I know your work's important to you but we've got to get our fair share of your attention. I thought things being quieter in construction would free you up a little to spend time with us. Instead of that you're here less and less. We matter most or have you forgotten that in your quest for Jacob Design to take over the city?'

'Oh come on, I've told you I'll make it up to you. It's just that it's all crazy and stressful at the moment and I can't afford to take my eye off the ball for a second. Please, Rachel, hang in there. For me? For us? For God's sake, I love you. I love you all. I admit I've cocked up lately but I'd never do anything to hurt you and the children. This bloody thing is just at a crucial stage and needs my full attention for now – but not for ever. I promise.'

She gazed at his pleading face. He seemed genuine. Surely that was worth a renewed investment of patience? Moving away from the kitchen to the furthest edge of the room, she curled her slender body into the cushioned softness of her favourite couch, and beckoned him to join her.

After his second glass of wine he relaxed a little, and Rachel thought it opportune to bring up their trip to Tobar Rock. He groaned dramatically at the mention of an entire month anywhere with Lottie and he was delighted when he found out that there would be others to dilute the overwhelming effect of the Miller family cocktail, announcing it to be an inspired plan to have other people to drown out the family noise. By midnight she had wrangled a promise from him that he would show up for as much of the annual holiday as work deadlines would permit. By midnight they had made love and fallen asleep together in the same bed for the first time in weeks.

CHAPTER FIVE

It didn't take Sadie long to track down her mother's American lodgers. They were the single unfamiliar presence in the decrepit lounge of the Tobarnaree Arms Hotel. It seemed the promised husband hadn't come, nor the son for that matter, because she recognized the pair in front of her as a stressed and somewhat crestfallen mother accompanied by a daughter in the full bloom of an exceptional sulk. It wasn't that complicated a scene for a teenager to analyse. Sadie imagined herself and her mother probably looked like that a lot, although perhaps not quite so miserable as the Carters seemed to be right then, marooned in a strange hotel with only each other, the stale air and the low ceilings for company. Fights with her own mother always tended toward fiery spats more than long-drawn-out and grudge-riddled affairs. It was a rhythm that worked for them, dissipating tension as it arose rather than letting it build only to later blow out of control.

'They've been expecting one of you,' Margaret Keane, the hotel owner, said, nodding in the direction of the two women sitting in the far corner of the gaudy wallpapered room around a clutch of expensive-looking suitcases. 'You can tell your mother that she's stealing valuable business from us. I would've told her myself if she'd bothered to turn up to greet her guests in person.' Margaret Keane's jibe was intended to be light-hearted but she failed to match her bitter expression to the easygoing sentiment. 'Years ago these kind of people tracing their family roots would have been more than happy to stay in my little hotel until your grandfather saw fit to set up his own little self-catering enterprise out there by that lonesome old lake.'

She had obviously interrogated the Carters about the purpose of their visit while they had waited for someone to come and escort them out to Tobar Rock. Sadie contemplated what she might say to Margaret Keane that would put her in her place, firmly but nicely. In her manners she was her mother's daughter while in her need not to be outsmarted by someone she simply didn't rate she was a teenager to the core. 'Who knows what attracts them to our lonesome old place, Mrs Keane? Still, my granddad must've known what he was doing because they obviously prefer the fresh air of Tobar Rock to being stuck here in this hotel with you, don't they?' she chipped with a serene smile, leaving Margaret to fume silently at the cheek of Nicholas Miller's grand-daughter and the faltering state of her season's reservations book.

Sadie thought Ellen Carter was quite glamorous, although in Tobarnaree putting on a slick of lipstick and wearing something other than a fleece and jeans counted as making a serious effort with one's appearance. Ellen was a significant bit older than her own mother, Sadie felt, a well-preserved fifty at a guess. She was certainly more substantial than Gina in a rich and well-fed sort of way. Her fingers were pink and plump, curled like sausages on a butcher's tray, her hands showing all the signs of a comfortable life unhampered by manual labour.

Her daughter Jessica was spiky and sullen and seemed deeply unimpressed by her mother's choice of holiday destination. If pressed on the issue Sadie would readily agree that to come from

Boston to Tobarnaree was nothing short of downright insane. Some things were just too ridiculous to understand. Indeed Sadie herself was mulling over making the exact opposite trip next summer if she could get the money together for the flight. Ellen Carter might turn out to be a useful contact. Getting to know her throughout this summer might prove to be a good move, not that Sadie would give her mother the satisfaction of admitting that. Her daughter felt that Gina was too fond of thinking she knew best, and consequently there was no way Sadie would say anything that would make her lose the run of herself entirely.

In order to justify their occupation of Margaret Keane's lounge for the previous forty minutes Ellen ordered afternoon tea and cake for the three of them, despite Jessica's derisory snort and Sadie's protest that she had just eaten and wasn't the slightest bit hungry. She thought it best not to mention that her last meal had been an extremely late brunch from which she was still chock-full. No need for complete strangers to know how lazy she had been. Hopefully, out of maternal loyalty, her mother wouldn't see fit to fill them in.

'We didn't get much lunch, did we, honey?' Ellen addressed Jessica, who could not look any more pissed off if she tried. Her blonde hair shone immaculately as if it had been recently and expertly straightened within an inch of its life. Its impressive sleekness was easily the prettiest thing about an otherwise exceptionally plain girl.

Sadie realized how relieved she felt that she wouldn't be escorting someone a good deal more attractive than herself around all summer. Her ego had taken enough of a battering recently; it certainly wouldn't be able to cope with the added injury of constantly comparing herself unfavourably to an exotic companion who would have the whole town gawking and talking. The sight of a belligerent Jessica Carter indicated a longed-for upturn in luck, although she hoped that appearances might be deceptive and she would turn out a bit friendlier than her bad-tempered face deemed possible.

It seemed as if Jessica was quite happy to ignore her mother's question about their lunch and so Ellen Carter addressed her again, a little louder this time, implying that she would not abide the rudeness of her continued silence. 'We didn't get much lunch, did we, Jessica?' she demanded, eyeing her daughter sternly.

Sadie felt the obvious rebuke was for her benefit but she really didn't want to be drawn into such unpleasantness. Managing the expectations of one mother was enough to cope with, she decided as she watched the pair in front of her trying to outdo one another. Besides, if she were to choose an ally from this unlikely pairing surely it should be the daughter?

Eventually Jessica answered with no trace of affection in her voice. 'No, Mother, we didn't. Not unless you count that lumpy swill that you ordered a small vat of in the airport. I can't believe you actually ate some of that crud. I think they may have served you up the food set aside for the sniffer dogs by accident. Those famished animals are probably munching on a small-time drug smuggler as we speak and all because of a missed meal that you inhaled.'

'I thought it nice to try a traditional dish,' Ellen explained, looking at Sadie and with overdone sweetness attempting to convey apologies for her daughter's bad manners, 'so I ordered us both a casserole of beef in Guinness.'

'Beef in shit more like,' Jessica interjected with gleeful disdain at her mother's fawning explanation to the naive-looking girl in front of them.

'Jessica Carter, you will not speak like that to me or in front of this young lady either. Have I not told you that the first rule of being a conscientious traveller is that you never *ever* insult what your host country has to offer? It's most ungracious and disappointing to hear you indulge in such talk. I sometimes wonder what purpose all your expensive schooling serves, I really do.'

'Me too,' Jessica retorted, throwing her eyes to heaven.

Sadie looked at the floor, trying hard not to laugh. She had no intention of taking umbrage on behalf of the whole of Ireland and she figured the Guinness family were big and bold enough to defend themselves and their sacred brew against an unimpressed consumer. The clinking of forks against china filled the gaping conversational hole for a few tension-filled moments. Sadie's full stomach meant she could not even bring herself to lift a fork and pretend to eat a morsel. Instead she watched as mother and daughter tried hard to think of something to say to or about the other that would indicate who exactly was in control.

'This cake is a heap of shit too,' Jessica added under her breath but far too loudly for anything approaching discretion.

Eyeing her closely Sadie thought she might have copped the slightest flash of a conspiratorial smile. Indeed she would have been surprised if it really had been anything other than revolting as the hotel's reputation for home baking was legendary for all the wrong reasons. Margaret Keane had, without a shred of irony, gone on local radio with her recipes for long-life afternoon tea cake. The 'long life' element seemed merely to consist of putting the baked-until-cinder-dry item in a plastic box and continuing to serve it until all was disposed of and another round of domesticity and the regrettable outlay on ingredients was required.

Ellen ate her own slice with alarming speed, her fork beating a regular and noisy rhythm on the hotel's ivy-patterned china. When she had eaten her own portion she picked at stray crumbs on Jessica's plate, saying how much she hated waste, before filling Sadie in about the plans she had for their summer break. They would be basing themselves mainly in Tobarnaree but she was considering trips around the southwest and to Dublin or anywhere else in the country that might take their fancy. It was their first trip to Ireland and she wanted to make it memorable. Sadie thought of all the words that might accurately describe her home town and even at the furthest stretch of sentimental goodwill 'memorable' certainly did not make the list.

Ellen Carter had engaged the services of an internet genealogy company to research her family tree and they had traced a great-great-grandparent back to Tobarnaree. 'I was hoping I'd find some Irish cousins for Jessica and Ben but unfortunately there's no evidence here of anyone belonging to us now. I think your Great Famine may have wiped my family out.' She stared at the untouched wedge of cake on Sadie's plate almost as if she felt the girl's seed and breed must shoulder a portion of the blame for the extinction of her family's bloodline in Tobarnaree.

The Tobarnaree Arms didn't run to a porter service so Sadie shared the ferrying of the suitcases to the car park with Ellen leaving a fed-up Margaret Keane clattering stained tea cups and salvaging an almost perfect slice of fruit cake to put back into the Tupperware box in the kitchen. 'You could have left the suitcases in the car, you know,' Sadie offered helpfully, 'they'd have been as safe as houses.'

'Well, I just wasn't sure. The car doesn't have a sealed trunk so I was a bit nervous about leaving the luggage visible in a strange town. Crime stats and all that.'

' "Strange town": cleverest thing you've said all day, Mother,' Jessica interjected but Ellen ignored her, having apparently decided to rise above her daughter's negativity and deal with Sadie who was pleasant and personable in all the ways her daughter was not.

'Nothing would have happened to your bags, honestly,' Sadie offered while pulling the heaviest of the cases toward the Carters' brand-new rented people carrier.

Jessica, peeved at being overlooked, which she wasn't accustomed to, walked on ahead of her mother and Sadie, ignoring the fact that between them they were hauling a good portion of her entire wardrobe. She kept her hands tucked firmly in her jacket pockets looking around the town that her mother had picked for this year's annual holiday torture. The dearth of anything even remotely interesting to see depressed her. A lone neon sign flashed advertising a two-euro shop with a partially inflated shamrock on the window; from what she could make out it was a dreary drugstore-type place. How grim a prospect was that? There was scenery, of course, and lots of it, but none of it interested her; one mountain tended to look suspiciously the same as the last. Natural beauty was overrated, she felt. She counted on the existence of a regular train service to Dublin. From the little she had seen of it as they made their way from the airport it looked like a proper city, a bit dirty perhaps but she would embrace all its unkemptness if it meant she could spend as little time with her mother as possible. She hoped her dad and Ben would actually follow them as promised. Their presence might manage to move this trip to Ireland up a notch on the bearable scale. She was a little bit suspicious that Jack Carter had just wanted his wife out of his sight for a while. He could barely conceal how much her mother irritated him and how happily he would agree to her taking a trip to anywhere anytime she liked. It would be another year at least before Jessica would be free to stay home alone in Boston and let her mother roam wherever she pleased. The further that roaming might take her, the better, her daughter thought bitterly. She had gone on way too many of these trips with her mother and on each one Ellen became ever more insufferable. Ben mostly got away now because he was older and a college student with a wealth of credible, if ultimately fake, excuses for not doing the good-son act at his mother's side.

'Oh it is so beautiful down here, isn't it? So wild and peaceful at the same time.' Ellen Carter parked the hire car in the courtyard in front of Beech Cottage where Sadie told her she would be staying. She was thoroughly enthralled by her selection of holiday location even if the house itself looked impossibly small. She knew it was silly but she had been kind of expecting something the size of the main house that looked even more divine in reality than it had done on the website. She loved the cut-stone finish and the hulking oak and ash trees that lined the curling avenue down to the main road. Although if that road was considered a major one, despite being riddled by water-filled potholes, she was not looking forward to driving on a country lane. The cottages were pleasant to look at, a little like miniature playhouses. She was quite sure that if Jack actually came to spend some time in Tobarnaree with his family this summer (and she knew it would be for Jessica and Ben's sake and definitely not for hers) he would not last a second night sharing somewhere this small with her. Space and plenty of it had been their salvation, allowing them to live just far enough apart for comfort.

As she followed Sadie into the cottage Ellen wondered if she doubled or trebled the rental amount would Gina Miller consider vacating Tobar Lodge for the duration and moving into the cottage instead? A single woman and her daughter hardly needed a house that size, she thought, gazing enviously at the main house and taking in all its elegant but lived-in grandeur. It was a little rough around the edges but she felt that only added to its authenticity. Affording the extra money wasn't a problem so it was certainly worth asking if her host was up for revisiting their deal. Not many people turned down Ellen Carter's requests. Her husband always said she had the knack; or at least he used to say it before he gradually lost interest in anything his wife said or did. Husband? How fraudulent that word sounded now when used to describe Jack.

They had grown apart in a way she would not have thought possible when she had first fallen for him. They had met on a creative-writing module that she had undertaken with some determination once she realized that the handsome sophomore

Jack Carter would be taking the class also. That was nearly thirty years ago now and she still hadn't finished the novel she began so self-assuredly that autumn, although the first pages with their well-faded typeface still lay in the top drawer of her desk, waiting to be fleshed out by the addition of a body and an ending. Jack on the other hand insisted that he had long given up on the pipedream that he would make a living writing fiction. Instead he churned out a steady stream of solidly written feature articles for a host of newspapers whose prescribed topics almost without exception bored him rigid, and lately a humorous column that through its syndication had been earning him an obscene amount of money for a scant half-day's work. It was a situation that might have made some others more than happy with their lot but every aspect of Jack's life (apart from Jessica and Ben, and Ellen knew to be glad of that small mercy) seemed to disillusion him in ways he couldn't even begin to explain. Ellen Carter was quite sure she didn't want him to either. No one needed it pointed out to them that they were the essence of someone else's unhappiness. There were times when silence was a far softer and safer option for all involved. Besides, she imagined that plenty of people lived just as they did, alongside each other to the eyes of outsiders but not together in any real sense of the word. Over the years she had found that having enough money made comfortable what with lesser means would certainly have been unbearable. Too many people thought that money was the answer to everything while she had come to realize that it merely made it easier to avoid facing up to the unpalatable questions.

Gina was startled to find Ellen wandering around the hallway of Tobar Lodge looking at the Miller family photo history as if she owned the place, breaking off only to introduce herself before resuming the intent examination of her surroundings. She couldn't have known that Ellen was indeed imagining what being resident, albeit temporarily, might be like. While Gina had been upstairs changing the sheets on Sadie's recently vacated bed, Ellen had taken the liberty of touring the entire ground floor, apparently seeking out her hostess but in reality relishing the opportunity to have a good and uninterrupted nose.

Gina hadn't heard their car pull up and she wondered if Sadie was with this woman's family down at the cottage or if she had missed them entirely at the Tobarnaree Arms. She would throttle her if she found out that she had just ignored what she had been asked to do and was now amusing herself in town or lounging around at a friend's house. Sadie could find another job in the morning if that was the case because Gina refused to throw good money after bad and be made a fool of into the bargain. How could Sadie treat her like such a soft touch when she knew how tight things were going to be for them financially?

'Did Sadie not meet you and show you to where you are staying?' she asked as gently as she could manage, though she was considerably annoyed that any stranger should make themselves so familiar in her home. She would have to stamp this behaviour out and make it abundantly clear that she was renting out her cottages and not subletting her life.

Ellen seemed glad of something to get the conversational ball rolling. 'Absolutely; yes she did. What a charming daughter you have! You must be so proud.'

'Well, yes I am,' Gina managed guiltily while wondering if Lottie was right and she really had invited someone a touch mad to Tobar Rock. She would never hear the end of it from her sisters or indeed an egged-on Sadie if it turned out to be true. She took in her guest's money-pampered appearance while hoping their summer wouldn't be ruined entirely.

'Sadie's taken my daughter down to see the rock and the lake. My son and husband are due to fly into Shannon at the weekend and I know they'll be as charmed with the place as I am. I showed Jessica the photographs on your sweet website but she is anxious to see the area with her own two eyes and Sadie was good enough to go with her. She told me I'd find you here.'

'Yes, this is my home so it's a good place to start looking for me.' Gina was hoping that her sarcasm would make her point that she didn't like her private space invaded but Ellen was too busy looking around to take any notice of her host's subtle attempt to chastise her. People were unbelievable, Gina thought before trying again. 'Can I do something for you? Everything you need to get started should already be in the cottage. Towels, tea, coffee, milk, brown bread, butter in the fridge and a bottle of red on the wine rack.' Louis Corrigan gave her the house wines at discount to stock the cottages and people always seemed grateful for the thought of a bottle of wine ready for their first night. She didn't tell Lottie about the arrangement because her sister would most likely drink a team of wine wholesalers dry if she knew wine was to be had at a bargain price.

Gina quickly realized that Ellen couldn't care less about her hostess's efforts at hospitality because she'd other things on her mind. 'I saw that and you're very kind to attend to all those little details but what I really want to know is if you would consider eight thousand for here?' Ellen clasped her hands together to her mouth as a child might do for luck in a hook-the-bear competition at a funfair and she flashed Gina her most fawning smile.

'What do you mean, Mrs Carter? I am afraid you've lost me entirely.' Gina feared this could be a very long six weeks indeed. Her guest seemed to be rambling and she had only just arrived.

'Call me Ellen, please. I cannot abide formality when I'm on vacation. Forgive me for launching straight in but I'm offering to double the rental we agreed if I can stay here in your house instead of down at Beech Cottage for the six weeks. This house is just too adorable for words.' She gestured noisily, sweeping a jewellery-heavy hand around the lodge's spacious hallway. Her loud voice seemed to echo back from the sage-coloured walls and Gina was aware that even though she and Sadie lived there together Ellen on her own could easily outdo them for volume. Guests generally stayed in their cottages once they had obtained the key, turning up for flying visits to the lodge's front door with simple requests for directions or for local information about buses or activities. The wide-open door was an integral part of the Tobar Rock experience but an aspect which Gina paused to regret as she looked, alarmed, at Ellen's expectant face.

'The cottages are much better equipped for guests. My house is a bit old and shabby. I think you'd find it less suitable, to be honest, Mrs Cart— I mean Ellen.' Gina struggled to take in the absolute ridiculousness of what she was proposing. Could this woman not see that this was her home and not something she could order up on a whim?

'I know my offer must come as a shock to you but I have always allowed my intuition to guide me and your house just speaks volumes to me. It would be just perfect for us. When Ben and Jack arrive we won't be all on top of each other. Beech Cottage is rather small,' Ellen added gently. She could see Gina was taken aback but she gamely continued: 'You must have a good number of bedrooms in a house this size?' She nodded in the direction of the stairs at what lay beyond and so far unseen.

'We have six I guess though I use one of them as a store room,' Gina answered, though her mind had now fixed firmly on the extra four thousand euro that would more than cover the dip in earnings from her job at the restaurant.

'That many? How wonderful. You see it's impossible to roster Jack Carter. He absolutely hates having to fit in to anyone else's plans, even those of his own family. If I am being charitable I say he's a free spirit. When I booked this holiday I presumed he wouldn't want to come all this way but just before we left he promised Jessica he would fly over with Ben this weekend. This house, or your home should I say, would just be ideal for our needs. Say you'll consider it, please.'

Gina was half listening to Ellen as she wittered on about her evasive husband but she was speedily coming round to the kernel of her guest's offer. She would have to lock away her private things into a spare room or the attic and she would have to maintain access to the office under the stairs from where she ran her business but otherwise there wasn't really a problem so far as she could see. The weeks would fly by, surely, and what harm could it do? The thought of extra money flowing into all the unpaid hollows of her life swayed the last of her doubts. There was a credit-card bill in particular that bothered her, not that anyone else would consider it out of control but she had been unable to clear the balance. The card had operated as a safety valve for her and Sadie's needs, used as a last resort when there was something they needed that her earnings could not cover. She paid as much more than the minimum amount as she could afford every month but she dreamed of clearing it entirely. As Ellen spoke Gina allowed herself to wonder what it would be like to be debt free. Her and Sadie's future could begin on a clean slate.

'Well, maybe we could come to some agreement. You've caught me by surprise but it might be possible, I guess, although I'll have to check with Sadie first as I can't really hunt the girl from her own home without consulting her. I'll discuss it with her when she comes back and let you know later on this evening.'

Ellen nodded but she was reluctant to leave the warm and inviting space of Tobar Lodge for what she clearly considered the rather suffocating scale of her assigned accommodation with Tobar Rock towering giant-like in the background.

Gina stood awkwardly in the doorway of her kitchen, not knowing what to say next. Gradually she realized that by failing to leave Ellen was obliging her to make the next move. 'I could boil the kettle. Would you like some tea or coffee?' From her guest's grateful smile she knew that she had hit on just the thing that would satisfy her.

'Tea would be superb and I know that you all take your tea-drinking very seriously in this country,' Ellen said with a triumphant smile, taking a seat at what she planned would be her dining table for the next six weeks. She quoted tea-drinking statistics and a barrage of glib facts gleaned from the in-flight magazine while Gina ransacked the cupboards looking for something that she could produce for an unplanned afternoon tea. Clearly this woman was expecting more than a cup in her hand. Well, if she moved into the lodge she needn't bother thinking that she had a full-time cook. She feared that Ellen had misconstrued what self-catering meant. Surely the term was clear enough?

'Do you mind me asking what it is you write?' Gina enquired, remembering that Ellen had said in her email that she was a writer and thinking it only polite to ask exactly what she wrote about. She furiously scoured the shelf for one of the unchipped mugs and rinsed a rarely used jug to decant milk from the two-litre carton in the fridge door. Her guest seemed to be expecting a serious effort so she was not about to plonk the carton on the table as usual.

Ellen ran her fingers through her chocolate-coloured bob and her pretty features puckered up as if overcome by a sudden spasm of pain. 'Did I say writer? I write a little but mostly I paint. I'm, em, a landscape artist,' she stuttered.

Back at their pipsqueak cottage Jessica thawed a little when Sadie suggested a wander into Tobarnaree later to have a proper look around. From what Jessica had seen of the town she doubted it had much by way of latent treasure to offer but anything was better than a quiet night in with her mother in a strange cabin in the middle of nowhere. Ellen would want to talk, plan some day trips or maybe play a board game and Jessica had no intention of partaking in any such activities. Her mother had outdone herself this time finding this dive but there was no point in taking it out on the earnest local girl charged with being her chaperone. If she put Sadie off she would have no one for company apart from Ellen and further isolation was a prospect Jessica would not bring on herself lightly. Sadie told her there were some good pubs and two nice coffee shops and that no one under the bingo crowd age ever went into the Tobarnaree Arms because it was a dead duck of a place. Having enquired what bingo was and lost interest during the protracted explanation (numbers, old ladies with their pens poised and clasping their handbags in anticipation; she really didn't care as much as Sadie about the quality of the answer), Jessica's most pressing issue was transport, independent of her mother's hire car. What means did she have of getting out of the backwater her mother had landed them in?

'I'll go back and ask my mam if you can borrow her bike while you're around. She doesn't use it much and it would be handy for going in and out of Tobarnaree. I cycle all the time. Otherwise I'd be stuck out here because Mam won't let me have her car much. Not that I blame her really because my driving is brutal. I just can't seem to get the hang of the whole clutch thing . . .' She tailed off noticing belatedly that her companion's eyes had widened alarmingly at the prospect of having to cycle into town.

'A bike? Great,' Jessica muttered in patent disbelief. She couldn't remember the last time she had been on one. Summer camp maybe about a million years ago. 'What time are you planning to head back into this Tubber place?'

Sadie sounded it out helpfully. '*Tobar-na-ree*. It's Irish. It means the well of the kings.' Sadie sounded a little proud of a heritage that she felt a lot closer to than she was often willing to admit. 'There's a local legend—' she began before Jessica cut her off abruptly.

'Yeah, right. Cute I suppose if you're into all of that stuff but I'm not. So what time?'

Sadie told her anything before eight was hopeless. If Tobarnaree was ever guilty of buzzing at all it tended to happen after that hour but she made it plain to Jessica that she couldn't promise anything too exciting.

Jessica smirked. 'As if,' she muttered, 'but away from my mother after the nauseatingly close contact of a transatlantic flight is all I ask.' She knew she should be grateful that Sadie was trying to help but the long journey had all but depleted her store of gratitude.

Sadie decided to text her friend Tara to join them for a bit of company. It might make the first night's conversation run a little more smoothly, although she already knew what Tara was likely to think of their summer companion.

When she came back through the open hallway door of the lodge and into the kitchen she found her mother buttering and spooning raspberry jam on a round of hastily defrosted and now steaming hot scones for Jessica's mother. After much chatter about her plans to pick up new oils and brushes in Cork the next day, their guest finally left, overcome by late-onset guilt that she had left her teenage daughter to fend for herself in a strange house, even if it was a minuscule one where she was unlikely to get disoriented. 'Poor Jessica, what will she think of me?' she squealed as she headed for the hallway. The heels of her shoes came down hard on the flagstones as she scuttled out the door and on to the gravel where she broke into an awkward trot.

Gina closed the door behind her dying to see if Sadie was up for the adventure of loaning their house to the Carters. 'She's offering eight thousand euro if she can rent this house instead of the cottage for the six weeks. You and I can move into the cottage they're in at the moment. It means we'll be close to Lottie, Rachel and the kids when they come to stay. What do you think, pet? Are you up for it?'

'Holy cow! Are you sure she said that much? That's insane money!'

'I'm positive that's what she said. She stopped short of saying she couldn't breathe down there in the cottage. It seems like the Carters live on a much grander scale than our little cottages at Tobar Rock and I think she wants to have a stab at being lady of the manor. With any luck she might give the place a lick of paint or have the loose roof slates fixed while she's staying here. Seriously, though, do you think we should go for it?'

'Mam, would you go on and bite the woman's hand off elbow and all before she has the lobotomy reversed? Who knows, after six weeks she might offer you a few million for the whole place and we could move to somewhere that actually has a pulse? Maybe even the big smoke? The excitement of Dublin would knock us out and let's face it that's never going to happen here, is it? If we can't bring Dublin to Tobar we have a duty to bring a bit of this godforsaken spot there. We could get a place close to Rachel, Orla and Billy but maybe a bus ride from Lottie just for safety.'

Gina couldn't afford to let Sadie's running down of Tobar Lodge continue. She was staying put and she hoped that Sadie would find enough in the place they lived to come back on more than the odd occasion when she had made the break for college. 'Don't be silly, why would we want to sell the place? I adore it and I know you do too but you'd die before you would admit it. And much as I love Lottie and Rachel I'm happy to live a good hundred and sixty odd miles away and see them when I can but not all the time. I just think that the extra money this year would be so handy. If it all works out, sure she might come back again next year and we would do the same thing. It's money for old rope really. With any luck this old house of ours will step up to the plate. Now would be an unfortunate time for the water pipes to burst in the attic or for Mammy's Aga to finally choke, splutter and die.'

'Yeah, go for it, Mam. You would be insane not to take her up on it but they better not touch any of my stuff, especially anything in my room. It's private and they shouldn't need to even go in there if they use the spare rooms. Nana Miller's ghost will probably haunt the strangers from the bowels of the simmering oven if they stick their nose where they're not wanted.'

Gina was amused at Sadie thinking that anyone would covet any of the stray belongings she had strewn everywhere in her bedroom. Her tone rippled with sarcasm but she managed to keep a straight face as she replied: 'Well, we'll have to see to it that all your valuable jewels, heirlooms and antiques are packed away, won't we? Maybe we could get Foleys Antique Rooms on Quay Street to value and catalogue them while we're at it. You'd never know what your treasure trove might be worth all told.'

'Jesus, you're hysterical, Mam, aren't you? I'm just saying I don't want them going through my private things, that's all. They seem normal enough but Auntie Lottie always says the real weirdos come wrapped in brown paper so just in case she's right I want to box my stuff and put it in the attic.'

Lottie would definitely know all about weirdos, Gina thought, but having just that afternoon surveyed the unfathomable chaos that Sadie liked to call her bedroom she guessed that the Carters would steer well clear if they had any sense at all.

'God, she got a good hard scrape of the ugly stick, didn't she?' Tara Hickey had made her way to the Wild Oat pub on McCauley Street to meet Sadie and to have a good look at the American girl who was staying for the summer holidays. While Jessica had disappeared to the toilet she had given her unkind if more or less truthful verdict.

Sadie felt a surge of loyalty toward her new charge that caught her unawares. 'She's kind of pretty in her own way, I suppose,' she offered in a weak-spirited defence of Jessica while making a determined effort not to meet her friend's incredulous gaze. She was anxious to stem Tara's cruel bluntness but knew that she probably wouldn't succeed. Tara always relished a frank debate.

'Yeah, in much the same way that my dad's pack of hounds in full chase could be considered pretty. Maybe she'll visit Crufts while she's on this side of the water? She'd fit right in.' Tara could not resist having the last word.

Sadie ordered two glasses of lager for herself and Tara while Jessica tarried in the bathroom. Quite what she was finding to do in there for so long puzzled them both. It wasn't the type of place that generally encouraged a long stay.

'Cheapskates,' the barman slagged as he set their drinks down before them but they knew he didn't mind really. The Wild Oat depended on drinkers of their ilk to keep it afloat on week nights. It was common knowledge that the town's pubs did serious trade only on Thursday, Friday and Saturday nights and even that business had begun to flag in recent months. Opening on any of the other nights was little more than community service, albeit one that the locals were very glad to see continued.

Eventually Jessica emerged from the toilets in the back corridor looking a lot brighter, even a little smug, Sadie judged. A layer of foundation applied with a heavy hand and a streak of gothic purple lipstick revealed that she had used the opportunity to apply make-up, a task severely hampered by the almost non-existent lighting. Soon, when she knew her a little better and could frame the words just the right way, Sadie vowed to explain to Jessica that a week night at the Wild Oat didn't warrant that level of effort.

'Woof and double fecking woof,' Tara said under her breath. Sadie shot a glance at her friend imploring her to keep her mouth closed on the subject of Jessica's odd appearance. Her friend grinned back disarmingly. Sometimes the target was just too damned easy and there was no satisfaction in that.

'A glass of lager?' Sadie asked, tapping the side of her own glass and hoping that Jessica would not ask for a drink that was beyond the Wild Oat's somewhat basic inventory.

'Oh, nothing for me, thanks. I carry my own.' She slipped her hand into the inside pocket of her jacket and winked at Sadie and Tara, who managed with some difficulty to smile back. She pulled out a hip flask and Sadie almost choked. She didn't know which was worse: being thrown out of the Wild Oat – one of only two nearly cool pubs in the town – for drinking from a hip flask, or bringing Jessica home legless to Ellen Carter on her first night in Tobarnaree.

'What's that?'

'It's a hip flask. My dad bought it for me in Rome for my sixteenth birthday. Pretty cool, yeah?'

'Oh for Jesus' sake, of course I know it's a hip flask, but what do you have in it and why would you bring it into a pub? They do sell drink, you know. That's the whole point of pubs. Irish ones anyway.'

Jessica stroked her hip flask lovingly as if it was a favourite pet, completely oblivious to the discomfort she had caused in her new companions. 'Right now it's full of Jack Daniel's. I tried to get Mother to buy a stash of it in the airport for Dad when he comes but she couldn't stop panicking about her brand-new suitcases getting soiled by proximity to all the uglier models in the baggage chute so there was absolutely no time for shopping. I nipped out of that dire kip you guys actually call a hotel over there and got a half-litre in the store. Surprised they had it, to be perfectly honest. I was expecting a keg of home brew simmering in the middle of the floor. Never even asked for my ID card so I didn't get to test out the fake one that Ben set me up with. I'm not all that keen on the taste to be honest but Mom

never detects the smell so it's neat from that point of view.'
She offered the flipped-open hip flask to both girls. They shook
their heads. Whiskey had made Tara vomit the one time she had
tried a mouthful and Sadie was too busy wondering was there
something she could do with Jessica Carter in Tobarnaree for
a whole six weeks that wouldn't involve them getting barred
from the Wild Oat for supplying their own drink. It was all very
well for Jessica because at the end of six weeks she was going
home but Sadie had to live there for another while at least.

'I bet you girls will fight like alley cats when you see my
brother Ben. He's a real hunk or so my friends back home
never tire of telling me. This town won't have seen anything
like him.'

'We don't fight about fellas, do we, Sadie? They're not worth
it.' Tara felt sure that if Ben Carter looked anything like his
sister she would most definitely not be getting into a scrap with
anyone about him. She winked at Sadie but got no response.

Sadie, despite her best efforts to focus on Jessica and Tara,
had fallen into a reverie about the night Leo McLean first kissed
her and was struggling with a ridiculous urge to cry her eyes
out. So much for thinking she was getting over him. Her mother
had said she would bounce back in no time, which proved just
how little she knew. Six months on and the slightest thought
of him still hurt so much. She hoped it might be better when
she could take herself to college in Dublin and not live in fear
of seeing him around every corner. The Wild Oat on a Tuesday
was a safe haven because he had football training midweek
and never drank in the run-up to a session. He took his sport
seriously, a lot more seriously than he had ever taken her, she
thought, biting her lower lip and willing herself not to cry. She
tuned back into the one-sided conversation to hear Jessica still
rattling on about her brother while Tara's eyes misted over from
the effort of curtailing her rising aggravation.

'You'll change your mind when you lay eyes on him, I swear.

Ben leaves a trail of broken hearts after him and he just steps over the carnage as he moves on to his next pretty target.'

'Sounds like a bit of a dickhead to me,' Tara said under her breath but she needn't have bothered with discretion. The impatient swilling of alcohol seemed to have dulled Jessica's hearing somewhat. Either that or she had no intention of taking offence on behalf of her absent brother and was simply glad to be free of her mother's company and spending time with girls of her own age.

'When's he arriving anyway?' Sadie ventured, feigning a sincerity and interest that she hoped might sound genuine even though she couldn't care less.

'He flies in at the weekend with my dad although quite how long Jack McKenzie *with a zee* Carter will stick this Tubber place of yours is anybody's guess. He doesn't do rustic as a rule and this place is like some forgotten outpost from the last century. I was quite surprised that my cell phone actually got a signal here. Mind you, if it didn't I told my mother that she could just drive me straight back to the airport because I was flying home.' She took another thirsty slug straight from the hip flask and a smug smile played across her lips. Sadie wondered what it would be like not to care an iota what other people thought. Did it take much practice or could someone be born that way? Tara was wondering much the same thing but had no intention of keeping her musings on the matter to herself.

'It's a provincial town, that's all, and I'd work on getting its name right if you're going to spend the summer here.' Tara was mightily pissed with the girl's superiority and was not going to let her rudeness pass unnoticed. There was a point where insistence on being well mannered just made you look dim-witted and she wasn't about to fall victim to such misplaced politeness. 'I'm sure you have something like it not too far from Boston.' Then she sounded out the name of the town slowly for Jessica, doing nothing to hide how much she had decided to detest her: '*Tob-ar-na-ree.*' It wasn't that difficult if you paid a bit of attention but she needn't have bothered because Jessica didn't think the dismal place deserved her memorizing its name in the first place.

'I take after my dad. I don't go beyond city limits if at all possible. I'm a city girl through and through except when I am forced to accompany my mom on her godforsaken trips to the backwaters she is so fond of discovering. My brother on the other hand will probably think this whole rural vibe is really cool. Camping and trekking in the wilds are just about Ben's favourite things at the moment. He has some sort of wilderness thing going on and I guarantee you two will fall helplessly at his feet. Just you wait and see.'

'Will you hit her or will I?' Tara fumed as they were leaving. Any brother of this Jessica article was hardly likely to be God's gift if her horse-ugly appearance was anything to go by.

'Stay cool,' Sadie implored. Jessica was more than a bit full of herself, there was no doubt, but remembering the plans her mother was making for the extra money from Ellen Carter she didn't want to rock the boat. 'They'll be gone at the end of next month. Do your best to ignore it and pray for me rolling her home rollicking drunk to her mother tonight. She's not going to be happy to see her in this state.'

Jessica was rather pleased that she hadn't forgotten how to cycle and even managed Gina's clapped-out bike. The two-mile journey and its attendant fresh air worked a minor miracle. By the time they reached the cottages she had almost mastered the role of meek daughter complaining of a jet-lag-induced exhaustion. Ellen fussed over her, giving her extra blankets from the generously stocked cupboard that she had discovered and broke the good news to both of them that Gina had agreed to surrender her home to the Carters.

'Your mother is an angel. I hope you know that, Sadie. What

a beautiful lady to rescue me in my hour of need. I've only un-packed what we need for tonight so we can move lock, stock and barrel tomorrow. Maybe you would be kind enough to help me with the bags? And do tell Gina again how grateful I am, won't you?'

'Absolutely,' Sadie agreed and she turned back toward the lodge planning a little packing herself before bed. That's if her neat freak of a mother hadn't got there first and divided her whole life into labelled boxes for the attic.

CHAPTER SIX

On the last day of June Gina strode impatiently into her bank on Quay Street after an unusually busy lunch shift at the Lime Tree. A bus of day trippers had arrived bang on lunchtime and Gina was thoroughly worn out from performing a miracle of the loaves and fishes variety with the mixed and somewhat uninspiring contents of the restaurant's stock and cold rooms. Her feet ached and her two middle fingers had been scorched from a too-close encounter with the salamander grill as she rescued a sizzling swordfish steak from its fierce heat. She knew that the red char mark across her knuckles would rise into an impressive blister before the night was out and would make the next day a bit of a struggle. Her hand would become shy of the oven and grill and all the usual fast-paced actions would become sluggish.

To add to her irritation Louis Corrigan had not shown the slightest scrap of gratitude as the unexpected order receipts piled in and she worked like a demon to fill them efficiently. Time for a new job, she felt. She had that thought at least once a season but there was nothing much to be had in Tobarnaree for someone who was a good cook (actually quite talented, she would admit on a good day), but had no real qualification other than endless years of on-the-job training. The Lime Tree would have to do for the moment, she decided as she noted with dismay the long queues for the bank's customer service desk.

Banking was an inconvenience and she always looked to complete her meagre business as quickly and as painlessly as possible, preferably without having to leave her own house to do so. Yet there were obviously matters deemed too delicate to deal with electronically or over the phone. Honestly, you would think that she had committed some crime the way Justin Flannery came to summon her away from the queue and into the inner sanctum of the manager's office.

She spotted Theo Corrigan at the business desk as she was directed by Flannery to his private room. She nodded at him and he smiled back, raising his hand to acknowledge her before turning to complete whatever transaction had brought him there. Gentleman farmer was the look he was going for, she decided, because he certainly looked nothing like the local farmers, who brought the unbecoming fragrance of their livelihood on their clothes and on their jeeps when they swung into town on business. A navy jacket, linen at a guess though she wasn't close enough to see for certain, over an open-necked shirt and a pair of worn denims. He was certainly dressing a good deal more snappily than his brother. Louis had inherited the baldness and gait of his father while Theo was a good deal taller with bulk suitably in proportion to his frame and a generous head of hair that looked as if it could do with the taming of a good haircut. Gina wondered how long it would take Lottie to get herself over to the Corrigans to check out her old flame. She knew her sister wouldn't be able to resist a gawk and, taking a final look at Theo before darting into the private area of the bank, Gina felt she might offer to accompany her sister. It would do no harm to curtail Lottie because after all Gina was the one who was going to be left with Theo Corrigan as a neighbour when Lottie, holiday over, hightailed it back to Dublin.

The walls of Flannery's office had been painted a crimson red and the smell of fresh emulsion hung in the air. Gina felt a calming and less abattoir-like shade might have been a better choice. Didn't banks usually try to market themselves as shiny friendly places where you could just drop in when you were short of a bob or two and they would sort you out? She made a mental note to stop watching so much television. She knew too many of the impossibly white-of-tooth characters that peopled the upbeat banking advertisements. They all smiled insanely as if giving away wads of cash was nothing but an exercise in supreme bliss. Reality fell short of fiction by a long way, she decided as she watched a pallid Flannery fuss with stray papers on his desk and carefully tuck a plastic pen into the breast pocket of his suit as if he had located a priceless gem stone.

'What seems to be the problem, Justin, and why have you hauled me in here? Are the Criminal Assets Bureau on my tail for laundering dodgy money in Tobar Lake? I suppose I should've known I wouldn't get away with my pocket of fraud for ever.' She grinned at him helpfully on the sad off chance that he wouldn't realize she was cracking a joke but the gesture was lost on him and his features remained decidedly glum.

'Not at all, Gina, your financial matters are, from what I can deduce, perfectly in order. Would that all my customers could manage the same level of self-restraint in these straitened times we find ourselves in.'

She felt as if she had been given absolution by a priest, an indulgence for good behaviour, and Flannery's superior tone grated. She fumed silently. Who the hell did he think he was? Gina had no money to speak of and what she did have she protected with a frugal hand so she was very sure that she was of precious little interest to the bank's bottom line, which made her summons all the more puzzling until Flannery deigned to speak again.

'However, there is an irregularity of sorts that I wanted to bring to your attention.' Clearing his throat he seemed to blush a little at whatever sensitive detail he was about to divulge. 'It's just that a cheque for a thousand euro that you lodged last week has bounced, so unfortunately we haven't been able to credit your account, which may cause some problems for your cash flow were you not alerted.'

On top of considerable irritation, Gina was now utterly addled. Flannery must have mixed her up with someone else. The only cheque she had lodged recently was Ciaran's annual payment for their month in Tobarnaree, one that he always insisted on making in advance. Who knew, he would joke, if by the end of the month anybody would be on speaking terms or indeed willing to pay good money for the experience they had just endured. Better to settle it up front so they could point the nose of their car at the gate and make a speedy getaway raising plenty of dust on the rough avenue if necessary. She keenly appreciated that her brother-in-law always sent a cheque and in so doing kept the arrangement between them strictly professional. By contrast Lottie could be heard moaning and groaning on the last Sunday, as she laboriously counted out the money she owed in the smallest denominations possible, that she never had a penny to her name when she left Tobarnaree after the month of July and would have to exist on dry bread and baked beans until she managed to sell a few paintings. It wouldn't have surprised any of them if she produced the rattling contents of her childhood piggy bank in her pitiful attempt to foot the modest bill for a month's holiday. Gina knew to expect the well-rehearsed charade every year but the intended emotional blackmail always irritated her. The year before, as the whining began to get out of hand, Rachel had chimed in that the Orla Kiely bag that Lottie was plundering for stray cash had probably cost at least half what she owed Gina for the holiday. Lottie had eyed her murderously before producing the balance owed a little more quickly than she had planned.

Justin Flannery knew who Ciaran Jacob was of course. How could he not? They had often met in the restaurant or in the pub during previous summers and she felt he was nosing for information or insinuating financial trouble for her brother-in-law and she didn't like it one little bit. 'Thanks but I'm sure there's a perfectly good explanation for this.' She was thinking to herself that someone in his office must have got him to sign a cheque book from a defunct account or a petty cash account had erroneously gone into arrears, but she had no intention of sharing her explanatory thoughts with Flannery, who was now eyeing her intently. Absolutely none of his business, she decided furiously. She was taken aback at how protective she felt of Ciaran and his reputation but then she reminded herself that he was family and of course that was the reason.

'Oh, without a doubt, Gina. Ciaran's own branch will inform him in due course I'd imagine, especially if yours is not the only cheque to have been met by insufficient funds. Anyway, I'll leave the matter in your brother-in-law's capable hands.'

'Do that,' Gina said with a bitterness she didn't mind revealing to Flannery, 'and shall I tell Ciaran that you were asking after him? Wondering how he's doing *in these straitened times*?'

'Oh, do, yes. I always look forward to seeing him during July. I take it he's coming to see us this year as usual?' He looked a touch embarrassed, fearing that she had seen right through him.

Gina nodded silently and left. There was nothing to be gained from taking the head off Justin Flannery, no matter how satisfying she might have found swiping at the pinched little spectacles perched on his pointed nose. Instead she would ring Rachel and get her to mention it in passing to Ciaran. No big deal except that it was all very well sending a bouncing cheque to your very understanding sister-in-law but it wouldn't look that good if his office was sending the duds out to all and sundry. Gina imagined that was the kind of thing a company's reputation could quite easily falter on so the sooner they were alerted the better.

She left a message on Rachel's mobile telling her about the issue of the bouncing cheque but insisting a few times that it was no problem at all; they could pay her when they arrived. She was ringing so that they could prevent an embarrassing faux pas with a client or a supplier. The beep cut her off mid message and she was irritated that she had left a message at all. It would sound badly played back and she hated the thought that Rachel might play it for Ciaran in an effort to find out what her sister was talking about.

CHAPTER SEVEN

Ciaran walked distractedly along Grafton Street immune to the atmosphere and noisy swell of the shopping crowds as he made his forlorn way from yet another posturing meeting at the nearby office of his bank. He wasn't sure how long either party could maintain the charade of business as usual when they were knee-deep in a shared debt with no obvious way out. He had spotted the bank manager's forehead wrinkling in betrayed stress while talking professional twaddle that neither client nor banker had the naivety to believe.

On strict principle Ciaran had always resisted the urge to invest money in the developments on which he had served as consultant architect, despite any number of opportunities to do so. Design was his thing and he had always advocated that people should stick to what they knew best. Life had not given him any reason to doubt the soundness of that theory but in recent years the profits made by people he thought considerably less bright than himself had become more difficult to take. A slow-burning envy of the effortless success of others, an envy he could barely admit to, had finally made him falter and give in to easy temptation.

The director of Cedar Build had talked him into buying three units in the Ivory Square development. Talked him into it might have been slightly overstating it because Ciaran's will to abstain had already begun to flag, but Emmet Kinsella certainly made the prospect of investment appear to be a no-brainer. Besides, Ciaran truly believed that there was nothing run-of-the-mill about the apartments he had designed at Ivory Square. From time to time he had been involved in a development that exceeded all the hype and promise of the sale brochure and he felt this was such an occasion. His fondness for the development meant he was more than ripe for persuasion when Kinsella began his compelling sales pitch. Only fools lacking a scrap of imagination left their money on deposit or sitting in stale pension funds, Kinsella counselled, when there was real money to be made on straightforward bricks and mortar. It was last chance saloon to buy in at a special discounted pre-release price for friends and sell again quickly to eager homebuyers at a considerable profit. The advantage for Kinsella was that he freed up funds for his next project by surrendering a sizeable but not ruinous cut of the profit on current enterprises. It was a dead cert, after all, and Ciaran had worked on projects with Kinsella a number of times before. He could personally vouch for the quality of the build and fit out because he saw to it that Jacob Design only involved itself in projects where the best finish was promised and delivered. It was time to bite the bullet and he was glad of the opportunity that Emmet Kinsella was offering him, even though he had never really thought of him as a friend before then. It was flattering to be cut in on a deal at such good terms and it made him feel as if he had arrived; an inside player on the scene at last.

Ciaran considered telling Rachel about his property purchase but decided that he would wait until he had sold off the first unit at a good profit. Then he would be able to tell her that he had had the incredible foresight to buy another two apartments on which the gains of the first would be replicated, or maybe even exceeded if the market continued to perform as it had. She would be thrilled for them, he knew, although she never seemed that bothered about money, happy to leave all that side of their affairs to him.

His role of taking care of business for his family was one that he had relished. He felt sure that the sale of the apartments would set them and the children up fully for the future. Getting loan approval for the project was staggeringly easy. He had waited longer for a steak to be cooked to the point of medium rare at De Quattro on a Saturday night. The speed at which the credit was extended to him redoubled his confidence. The fact that the bank was prepared to sanction his application so quickly made him trade innate caution for something approaching arrogance.

He had purchased the penthouse and two adjoining apartments on the first floor, signing on the dotted line almost exactly a year before. He remembered that the children had been excited about their annual holiday to Tobarnaree when he got home from signing off on the deal. He rambled into the garden, relaxed after a celebratory pint, to find his son had parked his tricycle next to the trampoline, confident as only a three-year-old can be that the desired items would magically shrink to fit into his daddy's car and come on holiday with them. A far savvier Orla had picked out books and DVDs she wanted to bring with her and from a hoarded supply of fancy paper she had wrapped the small presents bought for Gina, Lottie and her big cousin Sadie. He watched Rachel as she spun around organizing the packing of clothes and all the countless small tasks entailed in the smooth leaving of the house.

She spared him from a wealth of household duties and he was proud that he had taken a bold step to secure their future.

He hoped they might even build a holiday home in Tobarnaree in a few years when the Jacob Design practice was absolutely secure. His parents had moved from their adopted town back to England when their sons had scattered to college, jobs and finally to live with girlfriends and wives of their own. It would be sweet to have somewhere to go to that was a Jacob rather than a Miller house. Not that he wanted to be seen as petty but it would seem more appropriate to his sense of his own standing if they had their own place instead of feeling like perpetual guests of his wife's family. He looked forward to the time when he would tell her and they could celebrate properly with a dinner out in a fine restaurant and maybe a bottle or two of their favourite wine. He might even concede to join Rachel in a glass of bubbly though it was something for which he had never managed to develop a taste. The popping of champagne corks lent a desired razzmatazz to project launches but he was never happier when, job done, he could leave the straitjacket of the official reception, loosen his tie and go to the bar to order a pint of lager or a glass of good red wine. He knew the part he was expected to play and he did it well but he also knew enough to know the minor details that would never really suit him.

Sufficient wisdom to foresee that the Ivory Square apartment block would become one of the first high-profile casualties of the relentless financial downturn evaded him. Such lack of foresight could be forgiven, he supposed, as even the surest of bets had collapsed as easily as sandcastles overcome by the swollen flurry of an incoming tide. The property bubble had been threatening to burst for years but nobody could be precise about how much time was left to secure the last good deal. Because he was caught up in the market Ciaran was primed to seek out only the optimistic forecasts. It had all been an exercise in brinkmanship; no one knew when their last move would prove to be not the cleverest they had ever made but an act of outrageous stupidity. For so long it had seemed that you could name and achieve any price you liked in the right location and Ivory Square was most definitely in the right location. But then, almost overnight it seemed, properties began to just sit there in unattractive quantity, with ever decreasing numbers of potential buyers all waiting for the vendor to blink and sell for a good deal less than the purchase price.

After a number of hastily convened meetings with a fractious bank manager it became obvious that Ciaran had invested too much and far too late. Had he moved six months earlier he might have pulled off a master stroke and would have been feeling relaxed and smug rather than lost and directionless. It took him time and the gift of perspective to realize that it was not his specific loans that were causing his bank so much angst; his were merely a tiny detail in a wider and uglier picture of money offered, owed and now secured against vastly diminished assets. To be part of such a cohort of potential loan defaulters might have brought comfort to some but not to Ciaran. His predicament was too urgent.

He put through a call to Emmet Kinsella in the vain hope that he would know someone who might want to buy at least one of the units from him. He tried not to beg for a dig-out but in asking the pitiful question he realized that the over-confident swagger of a winner addressing a loser had a distinctive and sickening sound.

Kinsella seemed very proud of the killer deal he had pulled off on the Ivory development. 'It's tough luck on you, Ciaran, but in the building game timing, as you know, is everything. Still, I'd advise you to hang in there. Someone is bound to bite eventually.' He said it as if there really was any other option open to Ciaran except to stay put and hope for a miracle. Why would anyone bite when the banks had come over all coy and there was every chance that prices might well collapse even further?

Ciaran swallowed hard, trying not to betray how stressed he felt. Kinsella hung up after a feeble promise to stay in touch and put any interested party Ciaran's way. He wouldn't be hearing from Emmet for a long time, he imagined as he put down the phone. He rubbed his face furiously with his open hand and ended up chewing on the knuckles of his left hand to stifle a groan that threatened to otherwise escape.

Ciaran had never been shy of deploying his fiery temper but he couldn't summon enough anger to berate Emmet Kinsella because only a portion of this mess could be deemed his fault. Instead his ire was reserved for his own gullible self. He had risked the financial solvency of the firm he had worked so hard to create on a misjudged gamble. In hindsight it was all so clear and he marvelled at how he could have been so easily outwitted. He had mistaken his uncharacteristic spontaneity for inspiration. Ivory Square was dead in the water and with it Ciaran's plans for a secure future for his company and his family.

At the top of Grafton Street he ignored a red pedestrian light and darted through the slow crawl of afternoon traffic. Cutting through Stephen's Green he made his way to a confessional meeting at the office of his company accountant, feeling it was high time to come clean on his disastrous solo run. An in-house accountant might have stopped the plan in its tracks but it was too late to rue that mistake now.

'How long can I hold out?' he asked as he sat down.

Kevin Cooper was circumspect, poring over the figures for what seemed like an age. He was unwilling to make a snap prognosis on a client's business, although every document that Ciaran had produced was more damning than the last.

While he waited Ciaran sipped absentmindedly at the sour tar-coloured coffee provided in a generous-sized mug by Cooper's assistant. He wasn't sure if its pungent taste was making him feel sick or the thought of what he was about to have confirmed by his accountant. He wondered if anyone had ever felt like vomiting in this office quite so much as he did now. To occupy his mind he trained his eyes on the uneven gaps in the floorboards.

Cooper's barren basement rooms were an oppressively dark space not helped by the mean-spirited light of a dull afternoon. Ciaran had noticed the dreariness of the surroundings on previous visits because it offended every ounce of his design sense, but it was not lost on him now how apt that bleakness was as a stage to witness the retelling of the tawdry details of his own stupidity. He had flippantly offered to design a revamp of the offices a few years ago at a good price but Kevin Cooper had made it plain that his clients came to him for facts and figures and not to appreciate the very limited aesthetics the building had to offer.

Finally Cooper gave his verdict. 'Well, if you're planning to continue feeding these massive mortgages from the company's puny war chest then the first risk is not having enough left over to cover the monthly salary bill. Cash flow for that could be a problem as early as the end of this month, depending on what Jacob Design accounts are settled in the interim. But in the present climate I wouldn't be overly confident that too many clients will be beating a path to your door with cheque books bulging out the lines of their finely tailored suits. What in the name of God were you thinking of?'

Ciaran shook his head. It was almost physically painful to hear the precise detail of his misjudgement recited so baldly and unsympathetically by the smug Cooper. 'What can I say? I took a punt,' he said with a flash of irritation mixed with residual defiance. He hated being criticized, always had. Except now he knew in his heart and soul that he deserved it and that sickened him even more.

'A punt is one hundred euro each way on a hunch on the three twenty at Leopardstown or raising the stakes at a poker table because you've spotted a blatant weakness in the hand of the dopey-looking guy next to you at the table. A punt does not even come close to describing the mess that you have landed yourself in. Have you any idea how much of an all-out catastrophe this is for your future?' Ciaran couldn't bring himself to look the other man in the eye as Cooper continued; the accountant was unable to conceal his disdain at how profligate Ciaran had been with the future of a previously rock solid company. 'I wouldn't bother ringing the developer to thank him for putting a good deal your way either. At this stage I'd say Emmet Kinsella is teeing off on some salubrious golf course in the sun and paying the green fees with your money and that of other innocents like you.' He flicked the balance sheets and bank statements he had been furnished with accusingly and Ciaran wondered why he had never noticed before how sanctimonious Cooper could be. Maybe he only seemed insufferable when he was delivering bad news and up until now Ciaran's business life had been remarkably plain sailing.

Ciaran tapped the wooden floor anxiously with the heel of his shoe. He wanted to leave but couldn't bring himself to haul himself from the chair, unable to bear the scrutiny that such a move would invite. Instead he gave in to a temporary paralysis that he hoped might be mistaken for boldly standing his ground. His only movement was a nervous fidget with his wedding band that had gone from tolerably tight to loose on his finger.

'You'll have to tell Rachel,' Cooper announced suddenly. Ciaran shifted uncomfortably in his seat. Telling Rachel would be the final admission that he had really screwed things up. He wasn't ready for that and he hated having his wife's name mentioned in this context. He could not allow his family to be contaminated by the frightening scale of his stupidity. He felt as if he had been inhabiting another world for months now where he had no business to be. He had dabbled in property speculation and it had backfired spectacularly. There had to be a safe place for Rachel and the children in all of this; somewhere untainted by his mistakes.

Finally Ciaran answered, 'I was hoping to sort things out a bit, try and sell one property anyway before I said anything to her. Don't want to worry her unduly.'

Cooper let a smirk escape and Ciaran barely controlled the urge to lean across his desk and give him a good solid thump across his know-it-all face. He stood up to go at last but Cooper's voice stopped him; he was like a tenacious dog that had just sniffed out a buried bone still rich with meat. 'Expecting a miracle, are you? Have you sprinkled holy water on the place or slipped relics under the floorboards? Because a sale at the price you need is not going to happen anytime soon.'

'Well without doubt I own the most fabulously designed penthouse apartment in Dublin until I do manage to sell it. Though spending all your time here I doubt you'd appreciate it,' Ciaran said sharply. He realized too late how pathetic this last stand sounded. Defending his design to someone who would not know good design if it walked up and slapped him in the face was a new low in long weeks spent plumbing unimagined depths.

Afterward he thought briefly of returning to work at his office on De Courcey Row. The Macken Institute build could do with some reworkings of the drawings, even if it was unlikely the required funding would materialize for his efforts to come to fruition. Cutbacks on government-funded projects had stalled plans all over the city but a perfectionist streak within him wanted to make sure that his part of the job would not be found wanting should it be called upon. He was still a fine architect even if his timing in business could clearly not have been worse.

His low mood meant he couldn't face seeing colleagues and it was impossible for him to go in without being seen by everyone. Open-plan offices were a good idea when everything was going well but at times like this Ciaran would have welcomed a solid door and sturdy wall to hide behind. The community layout was ideal when you wanted a spirit of confident optimism to pervade the office space but right now he needed a dark quiet corner where he could hide the worst of how he felt from those whose jobs depended on his judgement. Recently the toilets in the service corridor had been the only safe haven in the building where he could manage five minutes alone, with the need to pretend mercilessly lifted for a few moments at least.

Looking to buy a bit of time he pulled into a nearby side street instead and sat in the car, glad of the privacy afforded by the tinted windows. Plundering the glove box threw up something to fill a gap left by a skipped lunch. He chewed on a once melted but solid again (if a little off colour) chocolate bar confiscated from a sugar-high Billy after a birthday party months ago and its sickly sweetness revived his flagging energies. The low hum of drive-time radio on the car stereo did a little to distract him from his plight and he valued not being totally at the mercy of his thoughts. Evidence of a world intent on proceeding as normal was all around him: traffic lights changing; lines of taxis weaving through traffic; and the sound of buses groaning at the colossal undertaking of getting swarms of people home from where they clung together in noisy, impatient bunches on the streets. For the moment he found such evidence of a city in chaotic routine comforting but he feared that there would come a day shortly when the sound of life at full measure would be more than he could bear to witness. He remembered an article he had read recently about a businessman who had taken his own life owing to the pressure of accumulated debt. The story had been all over the papers for a few brief days, a parable of how suddenly a change of fortune could befall someone perceived by others as an exemplar of success. His heartbroken wife had found the man slumped on waste ground at the back of their new and extravagant home. His fingers were stiff and cold against the metal barrel of one of a pair of hunting rifles he had bought but never found any time to use before raising it to his head that morning, as his family slept inside.

Ciaran was ashamed to discover he couldn't remember the man's name, just that he had been one of the swell of business success stories of the previous decade. He allowed himself to wonder how the slide to that awful place might begin and if the journey was a series of small successive steps or more a catastrophic slip-up blotting out any good times that had gone before. Was it the sight of other people achieving what you had thought of as your rightful expectation? Was it the disappointment in the faces of people who had believed better things of you or was it the progressive inability to raise your eyes to look at the world going about its business, immune to the loss of a single working part that could be readily replaced? With trembling fingers Ciaran traced the raised insignia on the central hub of the steering wheel and offered a quick and silent prayer to anyone or -thing that might listen. If there was a bigger and better power than could be plainly seen he was ready to admit that he had never needed its assistance more.

The speedy ingestion of stale chocolate left him feeling queasy. He hadn't eaten properly in weeks. Eating had become another leisure activity for which he resolutely didn't have time. He had survived on salty snacks and coffee grabbed at service stations when he was paying for petrol or buying a newspaper to scan another spate of depressing headlines implying that everything was set to get worse. Headaches and bouts of nausea took it in turns to plague him.

He couldn't go home just yet but, even though it sickened him to admit it, Cooper was right: he would have to tell Rachel soon. It pained him that he should have to draw her into a problem from which he previously had the power to insulate her. Part of the reason he felt so wretched was that they had always talked things through thoroughly in the past. He had suffered real loneliness in the previous weeks and months because he had slammed the door on all of his wife's attempts to get to the heart of what was bothering him. It wasn't as if he could confide in anyone at work either. They would immediately panic and wonder what it meant for the future of Jacob Design and their jobs. This was too bleak a prospect for Ciaran to contemplate. His misery weighed heavily enough on his shoulders without the added burden of feeling responsible for the livelihoods of others.

He picked up his phone and texted Rachel. It was a far easier if more cowardly prospect than talking, though he would have to find courage from somewhere tonight to tell her how badly they were fixed. His fingers shook as he attempted to key the message; his body betraying the stress that his mind was trying hard to contain. He attempted a casual upbeat tone because he wanted her to be in the best form possible for what he had to tell her. He didn't deserve her to be in receptive humour after the way he had treated her in the last while but he was hoping that all his luck might not evaporate at the same time. A stickler for detail, he checked the message over for spelling or space errors. He detested when people were slack with small things. It signalled a carelessness that he hadn't the patience to abide although he would have to admit that was an irrational stance for a man who had risked a hard-won enterprise with one poorly thought-out decision. The text message was perfect he noted with subdued satisfaction.

Hi, don't bother doing dinner for us. I'll pick up something from the deli. There's something I need to run by you. Will you put a bottle of white in the fridge? I'll be home in an hour. Xx

Chapter Eight

At their house in Shreve Court Rachel was relieved to read her husband's message. She would have felt lucky to get a single call during any of the previous weeks, as if he literally couldn't spare her the time of day. Orla and Billy would be thrilled because she would take the lazy route and give them their favourite ham and mozzarella pizza for tea and she could look forward to a late supper with her husband. Ciaran almost back to his old self two days in a row could only be good news, she decided. She resolved to mention Gina's puzzling message on the answering machine when she had given him a little time to relax.

When he finally worked up the necessary courage to go home Ciaran dumped the hastily purchased food on the kitchen counter. Far too much, he realized when he saw the haul stacked high. The shelves of the delicatessen were just too tempting; he had snapped up anything that looked familiar. It was all easy stuff that wouldn't need any preparation: hummus, chicken liver paté, Serrano ham, a wedge of Brie, stuffed black olives and crusty bread. He had deliberately chosen all of Rachel's favourite things and he hoped she would appreciate the gesture when she came down from settling the children upstairs.

Automatically he went to the fridge, scouting for the bottle of wine he hoped she had remembered to chill, but the soaring sound of Orla's hilariously off-key voice belting out a song in the bathroom filled him with a yearning tempered by guilt at his prolonged absences from his children. He suddenly realized how unforgivable it was to miss so many bedtimes when they surely looked forward to seeing him. The drink could wait, he decided as he climbed the stairs quickly, taking the steps two at a time to find his family. He gave Orla a huge hug on the landing, which stopped the mid-Atlantic singing voice, honed from watching her *High School Musical* DVDs back to back, for a glorious moment. Her father promised her he would be in for a chat and a story when he had tucked Billy up snugly.

Orla was happy with the proposed arrangement and gave it her enthusiastic endorsement. 'Yeah, you'd better do the little squirt first. He needs to sleep because he has been wrecking my head whinging all day. If I was Mam I'd have broken out the Calpol at lunchtime but she's far too patient with him for her own good.' Orla skipped into her hot-pink festival of a bedroom leaving her father gazing after her in amazement. A teenager in a little girl's pyjamas had arrived in their midst.

Rachel smiled broadly at Ciaran because she knew how much his presence would mean to the children. She had been doing the bedtime routine on her own for months now so she appreciated the company far more than the actual help she had long learned to manage without.

Their son was still resolute in his devotion to *Farmer Duck*, Ciaran noted with some dismay. 'Are you absolutely sure it's good for him to get the exact same story read to him every night for nearly a year?' he enquired with discreet urgency to his wife, not wanting to upset Billy though longing for a reprieve from a story he knew every sorrowful quack of by heart.

Rachel was staunch in her defence of the maligned duck that made her son smile every night before he finally agreed to give up on the day and fall asleep. 'It's perfectly fine. It builds his confidence because he knows what's coming next and he finds the repetition comforting. Besides, it's a great story and we do read other things as well. Not often but sometimes.'

'I bought the book for him I think you'll recall so I don't doubt for a moment that it's a great story but I'd say the poor fecking duck has another case for the European Court of Arbitration by now,' Ciaran said as he plucked the tattered book from Rachel and straightened the quilt on his son's chunky wooden bed.

'I promise if we happen to lose this copy of the book *you bought* I'll wait at least a week before replacing it,' Rachel said mischievously, winking at her sleepy but thankfully oblivious son.

'Your mammy's all heart, Billy, did you know that?' Ciaran said as he took a welcome seat on the yielding comfort of his son's bed. Billy beamed, delighted that it was his dad reading his story for the first time in ages, and his eager smiling face was a welcome antidote to all that his father had lately been through. He mouthed the words of the story, silently keeping time as his father read it to him. *There once was a duck who had the bad luck to live with a lazy old farmer.* The little boy in his soft-as-snow pyjamas snuggled into the welcome and comforting shape of his father's body and was reassured by the familiar cadence of the story. Absent-mindedly he rubbed the silky smoothness of his father's striped tie between his chubby thumb and forefinger and for a few short moments Ciaran very nearly forgot that he had a care in the world. The trusting body curled into him was all that mattered and he prolonged the story adding his own little asides so that the safety of the shared moment could linger between them.

Downstairs Rachel had sorted the groceries and prepared a tasty platter of delicious things for them. Earlier in the evening she had been unable to resist picking at the uneaten crusts of Billy's pizza but she was glad that she still had considerable appetite for all the lovely luxuries that Ciaran had brought home. She wondered why he had bought so much of everything and then remembered how absent-minded her husband had been of late and then the impractical amounts of food made a little more sense. Most of the stuff would keep well enough but just how much crusty bread did he think one couple, no matter how hungry, could put away during the course of a single night? Maybe a trip to feed the ducks at the weekend to bombard them with chunks of rock-hard bread would be in order. Although Billy would likely insist on staying at the edge of the water until he'd managed to make at least one keel over from gluttony.

As she disposed of the plastic bag in the back kitchen she wondered what he'd been referring to in his message when he said he had something to run by her. In the past he had frequently asked her advice about things at work that were bothering him, but such sharing of the burden had stopped completely in the previous months despite some persistent prompting on Rachel's behalf. She took it as a very positive sign that he was ready to begin talking again because she had missed her role as his chief, if alarmingly underpaid, adviser. She considered that raising her children had been absolutely worth every second of the time that she had devoted to it but she felt that even Ciaran sometimes forgot that it could be an isolating occupation and that the machinations of the world beyond the front door were a welcome distraction from the merciless repetition of familiar if useful chores.

When Ciaran was finally released and allowed downstairs by his sleepy and performance-depleted daughter Rachel handed him a glass of wine whose taste she expected he would relish. She had no intention of interrogating him again. It was enough that he was willing to be in her company and had put some effort into their night together. She tucked hungrily into the food, offering him slices of Brie and some olives on a plate. She was so busy savouring the delicious tastes that she wasn't at all prepared for the powerful wave of words that flowed from her husband. It was such a change from the sullen and dismissive Ciaran of late.

'There are things happening at work – well, not work exactly but related, I suppose. Investments I've made that aren't paying their way. Ivory Square – I invested big time in Ivory Square.' His voice caught a little in his throat as if he could scarcely believe the words that were coming out. 'It was so certain. Everything looked right and fell into place so quickly. You've heard me talk about the development so you know how special it is, or was anyway.'

'How much did you invest?' Rachel asked, her voice barely above a whisper, struggling to take in what she had been told.

'Close to a million for three units. A year ago it might have been a class move but it's nothing but a stupid mess now. The bank is getting jittery and I've run down whatever cash reserves we had servicing the loan. Jacob Design is in danger; we could even lose the house. I've ruined things for us.'

While he spoke Rachel barely got a word in. He had anticipated all her likely questions and with a flood of nervous energy he rushed to explain the details of his misjudgement. As he spoke Rachel remembered Gina's message that she had listened to earlier: the bouncing cheque, which she had casually dismissed to herself as an office error, suddenly appeared sinister. With a shaky voice she made her tone as gentle as she could manage. The flood of information had astounded her and she didn't try to hide the extent of her confusion. 'I haven't a clue what the best thing to do is but we will think of something, love. We could sell this house maybe and move into one of the apartments. The development is not far from here so Orla could stay in the same school – that might work for a while until the market improves. I don't know how we will get out of this but we're in it together and you shouldn't have had to shoulder the worry of this on your own. I'm not sure what I could have said but I would've wanted to help, you must know that?' She reached out and took his shaking hand between both of hers. It was a little clammy to her touch. He looked frailer than he ever had and it was suddenly obvious to her how the weight of worry and an erratic appetite had diminished him physically. The collar of his shirt stood shy of his neck even though its top button and his caramel striped tie remained neatly fastened.

The skin on his neck began to blotch in angry red patches. 'But it's all my fault, Rachel, how can you be so good about it? I may have fucked up our entire future. I messed it all up, don't you understand?'

Rachel squeezed his shaking hand in the warmth of her own. 'The most important thing is that we stick together no matter how bad things get. OK, so you made a bad decision but every proper and clever financial move we have made in the last ten years has been more or less all your doing too. This is a fairly massive cock-up by the sounds of it but you had the best of intentions for our future at heart. How can I be mad at you for that? We'll find a way through this as long as there are no more secrets. Trust me and I'll trust you.'

Ciaran moved to put his weary head on her shoulder and when she hugged him close and stroked his hair she felt his body giving in to heaves of despair and the wet heat of escaping tears as they trickled on to the softness of the crook of her neck. She held him until the shuddering abated but even when he moved away from her embrace she couldn't catch his eye. She watched as he cradled his head in his hands, massaging his forehead furiously with his fingers. It seemed to Rachel that he was in search of some magic that would erase all that had happened. Her head swam with panic and despair that for both their sakes she knew she had to conceal. She had spent weeks trying to guess what might be wrong, becoming steadily more frustrated at her inability to get her husband to talk. Now that he had she hardly knew what to say next. She would tell him about Gina's phone call in the morning but for the moment it was plain that he wasn't capable of dealing with another thing.

By the time Rachel picked up the phone to Gina the next night to apologize for the bouncing cheque and to tell her about the situation they had found themselves in she was feeling overwhelmed by a new reality for which she was very poorly prepared.

Gina listened sympathetically, asking a few questions to clarify what she could scarcely believe. Ciaran had always been the high achiever in their lives. Of course Lottie had had her fair share of impressively rich boyfriends but their presence was sporadic and their tenure generally brief. Unlike Ciaran, whom they had all known practically for ever. Until now he hadn't seemed to know what it was to put a foot wrong. He'd always been a success to his fingertips so it was hard to think that his magic touch had deserted him. Gina was wary of saying something that would upset her already bewildered sister; she asked carefully if there was anything she might be able to do to help. Perhaps Orla and Billy could come and stay with her and Sadie while Rachel and Ciaran stayed on in Dublin to sort things out? Although she knew it was unlikely that Rachel would be happy to be parted from her children for any length of time, especially given the situation she was in and how far away Gina lived.

Tears welled in Rachel's eyes at the thought of this one sure way to make her feel worse than she already did. 'Without the kids here making noise and all sorts of mayhem I don't think I'd be able to function at all. The distraction of what they're up to that they shouldn't be stops me thinking about myself for a few minutes even though there's a risk I might kill them for precisely the same reasons.'

'So there's nothing I can do then?' Gina felt her sister's distress all the more keenly because Lottie was always the one that was in an ongoing spat with life while Rachel seemed capable of keeping everything in order and running smoothly with very little fuss.

'About the only thing that will rescue us is finding someone who badly wants to buy three very expensive apartments when there's far cheaper ones to be had everywhere you look. Can you get your hands on about a million in a hurry? That would surely sort it all out.' Rachel managed a lightness of tone that she wouldn't have thought possible under the circumstances.

Gina was happy to extend the joke at her own expense if it would help to bolster her sister's spirits even temporarily. 'Oh yeah, sure, a million's no problem at all. Justin Flannery would have it arranged in jig time because I'm ever so well in with him, you know. He's only dying to do me a favour. The only catch is you'll have to collect it in person when you get here next week. Have we a deal? I need to see you so we can talk all this through face to face.'

'That's the other thing, Gina, I don't think we'll be able to afford coming to Tobar this year. I am sorry but there's no way we can manage it. Besides, having a holiday seems such a frivolous thing to do when everything is coming down around our ears.'

'Forget about paying me, for God's sake. We need to see you and I hope you want to see us too. Tell me you'll come, please? Billy and Orla won't understand if they can't come for their holidays. They love it down here and we love having you. Have mercy and don't leave Sadie and myself on our own with Lottie,' she added in a humorous attempt to secure her sister's agreement and feeling suddenly and unbearably lonesome for their summer tradition that she had taken so much for granted.

'Ciaran couldn't stand it if we didn't pay our way as usual. I know how he is and he just couldn't bear being humiliated even though I know that wouldn't be anyone's intention. He's not thinking straight at the moment. I just can't get through to him but I know a holiday we couldn't pay for would be the final straw.'

'Well, pay me when you can then. Come on, Rachel, you need your family now.'

'I'll try to talk to him but I'm not promising anything. He's in a bad way and I'm not about to leave him to his own devices while I head down the country to you with the kids. I doubt very much that I can persuade him to show his face at all. He feels embarrassed that he has made such a blunder and nothing I say seems to change that.' She was close to tears but she felt that if she started she might never stop and Ciaran was due home shortly from the Board of Management meeting at Orla's school. She knew without waiting to ask that he would have found it a hellish ordeal. Rachel had forced him to go saying that it was better to keep everything going as normal for as long as they could. He had relented at that point because he was grateful for her insistence on holding the shaky frame of their lives together with such resolve. He had nothing new to offer by way of solution but still she was refusing to allow their family to give in to despair.

Gina held her on the phone for as long as she could and filled her in with as many insignificant little bits of news about her and Sadie that she could manage. She told her how Sadie felt she had done well with her Leaving Cert. All had gone well apart from Biology and Geography papers that she had found tougher than expected, but she hoped she would still be in the running for the first course she had selected on her college application form.

Rachel tried to show genuine interest in her niece's exams but her thoughts were firmly trained on her own life, trying to imagine a resolution when none was obvious. While Gina nervously rattled on about Galway or Waterford maybe being grand for Sadie if Dublin didn't work out, Rachel looked around the house she loved and wondered for how much longer her family might have to call it home. She had grown firmly attached to it in the years she had spent looking after her children there. It had started as an old house smartened up and cleverly redesigned by a young, design-conscious couple but it had become a warm and treasured home, more cluttered now than she or Ciaran would have tolerated a decade before when a new item of furnishing was added to any room only for a specific reason and after much consideration and joint consultation. When Orla was born they had insisted on handmade wooden toys, pointing friends and family in the direction of suitable shops and websites for birthday and Christmas presents. Six years on with Billy now on board the house was awash with gaudy plastic toys of every description, idealism unceremoniously replaced with the untidy reality of what their children had the bad taste to actually want. Rachel knew the house's every creak and corner, the dodgy floorboard on the landing that she studiously avoided treading on when the children were asleep along the corridor and the crisscross pattern of light shafts that the sun made on the hallway floor when it flooded generously through the skylights on summer mornings. It was merely four walls, she reasoned, but she had taken the security of knowing it so intimately very much for granted.

When Rachel finally managed to get a concerned Gina off the phone with a promise to do her best to go to Tobarnaree she went to look in on the children and turn off their reading lamps, switching on the night lights whose secure glow they both looked for when they woke suddenly during the night wondering where they were. She tousled Billy's almost damp hair and softly kissed his toasty hot forehead. His hands were firmly wrapped around the scruffy blue dog with the soft felt nose that he always slept alongside. The grip of his fingers tightened noticeably as he became aware at some subconscious level of noise and movement in his space. She closed the door gently willing him to fall back into a sound sleep. In Orla's room she set about removing the bulwark of books that her sleeping girl had surrounded herself with on the quilt. Her arms were cold as ice from being outside the bed covers. Rachel didn't doubt that her daughter had refused to give up reading until she had finally faltered in the middle of a page she had willed tired eyes to finish.

Straightening the star-patterned comforter over her daughter's slight body she knew she was prepared to go through losing the house she stood in a million times over if it meant she could keep the family she loved together. Shreve Court was just an address, she tutored herself. A beautiful and treasured house it might be, but if it were gone in the morning she would have everything she needed in the coterie of people she was lucky to call her own. She hoped if she repeated the mantra to herself often enough she would eventually believe it. When Orla's door closed gently behind her she stood there for an age in the half-darkness wondering if she would look back on these days as the time when everything had changed for them.

Despite her temporary home in Beech Cottage Gina maintained her early-morning routine, collecting the post, checking her emails and making phone calls at the lodge. It pleased her that Ellen was keeping the place in strict order. In fact in some ways the fact that she had moved out to the cottages allowed her to appreciate the lodge even more since she wasn't witness to its array of failings on a constant basis. Suddenly what the house had more than compensated for what it had not. The inconvenience of the move hadn't bothered her that much except that she missed the comfort of her own bed. Everything in the cottage was new and therein lay the problem – she had been accustomed to all that was ancient and well used for so long. She missed her Tobar Lodge bedroom where the lumps and hollows of her own ancient mattress matched the curve of her perfectly. A crease of light generally shone through her mother's hand-sewn curtains on summer mornings, wakening her gently and long before her alarm clock had a chance to harshly confirm the arrival of another day. It was yet another heartening ritual that she hadn't realized how much she clung to until she had awoken disoriented in a strangely darkened room smelling of fresh paint and disquieting in its unfamiliarity.

If Gina's daily appearance bothered Ellen even the slightest bit she was polite enough not to show it. She had got into the habit of bringing Gina a mug of tea as she sat by her computer trying to attend to everything without causing too much interruption. This morning Gina felt might be somewhat different though because the Carter men had arrived the night before. She was curious to see what they might be like. Lying in bed in her cottage the night before she had watched the headlights of Ellen's hire car leave to collect them from Shannon airport; doubtless they had returned a couple of hours later although by then Gina had fallen into a shallow sleep.

In preparation for her husband and son's arrival Ellen had made up two beds the day before, asking Gina to locate spare sheets for the single beds in Lottie and Rachel's old rooms. Gina obliged and thought her hunch had been right about the Carters being a separated couple. She considered it civilized that they could still manage a holiday together under the circumstances; she wasn't at all sure that she could find within herself such goodwill and cooperation if she were in the same situation.

Ellen was in the hallway on her mobile phone when Gina went in. She waved her into her office under the stairwell, moving into the privacy of the kitchen to continue the call, and Gina took the none-too-subtle hint that she was far too busy to talk for the moment. There were a number of emails enquiring about availability for September, of which she hoped at least a couple might turn into firm bookings. August was looking healthy too and with the extra money it looked as if it was going to be a strong enough year. She was relieved that the worry about her finances had proved to be unfounded. It pleased her that she would be in a position to buy some new things for Sadie and send her off to college kitted out smartly. Top of her list was a soft leather travel bag which she had seen in a Paul Street shop. She hoped it might bring her daughter and her belongings home with some regularity.

Her phone call finished, Ellen heaved the cast-iron kettle on to the hot plate of the Aga, hauling up the heavy dome lid with a by now practised ease. She would make tea for Gina as she had every other morning of the past week. As she set out two of Gina's mugs on a tray and doled out a tea bag to each she decided she would not lie to Jessica about what had happened – or to anyone else for that matter.

Ben had shrugged his shoulders when he walked into arrivals alone. His dad had met him at Boston Logan to say he couldn't make the trip. That was all her son had offered, as if the detail of Jack's absence was no more remarkable than the fact that his flight had touched down almost an hour behind schedule. Ellen didn't ask why he hadn't rung ahead to warn her because if her husband hadn't shouldered the responsibility of breaking the news to her she certainly wasn't about to hold Ben to account for his father's bad manners and thoughtlessness.

Over the past number of years she had often wondered how she would find out Jack was leaving her because now that it had finally happened she could admit that it had never been a case of 'if' but always 'when'. It went without saying that it was he who would leave the marriage, not her, because Jack Carter was the only man who had ever truly interested her. There was no one she would choose over him. It wasn't that she couldn't see the attraction in other men, of course, but he was the only one who had mattered to her, and for such a long time. If a love affair that had started so full of promise could disintegrate as theirs had then she wasn't likely to try again with milder hopes and lower expectations.

And so in her head she had often rehearsed the manner of his departure in order that the pain might be diluted when the day inevitably arrived. Would it be prompted by him finding a younger woman who had with her vitality shown him what he had been missing? Or an exciting job that he couldn't turn down? Would she receive a phone call from some city he decided not to come back from? In imagining how he would leave she inflicted considerable damage on herself, cushioned only a little by the thought that she would at least have prepared herself. What she had never considered was that her husband would be cowardly and callous enough to simply fold a carelessly written note into an envelope for her and place it in a pocket of Ben's well-worn rucksack. He had asked Ben to deliver it for him; it was an incredible insult to her and an abuse of their son's un-suspecting but obliging goodwill. It was a telling indictment of their marriage that his wish to dissolve it was not even worthy of a stamp, a phone call or a face-to-face conversation to break the bad news.

Ellen read the note in Jack's harsh sloping handwriting three times before refolding it and placing it on the nightstand in her room. On top of it she placed her wedding ring, quite certain and a little saddened that she had taken it off for the last time. The still shining band left a dark welt on a much swollen finger. It was tempting to think that she had outgrown the restrictions of her marriage but the truth was that she would have remained in its familiar prison for want of somewhere better to go. She had thought that they were equally unhappy, and not catastrophically so, but in misery as well as everything else it seemed her husband had insisted on finally demonstrating that he had the edge on his wife.

As the boiling water scalded the tea bags in the mugs she recited his harsh message silently to herself as she squeezed extra colour into the tea: *clean break . . . look forward . . . best for everyone . . . friends always.* All of it meaningless. Why allude to a sense of friendship now when anything approaching it had been in such meagre supply for so long? In the note she found nothing personal about her or them, nothing that would indicate that their lives had been bound together for a quarter of a century. From the pool of words that she would return to time and again to define her husband's treatment of her, 'cruel' and 'heartless' would always feature at the top. She hoped there might come a time when she would not think of him at all.

Gina favoured her tea more black than russet and it gave Ellen an excuse to move slowly, delaying the moment when she might have to put a voice and words to the new life that had been thrust upon her. He was leaving her but he wasn't going to another woman, job or city as she had imagined. She couldn't deny that it hurt a little more because she had no one or nothing to blame. She carried the tray with the brewed tea and a milk jug patterned with sweet peas to Gina's desk. As Gina reached gratefully for the offered drink she enquired playfully if the boys had touched down safely and Ellen realized the moment had come to start telling everyone the truth. She opened her mouth and waited to hear what those words might sound like when said aloud.

'It's a stupid idea. I want to have a party with my friends in Boston when I go home. It's bad enough that you've chosen for me to turn seventeen in this hell hole but I will not endure a dinner party just so you can show off to your strange menagerie of new friends.'

Jessica had taken her father's no-show badly. In her heart she had feared he wouldn't come but the reality of his absence was still a lurching disappointment. Coupled with that was her mother's rather too chirpy announcement that together she and their father had taken the painful decision to part after twenty-four years of marriage. It wasn't that Jessica hadn't realized that they were unhappy; it was more that they had been miserable for so long she wasn't sure why there was any need for radical change. Nobody's parents were happy really; some were just better at covering it up than others, Jessica felt. She wished her own had the good grace to keep the pretence going and not be such a massive embarrassment to her.

Her brother of course didn't seem one bit disturbed by the news. 'Shit happens,' was the full scope of his reaction and she even had to wring that little gem of wisdom from him.

Ben raised his eyes from a fly-fishing manual he had found on the bottom shelf of the lodge's eclectically stocked bookcase. Ancient Mills and Boon romances were shelved shoulder to shoulder with bird-spotting guides, introductions to traditional Irish cooking and battered children's books with Sadie Miller's name etched on to almost every second page. When they moved from Melbourne Terrace Gina had kept those still in good condition so that she could put a selection into the cottages when she knew children were coming to stay. 'A party wouldn't be such a bad thing, Jess. Gina and Sadie are lovely and the rest of the people here seem fine too. Besides, I'm sure Mom will fund a big party in Boston when you go home. Won't you, Mom?' Ben winked at his mother who was ridiculously glad of the solidarity.

'Anything you want, honey, really, but I don't want the date to pass unmarked. We'll just have a dinner party. You'll enjoy it, trust me.'

'My life just gets worse and fucking worse,' Jessica stormed before she left, slamming the kitchen door with a bang that caused the plates on the dresser to shudder. Ben resumed reading and Ellen looked gratefully at the one person who seemed not to think she was an utter disappointment. Nothing she did or failed to do seemed to wildly irritate Ben. How ridiculous was it to think that that was probably the nicest thing anyone in her family thought about her?

CHAPTER NINE

As the rock of Cashel rose ahead of them in the skyline after a torturous car journey, Emmet finally revealed to Jill where he had booked them for their holidays. A sigh was her only discernible reaction and he thought he may even have imagined that when nothing else followed. He suggested that they might find somewhere nice to have lunch if they came off the bypass and had a look in the town. So far what they had seen had not inspired him to pull over but he looked keenly at everywhere they passed hoping something might stand out or, better still, that Jill herself might pick somewhere, but his optimism was not rewarded and she remained silent. Suspecting that her mind was wandering around the rooms and streets of her childhood home Emmet suggested gently that when they reached Tobarnaree she might like to have a look at the house the Cassidys had lived in. He was curious about what it might be like, of course, but mostly he was ready to do anything that might help Jill. Emmet had become used to her sluggish response in conversation. In fact it had become a sort of victory if she conceded to answer him at all and so he was relieved when she finally spoke; her voice bristling with irritation and anxiety.

'I'm not sure if I will. Maybe during the week . . . It would be too strange to go there straight away. I haven't been back here in such a long time.' Jill fidgeted with the cord ties on her linen trousers, pulling them into a series of loose knots before unravelling them and mindlessly starting all over again. The light fabric fell slack against the length of her thigh. They were last summer's trousers and a smaller size would now suit her frame better but she hadn't bought anything since Fionn had died except two jackets that she interchanged as work wear.

Unwilling to let the prospect of doing something together die away easily Emmet pressed on regardless of his wife's lacklustre reaction. 'Well, I'd like to go with you, if you don't mind. I'm sure it won't have changed too much from the way you remember it and it'd be nice to finally see where the Cassidy family sprang from.'

Over soup and sandwiches in a high-ceilinged pub lounge their conversation was stilted, despite Emmet's concerted endeavours. He just wanted her to talk; about what, it did not matter. Out of nervousness and impatience he pressed her on the quality of the lunch he had ordered for them, asking her pointedly if she was enjoying it even a little bit. Jill murmured that the soup was nice though she barely lifted more than one or two spoonfuls to her mouth. He thought, however, that she seemed calm that they were going to Tobarnaree. Happy would have been overstating it but he was willing to accept even the tiniest glimpse of progress. At least she hadn't snapped his head off as he had feared she might.

Jill was stunned at Emmet's plan for them because a self-catering holiday in the middle of nowhere was about the last thing that she thought her husband might arrange. She had felt sure they were bound for some exclusive resort where Emmet was planning to play golf while he left her alone in a comfortable suite to work through the grief that was paralysing her. The generosity of the gesture to her childhood was not lost on her but the thought of being in such a memory-filled place while so much troubled them was overwhelming. She hadn't been back to Tobarnaree for years. She had planned to bring Fionn there to see one of the spots where his mother had grown up but a busy schedule and far more exotic places to go meant that she had never got around to it. Besides, when a certain amount of time had passed she had begun to feel that she was such a different person from the one who had lived there that it would be risky to return expecting anything to feel familiar. Tobarnaree was a safe haven in her mind. It was enough to know that it existed and that it had meant so much to her.

As she watched Emmet eating his lunch she wanted to scream but she felt her survival depended on keeping the fist of her anger firmly clenched. Emmet was doing his best but she no longer knew if his best was anything that she was remotely interested in. She pondered the irony of being able to make a weak effort for outsiders while being unable to offer anything at all to the person that she had once considered not just close but part of herself.

A little over an hour later, they passed her home place on the way into the town and Jill raised her eyes, hungry to take it in. She was shaken by the bolt of familiarity the sight of it sent through her. Her veins seemed to tingle in dread. The house was in good condition, lived in and loved it seemed, but other houses had been built close to it so it no longer stood out as proudly as it once had. Or maybe it really was smaller and more insignificant than her younger self could reliably or readily remember? She knew of course that objects nearly always appeared impossibly small scale when returned to after a long absence. Statues in churches or streets that looked as if they might well eat you alive when examined with the eyes of a small girl often seemed remarkably shrunken and timid with the passing of years.

The house's red-brick wall that was the first thing she would spot coming home from school walking with girlfriends or later

hand in hand with Theo Corrigan had been replaced by a newly planted hedge whose light-limbed stems had begun to wrap
tentatively around one other, sharing a shy dance of solidarity
against the wind that blew through them. She and Theo would
walk at a deliberately slow pace so that the moment they would
have to say goodbye would be delayed for as long as possible
without either of them getting into trouble. Nancy Cassidy (at
her husband's strict if unspoken insistence, Jill didn't doubt) had
made it perfectly plain that she didn't object to her daughter
having a boyfriend who walked her home from school but she
would not abide them loitering around her front gate and giving
the neighbours something to gossip about. A bank manager's
daughter had standards to keep up, she insisted, and so Jill and
Theo found plenty of quiet places to linger with each other on
the way from school before saying the required prompt goodbye accompanied by a curt peck on the cheek at the Cassidys'
front gate.

The grown-up Jill looked through the familiar gateway and
examined the evidence of a new garden laid out by the people
who now called it home. A car was parked in the driveway
and a woman was crouched on her knees carefully tending a
flower-filled border. She looked middle-aged, but might have
been younger; she was dressed in unflattering gardening clothes
that aged her. If Jill could work up the courage she would call
there later in the week, ring the door bell and find out who had
lived in the house in the intervening years but she knew that
feeling that brave was an unlikely prospect.

As Emmet took the familiar turn for Tobar Lodge, choosing
to trust his top-of-the-range satellite system rather than test his
wife's memory, she didn't think to tell him that they had passed
by the house she had once lived in because she could not cope
with the thought of his insistence on seeing it. Questions would
surely tumble from his lips that she had neither the energy nor
the inclination to answer. As they turned into the avenue of

Tobar Lodge Jill tried to compose herself. A brightly painted, old-fashioned swinging sign directed them toward the cobble-stoned courtyard that housed the cottages. A neat semi-circle of cosy domesticity, a jail by any other name, Jill thought, and her sentence was to be two interminable weeks in the company of a man who insisted on calling them husband and wife despite the awful thing that had happened to them.

If the Millers still owned the place she didn't really want to show how upset she was to the first familiar face she might see in Tobarnaree. She watched as Emmet bounded through the open front door and emerged after a few moments with a set of keys followed by a slight mousy-haired woman who waved gently in Jill's direction but just as quickly ducked back inside the house anxious to allow her new guests their privacy from the very moment of their arrival. From a distance Jill couldn't be sure if she knew her face but Emmet didn't leave her in doubt when he returned playfully tossing the keys to Sycamore Cottage on to her lap. 'That's the owner, Gina Miller,' he offered. 'She says she remembers you from school?' After a pause which his wife didn't naturally fill he added, 'You could call up later and say hello? I said you might when we've done a little bit of unpacking. With you being a sort of a local and all that.' Jill didn't open her mouth but her silence gave away the answer just as clearly as if she had.

Lottie had attempted to arrange a convoy with Rachel and Ciaran but they had insisted they would be travelling alone this year. Rachel told her she wasn't sure if Ciaran was even coming and that struck her sister as incredibly odd. Could she not ask her own husband his plans or was Ciaran that shagging precious now with his big practice? It's not as if he was a transplant surgeon needing to be on call to fly with a heart or kidney across the country. The construction sector could surely spin on its own axis for a few days without her brother-in-law's presence even if he might find that almost impossible to admit. She knew that he was having some crisis at work, the details of which Rachel had sworn that she would fill her in about just as soon as they got to Tobar Rock. To Lottie it seemed like a bit of an overreaction because to be honest who wasn't having some sort of crisis? The rules had changed for everyone, not just her hotshot brother-in-law. Men were like that, she reflected, thinking no one's difficulty could be a match for their own. She was looking forward to a few opportunities to cut her brother-in-law's ego down to size if he did show up in Tobarnaree acting the big man amongst all the women.

Even well into the journey she was still quite peeved that she had missed the annual first day brunch with Rachel and her children that marked the start of their summer trip to Tobarnaree. They usually headed out of town a little and docked into whatever café took their fancy. There they would eat to fill the gap left by a rushed breakfast hampered by excitement and inevitable last-minute packing. Indecent mounds of sausages, rashers and scrambled eggs later the sisters would stagger uncomfortably to the cars swearing that it would be a light salad for dinner and healthier breakfasts for the rest of the holiday. By the following morning the savoury smell of frying bacon wafting from the open windows of Gina's kitchen would dissolve any good intentions and they would arrive ravenous for a gossipy breakfast and great wedges of buttered homemade bread to mop up the tasty juices. An enormous kettle would be on more or less continuous boil and refill for the month ready to offer a cup of tea to any thirsty mouth that might come in the back door looking for sustenance.

On the annual trip from Dublin Lottie would usually drive ahead with either Billy or Orla, who took it in turns as co-pilot to their aunt. Keeping them separated for the car journey meant a quieter life and lower blood pressure for everyone involved. About half an hour along the motorway journey to Cork Lottie would indicate and trail off to an exit and Rachel would know that her sister had relented to the pleas of her young charge for a mound of sweets, crisps or ice cream. Holiday pocket money always burned a hole in Orla's pink sequinned bag and Billy for his part believed that his sister had a magic purse that was never empty of coins. Their indulgent aunt didn't need much in the way of persuasion. 'Ah sure they're only children and it's their holidays. A Choc Ice or a Loop the Loop never did anyone any harm,' Lottie would say as Billy and Orla made short work of their haul. Their aunt would join them for a squidgy Brunch ice cream on the service station wall for old times' sake, being strict about the fact that she didn't want her car destroyed with sugary mess.

She didn't fully realize how much she would miss their company until she had undertaken the journey on her own and found herself checking the rear-view mirror instinctively looking for her sister's car tailing her at doubtlessly the precisely correct speed limit. She fiddled with the radio, searching for suitably upbeat holiday music, while trying not to think of Joe King. Every male driver that slowed her up or overtook her was cursed for being a waster and a loser. She insisted to herself that there was no connection really. People drove badly. She was doing a public service pointing that fact out and if she managed to vent some anger into the bargain then so much to the good.

If she could just get to Tobarnaree and away from the scene of being dumped for a few weeks she could begin to put the whole sad escapade behind her. She turned up the radio to its loudest setting, hoping that she would get to Gina's house in time for a late lunch. A girl couldn't be expected to start her holidays on her own. You had to set off with someone. Surely that was the whole point. Company was what she craved so she texted Gina to add her to the lunch pot. Coming down heavy on the accelerator she left a trail of smoke as she bombed along the motorway. The exits for Kildare and Monasterevin passed by in a haze of impatience-fuelled speed. The country twang of Tammy Wynette started to blast out from an easy listening station when she had been hoping for some light-hearted sunshine. 'Stand by your man', indeed. Run him over more like, Lottie thought as she flicked the dial to another station in search of more appropriate lyrics. She slowed dramatically at the points where she suspected speed cameras might be placed but she knew she was probably wasting her time. The odometer in the car had been on the blink for months so she was merely guessing what the correct speed might feel like were she to adhere to it. Too damned slow was her fed-up conclusion.

'Jill Cassidy's here? Staying in one of our cottages?'

Lottie had arrived and Gina was helping her bring in her bags into Rowan Cottage. Gina thought she would let her sister get away with her ownership claim on the business. Lottie had only just arrived and Gina felt they should get through the first day without a quarrel. Tomorrow all bets would be off on that score, although this was Lottie so maybe getting through lunch was a more realistic prospect, Gina thought, quickly amending her expectations. It didn't do to be too ambitious for harmony when Lottie was around. 'Do you remember I said there was a businessman, Emmet Kinsella, coming to stay? Well, he's arrived and it turns out that Jill Cassidy is his wife and he planned the trip here to cheer her up. Lovely man. Very chatty and charming. I'd say you'll like him. Apparently Jill was always talking about how much she loved Tobarnaree so he thought he'd surprise her with her first trip back in years. He said a family bereavement has left her feeling low. She stayed in the car while he checked them in and got the keys for the cottage so I didn't get talking to her. Maybe one of her parents, I was thinking afterwards, because they'd easily be as old as Daddy, wouldn't they?'

'God yeah, older if anything. Jesus, I really didn't think I would ever lay eyes on her again. Tell me she's aged horribly. Coarse thatch of hair, crow's feet, bulging bunions: the lot. I deserve that little victory after she snatched Theo from under my nose.'

'You were *thirteen*, Lottie. Over twenty-five years to salve the wound. Besides, if I remember correctly I think the bold Theo did the snatching and not the other way round. Please tell me you're over it and haven't borne a grudge this long?'

'Oh, I'm most definitely over him. Was never into him really but I didn't like to be the only one in my gang that had no fella to walk me some of the way home from school. You know me, I try to fit in at all costs.' Gina smirked but her sister ploughed on without clocking her sister's amused reaction. 'He bridged a gap nicely while I was on the lookout for someone a bit cuter. I'm excellent on grudges though; never let go of even the minor ones while you still have a bit of grip in the old fingers, I say. It's good practice for when somebody really pisses you off because your instincts are primed and ready to launch a spirited defence.'

'Hold the line there; I'd say the United Nations are bound to come calling for your noted ability to pour oil on troubled waters.'

'It's called spirit, Sis, and I'm glad to say I have it in spades, but the teensy weensy petty side of me does need the pointy Ms Cassidy to have suffered a little in the interim. Tell me she looks like a bitter old hag beaten down by the fags or the drink. One row of false teeth at least in her sunken jaw?'

Gina laughed as she hauled the last of her sister's bags inside, remembering the graceful woman she had spotted earlier foraging in the boot of their car looking for something before walking aimlessly away. 'She looks damn fine to me but I'll let you judge for yourself when you see her. And she's landed a gorgeous-looking man even if he does seem a little sad.'

*   *   *

Inside Rowan Cottage Lottie gazed appreciatively at the ceramic jug filled with pink mop-head hydrangeas that decorated the kitchen window sill. The garden at Tobar Lodge was littered with the generous shrub but there was something about seeing them inside her cottage in such abundance that always cheered. 'The flowers are lovely, Gina. It always makes me think of being here when I see them anywhere else. Big and agricultural and not at all delicate. A bit like myself actually, unyielding balls of stamina.'

'Well, I can't seem to kill them. As long as it rains in Tobarnaree they thrive without a scrap of help from me. Lots of guests ask to take home cuttings but I always seem to end up with more the following year no matter how much I give away. Coffee?' Gina asked, flicking the switch on the kettle, presuming the answer without waiting to hear it. Lottie was always gasping.

'Is it too early for wine?' Lottie enquired, sinking into the comfort of a couch in front of the small cast-iron stove in which Gina had already set the makings of a fire.

'Ah steady on, it's only lunchtime and I've still got loads to do. Whatever happened to pacing ourselves?'

'I was only asking. Go on, coffee so I suppose,' and then, panicking that there might be no food on offer: 'You got my text, didn't you? I skipped on lunch to get here early and eat with you.'

'And when exactly did I ever starve you or let you fend for yourself that you'd start doubting my capacity to feed you now?'

'Ah I know you never did but I thought maybe when you had moved out of the lodge you might have scaled back on the cooking. It's hardly the same working one of these little gas cookers when you're used to Mammy's range heaving and spitting in the corner of your kitchen.'

'Take your coffee and follow me,' Gina instructed and Lottie tottered after her sister and into Beech Cottage where the smell of fresh baked bread was enough to yield immediate relief.

'I wouldn't doubt you. What are we having? Nothing too healthy, I hope. I'm not in the mood for virtue, beetroot or much in the way of seeds.'

'Potato and lovage soup with Gruyère scones. Wholesome but delicious was what I was aiming for to give you a good walloping Miller welcome home.'

'Gina, you're a fecking treasure, do you know that?' Lottie said while helping herself to the welcoming warmth of a long-postponed lunch. Sitting with her sister in the shadow of her home place was a feeling she had been waiting to savour for weeks and she would enjoy this first day when the weight of expectation and experience were sweetly matched. It would have been better if Rachel had been there too, of course, but that it seemed couldn't be helped. She would let the coming weeks take care of themselves. It was enough to be at home and temporarily away from her serious life in Dublin. She asked after Sadie.

'Out with our American friends, showing them what Tobarnaree and Munster in general has to offer, I imagine. She'll be back for dinner. I can always depend on hunger and running out of money to bring her home.'

Gina seemed a little too delighted with the arrangement she had made with the Carters for her sister's liking. She felt like saying that money wasn't everything but instead offered, 'You mean the impostors in the lodge, acting like lords and ladies of our manor?'

'From my eldest sister I half expect some maturity.'

'Well, you were sold a pup, petal. Maturity is not my bag, I'm afraid.'

Of course Lottie couldn't wait for the meeting with Jill to happen naturally so after Gina had left for the shops to buy supplies for her sister's requested first-night dinner of cannelloni topped with acres of Parmesan shavings, Lottie fixed her eyes on a tall blonde woman walking slowly back from the lake. Statuesque now and transformed from plain lanky to perfectly slender, fair-haired and superior-looking, there was no mistaking her teenage nemesis even after all the time that had passed. Jill looked lost in her own thoughts but, deciding to ignore the hint that she might want to be alone, Lottie approached her anyway, not pausing for a second to consider good manners.

'Well, as I live and breathe if it's not the one and only Lanky Cassidy?' Lottie was chancing her arm being so familiar with a girl she hadn't seen for more than twenty-five years but she felt losing a boyfriend to her allowed for some relaxing of the normal codes of good behaviour. Infuriatingly she looked amazing and Lottie was even more self-conscious than usual about the extra weight that stubbornly clung to her own hips and belly. Jill's figure by contrast was perfect, rounded and flat in all the right places, but her face showed real evidence of weariness and sadness. Proof that no life was perfect, Lottie thought with guilty satisfaction. Black circles under her big eyes gave her a haunted look and Lottie regretted her flippant and over-familiar greeting.

Eventually Jill managed to speak but her voice was barely a notch above a whisper. 'I can't believe we're here, to be honest. Coming back to Tobarnaree was a surprise. Emmet – my husband – thought it might be a good idea. I was out here a couple of times when my dad would come to see yours but these cottages were nothing to look at back then. I barely noticed them, thought everything behind the lodge was outhouses, to be honest. Gina has done a really good job bringing the place to life. She had vision to see this working so far out here . . .' she trailed off, having offered as much as she could. Whatever slight colour she had in her face seemed to fade from the effort at conversation.

Lottie remembered how much Nicholas Miller had always valued his close friendship with Jim Cassidy and had laughingly refused his eldest daughter's demand that the whole family be blacklisted by the Millers when Theo had chosen Jim's daughter over Lottie. Nicholas had said several times that if Jim Cassidy was still bank manager in Tobarnaree when his farm ran into financial difficulty he could have counted on his friend to give him enough breathing space to turn the situation round. Instead his hand was forced. Somehow it seemed important to Lottie that Gina would not now get the credit for their father's hard work. 'It was my dad really. Couldn't settle when he retired without a big project on the go and this was it, I suppose. Gina just inherited it,' she said pointedly.

Not being family, Jill didn't pick up on the pettiness of the point. She was thoroughly wrapped up in her own sad cocoon. She remained silent and Lottie continued, not wanting the conversation to falter before she had wrung anything worthwhile from it. 'It's a bit mad all right for you to turn up in Tobar again when the world is wide, but home's always home, I suppose, no matter where you go. Mind you, your folks were prone to moving around weren't they, with the line of work your dad was in, so I guess Tobarnaree was never exactly home to you, was it?'

That comment seemed to plunge Jill firmly into silence and Lottie was wondering how she could possibly have upset her while being unfailingly polite. Hating the awkwardness that had settled around them she went on again: 'Gina said you'd a family bereavement. One of your parents, was it?' She knew that her sister had warned her about being nosy but she couldn't help it. The question was begging to be asked and Jill looked as if she would need to be prompted out of her rising distress.

'That's not something I can talk about now. Later perhaps but not now. Will you excuse me, please?' She clasped her fingers against her lips as if errant words might otherwise betray her.

In the space of moments Lottie had gone from feeling as if she was driving their chat and could find out anything she cared to know about her old teenage rival to utter confusion. Jill made her way briskly across the courtyard to Sycamore Cottage as if she had just remembered something urgent to which she should attend. Lottie watched her as she bowed her head a little to get under the low-slung lintel and then shut the door firmly behind her.

What had Lottie said to Gina? July was for the Miller sisters and that was the way it should have stayed. It wasn't for strange people like Jill Cassidy who wouldn't talk to you unless you dragged the words out of their mouths and that Carter woman who'd kept her on the phone for an hour when she rang a few nights before not knowing that Gina had given her the loan of their lodge to live in. It was going to be a bit of a strange month, she decided, before getting to grips with as much unpacking as would take her through the first day and night. Careless living out of a suitcase was one of the chief pleasures of a lazy month at home. It wasn't as if it mattered what she looked like anyway, she thought, allowing a shaft of melancholy to encroach on her effort to keep the bright side showing now that her holidays had begun.

'Are you going to tell me now why Daddy isn't coming?' Orla asked with just the right level of insistence that could not be ignored even by a parent with years of practice at dodging awkward questions.

Rachel thought her head might well split open from the strain of pretending to the children there was nothing wrong while at least one of them was making it plain that they didn't believe a word their mother was saying. She regretted not swallowing a couple of painkillers when she had packed the travel first-aid kit that morning because a headache had stuck fast like a metal band around the crown of her head. They were only about fifty miles into their long journey to Tobarnaree and Orla had begun her determined attempt to interrogate her mother and get to the bottom of what had changed her parents immeasurably before her very eyes. Nowadays they were either sad, mad or cranky and she didn't like how it made her feel.

Billy had taken the news that his dad would follow later in his casual stride, helped along enormously by his mother dropping a lucky bag on his lap and a punnet of raspberries to munch on while they travelled. Rachel studied his perfectly peaceful reflection in the rear-view mirror, his head back and ruby-stained lips pursing tightly while he slept. At least the youngest quarter of her family was content. Bribery was not having the desired effect on Billy's sister but Rachel was far from surprised by Orla's intensity. She had wordlessly taken everything her mother had to offer in the way of enticements: a new and much requested Rainbow Fairy book, a travel pad and sparkly markers and a packet of Love Heart sweets. Arranging the sweets on the empty seat between herself and her brother and reciting their cutesy messages to him had amused Orla until he had thoughtlessly fallen asleep and left her alone with only the back of her mother's headrest for company. As a concession she had delayed her questions until Rachel had negotiated the heavy traffic out of Dublin, knowing how addled her mother got when she was interrupted while she was trying to concentrate. But they were on the open road now and she had no intention of being fobbed off.

Her daughter was beginning to sound a little like Lottie, Rachel realized with some apprehension. Nature could be a cruel thing, she decided as she steeled herself against a thorough debrief. 'I've told you a hundred times already, Orla, he'd work in the office that wasn't quite finished. He'll come down on his own later. You can keep at me the entire way to Auntie Gina's but that's the whole truth and there's nothing else to tell.' She checked out her daughter's expression in her mirror but was disappointed at how unconvinced she seemed.

'So why were you fighting this morning when you were packing?'

'What makes you think we were fighting?' Rachel was thrown a little. She felt certain that her conversation with Ciaran that morning (heated definitely but not really a fight surely?) couldn't have been overheard by Orla.

'I heard the two of you. I was going to check if I could add a party dress to the bag we'd packed for Auntie Gina's. I could hear you fighting when I went to open your bedroom door.'

Rachel felt ashamed and angry almost in equal measure. Why couldn't Ciaran have told her sooner that she should go ahead without him? They were already a day behind schedule and could easily have travelled with Lottie except Rachel had wanted to spare her husband what he considered the agony of her sister's company for as long as possible. 'Daddy will join us at the weekend, Orla, when he gets everything sorted out.'

'I'll believe that when I see it,' Orla said, looking very unimpressed as she scanned the countryside from her car window. She counted cows, silage bales, bridges and buildings until she felt sleepy in spite of herself.

'Did you put in the party dress in the end?' her mother enquired eventually, trying to reel them back to the safe water of innocent mother-and-daughter conversation.

'I put in the blue one and the long red dress with the velvet sash because I couldn't decide which one was nicer. I hope Auntie Gina has some parties so I can wear them. Do you remember the barbeque last year and Daddy was showing off wearing Gina's apron and he burned all her homemade burgers and Gina was so mad?'

'I'll never forget it. There was steam coming out her ears when we were making the chicken sandwiches to replace the burnt dinner. Then Daddy got himself in more trouble when he told her the bread might have been just a touch stale.'

'I hope she has another barbeque this year and I hope Daddy comes and burns the dinner just for the laugh.'

'I hope so too and by the way both your dresses are lovely. You'll be gorgeous in either of them,' Rachel said, wishing she was next to her daughter and could help herself to the hug she badly needed.

Unseasonal sleeting rain pelted harshly against the windscreen, doing scrappy battle with the windshield wipers that had worn to near uselessness with age. Yet another casualty of their frantic life that had grown too complicated and busy for ordinary things. Unpromising weather for barbeques, she thought as she reached across to the passenger seat for a pair of sunglasses jutting out from the front pocket of her handbag. If she couldn't stop herself from crying she would be damned if she was going to allow her clued-in daughter to catch her eye and witness tears when she knew far too much already.

PART TWO

SCATTERING

A man travels the world over in search of
what he needs and returns home to find it.

(from *The Brook Kerith*, George Moore)

CHAPTER TEN

'These are pure rubbish.'

Ellen had dropped some of her hastily completed paintings into Gina's cottage in the hope that Lottie, in her artistic capacity, might pass positive judgement when she came for her holidays. Gina had offered the information about her sister's gallery willingly but now that Lottie had actually arrived she wished she had had the wit to keep her mouth shut.

'You've always said that the appreciation of art was subjective.' Gina tried gently to get Lottie to soften a little but her sister's opinion was not for watering down.

'Yeah it is and these paintings range from drivel to shite on my subjective scale and I would know – or have you forgotten what it is I do for a living?'

'Not even a hint of potential? That's a pity. Really it is,' Gina said, regretting intensely the thankless position she had negotiated for herself between her plain-talking sister and her hapless guest.

'Why so? I mean the woman clearly hasn't the first clue how to paint but I don't suppose there's any harm in dabbling as long as she doesn't inflict the result on anyone else. Is that monstrosity over there supposed to be the lake and the rock?' Lottie asked, pointing to a particularly crude effort where the distant mountain range resembled an upturned egg carton and the water was a uniform and, given the conventions of geography and climate, an unlikely Mediterranean blue.

'I think it is, yeah. It can't be that bad if you can make out what she was trying to capture.'

'Take my word for it, these are all shocking. Can't believe she's actually proud to show these off. To think there are young artists out there scrimping to buy oils and canvasses and she's holed up here wasting mounds of expensive material on utter claptrap!'

'No middle ground with you, Lot, is there?'

Lottie shrugged as if the truth would out no matter what. 'I call it like I see it. What's the point of pussy footing? All this woman needs is enough white spirits to clean her brushes so she can salt them away for good.'

Gina swallowed hard and moved a couple of steps away from her sister for safety. 'It's just that I told Ellen that you ran a gallery and that she could talk to you about maybe showing some of the best of these there. Granted that was before I saw any of them. I thought she was an established artist by the way she talked about herself but clearly she hasn't as much talent as she let on.'

'Best of these? Have you lost the fecking plot? There *is* no best in this lot! Good God, Gina, why don't I take up some of Billy Jacob's finger painting from playschool and frame them up into a fetching little collage? Although come to think of it someone would take his sweet pictures off my hands quicker than anyone would buy these crap efforts. What's got into you? I mean, first you give away your house to the woman in case she would die of asphyxiation in one of our perfectly sweet cottages and then you start offering my services as her agent. I run a gallery, not a fecking drop-in centre for the creatively deluded.

Do you know how long the list is of proper artists who would give their eye teeth to show their work at the Gaslight? Have you the foggiest idea what I do at the gallery? I'm not cutting nice pictures out of magazines to stick on the wall, you know. I know talent and this is far from it.'

'Shush! She's coming.' Gina gestured to the window of the cottage from where she could see Ellen approaching from the lodge with frightening speed. 'Could you say something slightly positive, for God's sake? Humour her. Humour me. Just don't say what you really think. Her husband has just told her that he's leaving her and without a scrap of notice as far as I can tell. She's struggling to put the bright side out but I know she can't be feeling great and she could do with a bit of a lift.' Gina turned to greet Ellen, hoping that she hadn't heard Lottie emit the vicious growl that she reserved for when fury had driven her to the brink of insanity.

Ellen seemed to have forgotten that she was an aspiring artist at all and instead was wondering if there was a good local restaurant that she could book to throw a birthday dinner for her daughter's seventeenth birthday. 'You and Sadie and your lovely sisters will be invited, of course. Rachel's sweet young children too and her husband if he's arrived by then and I'll ask that charming couple – the Kinsellas, is it? And their children too of course if they have any.' Ellen didn't wait for the answer before continuing, 'I've always felt that children should get used to how to behave in restaurants from an early age. Serves them well later on in life. You'll all come, won't you? Jessica will be so pleased.'

'Of course we'll come, won't we?' Gina gave her sister an elbow until she elicited from her a nod so reluctant it almost dislocated her shoulder.

As if we have a bloody choice, Lottie thought venomously. Honestly, she would suffer having her right arm dipped repeatedly in a pan of hot chip fat rather than go anywhere with this woman, but if Ellen Carter was her sister and niece's meal ticket for the summer then she had some duty to go. Besides, there was always Ben to gaze at whom she had spotted heading out the driveway looking all tanned and delectable as she drove in. Lottie considered him a wildly inappropriate son for this Ellen creature who definitely did not share the same gene pool at all. Adopted maybe, she mused. He was half Lottie's age but then again she was only looking – the safest prospect for a woman so disaster prone, she decided, trying hard not to be sorry for herself but failing in spectacular fashion.

Gina agreed to arrange the dinner party for Jessica's birthday with Louis Corrigan. She knew he would be more than happy to put on a special menu in the Lime Tree for the occasion. For a big booking when the restaurant would otherwise likely be deserted he might do the cooking himself and Gina could sit at the table amongst her family and not have to worry for once what was going on behind the kitchen doors. Indeed, if he had no pre-booking he would probably offer to close the restaurant for the night and cook at the lodge. Outside catering had proved a handy stopgap when business was slow at the restaurant: anniversaries; communions; birthdays and the like; nothing big but wherever families gathered needing food but not wanting to cook.

Ellen seemed inordinately fond of the thought of that plan and Gina was immediately sorry that she had mentioned the possibility without checking with Louis first. She listened as Ellen took the plan and ran with headlong enthusiasm. 'Why didn't I think of that? A catered party in Tobar Lodge? Well now, what could be more special than that? Gina Miller, I've said it before and I'll say it again: you're proving to be an angel in my life.' She held out her arms and Gina smiled but stood back a little in case she might lunge in for a hug.

Helping herself from a punnet of black grapes on Gina's kitchen counter Lottie was wondering whether, if she just wandered off while they were discussing the brat's birthday party, she could manage to avoid mentioning the brutal paintings at all. She hated lying but she would have to if this woman pressed her too much on the quality of her dismal efforts. She was inching toward the door when Gina hauled her back, saying mischievously to Ellen: 'Lottie wants to talk to you about your lovely paintings. She was just saying before you came in that she feels she understands the wavelength you're on, weren't you, Lottie?'

'Something along those lines, yeah,' Lottie replied sourly, throwing a vicious look at her sister before launching into an elaborate and almost kind fob-off while Gina escaped to imaginary administrative tasks at the lodge. Market saturated with good landscapes. Moves to more abstract work. Had she thought of maybe paring back her expression to its very basics? She really had trotted out the most desperate tripe and Ellen for her part didn't seem to mind. All she could talk about was Jessica's birthday party and how special she wanted to make it. Where might she buy a very special gift? Something local that would always remind Jessica of the summer they spent in Tobarnaree was what was called for. From what Lottie had seen of Jessica she doubted very much that the girl would require a Claddagh ring or a slab of pottery to remind her of her summer in Ireland. Hadn't she said to Sadie that she now knew that it was entirely possible to die from boredom? Out of politeness Lottie managed a few half-hearted suggestions but she was distracted by the sight through the window of Jill sitting in the glow of the lamplight in her cottage with her bowed head cradled in her hands. The Kinsellas' black jeep had been gone all day and Lottie had presumed that they were both out on one of the many scenic mountain drives around Tobarnaree and having a lazy dinner with a glass of wine in the lounge of a cosy pub, exactly what Lottie imagined she would be doing if only she had someone to do it with. The lack of a willing partner was a small detail but a deal-breaker nonetheless.

She gleefully excused herself from Ellen while the woman was still rattling on and bundled her out the door and back to the lodge, impatient to find out what was the matter with Jill in the cottage opposite. Of course she wouldn't get too personal but there was no harm in seeing if the woman was all right or needed some company. Besides, anything was better than sharing the same space as Ellen, who seemed to greedily work through the oxygen of every room she set foot in. Entitlement was the woman's problem, Lottie felt, a sense that there was nothing to which she shouldn't help herself, no matter on whose ground she was treading. If the opportunity arose before the month was out Lottie forecast that Mrs Carter would find herself on the receiving end of a few home truths.

Lottie darted quickly across the courtyard in an attempt to dodge the squally rain that was coming in fits and starts. Jill answered the insistent knock on the door of Sycamore Cottage and smiled weakly at Lottie, who was more than a little afraid that she was about to have the door closed firmly in her face. Jill stepped back into the darkened hallway offering a wordless and reluctant invitation inside, her silhouette momentarily disappearing into the shadows of the lowly lit corridor.

'I don't mean to intrude but I saw you through the window sitting all alone and you looked like you could do with someone to talk to. Am I right?' Lottie nearly called her Lanky again but stopped herself just in time. Jill didn't look as if she was in the mood to be teased with her less-than-flattering nickname. Lottie realized that the Kinsellas' cottage smelled perfectly fresh with no hint of any food having been prepared in the previous days. In comparison to her own cottage, which was already like a bomb site smelling of last night's garlicky supper, it was thoroughly neat and looked rather as if no one had moved in at all. In the Kinsellas, Gina seemed to have found the perfect guests: quiet, unobtrusive and quite unnaturally tidy. The only sign of life under way was a bottle of wine and a half-drunk glass on the cottage table. A fruit bowl in the centre was empty as far as she could tell although she judged it would be somewhat rude to peer all the way in from where she was sitting to check for sure. Her eyes were drawn to a pool of pills lined up close to the wooden bowl like a stolen horde of penny sweets. Thirty or maybe forty of them in a range of vibrant pretty colours. Lottie was speechless. Why would Jill not have put them away before she opened the door and what kind of woman didn't mind someone knowing the sheer madness of what she appeared to be planning?

Jill reached into the cupboard above the sink for a second wine glass and held it up to Lottie, who managed to nod in agreement despite her shock at what lay arranged in front of her. Of course she would have a drink. The situation called for it and not just a single drink either but the entire bottle if things were really as bad as they seemed. 'Have I interrupted something awful here? It certainly feels as if I have,' she asked as lightly as she could manage, in case there was a plausible explanation, though she doubted there was innocence to be found at the heart of what she saw.

'I take it you mean my assortment of pills?' Jill's tone was matter of fact as if there was nothing unusual about what Lottie had seen and was now frantically trying to count on the sly. Jill filled a glass of white for her uninvited guest before taking a seat opposite her at the table. Her tanned arms were bare, goose bumped but enviably toned. Her hands reached out and fingered the capsules, pooling the green and yellow ones together as if she were planning an elaborate beading project that had to be just perfect. She took a deep audible breath as she fiddled with them, first picking up and then dropping one after another, their plastic coating making a shy tinkle against the wooden table as they fell. Her eyes were sad and distress seemed to seep out through her pores. Her body shuddered noticeably.

Lottie wasn't sure if she was merely feeling the cold or if she was under the spell of some sort of panic attack. Coupled with her worn-out appearance it made uneasy and painful viewing even for Lottie, who considered herself to have a fairly high tolerance for other people's misery, it often being such a welcome relief from her own. Hating the silence and unwilling to give in to its power Lottie dived straight in to where she realized she mightn't be particularly welcome. 'If you're planning to do yourself in, Jill, I think you might've overshot the runway with this amount of tablets. I know for a fact you wouldn't need this many unless you wanted to take out a few of the natives with you. Us Millers wrecking your holiday that much, are we?' Humour might help, she hoped, but never having interrupted a suicide in progress or planning before she hardly knew what was prudent to say. Even in her lowest mood about another lost cause of a relationship or a life stubbornly going in a direction she felt she neither wanted nor deserved she had never contemplated such a bleak option. Murder, frequently, but never suicide. Could Jill Cassidy be so very different? She wondered what could have happened to drive her to the edge of something so desperate. What Lottie was absolutely sure of was that she wasn't going to have Tobar Rock ruined by something so awful happening there. What a cheek she had to pick an innocent spot like Lottie's home place to settle her score with life. When she heard about this Gina would have no option but to admit that Lottie having the good sense to be nosy might well have saved them from a tragic nightmare unfolding on their doorstep.

Jill flashed a slight grin at her guest signalling that she was ready to step into what had been the one-way traffic of Lottie's righteous monologue. 'And what exactly would you know about killing yourself? You don't seem to be the type to give in to despair. You look stubborn and stocky like nothing would best you.'

Lottie decided to discount the stocky comment. There was a slight chance that she hadn't meant it as a slur on her appearance and even if she had now didn't seem like the ideal time to trade insults. What irked Lottie most was that she knew Jill's description was pretty accurate. She *was* a solid kind of girl, and being a whisker under forty she felt she could refer to herself as a girl with impunity, who maybe could stop traffic in its tracks but for all the wrong reasons.

'I know you wouldn't need as many as this, that's all. Twenty, tops, would do the trick, I'd say. At least it always leads to a stomach being dramatically pumped on *ER* and *Holby City*.' Jill looked at her quizzically and Lottie felt she might have to explain her embarrassing familiarity with TV medical dramas. 'When you're single like I am at the moment and have only a sporadic social life every few weeks or so you get to watch a lot of TV to plug the gaps between engagements. Remarkably true to life usually because they consult with medical experts to guarantee authenticity.' She waited for Jill to respond and when she didn't nerves made Lottie rattle on. 'I liked *ER* a lot, the tragedy and trauma were laid on thick like layers of butter icing on a cake. When I watch it I feel sure my own life is not that bad after all. There's something to be said for distress attractively packaged in lovely bite-size and generally curable doses. The doctors and nurses are like friends. I mean Luka Kovac makes me think I'd *love* Croatia.'

Jill nodded as if she understood but watching television was something else she had added to the list of things she never did any more. Going into the living room where Fionn had so often sat entranced by a favourite programme or a computer game was still a world beyond painful. She found it unbearable to be surrounded by walls lined with family photos, a gallery of past smiles mocking all the stolen days of the future. She had always loved taking photographs, excited to record every moment of a busy life, but she hadn't touched her camera since Fionn had died. She knew it was still in the glove box of her car where she'd always kept it. In the past she'd appreciated having it to hand at a moment's notice to record the little events that made up her family's catalogue of memories. There were photographs of him she still hadn't seen because she could not bring herself to scan or download the images she knew it contained. Doing so would be as bad as the dream she sometimes had that Fionn had never gone away at all and it had been a dreadful mistake only to wake and discover the horrible reality crushing down on her with renewed vigour.

Emmet spent a lot of time hiding out in the living room and that in itself was an adequate reason for her avoidance of being there. It was up to him if he was going to pretend to lose himself and his thoughts for an hour in a football match or a movie but she was not about to enter into such a charade of betrayal.

Jill eyed Lottie, thinking it was far from ideal to have found herself in such strange company when she felt so utterly lost. Lottie was greedy for every detail but Jill had become expert at keeping herself to herself and couldn't help finding the pernicious enquiries invasive. Despite this she had to concede that Lottie was asking questions that there might be no harm in forcing herself to answer. After a pause through which Lottie found it almost painful to keep silent Jill began to talk, words flowing freely from lips that barely moved in the effort. 'I wasn't actually going to go through with killing myself, I think. It's just that I find it comforting that I could if I wanted to. My life has swerved out of my control but my ending could be my own design and there's some power to be had in that, I think.' She was happy with the candour of that explanation and it gave her the impetus to talk further. 'It's not that I want to die as such but I'd like to think that if I badly need to disappear then that would be possible. I want to know the steps to make that happen. I want to have the method at my disposal, plan ahead as it were, even if I don't ever go through with it. Do you understand what I mean?'

'No, I don't at all. I'd be lying if I said I did. What in the name of God is wrong? This isn't normal behaviour by any stretch of the imagination. It's mad to be thinking along these lines,' Lottie said while with a cupped hand she gathered the tablets in a neat mound close to her side of the table.

Jill watched as the stash of pills moved out of her easy grasp. Yet again she felt she was ceding control and her resentment rose. Exasperation that startled Lottie rang through her words as she spoke. 'Normal? What's that? I sure as hell don't know any more.' She took a quick gulp of wine before rounding on her guest and baldly asking, 'Have you got any children, Lottie? I need to know so I can work out if you've the foggiest idea what you're talking about.'

'Children? No, not me. Never got round to it. Never that sure that I wanted any to be honest and no man went out of his way to persuade me any different. I see Gina with Sadie and Rachel with her two and they're all great kids, don't get me wrong, but I doubt I'd have the required patience to care all day every day. It looks to me like children are just a big black hole of need and then they go and leave you when you're shattered and stony broke from the sheer non-stop effort of raising them. How about you and Emmet? Child-free too by the looks of it,' she continued, scanning the clutter-free living room which displayed none of the chaos of toys and belongings that littered Rachel's cottage across the courtyard. Then she suddenly drew in her breath. 'Is that the problem?' she asked, the soft lull of her voice full of fresh compassion.

Jill's brow furrowed and for a moment she didn't speak. 'No, that's not the problem. I have a child – or I did have one. A son, Fionn is his name. He would've been eleven by now but he died in an accident just before Christmas at a construction yard. Emmet's construction yard.'

Lottie's jaw dropped. She felt the uncomfortable words like a slap of a wet rag across her face. 'Oh dear Jesus, I can't imagine how awful that must be. Good God, I'm sorry for the things I said about children. Feck sake, what would I know? Talking through my hole as usual. You poor thing, it's no wonder—'

'No wonder I feel like topping myself?' Jill managed to smile at that incongruous moment and Lottie was knocked off balance by the incessant to and fro of her mood. One minute she seemed utterly broken and the next almost playful.

'But doing something stupid like taking this cocktail of pills won't bring your son back, will it?' Lottie said, picking up a handful of pills and letting them fall through splayed fingers.

'Nothing at all will bring Fionn back. I know that,' Jill murmured quietly. 'But I might get some satisfaction from causing Emmet as much pain as I can. I think he deserves to lose on the double. I want the hurt to wind him completely because at the moment he seems to think if I would just move on that we could in time be normal again. Well, I'm not about to step over the memory of my son that lightly even if that's what his father is attempting to do.' She looked at Lottie who, despite her efforts to be non-judgemental, was examining her with eyes widened in shock. 'You think I'm a cruel bitch, don't you?' she asked, and when no prompt answer materialized she continued: 'You think the poor man has enough on his plate without his half-mad-with-grief wife adding to his heartache, but you know nothing at all about either of us. We're so lost we hardly recognize ourselves when we look in the mirror. I'd find it a lot easier to live with a stranger now than to continue living with my husband, who thinks he knows me to the core when actually he knows nothing any more.' She smirked then as if she couldn't believe all that she had tumbled out to a shell-shocked Lottie. 'Look at me pouring out everything to you and I haven't seen you in twenty-five years – and even then I didn't like you. But ask me to talk to my husband whom I've lived with and loved for a good chunk of those years and I'm at a loss for words.'

Lottie took a deep breath and with some sober effort hauled herself back from the most attractive lure of a spitfire retaliation. *Even then I didn't like you.* This good Samaritan racket was a thankless task indeed. What happened to having the good grace to be thankful when you were lured back from the dangerous threshold of surrendering to your own stupidity? Still, she ploughed on, unwilling to walk away from such a troubled woman. Curiosity mixed with goodwill would keep her right there until she felt danger had been averted or she got herself thrown out, whichever happened first. She guessed that the latter was more likely, considering Jill's suddenly icy expression. 'You're absolutely right, I don't know the first thing about you or your marriage but I'm happy to listen if you want to tell me.'

Lottie was pleased with the conciliatory tone she had managed under the circumstances. Beneath her anger Jill's fragility was palpable. It was obvious that she was on the cusp or indeed slap bang in the middle of breaking down but somehow she managed to go on explaining how her heart had been torn in two. She fingered the stem of her wine glass, nervously rubbing it with fingers that seemed to want only to tremble. Now and then she took tiny sips to ease a painfully dry mouth. Lottie listened as she began to tell about a December evening the year before when she had been anxious to take a quick trip into Dublin.

'I always hated the crowds the last few weeks before Christmas. Used to be a bit smug about having all my shopping done before others had even started theirs but just when I thought I'd everything done Emmet told me that there was one company he was going to close a deal with before Christmas and he wanted their present to be a cut above the ordinary. I pretended to be annoyed but of course I wasn't really. I'd never complain about a few hours in town because I was a champion shopper. Shop, then coffee somewhere nice to relax, my idea of the perfect afternoon, to be honest.'

Lottie nodded, making it obvious she understood, which gave Jill the confidence to continue.

'I asked Fionn to come with me, promising him I wouldn't be long, but he had zero interest and begged me to let him stay home alone with his PSP. Some new game he had that he wanted to get his score up on. Now plenty of lads in his class were left home alone all the time but it wasn't our style. Another two years or so might have been a different story – I'd let him come and go as he pleased. In my eyes they were still just kids and anything could happen so I insisted he should come with me but I told him that I'd stop off at his dad's yard and he could stay with Emmet until I came back from town. Imagine, I dragged him against his will from his perfectly safe home to somewhere I thought he'd be safer. How ironic is that?' She laughed a bitter laugh, making Lottie distinctly uncomfortable.

'Go on,' Lottie nudged.

'Well, Fionn was delighted to be left with his dad. Emmet was cool as you like with him knowing that I was quite capable of fussing for the both of us and Fionn relished how his father treated him pretty much like an equal whereas I still thought of him as a child. Emmet's father was as hard as nails and I know that made him casual with Fionn. In any case he thought I mollycoddled him too much. When we got there Emmet was in the middle of a meeting with the Russell Consortium, that same crew that I was off to buy the special gifts for. The whiskey was out and that was always a good sign. When Fionn went in Emmet curled his arm around his shoulder and presented him as the future of Cedar Build. It was all a bit cringeworthy so I made my excuses and left. The wheeling and dealing I left to Emmet because he was so bloody good at it. I've always preferred facts and figures to dealing with people that want their egos stroked or their worries eased. So I left to go into town and that was the last time I saw Fionn. I called goodbye to him but he was distracted with the louder voices that I'd no interest in competing with. Besides, I didn't want to embarrass him looking for a hug or a kiss. He was at a bit of a delicate age and he'd begun to be sensitive about things. There was still plenty of affection between us in private even though there was a host of things more interesting to him now than I was. But I was proud of him, a bittersweet pride if I'm honest. I delighted in him growing up, of course, but I missed the small boy that tugged at my clothes for attention when it was diverted elsewhere.'

Lottie nodded and when she extended her hand across the table in solidarity Jill tried not to flinch when it cupped her own. She had become an expert at rejecting touch, pulling back from people who might expect affection. Her voice remained steady and calm, as if the recitation of the worst true thing she knew gave it a validation and a life that could never be denied.

'I drove into town. The drive-time news programmes were full of guff about the budget the following day and depressing stuff about how the country was going down the tubes. I put on a Bruce Springsteen CD that Emmet had given me a few days before. "Shenandoah", a song I just adored, was playing when my mobile rang. I was stopped at a set of lights that just wouldn't change at the corner of Dorset and Gardiner Street. Seeing Emmet's name flashing I reached across the passenger seat and answered it. I was sure he'd remembered something else he needed me to get in town but of course it wasn't that at all. "It's Fionn," was all he said at first. *Fionn. Fionn. Fionn.*

Calling out his name like a madman and then roaring at me to come back quickly, that he needed me back because Fionn had had a fall.'

At that moment Jill let out a startling animal-like wail and Lottie rushed from where she sat to comfort her. Standing awkwardly alongside her Lottie paused for a split second, hardly knowing what to do, before settling the open palms of her hands lightly on shoulders that were hunched in a taut ball of distress.

'Tell me what happened, Jill. I know it's hard but just get it out if you can.'

A few moments passed where the only sound in the room was Jill's laboured breathing. As encouragement Lottie pulled out a chair next to Jill and sat down. Jill swallowed hard and seemed to regain a little composure. 'I don't remember exactly what route I took back to the yard. All while I was rushing through the traffic, willing lights to change, I kept myself going with the certainty that I could fix things when I got there. Emmet was always useless with cuts and bruises, panicking at the first sight of blood. I tried to ring him back a couple of times to remind him that the first-aid box was in the cabinet over my desk but both phones went to voicemail. I knew Fionn would be heartbroken if he missed his under-twelves football game the following Saturday and I was wondering how we'd console him if he couldn't play. When I finally arrived there was an ambulance parked next to Emmet's car, light flashing and its back doors flung wide open. The client, Dermot Russell, was standing behind Emmet's desk talking on his mobile and his face was as white as a sheet. When he saw me he cut off whoever he was talking to and pointed out toward the yard.

'Emmet was standing with his back to me, his hands clasped around his head and he was rocking back and forth. The paramedics were kneeling on the ground around Fionn but there was an eerie quietness about the whole thing. I'd missed all the frantic activity, I suppose. The sight of Emmet's face told me everything I needed to know. I pushed past him to get to Fionn, ignoring him talking to me and his arms pulling at me trying to shield me from seeing him. There were lengths of metal scaffolding strewn everywhere and in the middle of it all was Fionn lying in his jeans and sweatshirt. He looked like he was asleep but my perfect little boy was broken on the ground. There was a tiny bit of blood around his mouth that I wiped away with the sleeve of my jacket. I heard myself scream, knew I should stop but couldn't.'

'He'd been climbing the scaffolding?' Lottie asked, realizing that she too was shaking.

Jill nodded. 'They found part of his runner caught in one of the scaffolding joints. They think his foot got caught and that when he jerked it free the whole frame came apart.' As Jill set out the horrible details a distraught Lottie was rendered speechless. She couldn't think of anything to say that would make the woman feel better because she had been so winded by the account of what Jill had been through. In contrast Jill discovered that she had plenty to share when she got started. 'I feel primed to do damage like a cracked glass that's been left to sit on the shelf and will cut the lip of the first person that drinks from it. Do you understand? It's not revenge I want because I'm not stupid enough to think that revenge would achieve anything. Fionn is gone and there's no going back whatever my broken heart might wish. In spite of myself I feel I'm dangerous and I want to hurt someone more badly than I have been hurt. There's nothing or no one left that I care about.'

The extent of her callousness spurred Lottie from her dazed silence. She couldn't let such reckless foolishness continue un-challenged. 'That can't be true. There has to be someone. Your husband, for God's sake?'

'It was always Emmet but our relationship feels stone dead to me now. What would we talk about? The future? The past? It's all ruined, every last bit of it. Neither of us have words for each other. God knows he has tried but I just don't have the heart for any of it. Giving in has never been Emmet's style so he persists and his persistence makes me angry at his blind bullheadedness. He forgets I can see through him and I don't like any of what I see.'

Lottie ploughed on, feeling it her duty to help in some way, although heaven knew that was unlikely, after what she had just heard. 'Give yourselves time. There are so many stages of grief that have to be gone through.' Lottie racked her brain to remember what they were. Denial? Anger? She couldn't think beyond those two though she knew there was definitely a whole list that wouldn't come to her addled brain. It wasn't a prime time to think about herself but it wouldn't take a genius to work out why she was a bit stuck in her own life if she oscillated between those two emotions and never made any progress. Instead she brought her mind back to the rather pressing matter of cheering somebody up sufficiently so that they might shelve the plan of swallowing a bellyful of pills in the Millers' back yard. 'Look, it's still way too early to be looking for an improvement in the way you feel. They say grief is two years long and if that's the case, well, you and Emmet have only just begun. Your marriage can recover from all of this if you'll just give it time. Be patient and kind.'

'I'm afraid I don't think we can recover. Not as long as he thinks that we can come through this anything like the people we were. He thinks we can go back to who we once were and exist without Fionn. Well I can't and I don't want him to either. It's bad enough losing my little boy. I won't pretend that it doesn't matter or allow his father to think that either.'

'Don't be mad. I don't know your Emmet from a hole in the ground but I know losing his son must matter to him. People grieve differently and you can't expect him to have the same feelings as you at exactly the same time. He could be suffering in ways you cannot imagine. He has guilt to deal with. What happened to Fionn happened on his watch. I'm not a parent but I can't think of anything worse than feeling responsible for the harm that comes to your own child. He has to live with that on top of the fact that you blame him for what happened. Did you ever stop to think that he simply loves you and can't face losing his whole life in one fell swoop? The question is do you love him enough to give him the benefit of the doubt?' Lottie was quite proud of her well-balanced intervention. She judged it kind yet provocative enough to elicit a response. Her therapist would have been impressed that she actually had listened to the pattern of her logic during their sessions and hadn't just whiled away the expensive hours plundering box after box of man-size Kleenex.

Jill rubbed away a single tear that had defied her self-control by running down her cheek. She was glad of the chance to unburden her thoughts about Fionn but she wasn't sure she was ready for Lottie Miller to start telling her what was best for her and her marriage. Though she had only herself to blame for spilling her guts out to her old neighbour, who seemed to have perused a few quack websites and decided she was a psychotherapist of sorts.

'I hate telling anyone their business,' Lottie said with hardly a shred of self-awareness, 'but you won't solve much if you come on holidays together but spend all of your time apart. Take a trip together. Try anything and everything but don't spend the whole time avoiding him and planning to do something daft.'

Jill was silent in the face of her guest's none too subtle coaching.

'Where *is* Emmet anyway?' Lottie continued, not willing to let the conversation fizzle out without some sort of resolution. 'When I saw the car gone I just presumed that you were both out together. Very pleasant drives around here but sure I'm forgetting that you know them all. They haven't changed very much except for the odd well-placed picnic bench.'

'I presume he's playing golf because he always has his clubs in the boot but now that it's getting dark he'll have to come home shortly. Even he can't pretend to be practising his putt in this light. Most likely he has met up with someone out playing and has gone for a drink or a steak. Emmet's very sociable; he can talk to anyone about anything.'

Lottie thought it very odd that a husband and wife would eat separately while on holidays. If there were no advantages of company to this marriage racket perhaps she had always overestimated what she had been missing by being on her own. It was a sobering thought that what she had keenly wished for might be nothing at all like what she'd imagined. Rachel and Ciaran's marriage didn't look too enticing at the moment either and Ellen Carter's had crashed and burned. For a few moments she felt that herself and Gina, single and alone, might well be better off than any of those with whom they were holidaying.

She gathered the assorted pills together on the table, dropping great handfuls into the baggy pockets of her scarlet jacket. She didn't want to outstay her welcome and have Jill dodging her the following day. By taking the pills away she was removing the immediate means for her neighbour to do something reckless.

'I can just buy a few more blister packs of any of those, you know. They're very easy to come by. No questions asked unless you try buying them all in one go or at the same place.' Jill felt she had to say something about the cheeky way Lottie was bundling her pills into her pockets. And if her pretentiously designed jacket indicated Lottie's taste in clothes Jill felt her artistic eye could benefit from a little retuning.

Despite Jill's increasing tetchiness Lottie was intent on ending their conversation on a friendly note. She needed to be able to approach Jill again tomorrow and check that she hadn't sunk any deeper into distress. 'Oh I know, and first thing in the morning you might well do, but the fact that Tobarnaree's esteemed pharmacist is so miserable that he'd close the chemist door on the face of a desperate case if his watch told him it was a split second past six o'clock I feel you're safe enough at this hour.' Tobarnaree had so far resisted the lure of anything approaching late-hour shopping and Lottie was hoping that by morning Jill might be thinking of ways to live rather than ways to die.

Chapter Eleven

There was a scattering of ancient archaeological sites dotted around Tobarnaree and by the end of sixth class in Colmcille's primary school Sadie Miller had seen enough of the lot of them to last her a lifetime. Every school tour had landed them at another formation that had their teacher in the throes of enthusiasm he was eager to share but left the pupils wondering why they couldn't go to somewhere a bit cooler or, God forbid, a bit more interesting. However, she had decided that if Ellen Carter was offering her money (possibly fifty euro, going on a past day's touring around the Beara peninsula) to accompany them on a trip to a few historical sites she was most definitely willing to give over her time.

It was hard to know if Ellen was trying to come up with a schedule most likely to torture her already dangerously bored daughter further or if it was just a case of hapless good intentions on her part that tended to backfire badly. 'Go on, Mother, let's check out all those random rocks, roll 'em over and see if anything interesting pops out from underneath. That Patrick guy and his bunch of leprechaun snakes maybe or are the snakes all supposed to be poisoned by now? Silly me, I just keep forgetting,' Jessica sniped sourly throughout a pre-tour breakfast at the lodge to which Ellen had invited Sadie. Her words were intended to deride her mother at every turn when they happened to be in the company of others. Left on their own she was perfectly happy to ignore her completely; a habit that Ellen seemed to tolerate, if not encourage, in the interests of a peaceful life.

Stubborn enthusiasm for undertaking a trip and coercing some good family memories from the six-week holiday made Ellen somewhat immune to her daughter's swell of negativity. 'I'm sure, darling, if you listen carefully you'll find all the history fascinating and Sadie here will be a fount of information for us. This is her heritage so we couldn't be in better company to explore it for ourselves. Nothing's more valuable in these matters than the keen eye of the local.' She looked at her daughter beseechingly but there was not a shadow of encouragement forthcoming from her dour expression.

If the inducement of money to be their paid tour guide was not enough for Sadie then the presence of a perennially smiling Ben Carter was. In fact, such was his attraction that she would have offered to pay for the privilege of accompanying them had Ellen not issued the invitation.

Tara Hickey had let out an impressively guttural wolf whistle the first morning she had clapped eyes on Ben striding across the cottage courtyard as if he owned the place. Sadie had told her he was good-looking but her friend's shy description of him had failed to do him a shred of justice in Tara's opinion. 'They must have kidnapped him,' she squealed from her perfect spying perch on the window seat of Gina and Sadie's cottage.

'I know what you mean!' Sadie giggled, still bowled over by her first meeting with Ellen's son a few days before. His mother had mortifyingly introduced him to her as 'my lovely boy, Ben'. '"Lovely man" might be a better description, if you don't mind, Mother,' he had retorted kindly before winking at an already more than impressed Sadie. Man indeed, she had thought to herself and looked away before she went puce and betrayed every sort of shyness and exhilaration that threatened to make a fool of her while she stood opposite him.

Tara pursued the kidnapping theory further as Ben disappeared down toward the lake with one of Nicholas Miller's fishing rods tucked against the hollow of one shoulder and a knapsack slung loosely over the other. 'There's no way that specimen can be a blood relation to the dog-ugly crew in the lodge. He's a fucking ride!'

Gina bustled in through the back door carrying a basket of cleaning materials just in time to catch Tara's none-too-subtle appraisal of their young guest. 'Tara Hickey! What kind of talk is that for a nice young girl like you?' she asked with exaggerated shock, knowing quite well that Tara was capable of much more shocking outbursts. She'd witnessed more than her fair share while in her daughter's company.

'I'm a lovely girl, Gina, really, you know for a fact that I am, but Benjamin Carter is, if you don't mind me saying, the finest thing Tobar Rock Cottages has ever seen. You need to put his face in the brochure and on the webpage. Trust me, you'll never have a vacant cottage ever again if they get a load of the vision that I've had the good fortune to just witness sweep before me. They'd flock here to admire the lad,' she said as she drank in one last look at him before he disappeared from sight. 'Has anyone thought to break it to him that the only way he'll catch a fish in Tobar Lake is if we go before him and toss in a few packets of battered cod before he casts his line?'

'Well, let's not put that bit in the brochure, Tara. People who fish only when they're on their holidays like to think they *might* catch something but it's not like they would come here if they were serious about fishing. The lake's just a bonus and there might be the odd fish I suppose if you stayed out all day and looked very hard.'

'Forget the fish, Gina, the *real* bonus walked through your courtyard just now and don't you forget it.' Sadie and Tara buckled over in laughter and Gina knew only too well that there would be nothing but giddiness for the rest of the day and not a shred of work done by anyone but herself. She could see the daydreaming look in her daughter's eyes and although it meant she was on cleaning duty on her own again she was pleased to see her girl so happily distracted. It certainly beat the living daylights out of the heartbroken look that she'd made her own of late.

She shunted them out in good humour. 'Get out in the air and dry out those brains of yours. They're getting soggy from the sheer effort of being in here doing nothing. Oh, and don't follow that boy to the lake like a couple of lap dogs yelping frantically at his heels begging for a treat. At least look like you know how to play hard to get,' she advised, hoping against hope that the extrovert Tara would not sneak the lovely Ben out from under Sadie's innocent nose. The purpose of her last schoolgirl summer at home was to perk her up before she went to college and not to sink her confidence entirely with another crushing disappointment.

'Oh we will, Mam. Extremely hard to get, I promise,' Sadie said, winking at Gina before disappearing out the door in front of Tara. For the first time in ages she had forgotten to think what Leo McLean might be up to on this first sunny morning that a damp July had so far offered.

Sadie had spent the night before the planned day trip with the Carters studying a local interest booklet that had been put together by the historical society that her Granddad Miller had founded. She didn't want to be asked anything that she couldn't answer. She could have easily bluffed it with Ellen and was fairly certain that Jessica wouldn't listen to a word she had to say but it mattered to her that Ben thought she knew what she was talking about if he asked her any questions. Gina watched her as she sat at the cottage table consulting maps and guides provided for guests. Diligently she drew up a proposed itinerary for the tour, taking into account distances between sites and places where the Carters might like to stop along the way for food or just to stretch their legs. The site of the fairy fort at Lisnarua was nearly forty miles from the *fulacht fiadh* at Bearna and if they didn't delay too long they could comfortably see a few other places of interest that she had selected from the guidebook. She set about the task with more enthusiasm than her mother could remember her showing for anything in a long time. In contrast the study for her exams had been methodical but characterized by negativity. She simply couldn't see the point of the future after what had happened with Leo. Study she did because she had to but there was no talking to her about the years that lay ahead.

Gina tried to stop herself mentioning Ben even though she badly needed to know how hard her daughter was likely to fall for him. It was part of her obsessive need to be prepared for the worst if that's what might decide to play out. She wondered if Tara and Sadie had come to an understanding about who would throw their cap at him or were they both going to attempt to outdo each other indiscriminately for his attention. Gina hoped their long-running friendship would prove strong enough to withstand the danger of someone they both found attractive. She tried not to think about how much damage one good-looking boy and two lovesick girls could do in the space of a few weeks and how much mopping up of bruised ego and hurt feelings might lie ahead. Just at the very second she was about to ask after him something told her to hold her tongue. Her own parents sticking their noses where they weren't wanted had done no good at all. She would endeavour not to make the same mistakes, feeling that she owed it to Sadie to at least be original with her parental failings.

As if she could read her mother's mind Sadie said with a shy smile, 'You know Tara is sure that Ben really likes me, says she knows by the way he looks at me.' In her daughter's words and in her excited expression Gina found all that she wanted to know but was glad she hadn't asked.

'And why wouldn't he?' She smiled back, mentally reducing the casualty count to one lovesick girl and a handsome boy who she hoped was in possession of a kind heart even if it was far from made of gold.

Jessica spent the historical tour hooked up to her iPod, sometimes humming along to a song but mostly silent and glum, looking as if she would shortly expire of boredom and it would be everyone's fault but her own. She wouldn't get out of the car despite her mother's pleas to take a quick look at the wealth of history that Sadie was doing her nervous best to fully explain. 'More stones, Mother? Well, who'd have guessed? Pretty much like the last lot no doubt.' She rebuffed yet another earnest plea before popping her earphones back in and closing her eyes tightly against her mother's attempt to engage her even for a moment.

Ben on the other hand bounded from the front seat of the car with his camera around his neck taking shots of everything he could see. Sadie couldn't take her eyes off him and was hoping that her devotion wasn't too obvious. He had persuaded his mother to stop at a butcher's and buy some meat for the makeshift barbeque he had packed into the boot of the car before they left the lodge. In a nearby service-station food store he added hot-dog rolls, mustard, tomato ketchup and chocolate biscuits to their lunch kit. Although his mother would have much preferred a nice lunch at one of the many pubs they had passed (arriving fully prepared and not raw and sweating in a carrier bag at her son's feet), she relented, seeming reluctant to do anything to dampen his refreshing enthusiasm.

They found a sheltered spot of strand that was almost deserted.

Their only companions were a group of teenage boys sitting in a sulky cluster further along the beach, passing a can of cider one to the next and raising wispy clouds of cigarette smoke above their heads. It was a typical summer's day, windy and showery, the sun behaving like a visitor that comes nervously to the door announcing from the off that they won't be staying very long and pleading for a minimum of fuss during their brief stay.

Ben set about lighting the amateur barbeque: a metal grill tray he had found in the shed, some kindling and a firelighter plundered from the coal box in the lodge's living room. Soon the smell of sizzling meat scented the air around them and even managed to coax a ravenous Jessica from her retreat in the back of the car. Sadie announced enthusiastically that the food was delicious but she was not sure she actually tasted much of it while she watched Ben taking care of everything. She felt sorry for Ellen caught between the two extremes of her children. Her face lit up when either of them addressed her as if she wanted nothing more in the world than for one of them to talk to her and then to listen to what she might have to say in return. She had even looked ridiculously grateful when Ben asked her to pass the ketchup around to him on the low rocks where he had perched himself to enjoy his lunch. Sadie thought herself and her mother lucky that they mostly got on and she promised herself that she would give Gina a big hug when she got home.

Jessica sneaked off saying she needed to find somewhere to pee because the backward beach didn't run to a public toilet. Sadie noticed that she took her jacket with her so she guessed that a sneaky drink was the real purpose of her disappearance. The length of time she stayed away convinced her that Jessica was behind the dunes with her father's hip-flask gift pursed between surly lips and undoubtedly a lit cigarette poised to take its place when the taste of the alcohol was no longer enough.

Sadie would have used the opportunity of Jessica's absence to enjoy watching Ben washing out the ad hoc grill pan in the sea

COME THIS WAY HOME

water before placing it back in the car but Ellen wanted to hold forth about her life and its selection of disappointments. Seeing as there was no one else to share the burden Sadie felt it only kind to offer an ear. She found the woman nice enough really and frequently she was a good deal more pleasant company than her fed-up daughter.

'I should never have forced Jessica into coming here with me. She's miserable and it was selfish of me to drag her away from her friends.' Ellen fingered a stray thread on the flower-bud pattern of her skirt as she spoke.

'Well, she says she misses Boston but sure it's only a holiday and you'll all be home soon,' Sadie offered while furiously searching for something more supportive to say. When the Carters had first arrived she had thought that she couldn't wait for them to be gone again so that she and her mother could go back home to the lodge, which she missed even though the house was in easy view across the courtyard. Ben's arrival had changed all that and now she planned to relish every day of their stay. She glanced again at him when it became clear that Ellen was in the throes of a self-involved speech and there was little need for any intervention on Sadie's behalf. It was enough to sit there listening while running soft handfuls of warm sand through her fingers. Ellen spoke about how she would have loved it if her parents had ever taken her anywhere when she was a child. They were both so busy that their young daughter, by her own recollection, had got little more than a look-in. Her father was dean of a Boston college whose numbers had swollen in tandem with a rising reputation for producing high-calibre graduates, and he worked long hours that kept him away from his family. As time went by and Ellen became a little more independent her mother had found plenty of charity lunches and social occasions that she could easily attend unaccompanied by her husband but to which it was simply out of the question to bring her daughter.

Sadie couldn't help butting in. 'You mean they left you at home on your own?' She was horrified, having spent her entire childhood more or less at her mother's side.

'Gosh no, there were any number of nannies passing through when I was younger and later a housekeeper so I was never alone as such but just not with my parents nearly as often as I wanted to be, that's all.'

Sadie nodded while hoping that Ben or Jessica would come back soon. In their presence Ellen might not let fall the tears that were welling in the corner of eyes that had grown heavy with sadness. She was fluent about her deficiencies as a mother; her own worst critic, Sadie felt, thinking that Ben at least was a sure sign that she had done something right. Sadie's eyes followed him to where he was crouched down examining something he had picked from the strand; a cockle shell or a stone polished to a soft shine by the sea, she guessed as she watched his intent face lost in the task of assessing what he had found. A sense of duty made her look back at Ellen whose shaky tone of voice seemed to suddenly deserve a kinder and more attentive audience.

'I tried to do things differently when I became a mother, tried to feed the need before it was ever voiced. I was terrified of doing too little, though it's plain to me now that I have done far too much and that wreaks its own kind of trouble. Different trouble, but damage all the same. My son and daughter are tired of me, tired of me wanting to be around them seeming like I have nothing better to do but inhale the details of their lives to make up for what is missing in my own. They think I live vicariously through them because I have no life of my own and they're probably right. I imagine I embarrass them though I try not to think to what extent. I'm strong in ways but far too thin-skinned in others. Ben's a sweet and kind son and he loves me and tolerates me well enough but Jessica has no such gentle sensibilities as you may have noticed. As a mother and daughter we are what could be termed a very poor match. I'm too needy and Jessica, well, Jessica is at pains to point out she doesn't need anyone; especially not me.'

Ben, as if he knew that his mother might require rescuing from herself, strode over to where she and Sadie were sitting in a somewhat uneasy huddle on the sand. Ellen, tears pooling in her eyes, didn't look up, but instead pulled her sunglasses down from where they were perched on her head. Sadie got to her feet quickly, brushing the sand from her trousers. She was glad of the reprieve and happy to be able to look at Ben and stand near him again. When he spoke he winked at her, a wordless apology for being called upon to act as his mother's confessor.

'Well, Sadie, where are we heading next? I'm getting a bit restless now.'

Sadie gave a rundown of one or two sites reasonable distances away that they could see and still be on the road home before darkness fell. Ben was happy with the plan and his smile meant everything to Sadie who was gleefully looking forward to another few hours in his company. His mother and sister would be there too but she could pretty much guarantee that both would be in a world of their own and so it would be easy to pretend that it was just her and Ben out on a trip alone.

'Come on then, Mother, we've got things to see and our guide awaits,' Ben said, offering a steadying hand to his mother to raise her from where she sat, her brown legs curled underneath the pretty fabric of her skirt. As she rose to her feet she turned automatically to seek out Jessica. Ben's frustration with his sister's brattish behaviour was plain. 'Let's start the car, shall we, that'll get her running this way pretty quick.' He told his mother to take a rest from the driving and instructed Sadie to sit with him in the front to navigate.

Sadie didn't have to be asked twice. She grabbed her atlas and her notes from the pocket of the back door where she had stowed them and tried in vain to conceal a smile so broad it made her entire face glow. Ben started the car, revving it dramatically, and Jessica emerged from behind the dunes looking slightly alarmed that she might be forgotten. Her jacket was slung over her shoulder and she was busily texting while keeping a stern eye on the car lest it should leave the beach without her. She reached the car a little breathless and irritated in varying degrees by every one of its occupants. The change of seating that allowed her mother to sit close by did nothing to impress because Ellen irritated her most of all. 'It's awfully good of you guys to wait so *patiently* for me,' she said with considerable acerbity, but no one responded, all deeply involved in their own thoughts.

Ben navigated the rough track from the beach and the car gathered speed when he had negotiated the junction on to the main road. Sadie gave a fast-paced summary of the route. She was grateful that she could sound confident, as if she was forever guiding tourists around. The clock on the dashboard showed it was a few minutes after three. There was at least a half day left in Ben's company and she intended enjoying every minute. She listened as the low hum from Jessica's earphones was adjusted upward to a considerable growl, no doubt intended to prevent Ellen from relaxing. When Tara sent a text wondering how the day trip with the sweetheart of a Yank was panning out Sadie texted back a single word that would tell her friend everything she was dying to know but would have to wait until later to hear. *Perfect.*

Alone and a little bored in her cottage Lottie wondered what she might do to entertain herself. Rachel had taken the children to an afternoon movie that would have been so painfully boring that their doting aunt had refused to accompany them. It would be another hour at least before Gina would arrive home from the afternoon shift at the Lime Tree. On a whim Lottie decided she would drive the half-mile up the road to Theo Corrigan's home place to see if she would find him up to his neck in renovations of his parents' house. She'd run into him in town a few days before, and he'd promised to call to the lodge to catch up with herself and her sisters, a promise that thus far he had not kept. His no-show had disappointed her because he had seemed sincerely interested in how all the Miller girls were and what their lives were like now. It bothered her that she still might be such a poor judge of character and that she had been fooled by a bit of charm. Finding out for herself seemed a brave if foolhardy thing to do, but curiosity and impatience got the better of her.

She texted Gina saying she was heading off for a while and wouldn't be too long. She knew her sister wouldn't approve and would be compelled to lecture her about visiting when she hadn't been invited and she had no intention of being put off by an unnecessary attack of her sister's good manners. If Theo was at home she hoped he would be up for a chat and even if he wasn't she intended to have a good snoop at the house and see what kind of state it was in. After all, sightseeing was part and parcel of holidays even if a few hundred yards from her own front door wasn't venturing very far.

Theo looked surprised when she pulled up but he gave a friendly wave. He was talking to his builder and they were examining a set of plans laid out on a makeshift bench made from an off-cut of timber straddling two well-rusted water barrels. The builder was pointing to the front section of the roof over the front-door porch that looked to Lottie's untrained eye as if it had been given a helping hand to cave in. The whole house looked sadder and more lacklustre than she remembered but then she reminded herself that it had been a very long time since she had been this close and not just spotting its outline from the main road where it lurked shyly in a knot of trees.

'I'm reroofing the whole place.' Theo gestured behind him as he walked toward Lottie over the rough layer of building stone that covered the ground where she recalled two rose beds had been when Theo's mother was alive. 'It's in a bad state. Nobody living in a place does shocking things to a house in a short space of time but the builder I have thinks he can make a real job of it in a couple of months. He comes highly recommended so I'm looking forward to seeing him get on with it.'

Lottie nodded but was unconvinced by the sorry state of what lay before her. 'Did you ever think of knocking this place and building from scratch?' she asked solemnly, thinking that's exactly what she would do if the unpromising pile behind Theo belonged to her. 'It might be a good deal cheaper in the long run,' she added as an extra enticement but he shook his head vehemently, obviously feeling she had utterly missed the point.

'God, no. What would I want with a new house in this place? What I want is the house I grew up in to be back to its best. Look around you: there's half-finished new houses dotted everywhere and I've no intention of adding to their number when I can do a job on a house that actually means something to me. Louis couldn't give a rat's arse about the house and he'd quite happily let it fall. Then again I don't blame him because he was up and back here all the time when Dad was sick and he got a surfeit of responsibility. When you're looking at a place all the time it's easy to see only the problems involved but this house has a history for me and I'm not about to let go easily of that.'

'Spoken honourably and like a true tourist, Mr Corrigan! But knocking it is what I'd do, I think. It pains me to say it but it looks like your sweet little renovation might be far more trouble than it's worth.' Lottie wondered what on earth had driven him home to take on this heartbreak of a project. If this was what he considered salvation what was he running from?

'Well then, we're about as different as different can be. I'm a glass-half-full type of person and I can see what this house has to offer even if some people can't,' Theo retorted pointedly.

Lottie bristled, feeling there was no need for him to be so

touchy about his precious little refurbishment. What did he know about her anyway? Time to put him straight. 'I'm a glass-half-full person too if you must know but I'm realistic enough to know when my sad excuse of a glass is shattered into smithereens,' she said, pointing to the doddery house behind them with a sarcastic sigh.

'Touché,' Theo conceded the point before breaking into a good-humoured grin that was so infectious Lottie had no choice but to return it. 'But admit it, you're spoilt having Gina keeping Tobar Lodge running like clockwork year round meaning you and Rachel can come home whenever it suits. You might sympathize a little more with this poor fool if you knew what it was like to see your home place disappear.'

'Yes, I'll give you that. Tobar Lodge beats your pied-à-terre hands down.'

'Well, to be neighbourly can I invite you to my temporary residence across the yard here for a mug of milky coffee and a round of chocolate biscuits? I'm the project manager so I get no breaks to speak of – there's no union to protect your rights when you're running the show yourself.'

'Can there really be that much to do?' Lottie was incredulous, thinking that Theo was exaggerating the project a little. The house simply looked like someone had tinkered with it briefly and hadn't exactly killed themselves with effort in the process.

'I've had three deliveries of materials to check this morning so nothing to eat since breakfast. When the kettle boils I intend making up for my privately inflicted famine.'

Lottie nodded and followed him to the battered caravan propped on block stacks at the corner where what remained of the Corrigans' front garden opened out into the expanse of trees that formed the beginning of Corrallis Woods, stretching from there all around the western edge of Tobarnaree. Her eyes lit on the open door of the caravan and while she was trying to get a preliminary look inside she stumbled on a rough stone and immediately regretted that she had worn her new wedge-heeled mules. Mud from all the rain that had fallen and the constant stubbing on rough stones was bound to ruin them. The fashion-conscious part of her was proud that she didn't own shoes suitable for a building site but she certainly would have rammed her feet into Gina or Sadie's wellingtons if she had thought to borrow them.

'All right there, Charlotte? Mind your footing on the rough ground,' Theo teased in an accent that no longer sounded anything like where they came from but not pure New York either. Quite an attractive hybrid of the two, she decided, watching him stoop to get his tall frame into the caravan whose door, fixed by a single hinge, slung hopelessly sideways.

'Never better, Theodore, never better,' she replied doggedly as she climbed the rickety metal steps and followed him inside to what she recognized as a homely swirl of chaos. She recalled how he used to make a big effort to call her Charlotte when her father was around them, who he knew didn't want a Corrigan next or near his precious daughter. Seated at the incredibly intimate caravan table Lottie watched as he filled the kettle and set about making the coffee. He tossed his high-vis jacket to the furthest corner of the caravan where it found plenty of company with the rest of his wardrobe. The table was cluttered with old newspapers, bundles of shrink-wrapped catalogues, a half-eaten bar of chocolate and a clutch of dirty mugs. By contrast Theo himself looked clean and well groomed and Lottie couldn't help but wonder how he managed to be at such odds with his surroundings. She decided that Louis must have extended the kindness of a spare room in his house and the caravan was merely a site office.

'Your father didn't like me much. Didn't like any of us Corrigans I think it'd be fair to say and sure maybe he was right. We were hardly up to the Miller scratch,' Theo commented as he rinsed the cleanest of two mugs under such a miserably poor flow of water that Lottie doubted it was capable of cleaning a thing.

'Ah, for the most part you Corrigans were grand but my father was a hard man to please and I should know,' Lottie answered quickly, feeling a little disloyal as the final words were spoken. She knew she was speaking the truth, but in her heart she thought it was letting her father down a little to expose his weak point to Bill Corrigan's son.

'Fathers want the best for us, I suppose, even if it's their idea of best and not ours. You've gotta make peace with that in the end or you could be bitter for ever and a day for the way life pans out,' Theo countered, sounding measured and magnanimous where Lottie had judged herself harsh.

'Sounds like you've been reading too many of those inspirational desk calendars,' Lottie chided. 'You must've swallowed an entire month's worth in one sitting too. Do they not give you anything to do running those banks except tot up your bonuses and benefits over and over again?'

Theo shook his head and a grin played along his lips. 'Thankfully my days of sitting at a desk are over for the moment at least and for your information the folksy wisdom wasn't gleaned from any calendar, I came up with that gem all on my own.' He pulled out a biscuit tin filled with half-eaten packs of cheap supermarket-brand biscuits among which were many of Lottie's favourites. She plumped for a custard cream, knowing if she were to start on the tartan-wrapped shortbread then she wouldn't give up until she had done shameful damage to his supply. With one sip from her mug of coffee she discovered that Theo had made it good and strong just to her liking. Into his own he spooned three sugars from the open bag and peered into the tin from where he chose a fistful of biscuits. Lottie was pleasantly involved in the task of dunking and eating when he launched a salvo that she wasn't expecting.

'Can't be much of a gallery you have up there in Dublin all the same.'

'Excuse me?' Lottie squealed at his cheek. The chunk of biscuit she had swallowed quickly in order to respond hurt her throat as it struggled to go down. If Theo was aware that he had annoyed her she couldn't tell as much from his nonchalant expression.

'Well, I'm just saying that if you can be in Cork for the whole month of July while your gallery is in Dublin fending for itself it can't be much of an operation, that's all. A bit of a sideline amusement in someone else's place, is it?'

'Are you trying to piss me off? What would you know about my business?' Lottie said, failing miserably to match his coolness and conceal her rage. She pushed the mug of coffee away from her, unwilling to partake of his snide company for a moment longer. He slid her a biscuit from his stash and it scuttled along the melamine tabletop before landing soundly on her lap. She stifled the urge to hurl it back at him.

'No, I'm simply making the very reasonable point—'

Reasonable or not Lottie was about to withdraw his licence to speak, cutting across him and jutting an accusatory finger in his direction. 'For your information, the Gaslight Gallery has, since its inception six years ago, closed the first two weeks of July for annual holidays. In my absence for the remainder of the month I leave in charge my two capable assistants, who are students from the College of Art and Design. In the unlikely event that there is something they can't handle I can easily be contacted and in a real emergency I could even fly back from Cork and be at the gallery in a matter of hours. Happy now about my professional arrangements, are you? Not that any of it is the slightest scrap of your business. Honestly! I think you've left your manners after you in the States.'

'All crystal clear and I really didn't mean to upset you. Just curious about what you're up to, that's all,' Theo answered, eyeing her cautiously as if he were checking on an overtired child to see if their spectacular tantrum had run its course and it was safe to re-engage their attention.

'Anyway, you're one to talk.' Lottie was intent on giving a cutting comment of her own now because he had shown himself undeserving of the benefit of the doubt which she had extended for old times' sake.

'Meaning?' he asked while reaching into the tin for another biscuit. He pushed the tin toward Lottie but she pushed it back just as quickly.

'Meaning at least I'm in the same country as my business should it run into difficulties while you're three thousand miles away on a pinched shkelp of your brother's farm. Priorities a little bit up your arse there maybe?' Faced with Theo's silence Lottie surrendered to an uncontrollable desire to press home her advantage. 'With the economy up shit creek shouldn't your hand be at the tiller trying to right the mistakes your banking crowd have got us into? Unless of course you screwed up big and they escorted you out of the building and out of the country for that matter.' She noted his shocked expression with satisfaction. He fumbled nervously with the cuff of his shirt, which, even through her temper, she had already paused to admire. Smart, exclusive, maybe even a little bit sexy, though she was far too irritated to get sidetracked by that for the moment. Rudeness dressed in a good shirt was still just rudeness.

'Exactly what line of work do you think I'm in, Lottie? Enlighten me please about my part in the downfall of the global banking system. I didn't realize you were so well up on economics on top of everything else.'

'Well, according to your late father's bragging you were practically propping up at least one side of Wall Street with your brawny shoulders.' As she spoke she remembered Nicholas Miller complaining about Bill Corrigan's incessant boasting in the pub on a Sunday afternoon. He'd told Lottie that even if he made his way to the inside corner of the snug in Duignan's for his weekly three-pint tradition Bill's booming voice would still carry through from the lounge, getting louder and more galling as the evening wore on. The subject was either his farm or his boys and since he could compete on neither score Nicholas Miller refused to give him the satisfaction of pretending he heard a syllable of it. Instead his neighbour's vain tirade would continue to exasperate him for days and he would tell whoever would listen that the man was insufferable, and for a quiet life they would heartily agree that indeed he was nothing short of it.

'Wall Street will survive pretty well without me, I'd say,' Theo offered with the merest hint of a smile at his news-hungry visitor. He dunked the biscuit and swallowed it in two generous bites.

'They fired you so,' Lottie countered, full sure that she had flushed out his shameful secret.

'No, actually I went one better than that and fired myself.' He was really smiling now, clearly enjoying the fact that she couldn't help her own curiosity – had not a scrap of control over it in fact.

'OK, so there's a black gloom of a recession and you walk away from a big shiny shit-hot financial job in the States *for no reason* to come and do up a run-down house and raise a few suckling calves or a couple of Rhode Island Reds in the middle of nowhere. Call me a miserable old cynic but I don't buy a word of your amateur fairy tale. We didn't come down with the last shower around here, you know. They fired you, which can only mean that you did something appalling and did it shoddily too in order to get caught out.' The last dig might have been a touch too far, she felt.

He seemed taken aback by her comments, not exactly wounded but considerably misunderstood at the very least. 'Sorry to disappoint but my job was a little less glamorous and far less influential, I'm afraid. I was a debt-collection manager for one of the major lenders. The recession has been manna for my job. Items to repossess all over the place; never been busier in fact. Houses, cars, boats: you name it. I could be arranging the pick-up and confiscation of assets every waking minute of my working day. I lost the heart for it, if I ever had it in the first place. On job satisfaction it doesn't even come close to making the list. So in a fit of decisiveness – or rashness, call it what you will – I decided to spend some time at home in Tobarnaree. Anything's got to be better than tailing people for cash who no longer have any to speak of. Believe me, a tumbledown house and a bunch of suckling calves are a spot of light relief in comparison. Now that you mention Rhode Island Reds I think a few hens might be just the thing. A bit of company and a few eggs to scramble if nothing else with the winter coming in and the nights getting long for me to be here all on my own.'

Lottie hardly paused to take a breath before deciding all of a sudden that she heartily approved and that Theo was a hero of sorts in her eyes. 'I think that's kind of admirable actually. I like it when people take a stand.' Her face beamed a generous smile.

'Well, it was less of a stand and more of an "I'm off now and can I have my severance package on the way out?" Not exactly as heroic as you might like to imagine,' Theo corrected her but Lottie liked when people surprised her in good ways. She thought briefly about telling him of Ciaran's financial plight but she knew neither Rachel nor Ciaran would thank her for it so she managed to hold her tongue. Instead she took the liberty of inviting him to Jessica Carter's seventeenth birthday dinner at the lodge the following night. Ellen Carter had specifically said the more the merrier or words to that effect; besides, she firmly believed that the undesirability of the female Carters would benefit from being thinned out a little by a few normal people.

Theo seemed reluctant to agree but when he heard that his

brother was acting as chef for the night he committed to come as long as Lottie cleared it with the host. He already dined on surplus food from the Lime Tree a few times a week at the restaurant counter or at night-time in Louis' house so he reasoned that he was merely changing the site of the hospitality he very much appreciated. Besides, he hadn't been at Tobar Lodge for years and she suspected he wouldn't mind going back for another look. She told him about Jill Cassidy and her husband staying at the cottages and was inordinately pleased when he appeared to have only a slight recollection of whom she was talking about. It never occurred to her that he might just be being polite and unwilling to go over the territory of who dumped whom and why when they were barely teenagers.

On the way back Lottie passed by the avenue to the lodge and instead drove into Tobarnaree. She had settled into a good mood and she felt like spreading it around a little. In Lavery's Delicatessen and Off-Licence she bought wine, a round of Camembert, an oaky Cheddar, a small terrine of pâté, a selection of biscuits for cheese and a few bars of really good chocolate. From there she went to the florist at the corner of McCauley and Quay Street and bought flowers for her sisters and a small bunch for Jill, freesias and tulips in bright colours to raise spirits all round. It was a perfect opportunity to host a little get together that evening in her cottage; a bit of chat might well oil the proceedings at the lodge the following night. The Carters were on a mystery tour conducted by Sadie and probably wouldn't be back until late if the extent of her niece's notes for the trip, which Lottie had seen that morning, were an accurate indication of the itinerary.

'I wouldn't be much company, honest,' Jill pleaded, hoping that it mightn't take too long to get her fixated visitor to turn away from her front door and leave her alone. She was happiest inside where her horizons were shrinking ever smaller from the lack of human interaction. Away from her job and from Dublin she felt the limited skills she had retained for dealing with people disintegrating from lack of practice. She judged that listening to the radio or reading a book was about all for which she had sufficient appetite or energy. Emmet had taken a drive to see a parcel of land that was for sale near Goleen so she couldn't pretend with any degree of credibility they had plans together. Surprisingly he hadn't even asked her to go with him so she hadn't been forced to refuse and that had been a relief.

'Don't be ridiculous. It's just you, me, Gina and Rachel. Something to eat and something to drink. Actually a lot to eat and a lot to drink,' she said, gesturing at the stuffed-to-the-gills grocery bags at her feet. 'Come on, it'll be nice. Tobarnaree girls all together again, thrashing out old times and catching up over a glass of wine. It might do us good?'

Jill bit her lower lip wondering how she might possibly frame a refusal that wouldn't seem too rude.

Sensing her resistance Lottie added, 'In case you're wondering I've told Gina and Rachel about Fionn but you won't have to talk about him if you don't want to. They will take their lead from you though they're mothers and they definitely understand how you must feel but it's totally up to yourself.'

'Look, I'm sure you all mean really well and it's kind of you to include me but I don't feel much like going.' Jill felt like adding that she hadn't gone out to stock up on pills again so her life was not in danger and it was safe to leave her alone, but she wasn't sure what good (if any) that would do.

'Come for twenty minutes. If we're unspeakably awful I give you full permission to up and leave us. I'll even escort you home?'

Jill knew she wouldn't get away with saying no so it was easier to pretend she had been persuaded. 'Well, maybe for a short while then.'

'Brilliant! Hang on there for a second, I've something in the car for you,' Lottie said before darting around to the passenger door and returning with a bunch of yellow and white freesias. 'I bought flowers for us all to cheer us up. We could do with a bit of brightness seeing our heat wave cancelled its tour and stayed at home.'

Jill took the bouquet and grinned at Lottie who looked mightily pleased with herself. 'Was I not going to get the flowers unless I played ball with your invitation?'

'Ah God you were, yeah, but I didn't want you to feel like you were under pressure to come if you really didn't feel like it.'

'Perish the thought.'

Lottie didn't let Jill's sarcastic jibe throw her off her determined course. 'I'll be receiving visitors anytime after eight,' she announced as she hauled her assorted refreshments to Rowan Cottage.

Watching from her doorway Jill was overwhelmed with a sudden flood of unexpected gratitude for being forcibly turned right side out by Lottie. She wouldn't have thought herself in the mood for counting blessings but she had to admit that being forced to pop next door might do her no harm at all.

Back inside the cottage she turned the lock in the front door and pulled the curtains in the back bedroom, blocking out the surly sky that had settled like a shroud over the lake. Pausing to kick off her sandals she climbed under the wool blanket she had brought with her from home. It had become a comforter that she wouldn't allow herself to be without, one of a small selection of items that she was glad she had kept from Fionn's baby things. The only way she could persuade her body to sleep at night was when she soothed herself repeatedly fingering its worn tassels. She pulled it high under her chin and in the silence drifted off to a light sleep. She was blessed with dreams where everything was as it should be.

By eight Emmet was not yet home so Jill texted him to say she was visiting the Miller sisters in Lottie's cottage in case he were to come back and wonder where she had gone.

Emmet read his wife's text while sitting in his car in the shelter of a garage forecourt sipping a strong coffee and eating a stale sandwich whose forgiving sell-by date had been rather optimistic. It was a message unprompted by him and it showed she was thinking about him. He wondered if it was progress of sorts and just as quickly he wondered if he knew anything any more. He replied *home shortly* and all the way back to Tobarnaree his eyes would glance away from the road and back to the screen of his mobile phone willing a reply that never came.

Rachel left her own cottage for Lottie's earlier than she'd planned. Tara Hickey had arrived to babysit Billy and Orla and was buzzing with incessant chatter about how delighted she was that Sadie was getting back into the groove after Leo McLean. The melodrama proved a little too much for Rachel whose mind was addled by her own family's predicament. She wished Sadie only the best but it all seemed so insignificant in the scheme of things. Ciaran was due down to Tobar Rock after work the next day and though she was excited at the prospect because she had missed him she was also consumed with anxiety about what kind of form he might be in. In night-time phone calls to the children he was doing his best but she detected a brittleness in his voice when the children had wandered off to bed and she got him to herself. He was due to have a meeting with the landlords of the Jacob Design offices on De Courcey Row where he hoped to negotiate a significant reduction in the rent. While trying to be supportive Rachel couldn't help but wonder if a rent reduction would solve anything at all. She had gently suggested that maybe the swish De Courcey Row offices might be a little excessive under such changed circumstances but Ciaran's aghast tone made her realize how resolutely attached he was to the offices he had designed. She told Tara to give Lottie's window a knock if she needed her before pulling the cottage's front door firmly after her.

'Jesus, Lottie, how many are you expecting?' Rachel asked when she saw the amount of food that her sister had laid out on the kitchen table.

'Oh, just trying to get us in the holiday spirit. Everyone's a bit stressed and we could just do with a good old night, don't you think?'

'You'll get no argument from me on that score. Here's Gina now.'

'Evening, sisters,' Gina offered cheerily. 'Brought a few bottles in case you ran short,' she said before plonking three bottles on to the kitchen table. 'Like the look of the grub, Lot. Glad I decided not to have dinner. You've knocked us up a feast here.'

'Oh, I've been slaving away taking the wrappers off things,' Lottie announced and her sisters knew that was about as domesticated as she was ever likely to get.

The knock on the door was barely audible but Lottie pounced on it, afraid Jill would lose her nerve and steal away if not whisked inside promptly. After brief small talk about the awful weather they settled around the stove to which Gina had added extra turf. She couldn't help fussing with the housekeeping duties even if this was her sister's realm and Lottie was not about to protest. Although Lottie had cautioned them against saying anything about Jill's dead son unless she expressly brought up the topic the mothering part of Gina could not help but try to broach the subject subtly. What kind of woman would she be if she could not reach out to another who had lost their most precious thing? Anything she might say other than that would feel dishonest and inadequate. She whispered an acknowledgement of Jill's awful loss when she took her glass of wine and sat next to her on the couch while

Lottie and Rachel fussed with a stubborn lid on a tub of sour cream dip.

'It must be so hard,' Gina said softly. 'I've only one child too and I'd crack up if anything happened to her, so I can imagine how you feel.'

'Well, I think I am probably cracking up a little bit to be honest,' Jill said quietly, feeling relieved that she wouldn't have to pretend that she could be normal when she was feeling anything but. The wine flowed and they talked about school, Colmcille's first and then St Brendan's Secondary. Jill became animated wondering about teachers and classmates whose names she barely remembered but between them the Miller sisters were able to stitch together the people she was talking about. Lottie offered food around at regular intervals, anxious that everyone should have a small taste of everything. Gina got up to make a pot of coffee when both Jill and Rachel complained that they had had enough wine.

'I'll have two squirts beating down my door in the morning with no mercy for my hangover,' Rachel said before spotting the alarmed look on Lottie's face. 'Oh Jesus, Jill, I'm sorry – I didn't think,' she added, mad at herself for her thoughtlessness.

Jill bit her lip. 'Don't be silly. I don't begrudge anyone else their children; it's just my own little man I miss.'

Gina handed around mugs of coffee and generous chunks of chocolate and slowly the conversation regained a comfortable momentum. Jill relaxed once more as talk returned to the safe topic of their childhood town and she filled the Millers in on where her family had moved afterwards. When she saw the headlights of Emmet's car pulling into Sycamore Cottage she knew she would stay as long as she could where she was, talking about lighter things while she waited for her husband to be safely asleep before she went home.

CHAPTER TWELVE

Rain came down steadily that Friday afternoon and during a brief lull in the showers Emmet decided to vacuum his car. It wasn't that it needed cleaning as such because he didn't think apple cores and chocolate wrappers stuffed into the hollows of take-away coffee cups counted as dirt. His car was always full of such things; he considered it merely the unavoidable detritus of a busy life. It was more that he couldn't think of another thing to do because he had already read both of the newspapers he had bought on the way back from a morning round of golf that he could barely recall playing. He had packed a couple of books to bring with him, the same ones he had been trying to read for months now, but he hadn't even taken them out of his luggage. They formed an accusatory bulge in an inside zipped pocket where the case lay open on the bedroom floor. At home he might have cut the grass, wandered to the attic office and gone online to buy things he only half needed or tried to watch a television programme in the living room. None of these distractions were available to him in Tobar Rock Cottages and the slow passage of time made him edgy.

Jill was reading in their bedroom. When he'd ducked in to

grab a jumper her back was turned toward the door. She looked over her shoulder and back again, a silent acknowledgement that she'd heard him coming in and a damning confirmation that she still had nothing to say to him. The sight of the curve of her back stirred something base within him. He wanted to touch her, make love to her and for her to want to make love to him. It wasn't much to ask of a marriage, he thought, not too much of an imposition, surely? The very core of him ached at the memory of the closeness they had once so casually enjoyed. For months he hadn't dared reach his hand out to lay it on her bare skin and yet he surrendered to the torment of thinking about the possibility of that touch all the time. On the nights when he hadn't fallen asleep on the couch he followed her to their bedroom, lying numb and at a loss alongside the curve of her sleeping body. Though inches apart they might as well have been at opposite ends of the world. In his heart he felt he would hardly know how to make love to her now, his confidence shattered by her coldness and paralysing disinterest.

Struggling with the knotted flex of the battered vacuum he had found in one of the cottage cupboards Emmet was aware of a car coming from the direction of the lodge and pulling into the vacant space in front of the neighbouring cottage. It was teatime so he guessed it was Gina Miller's promised brother-in-law from Dublin. In her fuss to make sure he knew he wouldn't be the only man at Jessica's birthday party Ellen Carter had told him that Rachel's husband was due late Friday afternoon and would definitely be attending, 'so there's nothing to be afraid of,' as if Emmet were the type to cower awkwardly in a corner if he wasn't gently teased out of himself. As Ellen had wittered on, ignoring the fact that, to shut her up, Emmet had quickly agreed to go to the blasted party, he realized he was envious of the traditional family arrangement she alluded to. The wife down the country with her children in the company of her siblings waiting for her husband to arrive eager to join in the relaxation of a holiday. It all seemed far more like family than Emmet had experienced as a child or that he was likely to glimpse again as an adult. He burrowed deep in the boot of the car pulling out old newspapers and pretending he was in the throes of a consuming job, anything to avoid contact with someone arriving in the first flush of their holiday.

'Daddy, Daddy,' he heard the little boy's voice call through the cottage's open window and he swallowed hard for the words that would never again be meant for him. Tears welled in his eyes and he caught up his bag of golf clubs, flinging them more roughly than he meant on to the ground, hoping he still possessed enough fight to prevent him crying in front of strangers. He realized he was missing work and the company of men where it was absolutely permissible to talk of things of no personal consequence and for that to be considered normal. Without such outlet the tight control he had over his feelings was threatening to fracture.

Billy Jacob ran headlong out the front door of Alder Cottage, diving into his father's lap before Ciaran even had time to extract himself from the car. The little boy was followed by a squealing Orla, behaving like an actress whose leading man, after much delay and speculation, had finally arrived. 'Daddy! At last you're here. Mammy, it's Daddy. Daddy's here.' Then just as quickly her sentimental tone changed to one of calculating avariciousness forgivable only in the very young: 'What did you bring us?'

Billy echoed his sister's concerns: 'Mammy said you'd bring us something.' From where she stood on the front porch Rachel cleared her throat. 'I said if you were both very good Daddy *might* bring you something if he'd time to stop at a shop, which is quite a different thing.'

'But we *were* good *all* week, Mammy.' Orla was indignant.

'Yeah, *we were* good,' Billy added, acting as unpaid echo

for his sister and looking at Ciaran with a heartbreaking earnestness.

Their father's voice was playful and indulgent. 'Good God, let me get inside the house before you strip-search me. I might've the odd treat if I were to get plenty of hugs and a hot cup of coffee.'

From the ensuing squealing Emmet assumed they were lunging at him for offered affection and then he heard Gina's sister's voice urging them to 'go easy on Daddy. He's had a long drive. Back off and let him get inside.'

Despite his incredible resistance to witnessing the happy family scene play out behind him a rogue instinct made Emmet raise his eyes from his private world to take it all in. He wondered afterward if he had subliminally recognized Ciaran's voice but decided probably not. He didn't have an instantly recognizable accent for a start but a vague country accent that had been neutralized by years of living in the city. He could have been from anywhere. It was the scene itself and not the players that had, against his stubborn wish, utterly enthralled Emmet. The kindest thing for himself would have been to let them disappear inside, which would only have taken a few short moments, but instead he found himself looking around and straight into the stunned eyes of Ciaran Jacob.

'What a coincidence!' Emmet blurted out. He had had a great deal of practice at being able to talk when he didn't feel like it but Ciaran said nothing as he stood near his car with his young children tugging at his pockets for anything he might have thought to bring them. 'What brings you here?' Emmet continued, cursing the way chance had shaken them so close together. He could have done without this on top of all he had to cope with behind his own front door.

'It's my wife's home place. Well, the lodge is anyway,' Ciaran managed, nodding in the direction of the main house, which had been lit up like a Christmas tree by Ellen in preparation for the elaborate birthday dinner. 'I come from around here too but a long time ago now.'

Emmet shook his head as if to say *small world*. 'So does my wife. Well, amongst other places anyway. Cassidy? Jill Cassidy? They moved a long time ago too so maybe you don't know them.' Emmet offered her name though he wasn't sure why. It wasn't as if he was hoping to find further common ground with Ciaran Jacob. They shared too much knowledge about each other already.

Ciaran shook his head. 'Can't say that I do remember any Cassidys but it's been a long time since my family moved from here.'

Rachel moved quickly to the side of the car to peel an overexcited Billy away from his father. 'Easy, Billy. Daddy's talking to Mr Kinsella,' she admonished before flashing a grin at Emmet. 'Billy's a bit boisterous, I'm afraid.'

Emmet gave a forgiving shrug for the little boy's understandable enthusiasm, replying, 'Not at all. He's grand.'

'But, Mammy, he's got sweets. He must have sweets!' Billy's plaintive voice stung Emmet and he moved quickly to throw the golf clubs and assembled debris from the boot back into the car.

'I guess I'll see you all later up at the lodge for this big dinner,' he said before disappearing into his cottage and banging the door behind him with considerable force.

Ciaran rooted under the jacket of his suit slung in the passenger seat of the car and produced two bags of pick'n'mix. He had a few other small things but these would appease for the moment. Orla moved and grabbed them both quickly and to torment her brother she set off around the courtyard with Billy squealing in frustrated pursuit.

'Didn't know you knew the Kinsellas,' Rachel commented lightly in between chiding her daughter to be nice to her little brother or all their treats would be confiscated until the following morning. A pragmatic peace broke out and she turned her attention back to her husband, who seemed deeply unsettled by meeting Emmet.

'He's the director of one of the building firms we deal with,' Ciaran said briefly. He knew he should say more but fortunately his wife interrupted.

'Oh, right. Well, the girls remember his wife from school but I don't. She was in Lottie's year, I think. Had a good chat with her when we were in with Lottie last night and she seems nice enough. They lost their only child in an accident before Christmas and it's left her in a bad way. Him too I imagine but he hasn't really been around much so I haven't talked to him except to say hello. Lottie has taken Jill on as this year's project. Determined to have her back in ship-mental-shape before she leaves here, which is hardly realistic given what's happened but you know Lottie. Won't be put off once she's got the scent.'

Billy and Orla perched themselves on the front step counting out their spoils and Rachel watched them thinking she would die if anything happened to either of them. At once she was flooded with renewed sympathy for the Kinsellas.

Ciaran inhaled deeply and he found the words to be as honest with his wife as he had promised her and himself. 'I bought the Ivory Square apartments from him. Sold me them at an insider price. Emmet Kinsella's the director of Cedar Build, developer of the entire Ivory project. *Very rich* director of Cedar Build, so you shouldn't feel that sorry for him. I'd have thought he would have the money to holiday somewhere a bit more upmarket than here,' he added with a bitterness and pettiness that, while embarrassing him, he simply couldn't help. With a beep of his key fob he locked the car and Rachel followed him in through the open door of the cottage, stepping over their sweet-chewing children as they went.

'Well, maybe we can talk to him about buying them back or a partial reversing of the deal in some way?' Rachel said brightly, feeling a solution had to be possible now that the faces behind the ill-advised deal were all in one place. She had warmed some soup through on the hob for Ciaran to tide him over until dinner and she set out a bowl and spoon ready on the counter while she waited for her husband to speak.

'I've already asked him weeks ago if he knew anyone buying. He's not interested. As far as he's concerned they're off his hands and they're my problem. Why should he buy them back? Nobody in their right mind is buying property at the moment or have you forgotten? Whatever you may hope there's no chance that Emmet Kinsella is my knight in shining armour. The deal's a disaster for me but nothing short of a coup for him.' His tone seemed derisory as if his wife just wasn't grasping what to him was perfectly clear.

Rachel swallowed hard. She didn't want to get embroiled in a fight when Ciaran had only just arrived and the children were within earshot. 'Does he know how serious this is for us? That your business is on the verge of collapse because of the deal you cooked up together?' To busy herself she ladled the soup into the bowl and cradled its warmth in her cupped hands.

Ciaran shook his head in frustration. Was it possible for him to feel any worse? It had been a mistake to come to Tobarnaree and Emmet's presence here served as a further mocking confirmation of that. He looked at Rachel, hopeful and eager for their circumstances to improve, and all he wanted to do was get straight back into the car and drive away from the weight of his responsibility and her uncomplicated expectation that things would surely get better.

Faced with his sullen silence Rachel spoke again. 'I can talk to Jill. As I've said, she knows us from years ago and I'm sure she wouldn't want you to lose your business over this deal. The fact that she knows who we are will make a difference. I bet if I were to go in there now—'

'Good Jesus, Rachel, you'll do no such thing. Don't you think

I feel bad enough already without you going begging Kinsella's wife to dig me out of a hole? Are you trying to make me feel like shit altogether?'

Rachel looked at his face distorted in antagonism and wondered just how they had managed to fall so far and so fast. Before she could think of anything to defend herself against the unfairness of his accusation Orla trotted past where they stood in the living room to throw her empty sweet bag in the bin. As she passed her parents on the way back out she announced pointedly to her brother, 'Let's play pretend, Billy. I'll be the mammy and you be the daddy and we've to fight about everything *all* the time.' Rachel tried to call her back but she said her name too softly and the little girl didn't turn around. Besides, her mother wasn't sure that there was anything she could say that would prove that things were all right when clearly they were far from it. At the kitchen table Ciaran ate a few spoons of soup hardly tasting it as he did so and wondered how on earth he could face the night ahead.

The pulse and hum of the electric shower carried through from the bathroom to where Emmet sat in the living room of Sycamore Cottage. On the kitchen radio a sports programme busy with scorelines, teams and possible substitutions simmered on low volume. Every now and then he would hear a detail of a jockey's name or a fixture change and waiting for the next recognizable snippet would prevent him from drifting asleep even though his eyelids were heavy with exhaustion.

Jill had surprised him that morning by saying that she would go to the Carter party having decided it would be awkward to sit in while everyone was gathering in the lodge. He was glad, of course, but he knew enough to realize her presence there would not have a thing to do with him but everything to do with being in her home place and the company the Miller sisters had forced upon her since they had arrived. It was after midnight when she had arrived back from Lottie Miller's cottage the night before. He had lain awake for some considerable time afterward wondering what she might have spoken to them about that she could not say to him. He wouldn't complain if peer pressure persuaded her to do things that he could not. Returning to something approaching normality was all that mattered. He would not quibble with whatever means would get her there.

He expected it would be difficult to keep Ciaran Jacob's company under the circumstances but he wasn't about to pull out and leave Jill to face the occasion on her own. Any effort on Jill's part would be matched with increased determination by Emmet even if that stretched to making small talk with Ciaran, whom he had been hoping not to meet until their shared business history no longer rankled. Seeing the man with his family made him feel guilty in a way for which he was unprepared. On paper it had all looked so straightforward but now it didn't feel too clever to have used a real family as collateral. Still, business was business, he reasoned, and if emotion were to cloud every decision he made he would never have turned any kind of worthwhile profit.

A glance at his watch told him he could sit for another half an hour before he too would have to shower and get ready. Earlier he had called into one of the off-licences in Tobarnaree to buy a few bottles of wine to take to the dinner and he briefly thought about opening one of them to give him courage and boost his spirits for the night ahead. The voices of the Jacob children, by turns soft and then shrill, echoed around the courtyard and carried through the open sash window to where he sat in lamplight. Emmet closed his eyes and tried fruitlessly to block out their carefree noise. The sudden sound of metal on the cobblestones startled him and he rose to his feet to see Billy Jacob repeatedly thump a galvanized bucket with a coal shovel. The harsh echoing noise made him think again of the evening Fionn had died.

Hearing a similar clattering sound from outside his office he had risen from his desk, drained whiskey tumbler in hand, and furiously scanned the sketchily lit yard for his son. He ran down the steel gangway from his office passing by a bank of Portakabins, their witnessing shadows set dark against the glaring streetlights of a humming city in mid-winter nightfall. His panicked heart thumped in his chest already stung by the bracing winter air hitting his body clad only in a light shirt. In the interminable seconds before he reached the back wall he knew in his heart what he would find. The relentless torrent of men's footsteps that followed from his office died away behind him as they reached where Emmet knelt crouching over his son.

Collapsing back on the couch of Sycamore Cottage Emmet allowed the image of his blond boy to visit him and alone in the half-light he let himself cry the stream of tears he had earlier withheld.

Chapter Thirteen

'When exactly did it occur to you that the Millers should act like some class of serving troop to this Carter woman? I'd hazard a guess that our family come from far higher stock than her steerage crowd.'

Lottie was applying her lipstick while nitpicking at Gina for the arrangements she had made with Louis Corrigan to take over the catering of Jessica's birthday dinner. Gina felt obliged to put her sister straight. 'A big table booked for the Lime Tree earlier today so he's staying there but he's prepared all the food and dropped it off to the lodge. It's in the range heating through now. All I'm doing is making up a salad and serving it all up and if I don't mind doing that I don't see why it should piss you off so bloody much. I just thought you might help me, that's all, but I'll ask Sadie instead although she's not the best at waitressing. Always dropping things. Don't want her drenching Ellen, or worse still Ben, with a jug of gravy out of nervousness.'

'I suppose I could stretch myself and help but it's a favour to you, mind, and not to them. I was just looking forward to us all sitting around the table in your lovely kitchen and having a nice meal even if it is for that wretched little brat. Besides, I wouldn't make Sadie do it when she's so keen on Ben. She'd be mortified whereas I don't have the sensibilities of a mere teenager. Happily I possess the constitution of a mature ox. I'll don a frilly apron and serve like the charwomen of old if that's what's required to make the night a success.'

'Good God, I can't think of any occupation to which you'd be less suited, except maybe a nun. By the way, dinner is lamb shanks braised in red wine with roasted vegetables and herby potatoes, a Lime Tree special, which will be delicious if Louis didn't go tinkering with my recipe. I hope Theo will enjoy the night. He's still coming, isn't he?' Gina enjoyed teasing her sister, knowing that the low-cut navy wrap dress Lottie had put on was for someone's benefit and certainly not for anyone in her family, who were more used to seeing her in jeans when she was holed up in Tobarnaree. Her chestnut-coloured hair, usually ponytailed for tidy simplicity, hung around her shoulders in wild waves. Gina thought it was the best she'd seen her looking for a long time.

'Don't know,' Lottie answered, twirling the open lipstick in her fingers while taking in the job she had made of her make-up in the mirror of her compact case. 'Haven't heard otherwise but if he's like his brother I suppose we can't discount a no-show at the last minute leaving us Millers to handle everything.' Eyeing her lips again she added another coat for good measure, determined not to catch her sister's keen eye in the process.

In the lodge Ellen had got Ben to string lengths of white fairy lights around the banisters of the staircase; foil helium balloons clung together in weighted bunches along the hallway. There were bought flowers on the hall table and another vase was visible on the huge oak sideboard inside the living-room door. Gina was proud of the way the lodge looked as she strode in ahead of Lottie and Rachel and headed for the kitchen to check on the food. Ciaran lurked behind the children and Sadie, saying little and acting thoroughly preoccupied by the photographs in the hallway as if he were seeing the faces contained there for the first time. He was unable to disguise how disconsolate he felt and had barely murmured a greeting to his sisters-in-law when they'd met. Yet moody silence wasn't his usual form. Before, he had always animated their gathering with plenty of stories and sarcastic humour when he joined them, unlike this time when he was making it awkward and stilted. Gina wanted to say something to him about the problems he was having but couldn't; she felt it wasn't her place to say she was thinking of what it meant for him as well as her sister and her niece and nephew. She wasn't sure of the etiquette of sympathy in the circumstances and instead plumped for silence and hoped no one would blame her.

Lottie paused briefly outside the open door of the living room where the Kinsellas were standing some distance apart with glasses of wine in their hands but without a thing to say to one another. 'Here's where the rousing pre-dinner drink session is going on, obviously.' She beckoned to Rachel and Ciaran, who had no real choice but to follow where she led. Lottie and Rachel each took a glass of wine from Emmet whom Ellen had cajoled into being her barman, saying that she didn't have the heart to drag her son away from the girl he was sweet on. Ciaran sulkily insisted on pouring his own, scoring a petulant point against a somewhat amused Emmet.

Jill had taken up a position by the blazing open fire whose warmth was appreciated by everyone because the evening had turned suddenly cold. Lottie and Rachel approached her and clinked their glasses to the enjoyable time they'd had the night before.

Rachel appreciated that some small talk would have to take place before she could mention their husbands' dealings to Jill and she had no clue how she might easily bring up the topic of

Ciaran's ruined business while he was within earshot. Yet she was determined to do so whatever his misgivings. Jill should know and she would tell her every detail even if her husband hadn't. She liked the woman well enough and understood the horror of what she had been through but Rachel had a family too and she would see to it that they came first.

Emmet returned to his position at the curved bay window looking out on to the tree-lined avenue that threaded in a lazy curve up from the main road. The windows were dressed with heavy tapestry curtains, settling in definite pleats that betrayed the fact they hadn't been drawn across in some time. Two of the massive oak trees at the entrance gate were up-lit with floodlights but most of the garden had faded into the gathering dusk. While he stood taking it all in Emmet considered that with a bit of money, and not that much all told, the place could be spruced up and made very special indeed. In an effort at neutral conversation he said as much to Ciaran, who took a slug of his wine before replying that the problem with builders was that they never appreciated the true value of anything except turning a profit and that the lodge was perfectly lovely the way it was. *What a fucking plonker*, Emmet thought as he helped himself to a generous top-up of the decent French red he was glad he had brought with him. He hoped that dinner wouldn't take long and they could all go home. He watched as Jill talked easily to the Miller sisters, her eyes showing a reasonable amount of interest and engagement. He drank the second glass more quickly, holding lonely jealousy inside him with every angry swallow.

Orla and Billy followed Sadie and Gina to the kitchen where they found Ben tucked at the far corner of the rough wood table. Without waiting to be told the youngsters climbed up to their usual seats at their aunt's table and Orla launched a barrage of questions at Ben about who he was and where he'd come from that he proceeded to answer with patient good humour. Sadie egged her little cousin on winking at Ben as the interrogation became steadily more insistent.

Gina had popped into the kitchen earlier to put a chicken in to roast, guessing that the Lime Tree's lamb dish might well be too adult a taste for Rachel's children, steeped as it was in wine and herbs. Ben amused Billy drawing doodles of cowboys and horses on paper napkins pulled from the dresser drawer and the presence of the children promoted easy playful chatter between himself and Sadie. The patent adoration of her young cousins helped ease Sadie's nerves. They thought she was brilliant so it was easier for her to relax and believe that such a thing might feasibly be so. Tara Hickey had jokingly said she would give an eye tooth to be a fly on the wall to see the night unfold but when Sadie had offered to arrange an invitation Tara was adamant that she had no intention of being there.

'God no, Sadie, you need to be putting all your effort into charming young Ben and not distracted chatting to me. You go in there and snare that boy, do you hear?'

Sadie grinned to herself, remembering her friend's encouragement. Ben congratulated his mother on hiring a caterer. Gina agreed that it always made for a more relaxing occasion if no one had to fuss about the food. Ben winked at Ellen before revealing that she had attempted a wildly ill-advised lasagne interpretation the night before using a brace of rabbits that a local farmer had dropped to the lodge. 'I told Mother that even though the recipe hadn't specifically said so it was presumed that the rabbit fur would be removed before cooking. Would have done wonders for the texture, I think.' Gina stifled a laugh and stole a look at Ellen who, while a little embarrassed, seemed disarmed by her son's easy humour.

Jessica appeared at the doorway of the kitchen looking bored and unkempt, as if she had reluctantly roused herself from a nap that hadn't done her the slightest bit of good. Ellen's disappointment at her daughter's lack of effort with her appearance showed in her crestfallen face. 'Jessica dear, you've so many nicer things to wear. What about one of the tops you bought when you were in Cork the other day? Run back up and put on something else and while you're there brush your hair, won't you? Look at how smart everyone else looks and you *are* the birthday girl, after all.'

Jessica neither answered nor looked at her mother as she slid on to a kitchen chair between Sadie and her brother. 'I'd say you look lovely, Sis,' Ben teased, 'but you know I'd be lying through my teeth.'

His sister flashed him a sour grimace. 'What's that song? "It's my party and I'll cry if I want to".' Sadie caught Ben's amused eye and looked down at the table, stifling a smile that might hurt Jessica's feelings when she really didn't want to add to her bad form.

The shrill sound of the front-door bell sent Ellen scurrying out into the hallway, glad of the reprieve from her daughter's sulk-ridden face. Gina felt that dinner should begin shortly so she chose her largest wooden bowl from under the counter and set about preparing a salad with the assortment of greens she found in the fridge's salad drawer. Grabbing a jar she mixed up a salad dressing, glugging in olive oil, wine vinegar and seasoning by experienced eye and without recourse to the barely used measuring spoons hanging from a butcher's hook on the rack above her head.

At the table Orla stared in wide-eyed disappointment at Jessica. The little girl had dressed in her blue party dress, put on a fairy necklace that Lottie had given her, borrowed as much make-up as her mother would allow and quite frankly expected a bit of exotic glamour worthy of her aunt's gloriously decorated house. In ill-fitting track pants and a dirty-looking jumper Jessica was an utter letdown. Billy, cute in a shirt and loosely fastened tie, only had eyes for Ben as he expertly folded a sheet of old newspaper from the magazine basket to fashion an aeroplane for his newest fan.

Sadie turned to Jessica and whispered, 'Happy birthday.' In spite of herself Jessica smiled, noticing how lovely Sadie looked and allowing herself to give in to a little disappointment that she hadn't gone to some effort herself. Just as quickly she decided to have done so would have been to give her mother encouragement when the woman needed none.

Gina stood at the Aga, the heat of the open oven welcome against her bare legs. Having seen Lottie's dress and knowing before she even saw them that Jill and Rachel would naturally make an effort she had decided to flout her normal habit and wear a skirt. Sadie hadn't been able to conceal her surprise when she walked into her mother's bedroom in Beech Cottage. 'Jeez, Mam, there's actually a pair of legs under there?'

Gina had laughed, enjoying the teasing moment. 'Miller women have good legs, Sadie. I've hidden mine for years so don't you go and make the same mistake and only take them out when you're close to forty, do you hear me?'

When she pulled out the oven tray to check the lamb shanks the delicious smell almost made her swoon. With a gentle nudge of a metal skewer she found the meat exquisitely tender. She would have to give Louis his due, there had been no skimping on quantity either and a generous feast lay before her ready to dish out. Ellen Carter had obviously thrown wads of money at him and Gina was disappointed for her that Jessica was so un-impressed and ungrateful for the effort and expense involved. From the table Sadie caught her mother's eye and grinned at her before quickly returning to look at Ben who was involved in a serious arm-wrestling battle with Billy. The young boy's face shone with sheer competitive pride as he began to win the struggle.

Ellen returned from answering the door carrying a few elegant calla lily stems and was followed into the kitchen by

Theo Corrigan. 'This good man has said we must all sit down. He's here in his brother's place and you, Gina, won't have to lift a finger.' Her tone was embarrassingly triumphant, as if she had pulled him out of a hat. Jessica let out an exaggerated sigh. Exactly how many strange people had her insufferable mother invited?

Gina stepped away from the stove to take in their final guest at close quarters. He was dressed casually in an open-necked black shirt and jeans and his dark hair betrayed that yet again he had postponed having his hair cut. He looked boyish and eager and Gina smiled at him, thinking it really had been a sweet idea of Lottie's to invite him. 'There's no need, honestly, Theo. I'm well used to this temperamental range and to where everything is kept in the kitchen so sit yourself down with the others and I'll dish up.'

Theo stepped forward and grabbed a faded pinstriped apron from the back door where it hung on a nail. 'I insist. The least I can do is sing for my supper. Otherwise how on earth will I justify my being here? Sit down, both of you. Grab a glass of wine for the toast and we'll get this party under way. Louis said we are eleven adults and two children. That right?' Gina nodded, having already done the mental head count and put the required plates in the warming oven.

From the hallway they heard Ellen summon those drinking in the living room to the kitchen. 'Dinner's about to be served.' The drinkers came through clutching their glasses, each of them wishing Jessica a happy birthday as they took their seats. She felt no compulsion to answer any of them despite her mother's obvious unease at her lack of manners. 'Jessica—' she began but thought better of it when her daughter refused to even catch her eye.

'Sit here next to me,' Rachel offered and Ellen looked at her gratefully and did as she was told.

'You two make quite the double act,' Gina teased when Lottie finally sat down to the dinner table, having spent the previous minutes, sauce ladle in hand, acting as Theo's servile shadow as he placed the meat and roasted vegetables precisely on each of the plates.

'You're just jealous,' Lottie murmured under her breath, tapping the seat of the vacant chair at the head of the table. 'Stop working, Theo. Come and join us. We've everything we need except yourself now.'

'I think I am yeah,' Gina joked, delighting in the feeling of her kitchen being full and hospitality being enjoyed when she and Sadie so often sat at one corner of the table on their own.

Theo pulled off his apron and hung it back where he had found it while quickly scanning the table and taking in the mixed company he had found himself in. He raised his glass to Jill across the table murmuring that it was good to see her again.

Jill smiled at him and then at Lottie and Gina to his right. 'I'd never have imagined that we'd all be here together,' she offered before lifting her cutlery and beginning to eat.

Lottie raised her glass in a toast: 'To coming home.'

'Coming home,' they chimed and Jill wondered silently at the searing power of two harmless little words that said together could make her heart split in two.

Seated next to Orla Ellen offered the little girl a sliver of the lamb from her plate. 'Would you like to try it, honey?'

Orla gave the meat a poke with her fork, wondering if it was at all wise to take the strange lady's advice. She looked up the table toward her mother for guidance and Rachel nodded encouragingly.

'It's delicious, Orla, you'll like it.'

Jessica snorted, unable to stay silent any longer, having realized that in doing so she might allow her mother to feel smug about the horrible night she had gone to the bother of arranging. 'Trust me, you won't. It's disgusting. They've taken a field of big tired old sheep, chopped their legs off and stewed them up for my birthday dinner. You're safer with the little chick you've on your plate, or maybe you should wait for the cake. Mother bought that in a bakery so it should be safe enough. Nothing dead in cakes usually.'

Ellen was so taken aback by her daughter's offensiveness that, overcome with humiliation, she was momentarily unable to take her to task. It was left to Ben to upbraid his sister. 'Jess, do you *have* to be such a pain in the ass always? We're trying to have dinner here. Forget the whole night's for your benefit if you must but if you can't be nice just shut the hell up!'

Orla moved the offending piece of lamb on to her side plate, suddenly realizing that she wasn't hungry for any of the dead things on offer.

Across the table her brother was gnawing the last bit of meat from a chicken leg with determination, the import of the conversation having quite gone over his head.

'Another roast spud?' Emmet offered the ravenous little boy at his side who nodded gratefully as he drenched the remains of his dinner with a pool of gravy. Emmet popped the child's dangling tie over his shoulder so he could enjoy his food without the nuisance of his clothes getting in the way.

At the head of the table Ciaran watched Emmet's gentle interaction with his son and regretted his earlier conduct. Maybe they could talk later, he decided, before falling into a quiet conversation with Theo Corrigan about the project that had brought him back to Tobarnaree. Pressed on the issue of renovating an old house Ciaran slotted back into his professional role and discussed with a very appreciative Theo the pitfalls to be avoided. He promised that he would call up to the Corrigan home place while he was in Tobarnaree and answer any questions that Theo might have on site.

'That'd be great, Ciaran. Don't have an architect as such. Just winging it between myself and the builder, cutting out the middle man if you will. You probably wouldn't think that's a very good idea, do you?' Theo asked playfully.

Ciaran grinned. 'Well, an overseeing architect would be better by far but sure, wing away, just don't hold me responsible if it all falls down on top of your head. Seriously though, I'll come and have a look.'

Lottie's sarcastic voice held forth about good manners clearly being an art lost in some of the younger generation at least. Gina dug her sister in the ribs, unwilling to add any further to Ellen's discomfort; Ellen looked as if she was on the verge of tears. 'I'm sure Jessica didn't mean to be rude so let's forget it, shall we, and enjoy the rest of our dinner.'

Unwilling to let peace break out so easily Jessica rose from the table, kicking her chair roughly as she got up. 'Thanks for the lovely party, Mother. It's been a blast even if I can't stomach the dead sheep. I hope you bought plenty of wine 'cause your new batch of friends look thirsty as hell. Save me some cake for breakfast if it's not too much bother.'

Ben got up from the table and escorted his sister out to the hallway where he heatedly told her not to be such a spoilt brat. 'Go to bed and grow up while you're at it,' he instructed, much to the mental applause of those seated around the table. When he arrived back he apologized for his sister's behaviour. 'She likes being the centre of attention, guys. Too bad she doesn't realize that she could be nice and be the centre of attention all at the same time.'

There were murmurings – 'Not to worry, these things happen' – and eventually awkward silence gave way to rising clusters of conversation around the table. Sadie nudged Ben under the table and smiled at him when he looked up. He smiled back before playfully asking Billy if he would like a straw to get the last of the gravy from the jug. Ellen looked at her son, grateful he had taken control of the situation on her behalf. She ate her food quickly, nervously swallowing huge mouthfuls at great speed;

feeling too full and somewhat nauseous was at least a respite from all the other things she felt. Try as she might, she couldn't muster any conversation for those seated around her. To keep herself busy, she picked the bottle of red from the middle of the table and the bottle of white from the cooler on the shelf of the dresser and set about filling the glasses of her company while fighting back tears. She negotiated filling Sadie's glass, but when she tried to switch the wine for Ben's both bottles slipped out of her grasp and on to the floor. Her resolve to hold things together for the sake of her guests shattered along with the glass, and she gave into a dramatic bout of sobbing. Gina sprang into action, gingerly placing the broken glass into the dustpan, while Theo asked Lottie to point him in the direction of the mop bucket. Sadie offered to make Ellen a cup of tea, and when she didn't answer Ben nodded in her direction while pleading with his mother to calm down a little.

Seizing her chance during the confusion of Ellen's mishap, Rachel whispered to Jill, 'Can I talk to you about something?' Jill nodded. It would be good to have the distraction of thinking of someone's life other than her own. Rachel kept her voice low, not wanting to draw her husband's attention to what they were discussing.

As Rachel outlined the Ivory Square deal that had gone sour for Ciaran Jill felt her hackles rise a little. She couldn't remember the last kind thought she had had about Emmet so she was surprised that she felt like defending him against Rachel's insinuation that he had conned her husband. 'I'm sure that can't be the case,' she whispered firmly, 'but tell me what you've heard.'

On a hook on the painted frame of her bedroom door Jessica found a key which locked the door from the inside and would keep her mother out. She would be embarrassed for a while, weeping at the kitchen table no doubt and looking for consolation anywhere she might find it, but once everyone had gone home and Ben had gone to bed Jessica was afraid she might come looking for an explanation for her behaviour or an apology, which she had no intention of offering. She reached into the top drawer of her nightstand and took a slug of vodka from a quart bottle that she'd swiped from the drinks cabinet downstairs.

Above her bed was the trapdoor to the lodge's attic. She had examined its minuscule dimensions every morning as she lay awake daydreaming but reluctant to get up and join her family downstairs. With no inclination to sleep just yet she stood on the patchwork bedspread and reached up to jerk the half-moon metal handle. The attached ladder unfurled as the trapdoor opened and an automatic light switched on, lighting the spacious loft above her head. A network of beams lit by the harsh glow of a bare bulb was all she could see and curiosity moved her to find what was hidden from easy view. In the absence of something better to do she had never underestimated the attraction of snooping. She'd already been through all the photo albums on the book shelves in the lodge's living room, it mattering not a jot that she had no idea to whom most of the faces belonged. The day Rachel and her children had arrived Gina had left her email account open on the computer screen under the staircase and Jessica had taken guilty pleasure in running through scores of her mails while Gina helped her sister unpack and settle in.

With a firm shove of her knee she pushed the narrow single bed aside to let the ladder extend itself with a solid thud on to the carpeted floor. She climbed up the ladder into the loft. The beams creaked a little when she stood on them at first and she had to spit out a dangling cobweb that clung to her face. On the softness of a roll of fibreglass insulation she sat and began to sift through boxes of other people's things: photos, invoices, copies of tax returns, bank statements and lovingly bound school work that belonged to Sadie, the childish drawings of a Senior Infants folder giving way to more neat and precise offerings of an older girl. At first Jessica was careful to replace things as she found them but she became overwhelmed by a creeping sense of tiredness. She grew more careless with the Millers' belongings but her curiosity never waned.

In the kitchen Ellen's growing distress brought the dinner party to a rather awkward conclusion. The more wine she drank the more upset she became until finally Ben led her away from the dinner table to an armchair in the living room, telling her as they went that everything would surely look a little brighter in the morning.

The Kinsellas made their excuses first, Jill murmuring that it was late and they really should go and Emmet nodding in agreement while wondering exactly what they might have to get up for in the morning. Rachel and Ciaran set off across the courtyard after them carrying their exhausted children to their beds.

Gina suggested that she and Sadie should join the Carters in the living room and see if they could say anything that might cheer Ellen and ease the pressure on Ben. As she held open the door into the hallway for her daughter she paused to give Lottie an encouraging wink. 'Give me a shout if you need a hand clearing up, won't you?'

Lottie winked back, glad of the opportunity to have Theo all to herself for a while. 'Save us some wine, Gina. We'll be right in when we've straightened this place up.' She watched him scrape the waste food from the plates, methodically clearing the table, and commented that there was nothing like a dose of wash-up to clear a room like lightning.

Theo grinned. 'A team like myself and yourself will make short work of it. What's your preference, Charlotte, washing or drying?'

'Neither if I can help it usually but in order to preserve my manicure for another day maybe I'll dry.'

Theo whisked one of the tea towels from the rail in front of the range and threw it across the table to her. 'Right, the quicker we get this finished the quicker we can have a drink so let's get a move on.' As they worked Theo spoke about Jill. 'You can see in her eyes that she's in a very sad place. Husband seems like a sound enough guy too but losing a child – well, I can only imagine what that might do to somebody.'

'The girls and myself are working on her. Can't help feeling a bit responsible for her, to be honest. Hopefully Tobar Rock will weave a bit of its healing magic,' Lottie added. When everything was washed and put away they stood together at the counter munching on wedges of Jessica's birthday cake. Lottie thought it far more pleasant to steal their dessert there than have to sit at the table in the company of the ungrateful girl for whom the cake was bought. 'Good cake,' she enthused, savouring every delicious morsel.

'Even better company,' Theo countered with a smile. Lottie caught his flirtatious eye and did her best to hold her nerve under his intent gaze. 'Seriously, Lottie, I've really enjoyed tonight. Thanks for asking me,' he said, raising a forkful of chocolate cake to her lips.

'Very good cake,' she repeated as she struggled to maintain her composure. 'Come on, let's grab a drop of the wine before Mrs Dysfunction herself pours the whole lot down her depressed gullet and we're left with the tap water.'

'Must we go in there? I could make some Irish coffees for us here and we could join them in a bit.' Theo's voice was playfully plaintive but much as Lottie would have liked to spend more time alone with him she thought it might be no harm to take back control and try to play things a little bit cool.

'Jesus, Corrigan, where are your manners? Of course we must. The woman treated us to dinner, talking to her is part of the terms and conditions. You bankers should know all about those.'

Jessica's watch and phone lay below her on the bed so she couldn't be sure at what time Ellen came pleading to the bedroom door to be let in. Her mother's distressed voice sounded mercifully muffled from where Jessica was perched above the rooms of the house, lost and uninvited in the lives of others. Her mother's irritatingly persistent knocking died away eventually, the way most things do when they are ignored for long enough.

Chapter Fourteen

'So you do eat then?' If he had been less hung over Emmet might have attempted to find something appeasing to say to his wife when he emerged from the bedroom and a blackout sleep late the following morning. Coping with a throbbing head and the strange sight of his wife engaged in the homely task of buttering a round of toast it was the best effort he could manage.

'The toast's for you actually. I've eaten already.' Jill didn't look at him when she talked but continued with the job as if she was engrossed in a favourite pastime that required no further explanation.

'Toast for me?' Emmet shook his head in disbelief.

'I counted the empties,' Jill said, gesturing at the brigade of wine bottles standing on the floor next to the bin, 'and I decided I could feed you or call an ambulance. In the outskirts of Tobarnaree on a Saturday morning feeding you will cause far less fuss but we can do the ambulance later if necessary.'

Emmet emitted a low sarcastic laugh, the effort of which made his delicate skull ache. Ellen had filled his arms with bottles of wine the night before as they left the lodge in a clumsy attempt to make up for her daughter's bad behaviour. He had drunk the lot in great big numbing mouthfuls before staggering to bed as another day began to throw its infant light across the cottage's stone floor. 'Are you for real?' he asked, wondering if he was in some bizarre dream.

'Meaning?' Jill asked, her buttery knife stilling in reaction to her husband's obvious anger.

Blinded by agitation Emmet didn't pause to take good stock of what he said next. 'Meaning you've barely spoken to me for months. I've dragged any smidgen of conversation I could out of you but you've been as sour as a pig and I'm not for one minute saying you don't have good reason because we both know you do, we both have every reason. But now you go and make me breakfast and I'm supposed to think that's normal. I could've starved for the last seven months and four days and you wouldn't have given a flying shit so why the change, Jill? Why all of a sudden have you realized that your husband is a human being when you've gone all out to deny any feelings I might have? Go on, tell me,' he challenged. 'Your shit of a husband is curious about your Damascus conversion. Tell him what the hell might be going on in your fucking head 'cause he's a tad anxious to know.'

Jill blushed. She was unused to his temper, never having been subjected to it in good times and thus far having been spared it in the bad times that had awkwardly settled with them like a tongue-tied friend.

'Got talking to Rachel Jacob last night,' Jill quietly explained.

'Oh yeah, I saw that sincere little huddle develop at your end of the table and I presume I'm the villain of the piece. I can give a good stab at the script, if you'd like? Might save you the effort of recalling every detail of how you helped her hang me out to dry.'

'How do you mean?' Jill asked, smiling awkwardly.

'I mean I think I know how it goes. Let me see. Evil property developer tries to turn a profit on a perfectly good apartment block that's finished just a little too late to hit the market running. Had he cut a few corners, been satisfied with a slipshod finish it could have come to market a full six months earlier but this little fucker is a bit of a perfectionist. Likes things to be just so and therefore the apartments are ready just that tiny bit too late to take advantage of the market's fierce appetite.' Emmet was surprised at his ability to speak. When he rolled out of bed he would have doubted his ability to string two coherent words together but pent-up fury befriended him and angry words flowed from him with unrehearsed ease.

'Emmet, let me talk,' Jill pleaded. 'Yes, Rachel and I did talk about you and Ciaran's dealings but—'

'No, you'll let me finish before you tear me to ribbons. I'm fucking sick of hanging in there hoping things will improve between us. What's the point? You want us finished because of what happened to Fionn and maybe you're right. Maybe we've no business together. Now where was I with your little parable of greed? Ah yes, enter the handsome and blameless architect by the name of Ciaran with lovely and perfectly happy family and your husband, the evil builder, double-crosses him. Persuades him to be greedy, if you will, forces him to remortgage what he can't afford and chip by little chip his perfect world starts to disappear. I appreciate the tragedy and I have rehearsed my grubby part in the lovely Ciaran's downfall. Guilty as fucking charged! Happy now, Jill? You married a monster. God, you must be truly sorry you've had a thing to do with me.'

'Emmet, shut up,' Jill commanded.

He laughed, realizing that he was still more than a little drunk but also that he wasn't a bit sorry that this verbal flush-out had come to pass. The last months had been like waiting for a drawn-out death and the last breath had come with a relief that was satisfying more than sad. If he and Jill were finished then surely knowing that was preferable to the heartbreaking half-living they had been doing and he was to blame for the delay. Jill would have walked away months ago, of that he was certain.

'Eat the toast and have coffee. We'll talk when you've calmed down a bit.' Jill's voice was firm. The release of tension made Emmet feel unsteady on his feet and he sank on to the kitchen chair. He buried his face into the open palms of his hands and closed his eyes for a moment against what the day might yet bring.

The fight he had surprised himself with earlier had been only a surge. There was nothing left in the very core of him except a well of sorrow. Raising the mug of coffee to his lips and swallowing a huge mouthful of its bitter heat he was startled enough by Jill's voice to look directly at her when she spoke. She had taken a seat across from him, cradling a mug of her own.

'"Seven months and four days." I didn't know you counted it out like that too,' Jill said in a low whisper, referring to the timeline of private grief that had taken over their lives to the exclusion of the calendar to which the rest of the world moved.

The power of Emmet's grief embarrassed him and the habit of concealing it from outside eyes had become ingrained. But he had things to say about Fionn, things he had long postponed telling his wife, and he was resolute that fear of saying the wrong thing would not now deter him. 'I try not to track the days so closely but I can't help doing it. I remember how we counted the weeks when we were expecting him and how we measured his progress after he was born. Seven months old and he was sitting up. A little tuft of soft golden hair was growing long enough to cover that pesky little bald patch that he had on the top of his head. I used to comb it over like he was an auld fella struggling against baldness.' He smiled a little as he remembered. *And I used to go mad,* Jill thought but she voiced it only in her head while she listened to her husband. 'The photograph on the piano of him in the red cord dungarees would've been taken about then. Two huge teeth jutting out from his bottom gum. Maybe he had more but two is what you can clearly see in the photo. I know because I look at it every time I pass by. I do my very best not to count out the days or the weeks but I can't stop myself. There's no end to the ways you can torture yourself but then you must know that.' He knocked back the remains of the coffee and pushed the uneaten toast to the centre of the table. No hunger within him would allow him to eat. His head and throat hurt the most but there was hardly a part of him that didn't. Tears stung the back of his eyes but he could not let them fall.

'I blame you for what happened.' The baldness of Jill's statement made her husband look up again and notice the tears that were streaming freely from her blue eyes. 'I blame you for being careless, for drinking when you should've been looking after him. You destroyed Fionn and you've destroyed us.'

Emmet shook his head and looked down at the table. The words had been worse in the frequent imagining than they were now in reality but he considered that a negligible gift in the circumstances. It was a relief of sorts to have her admit what he had been certain of all along. 'I *know* you blame me. That hasn't been hard to work out. There's been a week's worth of talk between us during all of these months and most of that has come from me. I know what you think of me, Jill, and it doesn't amount to all that much.'

'Can you not defend yourself? Can you not say something that would make me think for a moment that I've wronged you just a little?' Her voice crackled with frustration. She needed him to counter her version of events with his own but her husband didn't look as if he had enough spirit to accept her late invitation to the fray.

In the courtyard the beep of the Jacobs' car alarm sounded as the car doors clipped open. From his seat looking out their cottage window Emmet could see the children spar with each other as Rachel urged them to get into the car, leaning in across them to check their seatbelts were properly fastened. Ciaran threw boots and a bundle of coats into the boot and slammed it shut. He walked around to the driver's door saying something over the car roof to Rachel who nodded as if she understood before they both climbed in. It wasn't weather for the beach so Emmet presumed they were off on a trek somewhere to get some fresh air and kill a few hours. Normal things. Witnessing the simple scene moved Emmet to think of his son and all the little trips they had lightly taken with one another never knowing how those allotted opportunities were steadily being used up.

Jill was asking for a defence and he had none to present. He would leave here today with or without his wife, he decided then, the clarity bringing with it a flood of relief. All these months he had believed he had the resilience to see his marriage through its difficulties but he was realizing that he had nothing much left to give. Coming to Tobarnaree was a last-ditch effort and he was certain now that it had been a mistake. With nothing left to lose he spoke, his tone matter of fact and final. He was getting out.

'What happened to Fionn was my fault. I can't change that. He got hurt while he was with me. I wouldn't have scheduled the meeting with the Russell Consortium if I'd known he was coming in but you know Fionn often played in my work yards and had never come to any harm. I got used to him being able to take more and more care of himself. I was lax but it was experience and not carelessness had made me that way. Fionn was so independent and I was proud of that urge within him but I hate myself for what happened. You hate me too and if I thought nothing could possibly be worse than the day Fionn died I know now it can because in losing him I lost you too.'

He rose to his feet quite unable to think of anything else to say and so he turned away. If he packed now and drank the rest of the pot of coffee that was brewed on the counter he might, with any luck, be fit to drive by lunchtime. With the help of light Saturday traffic he would be back at home in Lighthouse Road in a little under four hours. Getting as far as the house was the extent of his plan. He had no notion what he might do afterward. Jill's voice brought him back inside the cottage from where his thoughts had already fled.

'I don't hate you even if I act like I do. I hate what happened to us and that's a very different thing. I cannot bear that we couldn't protect ourselves from something so awful. Two capable and clever grown-ups and we let a child slip through our fingers.' With the open palms of her hands she wiped away tears from her face leaving the print marks of her fingers on her blotched skin.

Emmet clung to the high back of the kitchen chair for support. His heart raced. It was as much as she had ever offered and it had come just when he'd given up hope. He waited for more, not wanting to put her off by interjecting. If this was the last thing she would say to him he knew he would replay the words for ever so he concentrated on hearing every word and absorbing exactly what she meant by them.

Jill seemed to warm to the liberating power of explaining herself. 'I've always clammed up when I'm hurt. That's what I do. I pull the shutters down and I swear as long as I live I'll never find myself in such a place again. I did it every time my father took another stupid job somewhere I didn't want to go. I'd tell myself the next time I'd be strong enough to rely on myself and no one else and I became good at that. Very good at taking care of myself, staying in control. Until I met you and we had Fionn. You first and then Fionn opened up my heart without me even realizing how much. Then I wasn't prepared for anything. I was stupid to trust that what we had was ours and could not be touched. I was cocky, worrying about silly things that never happened while never imagining the awful thing that did.' And she began to cry fully as her words burned in the telling.

Emmet walked around to where she sat perched on the edge of her chair and fell to his knees in front of his wife, ready to help but hardly daring to trust his instincts and touch her. Her whole body shuddered as she sobbed. When he put his arms gently around her he felt her frail weeping body steady a little. He didn't move a muscle to pull her any closer to him because the promise of what he had within shy grasp was enough.

After a few moments Jill straightened herself up and away from him, determined to finish what she had started to say. 'Listening to what Rachel Jacob told me last night has made me admit something to myself. I'd no way of seeing you and me becoming an "us" again or even *trying* to become us again and I still don't even know if we can. But it's like I needed a map, a starting point for us to attempt to begin again. She gave it to me and I am giving it to you. It may not work but it would be wrong not to try. We owe it to Fionn, to ourselves.' She could see from Emmet's expression that he was struggling to see the connection, his face a soup of eagerness and frustration. At a loss he collapsed back on his heels searching the face of the woman he clearly adored but barely understood.

'What do you mean? What have the Jacobs got to do with you and me and Fionn?' His voice conveyed all the bewilderment he was feeling.

'They're a family in desperate trouble and despite what you might think I don't hold you responsible for what's happened to them. It's a free world and Ciaran Jacob exercised very poor judgement. He overstretched himself and went in way over his head. Rachel knows what I think because I told her that nobody forced him to take out huge mortgages. You don't owe him an explanation or charity but it's very plain to me that we can do something for them and in doing so we can begin to improve things for ourselves.'

Nervously he nodded as if he was beginning to understand. 'I want above all, Jill, for things to improve for us. Tell me what it is you think I should do and whatever it is I'll try and do it.'

'We don't need all the money we have while they need far more than they've got if they're going to pull through all this. We can afford to buy one or more of those apartments back or inject cash into his practice maybe to ease the pressure they're under. It may well be too late for his business but those children could lose their home. My husband would never let that happen to them. Do I know you at all, Emmet? Please tell me I do.'

Into her hair he whispered, '*You do, you do,*' and when her arms went around him for the first time in months he wondered if at the heart of being loved was someone thinking far better of you than you might ever think of yourself.

CHAPTER FIFTEEN

A few evenings later, Jessica abandoned Gina's bike on the main street of Tobarnaree, flinging it roughly against the monument to a whole host of dead people. War heroes, fairies, saints, goats: a monument to anything was possible in this hellhole, she thought sourly. She didn't pause to read the inscription because she had less than zero interest in knowing who any of the fallen were. The town – or the country for that matter – was not somewhere she ever planned on returning to. She doubted that any of the residents of Tobarnaree could rouse their energy levels high enough to steal the rust bucket of a bike and most likely Gina Miller would be reunited with her sad little antique in a matter of hours.

The days since the disastrous birthday dinner her mother had insisted on throwing had been hellish. Ben hadn't even spoken to her much since, apart from a smart comment the next morning about the Carters 'always knowing how to work a room – or was that clear a room?' Every time she saw her mother her disappointed face nearly made her feel guilty until she remembered that it had all been her stupid fault in the first place. Avoiding her mother and Ben and hiding out in her bedroom listening to her iPod had given her plenty of time to examine the letters she'd found in Gina Miller's attic. She had even gone to the trouble of reading them in chronological order and though she didn't fully understand what they meant she knew that they contained what Sadie's mother had wanted hidden. Not that she had anything against Gina as such but keeping secrets from people who had a right to know was just not fair in her opinion. Just as she would have been far better off if her father had never pretended that he was coming to Ireland in the first place. Instead she had foolishly raised her expectations and was now suffering the heightened disappointment.

She made one final check of her belongings: passport, cell phone, a thick fold of euro notes from her mother's wallet and precious flight reservation details from Cork to Dublin and onward to Boston. A few short hours and her mother would be on her trail but it would be too late and the thought of evading Ellen Carter satisfied her as she made her way to the bus stop. She waited in the cold breeze for the bus promised on the timetable to arrive. Her father would call the place a crock of shit and imagining him announcing his barbed conclusion amused her until her mind snagged on the fact that he hadn't kept his promise to spend at least some of the holidays with herself and Ben.

The trip to Rome the year before, which he'd billed as a sixteenth birthday treat for his daughter, leading her to boast long and hard to Ben and her girlfriends, proved instead to be a chance to meet up with a woman called Lydia with whom he appeared to be having an affair. Treating his daughter turned out to be just a sham. She trailed the streets after them, settling in terrace cafés eating ice cream and drinking hot chocolate while accepting bribes of cash from her father at every turn. At night she sat eating dinner across from them and watched as her father drank too much wine and forgot his habit of discretion, calling Lydia sweetheart and baby. He didn't seem to notice that his daughter had started to drink from the wine bottles that he called to the table.

Jessica's hip flask was bought not by her father, as she'd claimed to Sadie and Tara, but by herself while she watched her father and his girlfriend bicker at the corner of a pretty piazza, doubtless, she felt, about the way her presence was spoiling things. When Lydia left in a temper, pointedly telling Jack she would see him back in Boston when he'd finished babysitting, she never even said goodbye to Jessica. Waiting for their flight home from Da Vinci a sulking Jessica was planning when and how she might tell Ellen about Lydia but as if he could read her mind her father announced he was doubling her monthly allowance. His crafty offer proved too tempting and when she replied, 'Wow, thanks, Dad,' they both knew that she wouldn't utter a word to her mother. What annoyed her more was how little Ben seemed to mind what his father got up to, as if his father's attention was something he could just as easily live with as without.

Thinking of Ben, she wondered how long it would take him to persuade Sadie to sleep with him or if indeed the girl might discover some mettle and make a move on him herself. Part of her wished she could stay long enough to find out but she was somewhat compensated by the fact that in a matter of days or weeks her brother would definitely have lost interest. Sadie was nice and all that but hardly the kind of girl Ben would fall hard for.

She had waited until her mother was halfway down a second bottle of red wine and in the middle of a huge philosophical conversation with the Miller sisters in Lottie's cottage before slipping out the door of the lodge with a packed knapsack. Enjoyment of wine had made her mother forge the most unlikely of friendships; Jessica considered the Millers curious company for Ellen. In the cold light of day none of them wanted to spend much time with her, Jessica noted, but the promise of a shared

Merlot and some snacks to nibble on papered over the cracks of their incompatibility. Oiled with a few glasses of wine they would happily bullshit each other for as long as the bottle might last.

She rummaged in her holdall checking that she had the bundle of letters from the attic. There would be hell to pay when it all broke and part of her would like to be there to witness the discomfort unfold but mostly she wanted to get back to the house in Brookline and as far away from her mother as she could manage.

First she had planned to go down to the lake where she knew she would find Ben with his tent pitched looking out over the water and pretending that there was something profound to be gleaned from the backward place they had been landed in by their mother. It would do no harm to tell him that she was leaving because if he knew it might call off the worst of their mother's excessive attempts to track her down. It was the type of rash gesture that he would appreciate. It took a bit of gumption to plan to run away, she had decided, even if she was only running home to the safe house of a waiting father.

Besides, Ben might help her out with a little extra cash because he always seemed to have more than he knew how to spend, priding himself in keeping his needs a bare notch above basic. As she approached she heard voices and laughter and she knew without having to see for certain that Sadie was there with him. The bashed-up lamp that her brother had spent hours fixing and cleaning had been lit and in its shadow she could see two figures sitting together on a blanket.

In the depths of her holdall her hands played nervously over Matthew's letters, bulky in a thick brown envelope that she had pulled from the drawer of Gina's desk. She had written Sadie's name on the outside with a bold pink marker. Inside she had written a brief message on a slip of paper ripped from one of her mother's blank journals. Ellen bought new ones for every trip so that she could record thoughts and insights but they rarely contained anything other than a hastily copied recipe for a dish that would turn out nothing like the original or a scribbled address for someone she might scarcely remember when her flight home had touched down. She owned stacks of them and Jessica wagered she would not miss a torn page from a single one.

Sadie,
I thought you should know about these letters. I found them stashed in your loft when I was on a bit of a snoop! I'd want to know if things were being hidden from me. I'm going home tonight on a credit card loaned from Mother dearest. She writes a list of her pin numbers in all sorts of places in case she forgets so I'll have free rein for a few days at least. She's got a half a dozen others so don't let her fuss too much that I've cleaned her out because of course I haven't. If you make it to Boston next summer like you're planning, look me up. I'll show you a good time and who knows you might never go back!

Jess

Jessica knew that Ben would go crazy if he caught her spying on them so she moved away quietly in the direction of the path around the rock and back to the cottages. As much as she liked to talk about her brother's prowess with girls she hadn't the slightest inclination to witness personally his seduction technique in action. She had to admit she was glad he had chosen Sadie above Tara because she could probably do with whatever comfort he had to offer after she had read everything. As she returned from the lake she could see that Gina was sitting on the couch in her sister's cottage with a glass of wine in her hand. The whole place was a haven for sad lushes, she concluded, not pausing to include herself in their number.

Oblivious to the fact that his sister had been standing such a
short distance away from them, Ben moved closer to Sadie.
They had kissed at the back of the lodge the night before and
he had told her that he would be camping by the lake the next
evening if she felt like visiting him. She knew all day that she
would go and when Gina had told her that she was knocking
in to Lottie's cottage for a glass of wine Sadie realized that she
could go to Ben without having to explain herself too much or
at least tell any lies.

She hadn't seen Jessica since her birthday dinner though she
didn't mind as it had allowed her plenty of time alone with
Ben. Like a violent thunderstorm his sister's mood would have
to burn itself out and Sadie was wondering how the girl would
manage to put the incident behind her. She knew if she had made
a spectacle of herself like that she would rather die than show
her face again but retiring into herself permanently was never
going to be Jessica Carter's style. She had more confidence than
that. Her return would be spectacular, Sadie felt sure.

Ben had lit the paraffin lamp that he had found in one of the
lodge's outhouses that morning and which Gina had told him he
could have. Gina had been touched by his interest in exploring
the outhouses that had remained more or less undisturbed since
Nicholas Miller had died. There was a canister of paraffin
oil hanging from one of the rafters which she handed to Ben,
knowing that her father would approve of it finally being used
after all this time. He had always hated waste, a trait that his
daughter had inherited, but even so she had found no use for
a paraffin lamp in the years since she had moved back home.
Ben also found an old metal camp chair, shabby but solid. Gina
watched faintly amused as his tall figure headed through the
cottage courtyard and on toward the lake carrying his mixed
bundle of salvage to the spot where he planned to set up
temporary home.

Ben cut an overhanging branch from the sally trees that were grouped in stark lonesome poses around the edge of the lake and he was pushing the makeshift light pole into the ground when he noticed Sadie approach. She attempted a casual attitude, which she quickly realized was impossible while her heart insisted on beating so loudly in her chest. Her mouth was dry. Tara had earlier texted, telling her not to do anything that she wouldn't do and adding as a postscript that that allowed her a good bit of scope, all things considered.

Sadie was glad that Ben didn't make a fuss of her straight away, continuing with the task at hand as if her being there watching him work at the lake as the summer night reluctantly fell was the most natural thing in the world. With his attention divided she felt comfortable taking in the lovely look of him. He wore baggy cut-offs and a frayed blue cotton top whose stitching was undoing itself at the nape of his neck. Only the faded outline of a logo remained, the colours worn away by countless washes. His feet were slung casually into a pair of shabby brown boating shoes; their leather heels sunken by frequent and careless wearing. She was sure that nobody quite like him had ever stood on the edge of what she would always think of as her Granddad Miller's lake but he looked naturally at ease in a place so far removed from where he came from. She wondered how he and Jessica could have sprung from the same parents. Ben made things smoother for everyone in his company while his prickly sister thrived on creating an awkward atmosphere, always ready with a provocative comment or a hurtful putdown. Sadie was sure that to show the gentle confidence Ben possessed you had to forget about yourself totally. Sadie feared her own self-consciousness would mean that she would never feel so relaxed in the company of others.

She had showered and put on the nicest clothes she could find. Trying to work out what to wear was one of her worst nightmares; this time, in her bedroom at the cottage, she had pulled on a soft and flouncy white cotton skirt that she had bought quickly in a sale rack of a cheap-as-chips clothes shop in Dublin the summer before. To her relief it looked OK if she held her stomach in, not exactly gorgeous but then in her opinion nothing ever did look more than reasonably nice on her. Her stock uniform of jeans fastened too tightly on a rounded stomach were definitely not an option. If she planned on taking them off (and that was most definitely possible, she knew, even if the thought both terrified and exhilarated her) they would leave unbecoming welts across her stomach and she could do without the humiliation of that when she wanted to appear sophisticated.

Ben's attention was a gift to score out the memory of being dumped by Leo McLean and she was grateful she wouldn't have to tell lies or make excuses to cover where she was and how long she hoped to be there. Her nerves, playing up already, might well overwhelm her if she tried to put on an elaborate act of deception. Ben Carter was far out of her league but the fact that he was interested in her was a consolation – even a treat. If she had met him anywhere else she supposed he wouldn't have looked at her twice, but somehow this place, her place, had beguiled him. He *saw* her here when otherwise she might so easily have been invisible to him. Leo McLean's hurtful words constantly replayed in her mind, the taunts sniping at her. She hoped she could drown them out with the memory of this last summer before she left her mother's house for a new life.

Ben gave her a bottle of beer from a cool box that Sadie recognized. It was strange to see her family's belongings in the hands of others who treated the stuff as if it was their own. Her grandfather had always taken the box on his fishing trips to keep the day's catch refrigerated and her mother used it to pack picnics to take to the woods at Corrallis or to her favourite beach in Aughasallagh, although they hadn't been to either place in a very long time. Thinking of those days made Sadie a little sad not only for herself but for Gina also. She wondered if her mother missed those outings or if all that time she had been just finding ways to amuse Sadie until her daughter was old enough to find her own entertainment. Maybe she would suggest that they go on a trip to both places before she had to leave for college. If her mother enjoyed it, it would make her feel less guilty about leaving her to the mercy of a winter mostly alone in Tobar Rock. Sadie planned to return as often as she could, of course, but for so long it had been just the two of them and she worried about her mother rattling around the house without even the pressure of summer guests arriving at the cottages to distract her.

Ben flicked the bottle cap with an opener attached to a Swiss army knife hanging from a chain on his rucksack. Sadie took a welcome sip of its cold sourness and handed it back, hoping to keep the playful back-and-forth ritual going. He reached for it but instead of drinking any he leaned toward her as if he was not remotely interested in the beer while he had her sitting there with him. The tips of his fingers were hot when they briefly brushed the skin under her collar bone and above the trail of buttons that fastened her gingham shirt.

'You're beautiful, Sadie,' he murmured softly.

Her face flushed and she looked away from his intent gaze, her courage cruelly evaporating when she needed it most. Nut-brown eyes set against the sallow skin of his face overwhelmed her; she couldn't look directly into them. She willed herself not to blush or at least if she did that it might not be noticeable in the fading light of a summer day on its last and lazy legs.

The night before had been different. They had sipped bottles of beer sitting on the outhouse steps behind the lodge and she had been brave enough to respond to his unexpected kisses but tonight she knew more was going to happen if she would allow it. Without the soothing effect of alcohol all her inhibitions returned and she felt big, awkward and frumpy when she longed to feel smooth and enticing.

He stroked the soft skin of her face with his fingertips before kissing her cheek, which had begun to flare crimson. Between her thumb and forefinger Sadie fingered the charms of the bracelet that Lottie had given her. Touching them allowed her to look somewhere other than at Ben's face. 'Nothing more has to happen if you don't want it to, you know,' he said tenderly as if he could sense the well of panic surge within her. 'This place is magical and I'd be quite happy sitting here with you kissing, sharing a few bottles of beer and looking out on to this beautiful lake.'

Sadie managed a smile but knew that words would probably fail her so she didn't try to speak, content to let him talk if that was what he wanted. Ben seemed happy to fill the gap that her stream of shyness had opened up between them. 'I know Jessica has told you I'm some sort of stud because my little sis thinks it's beyond amusing to dine out on tales of my expertise, but I don't tell her anything so whatever she's said is straight from the little rooms of her mysterious mind. Boredom's a terrible thing and it does strange things to Jess. I just keep myself to myself. It's a whole lot less hassle in the Carter house if you stay well under the radar and keep the hype level down. Some of my family veer toward excitable, as you may have noticed.'

He had indeed hit on the best way to live with Ellen Carter, Sadie thought, because in contrast there was more or less a constant air of tension between his mother and Jessica. She began to relax a little. For a moment she thought she was breathing normally and the frantic thudding of her heart had abated to a more normal level. 'Intense' and 'desperate' Leo McLean had called her to her face, and probably plenty of other things had been said to others in his anxious need for everyone to know that it was he who had done the dumping and not the other way round. Not that Sadie's shipwrecked demeanour could have effectively pretended it had happened any other way. All his harsh words had filtered back to her over time as only unfavourable comments do. In the meantime sitting in front of her was someone who had made it plain he liked her and wanted her and she was absolutely going to reach out to grasp what was offered. Nothing wrong with a holiday romance, she reasoned. Ben wouldn't be here for ever and there was no point in regretting her inhibitions after he'd gone.

Sadie took the cool beer bottle from his hand and swallowed a greedy drink. She was parched and nerves made her gulp quickly. A few drops escaped her lips and ran down her neck and chest disappearing inside her collar where her brightly checked shirt gave way to the milky softness of her flesh. When his thumb and finger reached out to touch the droplets she didn't stop him. Nor did she resist when he began to open the buttons of her shirt and pull it back, exposing her snow-white shoulders. After he had unclasped her bra but before he had pulled it away from her breasts he whispered a question. *Was she sure?* When she nodded at him, meeting his eyes with a rising assurance and excitement, she knew that whatever happened next she would deliberately choose not to regret it. Each touch of his fingers seemed to almost burn yet filled her with anticipation for the next place they might reach for. She'd slept with Leo at his stubborn insistence that it was about time she did or he would begin to think she was weird and uptight. When it didn't feel great or even the slightest bit special she had blamed herself and her lack of experience. After all, Leo had seemed pleased with himself and in his smugness spectacularly uninterested in how Sadie had found the experience so she judged the shortcomings must have been all her own.

Eagerly turning her near nakedness into the welcome heat of Ben's body she felt an unexpected freedom. Through the flimsy ground sheet of the tent she could feel the rough uneven turf rubbing against the flesh of her back as she moved underneath him. The paraffin lamp cast a feeble almost haunting glow from its pitch on the sally rod. She listened to the familiar lapping of the water outside before losing herself entirely to the gentle persuasion of his touch. He took off her charm bracelet and for safety placed it carefully in the crevice of an open book that he had been half reading that afternoon while hoping that she would come to him.

CHAPTER SIXTEEN

It was after one in the morning when Ben walked her to the door of the little cottage to stand under the porch light that Gina had left on for her. She was glad that her mother had taken herself off to bed but she would take bets on the fact that she was lying wide awake in the back bedroom waiting for her daughter's key to turn in the lock. All the other cottages were in darkness except for the Kinsellas'. Their living room and bedroom threw their lights across the courtyard casting Ben and Sadie's distorted shadows on to Gina's cottage wall where they clung in a tight embrace.

'They're a wild lot, the Kinsellas. I'd say they're having a party over there in Sycamore,' Sadie joked, having earlier discussed with Ben how ill at ease and unhappy the couple seemed.

'Yeah, odd city,' Ben agreed, 'they're not exactly a good promotion for the magic worked by your mother's cottages, though she'd do well to sue the Carters for bringing down the contentment scale a notch or three. I really think a pre-booking psychological assessment would be in order to ensure all guests are relatively sane. You should suggest it or will I? Out of my mother's earshot, of course, in case she takes offence, though the Carters would never have got in were your guidelines a little less lax.'

Sadie laughed quietly, enjoying his humour but most of all relishing how natural it felt to be close to him, their arms linked, fingers intertwined and her head turned into the hollow of his shoulder. Her hair was tousled she was sure and she had plucked the white cotton skirt wrinkled and shabby from the floor of the tent but despite all of that she felt infinitely more attractive than when she had set out from the same doorway earlier that evening. It wasn't so much what he thought of her that mattered. It was more that being with him allowed her to forget to be critical and be gentle with herself. She was moved to recognize how much of a habit that unkindness to herself had become.

He toyed with her hair, coaxing strands of it around his index finger before releasing it to settle in short-lived curls against her cheek. He gifted her a long unhurried kiss on the lips before teasing her about being invited inside for a nightcap. There were limits to Gina's tolerance for her daughter's independent life and Sadie knew she would be crossing a plainly enunciated one if she brought Ben into the cottage for the bourbon whiskey he told her he quite fancied. Besides, she needed to savour what had happened between them in her own company, almost as if she had to fully capture and understand it before she could give any more of herself. He had a home to go to, two in fact if you were to count his rudimentary pitch by the water, so she told him she would see him in the morning at the lake if the cold night air hadn't driven him to the comfort and heat of his bed in the lodge.

'Are you insinuating that a mere Bostonian like me won't be man enough to withstand the stunted temperatures of what you humorously call summer nights in this neck of the woods?' he asked, doing a poor job of pretending to be mortally offended.

'Not at all,' she said, touching her fingers to the light stubble on his cheek, 'and just to prove it I'll bring you a flask of scalding hot coffee in the morning to thaw you out. You'd better zip up that tent or you'll have a hail of midges coming in to feast on your face and arms at the crack of dawn and hot coffee won't cure that.'

'Midges? I'm not even going to ask what the hell they are but I'll do what you tell me and zip up tight!' He stole another lingering kiss after she had turned to put the key into the Chubb lock. 'I look forward to the early-morning coffee delivery. Hope it comes with plenty of kisses.' He winked before setting off back toward the lake.

Inside she leaned against the closed door in the darkness for a moment before flicking the switch on the table lamp. It cast enough light for her to be able to move about the room but not enough to break the spell of what had just happened. Her body tingled at the memory of where she had been and what she had done. On the wide planks of the kitchen table she saw some chocolate left there by her mother and suddenly she felt as utterly ravenous as if she hadn't eaten for days. She helped herself to a few squares, greedy for their sweetness, while she read a short note from Gina that sat on top of a small parcel.

Hi Hon, help yourself to the slab of chocolate. It's courtesy of Auntie Lottie so there's plenty more where this came from. Someone stuffed this package through the letter box for you. Tara maybe? Nearly broke my neck on it coming in the door tonight. Talk tomorrow and make sure you lock the door before you go to bed.

PS. Hope you had a nice date with Ben! Of course we knew where you were going! I'm your mother and your aunties are as nosy as hell!

Mam x

Sadie grabbed the package and grinned to herself. There she was thinking that Gina hadn't a clue about her secret. It was amazing what her mother could glean without being told a thing. She had until morning to decide what harmless details she might divulge to Gina (and her aunts whose questions would come in gleeful pairs, she didn't doubt) but for the moment she was happy to keep it all for herself. In her mind she pictured his face looking down on her and the recollection of his touch made her feel giddy. At the sink she filled a pint glass of water and swirled it around her mouth to wash away the worst of the chocolate before she went to brush her teeth. From an underneath cupboard she pulled out a camping flask from the cottage kit and placed it next to the kettle for Ben's promised morning coffee before picking up the parcel and carrying its contents to read in the comfort of her bedroom.

Jessica's handwriting was unmistakable, bubbly dots on her i's and fanciful flourishes at the end of every word. All very sweet and neat and quite at odds with the girl to whom the writing belonged. She had promised Sadie she would print her off some details about work and accommodation in Boston for the following summer and Sadie felt sure that these were the promised printouts; a peace offering perhaps for her behaviour at the party. She scanned the note, lighting on words that jarred with what she expected. *I'd want to know if things were being hidden from me.*

With her head resting against her plumped-up pillows she set about examining the contents of the parcel as they tumbled out on to her lap. Some of the letters were brief notes about changes of address and Sadie was enthralled from the moment she began to look at them, quite unaware that they were anything more than an exchange of letters between her parents which for some unknown reason she had never seen. Each letter in the bundle was signed by Matthew and addressed to her mother at 36 Melbourne Terrace. She looked at the dates trying to make sense of when he had been where and why she had never known any of it. It wasn't that she had been told and had forgotten because she knew she would have remembered if she had ever seen any of this before. Different addresses were listed, Scotland at first and then southern England. Sometimes the contact details were all that was included but Matthew's signature was always jotted at the end, a witness to the information contained there. In one or two the bold capital M tailed off into a mostly illegible squiggle as if the reader should require only an elementary clue about whom it was from. On a short note dated August 1996 he had written *In case Sadie ever wants to get in touch*. Sadie scrambled through the letters trying to soak in what it all might mean until she came across a small envelope with her own name written in the corner in block capitals. From the wrinkles in the gummy flap it looked to Sadie to have been opened and somewhat clumsily resealed. Jessica? Her mother? Had both of them read a letter that was meant for her? Impatience shot through with a bolt of nerves made her fingers tremble and she struggled with what should have been the undemanding task of opening the envelope.

All thoughts of the hours she had just spent with Ben rushed from her mind, hunted out by the immediate confusion of what she was looking at. Matthew had taken particular care with the letter addressed to her, in it his signature was as clear as day. Sadie swallowed hard and painfully, her tongue feeling swollen in a mouth as dry as sawdust. She read the letter quickly, mouthing the odd word to herself silently at first and then a little louder to outdo the clamour beat of her heart.

5 Wellbridge Mews,
Kindling Way,
Starkhill,
London

7th August 1996

Dearest Sadie,

I know you're not old enough to understand me leaving you and your mother but I hope that she can find words to explain to you why I've had to go. I've asked her to give you this letter sometime in the future at a time she feels is right for you to know everything. I trust her to know the right time because she loves every hair of your head and in all of this she wanted only what was best for you. She was young and what happened was not all her fault but I could never think of us together knowing what I know. The words of explanation I'll leave to her because it's her story to tell. I know she thought that we could withstand her telling me what happened but that strength I simply could not find. It all cut me to the quick and I thought some time away with friends and family in Aberdeen might help me come to terms with the truth but it only made me realize why it would be impossible for me to come back to Tobarnaree and to you both.

I hoped I wouldn't have treated you differently but I couldn't be sure of that so I thought it best to leave before I risked behaving in a way that you didn't deserve. You must remember that you didn't do anything wrong. None of this is your fault. I hope one day we can meet as friends. I loved you, Sadie, and I always will, and I'd give the whole world for things to be different but that can't be. Your mother knows where to find me and I'll make sure if I move that she always has my new details. If I hear from you I'll be delighted but if I never do I'll understand why that is so. I keep a photograph of you chasing the butterflies with a net at Corrallis Woods in the window pocket of my wallet. I look forward to the day that you send me a new photograph that I can place there too. Mind yourself and remember the world is wide. You can be anything or anywhere you want to be. I so look forward to seeing what and where that turns out to be,

Always,
Matthew Gordon

CHAPTER SEVENTEEN

When she awoke in the morning feeling in her bones that her daughter was not inside the cottage with her as she should be, Gina went straight to the box bedroom opposite her own to put her fretful mind at ease. She was hoping to find Sadie's familiar form curled under the blankets with all of her, save a few strands of hair, buried for warmth in the way she habitually slept. Instead she found the letters spread across the tumbled covers and Matthew's name everywhere she looked.

Despite countless attempts to blot the memory out Gina vividly recalled the day she had told Matthew how everything had happened. It was a lovely Sunday afternoon spent together with no elaborate plan other than to have a picnic lunch, wander lazily through the trees and over the timber bridges that arched across the trickle of a river that fed onwards to the Blackwater. It was the type of day on which Gina could not have imagined anything bad could happen. Together with Sadie she and Matthew had set off to Corrallis Woods to walk the track surrounded by the sycamore and oak trees followed by a picnic and cold drinks devoured in the commanding shadow of the giant broadleaves. The simple food that Gina had prepared tasted delicious, its flavour heightened by the joy of being eaten out of doors. The butter had melted somewhat into the thickly sliced crusty white bread and the tomatoes that Nicholas Miller had cared for meticulously in the greenhouse behind the lodge were seasoned to perfection, their salty juices seeping into the pliable dough. They ate until they were happily full, comfortable in the knowledge that the day held nothing urgent for which they needed to rush away. Tobarnaree were playing in an underage football league final at the other end of the county but neither had more than a passing interest in sport so they were able to take advantage of having the popular wooded area almost entirely to themselves. The skin on Gina's bare shoulders and arms tingled from the heat of a lingering sun. Sadie took frequent rests on the picnic blanket in between chasing the butterflies that emerged lazily from the canopy of leaves above with a net that Gina had bought her from a bargain basket outside the supermarket on Quay Street. Eventually exhausted, after eating an entire tub of cubed mango and pineapple that had been planned as a refreshing dessert for all of them, the little girl had fallen into a comfortable sleep on Matthew's lap. Gina paused to soak in the look of both of them so obviously belonging together and she thought that their unity could withstand Matthew knowing everything. She convinced herself that if she could divide her secret in two then its suffocating power might dissipate and she would be able to breathe freely again, knowing she had nothing left to hide. Matthew looked over and smiled contentedly and she took that as encouragement to speak. It was as if something deep within her thought that Matthew had always suspected what had happened and he would welcome her honesty, better late than never. Of course she would always regret how much the revelation of her secret had ruined for the three of them but more than that she was sorry that it had been her confusing story to tell.

Matthew was right in what he had said in the letter to Sadie, the words of explanation belonged to Gina and Gina alone, but he was wrong to expect her to know the right time to tell her daughter. No mothering instinct within her would consciously seek out a time to deliver the words of explanation that were now forced upon her. Given a choice she would have let the issue lie as it had done, imperfect in its incompleteness but harmless in its fragments.

Overwhelmed by nerves and sadness she went to find Sadie. She had only one explanation and she prayed her daughter would forgive its belatedness and think it good enough. Perhaps it was cowardly to have kept the secret for so long and yet even with the benefit of hindsight she felt that cowardice had been her only option. Courage would have been to own up to what had happened immediately and never lie to Matthew or alternatively have the strength to lie for ever. Such things were for a different life and one that Gina knew she would not have known how to live.

Through the kitchen window of the lodge she could see Ellen fussing at the range stirring a pot of something but there was no sign of anyone else in the kitchen. Gina had hoped that she would find Sadie somewhere without having to go and ask the Carters if they'd seen her. She looked forward to taking Jessica to task for going through her private things for instinctively she knew that it was she who was responsible, but finding Sadie without delay was her immediate priority. If she had gone back down to Ben at the lake Gina wasn't sure what she would do. She needed to speak to her daughter as soon as possible but didn't want to add embarrassing her in front of her new boyfriend to her list of sins. She judged there might be quite enough to atone for already.

She breathed a sigh of relief when she found Sadie on the stoop of one of the sheds at the side of the lodge. Nicholas Miller used to call it the car house because that's where the car and tackle for the working horses had been stored in the days when they formed an important part of the farm's livestock. The stables similarly had never held a horse in Gina's memory but they were nevertheless called the stables in faithful and honoured memory of a time when previous Miller generations had lived a very different life at Tobar Lodge. Sadie was crouched puffing on a cigarette, its fiery butt glowing in the sulky morning fog that had yet to lift off and allow the day to get properly under way. Her awkward hold revealed a lack of experience at the task for which Gina was grateful. She had no doubt that it was Jessica who had introduced Sadie to the smoking habit. The sooner that girl was out of their lives the better. It had only taken two weeks for her curiosity to turn their world upside down and with all her heart she regretted handing over the keys of the lodge and her life. Still, there was no point in blaming Jessica for what Gina had made possible by leaving Matthew's letters in the attic and risking them being found. She wondered if she hadn't avoided destroying them on purpose, willing the truth to be revealed even if she hadn't the strength to be the one to do just that.

She sat down next to Sadie, her tiny frame curling itself into the small space between her daughter and the squat stone trough filled with summer flowering heathers. Tucked under the eaves of the outhouse they badly needed watering, yet they seemed to be thriving despite neglect, their blooms defying the drought enforced by their owner.

'Can I have a cigarette from the box?' Gina ventured, prepared for the smart remark she knew her daughter might spit at her. Yet she had to start somewhere on the most uncomfortable conversation they had ever had.

'Don't have another one to give you. Jessica keeps a spare one on the ledge inside the door here for when her mother is driving her mad,' Sadie said, motioning to the outhouse behind them.

'Now that she's taken herself back to Boston she won't mind if I use it up I guess.'

'Jessica's gone home?'

'Yup. Probably on a flight just about now. Left last night. Never to return, she said, and you know what? I figure she's dead right. Not much to keep a person around here when you come to think about it.'

'Does Ellen know she's gone home on her own?' Gina was incredulous. She worried when Sadie went away to concerts with her friends so she couldn't really get her head around the young girl having run away while her mother was still here. Besides, it seemed easier to concentrate on the Carters initially until she could fully gauge her daughter's mood.

'Well now, Mam, you better tell me seeing as you're the expert on secrets and on what information is allowed to flow freely between mother and daughter,' Sadie sniped, but then looked a little ashamed; she was unused to being unkind. 'I suppose I could let you have a drag if you're that desperate,' she offered as a sort of apology. She handed the cigarette to her mother who gave one slow pull. Still as rotten as she remembered and as a distraction from the matter in hand it only lasted a futile second. Matthew used to smoke a little, she remembered. There would sometimes be a half-smoked packet in his jeans after a night spent in the pub. Gina had nagged him a little to give them up.

'You know how bad they are for you,' she would counsel gently but Matthew was having none of it. Smoking was simply something to do with his hands in company before conversation had properly kicked off and eased the nerves that sometimes troubled him, a prop he was unwilling to do without whatever the extent of his girlfriend's disapproval. Gina wished dearly that he was here to help her explain things to her daughter but she realized that in this as well as everything else it was always just the two of them.

Her daughter stared straight ahead, watching the marmalade cat that had tenaciously insinuated himself into their household play with a piece of farming twine on the back-door step. She could not allow her mother's silence to run unchecked any longer. 'The truth would be a good place to start, Mam.' Her shrill voice betrayed a good deal of her bruised feelings. 'I've spent years wondering why Matthew left, always afraid to ask you in case you got upset. Worse than that I have spent years thinking he hadn't the slightest interest in me when for a time at least obviously he had. Why would you let me think that? Why would you let me think badly of him when he didn't deserve it?'

After years avoiding telling the truth and hoping such avoidance was the best thing for her daughter Gina now knew that the blunt force of those damaging words was about to overwhelm them. She took a deep breath and heard herself say what she hoped she would never have to reveal. 'Because Matthew has chosen to believe that he's not your father.'

'What do you mean "chosen to believe", Mam? For God's sake, is he or isn't he?'

'Come back to the cottage and I'll tell you everything, I promise. It's cold here. Besides, I think the Carters know quite enough about us already.' Gina got up from the stoop and held out her hand to Sadie to help her to her feet from her low perch. Slowly her daughter got up without accepting her mother's offered support. She nodded in the direction of the cottage and Gina led the way, dreading every step that brought her closer to what was about to unfold.

Chapter Eighteen

Tobarnaree, Summer 1990

When his wife asked that she be allowed home from hospital so that she could die in their house and in her own bed Nicholas Miller decided he would move heaven and earth to make her wish possible. The doctors and nurses in the Regional Hospital left him in no doubt how huge an undertaking he was proposing for himself and his three young daughters but he was having none of their kind and well-intentioned discouragement. While their mother slept facing inward toward the duck-egg-blue wall of her hospital room, Nicholas addressed his girls in the corridor outside as if he was mentoring a team for their next bout of competitive action. 'We'll mind your mother in every last way just like she's always minded us.'

Gina remembered how through their distress they had all nodded in silent agreement. Going along with their father seemed the kind and right thing to do though they had considerable misgivings. They didn't have the first clue how to nurse somebody, having always been on the receiving end of their mother's tenderness, but they silently promised themselves that they would do their absolute best for her and not just because their father would expect nothing less of them. All three were struggling with the idea that their mother was gravely ill and now their father was asking them to make the mental leap that they were going to aid the process of her leaving them for good.

In a cramped 'Family Resource Room' they were professionally and kindly led through the various support systems that they could call upon if things became too tough to cope with on their own. The name of the room irritated Gina. The word 'family' seemed like a cruel joke when no one was ever led to a private corner of an oncology department except to hear that something incurable was about to tear their family clean apart. As usual Lottie swung into deliberate action making sensible and beyond-her-age enquiries about home help, drug dosages and public health nurse visits, stubbornly withholding tears while asking questions that might otherwise be forgotten in her father's determination to proceed with the plan without fully thinking through all aspects of it.

Gina might well have stayed in her own miserable cocoon, setting herself apart in order to survive, but she was shaken by the sobs of Rachel, who clung tightly to the sleeve of her shirt and gave in to waves of distress. 'No! Mammy, no!' she kept imploring softly over and over again as Lottie and her father discussed unthinkable but necessary details with the hospital staff. She rocked back and forth, the rubber soles of her runners alternating squeaks and squelches on the polished tiled floor. Gina tried hard not to be annoyed by her sister's upset being more evident and physical than her own. Just because she hadn't cried yet, couldn't cry a drop in fact, didn't mean her heart wasn't breaking too. But tears came easily to Rachel – just like everything else, Gina decided bitterly. As soon as she had lived with the thought for a moment she was ashamed of herself for its pettiness. After all there was no competition, nothing for either to win.

Finally, when it all got too much for Rachel, the stuffiness of the small room making nausea rise in her throat, she fled from the spot where she had leaned into her sister for support. She startled those seated in the waiting area by darting away like an injured animal from the point of impact. She stumbled over a handbag that jutted out from under a chair and didn't turn back when its contents spilled messily and noisily across the tiles, much to its owner's vocal annoyance. Gina sprinted in pursuit of her sister without waiting for her father's inevitable nod to do so and spotted her making for the public toilets further along the uncomfortably hot corridor. Inside she found her in an open cubicle retching into a toilet bowl reeking of disinfectant. Gina crouched down close to her and gathered the dark waves of her hair away from her face, stroking the clammy skin of her cheek.

When the retching subsided she whispered gently that everything would be all right. As the words escaped her mouth she knew that she had no scrap of faith in the comfort she was offering. Her sister didn't answer and a depleted Gina could think of nothing further to say. Instead she rubbed the back of her sister's pink T-shirt in small rhythmic circles while waiting for Rachel's sobbing to wear itself out. When it had she got to her feet and in the wash basin she soaked a thick fold of tissue paper under the ice-cold tap water. Armed with it she dabbed her sister's face until the worst of the blotching subsided. 'Let's go and see Mammy. She might be awake by now and wondering where we've all got to,' Gina said in as cheerful a voice as she could manage. Rachel shuddered but gave a feeble nod and Gina held her hand tightly all the way to the side of their mother's bed.

*   *   *

'Jewel colours, Gina. Emerald green or a rich damson. They're the colours for you and if we can't get what we want in Cork we'll just take the train to Dublin instead,' Sarah May Miller had said when months before they had planned a trip to purchase the fabric for Gina's debs dress. 'Exactly the right shade will bring out those brown eyes of yours and you're so slight you'll be able to carry off a lovely straight dress or maybe an Empire line. I'll pick up a pattern though I'll hardly need one because it'll be easy to cut. Matthew Gordon better know how lucky he is to be having you on his arm.'

Gina was delighted that her mother had agreed to make her graduation dress and that she had dismissed out of hand her father's plan that Lottie's shell-pink nightmare from a couple of years before might be remodelled in some way that would make it suit her sister. Gina wanted to look pretty and special and not as if she had been sent out in her big sister's hand-me-downs. Besides, even Lottie hated the dress and had removed the framed photograph of her wearing it that their mother had proudly hung in the hallway. Some outfits were best forgotten, she knew, even though her mother had made the dress to her daughter's exact, if misguided, specifications. 'Your middle daughter deserves a new dress, Nicholas, and that's all there is to it,' Sarah May had announced boldly, brooking none of her husband's attempt to sway proceedings in this matter which she saw as rightly her domain. Her husband was in the habit of bossing and mostly she didn't mind letting him think he was in control, but in this instance she was having none of it. Sarah May winked at her daughter and Gina thought her graduation dance could not come soon enough.

So much had changed by late that August when Gina pulled on the silk dress in her neat-as-a-pin bedroom at the top of the landing in Tobar Lodge. It was Rachel and Lottie who helped her get ready, her sisters loving the relief of their girlie chat. Their mother had weakened further and had been sleeping even more since her doctor had once again altered the medication he insisted was keeping her comfortable. Nicholas Miller was anxious to get a photograph of Gina sitting with her mother before she left the house but his daughter pleaded with him not to wake her mother for the sake of a picture. 'I'll dress up again for Mammy in the morning, Daddy, but please let her rest now. I'd hate if she got upset before I go.'

Nicholas looked at his daughter, who was unrecognizably grown up by dint of the make-up Lottie had applied and the dress that his wife had expertly sewn before she had any inkling that she might not live to see this same night unfold for her youngest daughter Rachel. 'Maybe that would be best, love. She might have more energy in the morning and the hospice nurse will be here too. By the way, you look lovely except for the pair of black eyes you've painted on yourself. I think you might have over-egged the pudding with eye shadow or whatever it is you girls like to plaster yourselves with. No need to make yourself look like a scarecrow on your special night, Regina.' He left his daughters to their giggling preparations and as he shuffled down the stairs he wondered sadly how he would manage to finish rearing them alone.

'Don't mind him; you look lovely,' Lottie counselled, disgusted at her father's unhelpful evaluation of the smoky eyes she had created for her sister. 'As if he's got the first clue what good make-up would look like. I copied your look exactly from a photo shoot in a glossy magazine but then again *Vogue* and the like are wasted on a dive like Tobarnaree. Everyone in college does their make-up like this; well, anyone with an ounce of style anyway.'

'So I don't look like a scarecrow then?' Gina asked while taking in the look of herself appreciatively in the full-length mirror of her wardrobe door, delighted with how grown-up she looked.

'A scarecrow in a very fetching shade of plum,' Rachel

ventured cheekily from the window seat before getting a pillow flung across the room at her by a radiant Gina.

Some of the boys met for a drinks party in Ciaran Jacob's parents' house before arriving at the laughably non-alcoholic punch reception laid on by their class tutors in the school canteen. The whole group had been instructed to gather there to wait for Mick Devlin's coach to pick them up and take them to the Edengrove Hotel. Marcus and Valerie Jacob had already seen three sons through this graduation milestone and they had been insistent on hosting a little get-together for their youngest son and his friends to send them merrily on their way. Being in the company of Ciaran's youthful friends made them feel in touch with life and they had taken considerable part in the refreshments, much to their youngest son's embarrassment. Maybe the mooted plan of his parents going back to England was not such a bad one after all. As they had both retired and his brothers had left one by one, Tobarnaree seemed to have become far too small for their needs and personalities. They craved more social activity than any small town could give and Ciaran had no intention of plugging the gaps in his parents' life with fragments of his own. He was happy that his friends enjoyed the free drink but when the time came to be at the school reception Ciaran moved promptly to the door, shunting the boys out of the house in case they would be late. He didn't look back when his mother begged a kiss from her handsome baby. 'We're late already, Mam,' he pleaded, hoping that none of his friends were alert enough to have paid any attention to her slurred request.

Gina knew before she even spoke to Matthew in the canteen of St Brendan's that he'd partaken of far more than his fair share of the Jacobs' hospitality. The giveaway was his stupid crooked smile and the fact that he barely noticed her all dressed up, which annoyed her beyond measure. When pressed by Gina for a compliment all he managed was 'You look grand' while raising his tumbler of sickeningly sweet punch to toast an equally bleary friend across the canteen. When the bus came she wondered if there was a way she might sit with any of her friends instead of Matthew but as the couples paired off she had to take her designated seat, fervently wishing that the night might yet improve. A lot. When he half-heartedly started a drunken kiss and grope about a mile into the journey she pushed him away, telling him he would ruin her make-up. He shrugged his shoulders as if her knock-back didn't bother him in the slightest. Looking through the bus windows blurred with condensation at the yellow streak of street lights and listening to the excited chatter behind them, Gina wondered about her feelings for Matthew. If she loved him as she had begun to think she did then surely that shouldn't be ruined by him being drunk like practically three-quarters of the other lads on the bus. The difference of course was that she had come to depend on Matthew during the course of the summer when everything in the Miller house had begun to painfully unravel. Tonight she had loads stored up to talk to him about while Matthew was simply intent on enjoying a memorable night out. The heartbreaking changes in her life had made her suddenly older and more serious than any of her peers while Matthew and the others had remained carefree and optimistic. That attitude was exactly what Gina craved for herself but her mother's illness had erased that possibility.

In the last weeks of the summer she and Matthew had met in town a few evenings a week and Gina had taken considerable advantage of the fact that her father had eased his rules a little, thinking it important that his daughters had outings to distract themselves from the melancholy of what was going on at home.

Matthew had borrowed his father's car a couple of times. A fiver's worth of petrol was enough to allow them to go for drives out along the Saltway Road. They would end up parking on the height overlooking Carty's Inch and there Gina would unburden herself, describing to Matthew the awful way her mother was deteriorating before her very eyes. Sores had developed despite the fact that her slight body was regularly turned in the bed and she was plagued with a dry mouth, which they could only relieve by running a wet cotton bud over her thin lips because she had lost her power to swallow. Though he couldn't imagine what it was really like for Gina, Matthew attempted to do just that, tried to say the right thing to raise her spirits. Alone in the darkness, the lit houses of the town shining down at them like stars, they kissed and listened to music before making love in the back seat.

On the bus to the debs, Gina tried hard not to cringe as Matthew and their classmates bawled out a rebel ballad as they crawled into the hotel car park. Summoning the spirit of Robert Emmet and Wolfe Tone was usually saved for the trip home and Gina struggled with the desire to tell him to be quiet and stop making a fool of himself. He was in good and cheerful company, and she had never felt so alone.

She wanted to tell Matthew that she had seen her father crying in the rear-view mirror while they drove to the pharmacy to pick up a prescription for new drugs for her mother earlier that day. She had seen him wipe his eyes on the sleeve of his jumper before they got out of the car so that his daughter or anyone they might meet on the street could not accurately gauge the extent of his distress. The doctor was coming nearly every day now and Lottie was saying that might mean that their mother was going downhill faster than they'd expected and that she could die before Christmas and they should be prepared. Gina wanted to say to Matthew that she wouldn't die before Christmas, would she? The unasked question tightened like an awkward knot in the pit of her stomach. Her girlfriends all asked her was she feeling OK, anxious that she would enjoy herself despite the fact that her mother was so ill. She nodded, giving her best attempt at a convincing smile. It was their big night, anticipated for so long and prepared for so carefully that Gina kept her distress under wraps, unwilling to spoil what was meant to be special.

She drank a glass of wine, picked at her dinner and had a few more glasses of lager until she thought her forced high spirits could be mistaken for genuinely having a good time. When the meal was over she danced like a mad woman with her class-mates, determined to block out all that was upsetting her.

When Mick Devlin's bus was ready to go home Gina was almost relieved that Matthew and a few of his friends didn't make the driver's strict curfew and he left without them as he'd warned them several times over the course of their journey to the hotel that he would. She had planned to go as far as Tobarnaree on the bus with Matthew and stay in her friend Sally Gilligan's parents' house, but as they neared Tobar Lodge she decided it would be better to get off there instead. There seemed little point in extending the party when seated behind her Sally had belatedly decided to give in to Oliver Coady's persistent wooing and was now wearing the face off him, barely pausing to come up for air. The only singleton amongst her coupled-off friends, Gina didn't fancy hanging around Tobarnaree until Sally decided to call it a night and go home. She said as much to her friend through the gap in the velour headrest. Sally broke off what she was doing for a moment to say goodnight and give her friend a giddy thumbs-up. 'No worries, darling,' she said before diving back in. Gina shook her head in disbelief. Good God, Sally could surely do better than Coady and she would tell her so in the morning when she rang her for a full post-mortem on the night. She stood up and walked to the front of the bus as it approached the avenue of Tobar Lodge.

'I'll get off here, Mick,' she said, hoping that the driver wouldn't make a fuss of a young girl on her own legging it home in the dark.

'Ah, love, are you sure? Is there no one at all with you?' The innocently meant question niggled. Gina hoped that all on the bus were too occupied coming to terms with their mixed romantic prospects, their sore heads or their curdling stomachs to take note of what she had been asked. She could swing for Matthew for showing her up.

'Nah, Mick, but I'm grand. I can sprint up the avenue in two minutes though it might take a minute longer in these heels,' she joked.

Spotting the lodge's yard light through the trees Mick Devlin was reluctant to agree until Ciaran Jacob peeked over Gina's shoulder and said, 'Sure I'll walk you home, Gina. My place is not far from here.'

'Good man yourself, Ciaran. I feel better than letting you tear up there on your own, Gina, but if I took this bus up there I'd never get the shagging thing back down and I know your father well enough that he wouldn't thank me for landing this rowdy lot like a plague of locusts on his front lawn.'

As the bus pulled off to finish the journey into town leaving them standing at the lodge avenue gate, Gina thanked Ciaran. As brave as she'd pretended to be she was glad that she didn't have to run up the avenue on her own in the dark. 'You didn't have to do that, you know. I would've been fine.'

'Oh, I know that but sure it's no bother. Besides, I do feel a bit guilty about the way Matthew ended up. My old pair were plying all the lads with drink and out of good manners Matt just kept throwing it back, so apologies for the state he's in. I tried to get the boys to slow down the pace a bit at the hotel bar but they were having none of it. I just couldn't keep up. Think I've had a sheltered life compared to the lads in St Brendan's but the amount of drink they've had is mostly my folks' fault really. Lost the plot trying to "hang with the young people" as Dad might mortifyingly put it. The man's a disgrace since he retired. All that time on his hands is doing him no favours. I wish to fuck he'd discover a passion for something that didn't involve me.'

'Well, no one forced the drink down Matthew's neck but I do hope he gets home all right. They were all in such a state when we left the Edengrove. Never seen him so bad.'

'Sure he's with Pentony who'll probably ring his arsehole da to pick them up in the Beemer and they'll have a much more comfortable spin home than we had on Mick Devlin's gut-churn bus.'

'Bad, wasn't it?' Gina commented, glad of the opportunity to change the subject away from Matthew. 'I thought I was going to spew coming around the bad bend after Corrigans'. Made up my mind to get off here after that fright.'

By the time they reached the lodge Gina had asked Ciaran in for coffee or maybe a beer hoping everyone was in bed. If her father was still up she would make up some story about Matthew getting sick and having to go home early because he would think it untoward for his daughter to go with her boyfriend to the debs and be escorted home by a young man who had never stood in his house before. If truth be known Gina wasn't too impressed herself even if she was very touched by Ciaran's kindness.

When she saw her Uncle Paddy's car pulled in at the back door she groaned, deciding the night had now disappointed her in every way possible.

'Lousy visitors?' Ciaran asked, noticing how agitated Gina seemed.

'Nah, just my Uncle Paddy but he's a pain in the arse. When we go in he'll be hopping questions off us now about the night, right down to how many peas were on the dinner plate and telling us that young people don't know how handy they have it. He'll go on about spending all his young days thinning my granddad's turnips on his knees until they bled. He's misery on a stick and on top of that he gives me the creeps. Don't have any damning proof as such but my skin crawls anytime he's around.' She was steeling herself to face the sorry scene when Ciaran proposed an alternative plan.

'Come on, we'll take a bit of a walk around the place and he might go in a minute. Matthew tells me you guys are so posh you've a lake and seeing as I know no one else that has a lake of their own maybe you'd be so good as to give me the guided tour?'

Gina explained that her family didn't actually own the lake but the fields around it and the fishing rights.

Ciaran was playfully insistent: 'Ah listen, Gina, it's right here in your back yard so I think you Millers can safely lay claim to it.' When she showed him the path past the outbuildings and the derelict labourers' cottages he asked if it was too mucky and would her dress not get destroyed.

'Don't worry, I'll hitch it up. Besides, I'm a farmer's daughter and this is what we'd call clean dirt!'

'Clean dirt? I always knew farmers were an odd breed but I held out hope for their daughters. Foolish, obviously. Come on, let's have a midnight twirl on this clean dirt of yours.'

'Don't be cheeky. You're on my turf now,' she countered, feeling a little light-hearted and loving the feeling of release. By the time they reached the lake Gina had responded to all of Ciaran's gentle questioning about Sarah May's poor health and in the process telling him much of what she had meant for Matthew. Her instinct told her she could not step back inside the door of Tobar Lodge and to what waited for her there without unburdening her troubles to someone. She would never have dreamt she could talk so candidly to Ciaran, whom she knew only as Matthew's handsome but, until this evening, somewhat aloof friend. She hardly knew him at all because he had been at an out-of-town boarding school and had only come to St Brendan's in Tobarnaree the previous September to repeat his Leaving. He was bound for some college course in Dublin for which he had managed to secure the extra points through repeating. He would be heading off soon, she knew, unlike herself who would be remaining at home in her parents' house, all plans for the future on hold because of her mother's illness. She had got her first choice studying commerce in UCC but she was still waiting back to see if the place could be deferred at short notice. Otherwise she would have to apply again the following year, though no part of her could look forward to doing so because if she did she would have to deal with what might have happened to her mother in the interim.

'Is this rock of yours safe to climb?' Ciaran wondered, his question bringing her back from the depressing thoughts of what the future months might have in store.

'Yeah, I've done it loads of times in daylight but I'm certainly not going to chance it in these shoes,' Gina replied as she watched him, hands dug deep in his trouser pockets, appearing to consider the quickest way up.

Ciaran shrugged. 'Fair point. I always find wearing stilettos holds me back from things I want to do. The price we have to pay for fashion.'

Gina giggled at the thought. 'Not much to see at this hour of night anyway but it's fairly spectacular on a clear day.'

'Oh I don't know,' Ciaran joked, 'what about the glitz and glamour of the nightclubs of Tobarnaree laid out before us like a stretch of Broadway?'

Gina smirked at him. 'Yup, it's a dazzling sight all right. You'd need shades.'

'I suppose you're going to tell me it's too cold for a swim too?' Ciaran said as if she was intent on spoiling all his fun.

'Yeah, definitely, and we've no towels. Come back here during the day and you can do all the exploring you want. Daddy put in a seat for Mammy over here,' she said, gesturing to the right of the rock and Ciaran followed where she led. 'She loves to read down here or just sit in this hollow by the lake when we're all out of her hair. Says it's the only time she gets to herself because if she stays in the house there's always something that needs doing. She hasn't been able to come out here since she came home from hospital though. Probably won't be out here again either . . .' Gina trailed off knowing she was being too brave saying things that broke her heart. She sat down on the stone bench fruitlessly double wrapping the flimsy fabric of her skirt around her knees for some warmth.

Taking a seat beside her Ciaran asked if she was cold. When she nodded he took off the jacket of his rented tuxedo and swamped her neat shoulders as he wrapped it around them. She whispered a timid thanks and his kindness coupled with how miserable she was feeling finally unleashed her sobs. Ciaran searched his trouser pocket in vain for a tissue but Gina waved at him not to bother, furiously wiping away the tears with the back of her hand. 'Sorry, I'm just a bit messed up about things here at home at the moment.'

'Jesus, don't apologize, it's fine. Your mam's very ill. Give yourself a break, why don't you? To be honest I'm kind of surprised you even went to the grad tonight with the way things are.'

'I think I just wanted to pretend to be a normal girl for a night, you know? Dress up, slap on the make-up and go out without a care in the world – except my worries marched after me like a devoted nest of ants. Some chance of normality with what's going on in my life.'

'What do normal girls do anyway? I come from a house of lads and an all-boys boarding school so you girls are a bit of a mystery to an innocent like me,' Ciaran commented, looking at her playfully and hoping to cheer her up.

Gina shrugged her shoulders. 'Well, they kiss boys, I suppose, for one thing,' she said with strange bravery and then surprised them both by reaching across and kissing him tenderly on the lips. He shivered, and then kissed her back, knowing that he shouldn't but not being able to resist the tempting taste of her. Several times she thought they would surely stop themselves before what was ultimately harmless went too far but neither found the will to pull away. She welcomed the touch of his hands resting on the curve of her waist, feeling their heat through the snug fit of her dress.

She tugged at his shirt, pulling it free from the waistband of his trousers, feeling the smooth skin of his stomach and enjoying a sense of freedom in being with someone who didn't know how little experience she had. She felt nothing like herself and as their kissing and caresses became more insistent she realized a break from being Gina Miller and the restraints of what that had lately meant was what she needed.

When cold discomfort drove them from their seat at the rock it was Gina who led the way, knowing that they could sneak into one of the outhouses and find some shelter there. They each held their breath inside the shed when they heard Nicholas say goodnight to his wife's brother at the back door. There were promises from both men to be in touch at some stage the following day and Gina heard her uncle bossily instruct her father to go on to bed and get a few solid hours' sleep. Nicholas agreed that he would do just that.

'Must you wait up for Regina to come back from the dance?' her uncle asked and in the car house Gina swallowed nervously. The man's curiosity was insatiable.

'Not at all,' her father answered. 'It's all arranged; she's staying with Roy Gilligan's daughter in town. Won't be a trace of her until close to midday tomorrow, I'd imagine. There's no accounting for the way teenagers conduct their lives but sure we were all there once so it doesn't do to criticize too much.'

'No indeed! Go on inside with you so. No point in wearing yourself out. Tomorrow's another day.'

Through a crevice in the shutter of the car-house window Gina saw the red tail lights of her uncle's car edge sluggishly down the driveway and the yard returned to silence and darkness save for the back-door yard light. From under the gable-end eaves the cattle dog roused himself from sleep, disturbed by the commotion made by the car, and offered a lazy, unconvincing wag of his tail to his owner. Gina watched Nicholas pat the dog's head for a few moments before turning on the outside tap to fill the empty drinking bowl with water. When her father went back inside the house, knocking off the porch light as he went, the only sound to be heard was the to and fro scraping of the metal bowl across the concrete as Crosby energetically lapped up every last drop. Gina watched as he wandered back to the spot under the eaves and collapsed in a heap on the still warm canvas sacking.

Ciaran spoke, his voice barely above a whisper, 'Am I going to be eaten alive by your father's dog? What a way for the lights to go out on graduation night! Here lies Ciaran Jacob, torn to shreds at the edge of Tobar Lake by the Miller family mutt.'

Gina giggled and shook her head. 'Crosby's so old and lazy he only gets up if there's food or drink on offer. He won't come sniffing us out, if that's what you're worried about. He must have been on the mitch in dog school the day they did guard-dog training.'

'We're safe so,' Ciaran said, pulling her back toward him and into an embrace. They didn't talk about Matthew even though both were trying not to think about him while they stood with their arms wrapped around one another. *We won't tell him*, Gina wanted to say but in the silence and the darkness she convinced herself that he wouldn't breathe a word and of course neither would she. Ciaran lifted her slight body up on to the high work bench inside the door and she curled her legs around him inviting him to continue what they had started in the shadow of the rock, blocking out all the impending sadness for the briefest of moments.

CHAPTER NINETEEN

'You slept with Uncle Ciaran?' Sadie bleated, having listened appalled to her mother's confession of her teenage indiscretion.

'Jesus Christ, Sadie, would you keep your voice down?' Gina pleaded, moving quickly to slam shut the sash window to the courtyard that she had earlier opened when she felt she couldn't catch her breath for all that had happened. 'This is our business, yours and mine, and nobody else's, do you hear? He was nobody's uncle then, nobody's father or husband for that matter. Just a young lad. Just Ciaran. He was nineteen years old and I was your age. We were kids messing around and we ended up doing something we probably shouldn't have done. I was upset and my head was all over the place. Mammy was dying—'

'Does Auntie Rachel know?' Sadie was deaf to her mother's attempt at a mitigating defence and wanted only the facts of the story laid out in boldest black and white.

'No, of course she doesn't! I certainly never told her and there was no reason for Ciaran to either. They didn't meet for ages after that and by then it was just something that had happened years before that she had no reason to know. It would've just been embarrassing for everyone and utterly needless. Nobody tells exactly everything they've done in the past. I'm sure Rachel has things she has kept from Ciaran. That's life, you know, not neat and tidy but messy as hell . . .' Gina subsided into silence, cursing the situation she had found herself in.

'So am I his then? Is Ciaran my father? Is that what Matthew thinks? Is he right?'

Before Gina had a chance to answer Sadie's beseeching questions, a shook-looking Lottie cruised through the unlocked front door pleading for the kind attention of painkillers. 'Have mercy, Gina. My head's opening and I've used all mine up. Rachel and Ciaran have gone out already and seeing as drugs are a bit of a sensitive topic between myself and Jill I can hardly go begging to that door. Wouldn't look good.' Clocking the awkward atmosphere that hung between her sister and her niece she clean forgot about the headache that was troubling her and fell headlong into the furrow of her sister's private business. 'Something wrong, Sadie darling? You don't look too good this morning.' From experience she knew that tackling her niece was far more likely to get her to the crux of the issue. The girl was, in her aunt's opinion, without guile. It was clear from Sadie's reddened eyes that she had been crying but she was bristling with edgy nervousness too. Her aunt judged that she was as mad as hell about something.

Sadie managed a stiff, unconvincing smile and a shoulder shrug that divulged far too little for Lottie's liking. Gina returned from the bathroom cabinet with a blister pack of paracetamol and thrust them at her sister. 'Here you go. Take some and go back to bed. You'll be grand in an hour.'

'Ah Jesus, a couple would've done, I'm not that bad.'

'Just take them,' Gina said impatiently, showing Lottie the

door. 'Sadie and I have one or two things to talk about so just give us a little while. I'll knock in for coffee later maybe.'

'Are you working in the Lime Tree today?' Lottie asked, buying time and trying hard to work out what was going on while she was still in a position to examine them at close quarters. Though they both looked as if they might explode there was a disappointing lack of clues as to what could be the matter. It had to be Ben, Lottie decided, because Gina and Sadie didn't fight as a rule. It made sense to blame the new boy for whatever was causing such tension between them. She watched while Gina became more and more exasperated.

'Supposed to be covering lunch, yeah. Not sure though. Might try and sort some time off with Louis . . .' Gina tailed off, knowing well how badly her boss would react to such a late request.

Stopping dead in the doorway to glance over Gina's shoulder at her niece Lottie couldn't resist whispering, 'Don't like telling you your business but I think you might've left it a bit late for the birds and the bees talk. Wouldn't be surprised if the bold Ben hadn't got there before you with the practical. So I'd save your breath.'

'*Not even funny*,' Gina intoned sourly and when her sister didn't move even then she added, 'Get out and give us a bit of space.'

With a reluctant Lottie gone, Sadie got up from the kitchen table and announced that she was going down to the lake to see Ben.

'I thought we were going to talk? We can't leave things like this,' Gina implored, not knowing why on earth she was pushing the issue when she had no stomach for the topic apart from thinking that if the conversation had to happen it might be best if there was no further delay. She was nervous enough already.

'I told Ben when he left me home last night that I'd take him down a flask of coffee to the tent when I woke up. He'll be wondering why I haven't gone down already and seeing as none of this is his fault I think I should keep my word.' She strode across to the kitchen counter and busied herself scalding the flask that she had taken out the night before when her life had made some sense.

Gina watched, hypnotized by her daughter's seeming engagement with a commonplace task. The smell of brewed coffee filled the room and Gina longed to be doing something mundane like sitting down to a bowl of cereal with one eye on the morning newspaper taking a leisurely dip into the goings on of the outside world.

While she tightened the lid of the thermos Sadie spoke without bothering to catch her mother's eye. 'When I come back up I think we should go for a drive and get away from here for a few hours so you can finish telling me who I am. I wouldn't mind knowing for sure if that's not too much bother.'

Gina flinched at the sharpness of her daughter's comment. 'Where do you want to go?' she enquired, needing to know at least some of the shape the day might take. If it was up to her she would stay at home and deal with everything inside their own four walls but in this she knew she would have to defer to her daughter's wishes. She couldn't help feeling that their self-imposed exile from the lodge was contributing to how ill at ease she felt and none of this would have happened if they had stayed put.

'Well, I'd been thinking over the past while that we should go to Aughasallagh sometime before the summer finishes. We haven't been there in ages and I thought it might be nice before I head away to college. For old times' sake, you know, and sure maybe while we're there you can explain to me all about those old times because I think I've had the wrong end of the stick all along.'

'Sadie . . .' Gina pleaded but her daughter was gone, clinging to the warmth of the hot thermos, walking away from her mother and into the arms of someone she hoped she could trust.

When it became clear that Sadie was going to take her own sweet time to return Gina abandoned her sentry duty at the kitchen window and set about routine jobs in the cottage. In Sadie's bedroom she gathered the letters together in a pile and placed them on the nightstand. When the bed was made and the pillows arranged to her satisfaction she had a cursory look through the letters and then put them back where she had found them.

'Do you want to get some food first?' Gina asked as they drove out of the lodge's gate and headed in the direction of Aughasallagh. 'There's a couple of places we could go. Daly's do sandwiches or there's the café across from the church though it wasn't that great the last time. Do you remember we had quiche and they put melon and all sorts of odd things in it?' Gina chatted nervously but her daughter was having none of her idle attempts at distraction from the matter in hand.

'Nothing to eat, Mam, and nothing to drink. The truth's all I'm after. Matthew or Ciaran? Or now that we're on the open road maybe you're going to confess that's not the full list of potential candidates?'

'Jesus Christ, of course it is. What do you take me for? How dare you?'

'Sorry, but what would I know?' In the pocket of her hooded top Sadie fingered her phone, willing it to beep. Ben told her he would text to see if she was OK and that she was to come and find him the minute she came home. He wagered he would spend most of the day at the lodge calming his mother down about his sister's overnight flit back to Boston. Sadie had tumbled the bare bones of the story to him as he took welcome sips of the scorching coffee and even though he had been sweet and kind to her he couldn't seem to get past the issue of the grotty part his sister had played in the drama in which Sadie found herself mired.

'She'd no fucking right to go through your family's things. Sometimes I wonder about her brain and the sick way things are wired up in there. Just as well she's gone home or I'd be putting her on the plane personally. Head fucking first.'

'She might have done me a favour,' Sadie had offered quietly, doing her stubborn best not to bawl her eyes out. Why couldn't her poxy life just have behaved itself for a few weeks while Ben was around?

'You think?' Ben had answered, pulling her into a hug and telling her not to worry about a thing. He'd confessed he was perished with the cold but had been determined to remain camped out until she arrived with the coffee in case she thought he was soft and couldn't handle the Irish elements. She told him to go back up to the lodge and stand with his back to the range because that was what she always did when she wanted to thaw out after being outside.

Gina's voice pulled her back to the present, its fragility doing battle with the rattle from some wayward part of the dashboard that always insisted on announcing itself when they attempted to travel at anything above a crawl speed. Her mother's car was on its last legs but it had been that way for years; there was no reason to think it would give up on them now when it had soldiered on for so long. 'The truth is, Sadie, I don't know for absolutely sure but I've always thought it had to be Matthew because that's the only thing that makes sense. You look like him, for God's sake: the same eyes, the same colouring and build. I can't prove it except to say in my heart I'm sure you're Matthew's. Ciaran and I slept together twice while I was going out with Matthew. It's not something I'm proud of or ashamed of either for that matter. It's just something that happened when I was young and confused.'

Sadie didn't answer or make any sign that she had heard or

understood what her mother had said so Gina continued while navigating the familiar route to Aughasallagh. 'I was a good few weeks pregnant before I realized. More like months actually. Sounds a bit odd maybe but that's the truth of it. Your granny Sarah May died the first week in November and the whole lot of us just fell apart. I didn't keep any track of my periods; it was the last thing on my mind, to be honest. Dad was just miserable. He went from being in absolute control to falling into a total wreck. The house was full of visitors more or less all the time. We had such a lousy time that Christmas and Lottie, and she was no better at subtlety then, told me I was getting as fat as a pig and to stay away from the tins of sweets and biscuits that lay open on every table top. There was food everywhere. People insisted on feeding us because they didn't know what else to do. But I hadn't been eating that much and the penny dropped and I knew even before I dared to do a test. I looked at myself in the long mirror on the outside of my wardrobe door and I saw my belly swelled a little. Not much – Lottie was exaggerating, of course – but enough for me to know and I was scared as hell.' Gina shivered at the memory of how she had sat on her bed hugging her knees to her chest and wishing that she too was dead like her mother and that she would never have to feel anything ever again.

'What did Granddad say when he found out?' Sadie enquired.

'Very little, to be honest. Couldn't take it in, I think. Just another thing that try as he might he couldn't handle. In fairness to her Lottie came and told him with me. Rachel was only fifteen so we kept her in the dark for a bit. I think Lottie thought he might kill me but he didn't go mad although I know he must have been disappointed. With Mammy gone the worst thing had already happened to him and that had knocked him sideways.' Gina knew if her mother had been still alive he would have lost his head, relying on the safety valve of her kindness to temper the worst of his reaction. Without her he didn't seem to know what to say, almost as if he had forgotten his lines and was waiting for prompts that never came.

'Did you ever think about not keeping me? The baby, I mean, before you knew it was me?'

'Not for a moment,' Gina answered quickly and truthfully. She remembered how her sisters, while shell-shocked at her news, became excited in spite of themselves. It was good news where there had only been bad and their girlish positivity began to rub off on Gina. Nicholas Miller had urged her to consider the possibility of adoption a few weeks later, as if he had only then realized the full import of what she'd told him in the lodge's living room where she had stood trembling with anxiety about the moment and the future.

'You're only a girl and you can have any amount of babies. There are older people out there, married people, who'd only love the chance of a child. Tell me you'll think about it, Gina. For your sake but for this baby too.'

But she wouldn't repeat his words now to Sadie because she might think badly of her grandfather and that would be unfair. As a parent herself she knew she might say exactly the same thing if faced with Sadie in a similar situation. Age had only added to the confusion of life rather than taking from it as she had imagined it would. Neither would she defend herself with the response she had given him. 'But not this baby, Daddy. I'll never have this baby again.' Instead she proceeded to tell her story as she drove through the slate-coloured mountains and toward the sea where they would finally have to stop and she would have to look into Sadie's eyes and see clearly what damage had been done.

'By the time I found out I was pregnant Ciaran had gone off to college and his family moved back to England shortly after so he wasn't even back here at weekends. He was out of the picture completely and I never told anyone what had happened between us. It was one thing left to me that no one could have an opinion about because nobody knew. Matthew was brilliant when Mammy died, so kind and so good, though it can't have been much fun hanging around here with me where if I wasn't crying I was comforting one of the others who were. Everyone, including Matthew himself, presumed he was the father when I found out I was pregnant. I never thought any different. You were just a little over five pounds when you were born and the doctor wasn't sure if you were a couple of weeks premature or just a teensy little thing and I could only guess at the dates. But none of that was important anyway because what mattered was that you'd arrived and you were perfect.'

'So Matthew stood by you from the beginning?'

'Well, not exactly. Dad kind of made it plain that he didn't think Matthew was good enough for one of his daughters. I'm not even sure he thought that really, though he could be dreadfully snobby, but I think it was his heavy-handed way of trying to make sure we didn't rush into getting married just because I was having you. He wanted me to stay on at Tobar Lodge and it was my home so I wanted to stay there. I didn't want to live with anyone else. Besides, we didn't have a bean so there was no point in us thinking of branching out. One step at a time, Daddy used to say, and I'd neither the will nor the gumption to rebel. I was already handling as much change as I could manage.

'Matthew got a driving job on the continent and he was back and forth until after you were born but we weren't really together much after that. We saw each other and talked but neither of us had a clue what to do next. I was overwhelmed with minding you and had no time to nurture a relationship, wouldn't have had a clue how. He was a good father to you any time he was around; I couldn't have asked for better. He brought home the odd outfit for you from his trips. Some of them were frightful-looking old-fashioned things with shiny bows and big sailor collars with god-awful matching hair bands that I never let you wear. Lottie and Rachel clubbed together to buy you far nicer things. God knows where he got them but he meant well. Matthew always meant well.'

'So how come he ended up living with us in Melbourne Terrace if you and he had broken up?'

'That was later. I got the flat when you were a little over two years old. Rachel left for college and Lottie was having a great old life in Dublin so I moved out of home trying to prove that I could be independent too. Besides, I thought town might be better for you then with the playground and other children on the street to play with. Dad protested a lot and made it plain that we would always be welcome back to the lodge at any stage. He missed you so much. Missed me too, I suppose, but you really got under his skin. Loved that you were called after Mammy, didn't even seem to mind when I chose Sadie over Sarah because it suited you so much,' Gina explained. While she spoke she recalled how her father had told her that at first he thought he would never again get used to the noise of a small child in the lodge. By the time they left he hated the oppressive silence they left behind and he missed the squealing company of his toddling grand-daughter intent on following his every move.

But Gina found she had needs of her own that could not be satisfied in her father's house. 'I wanted a home that was just yours and mine and I turned that flat into a little palace. Little of course being the operative word. Granddad Miller would wolf his dinner down when he came to us on a Sunday so that he could take you out for a walk along the river. Wasn't good for a child to be cooped up somewhere so small, he used to say, and that drove me up the wall. I mean we were out and about all the time when we lived in Melbourne Terrace and he made it sound like I was holding you prisoner there.'

'I loved living there. I remember Matthew a little but mostly I remember the two of us curled up on the couch watching television and me making you watch things with me. Do you remember *The Beachcombers* every evening at half five? Never thought of it as small at all until we moved to the lodge and it was so massive by comparison.'

'Me too but I'd managed to block out *The Beachcombers*,' Gina said wistfully, thinking back to a life which, though appearing difficult at the time, seemed utterly straightforward now. Each day would be safely packed away when her daughter's body gave into dreamy sleep in the small bedroom down the hallway from her own.

'So when and how did you and Matthew get back together?'

'He came back to Ireland and had a go setting up a courier company. Rachel and Lottie used to compete about babysitting you when they were home at weekends and I just started to see more and more of Matthew and we kind of fell back together. He was brilliant with you. Playful, acting the eejit on the floor, making those chunky wooden puzzles over and over again and never losing his patience even when I was going mad about the mess you two always made. It helped that he was just a big kid himself. He stayed living in his brother's house out the Saltway Road at first but eventually he moved in with us. No big decision, it just happened gradually. It seemed like things had taken their own sweet time to right themselves but they were right and that was all that mattered.'

'So why did you go and tell him about what happened with Ciaran? It seems to have ruined everything.'

The blatant question took Gina's breath away. Why indeed? It had been a long time since she had tortured herself about the issue. 'Rachel got together with Ciaran in Dublin in a whirlwind romance, brought him home to the lodge to meet Dad after a few weeks. Friends introduced them, knowing that they had both lived in Tobarnaree at one stage or another. They were just totally serious about one another from the get-go. Confusion and guilt started to well up in me until I thought I was going to choke. I couldn't believe he was back when I had him so firmly in my past. Matthew was delighted to meet up with Ciaran again and they were drinking together any Saturday night when Ciaran and Rachel were in Tobarnaree for the weekend. I felt I had to tell Matthew what had happened, that anything else wouldn't be fair. Of course I didn't have to do any such thing. I could've kept my mouth shut and maybe we'd all have been better off. Certainly feels that way now.'

The car chugged over the rough gravel roadway to the strand and Gina found a convenient space just next to the walkway through the dunes that led on to the beach. A horsewoman on an early canter and an elderly couple walking a pair of dogs were the only others out and about on a cold and snappy morning. 'Do you want to go for a walk? A bit of air might be nice?' Gina suggested, thinking they could both do with it, but her daughter was brimming with questions and had no interest in leaving the car until they had all been asked and answered.

'When you said this morning that Matthew had chosen to believe I wasn't his, what exactly did you mean?'

'Matthew tried to persuade your Granddad Miller to invest in his courier company. He had a crew of banged-up vans on the road and he thought he would surely get more business if everything was newer and sharper-looking. I think hanging around with Ciaran again made him restless because Ciaran was so obviously on the up career-wise. Ambition has always just been like breathing to him whereas until then Matthew had been happy with a small operation to call his own. He'd a brand-new fleet in mind and all he lacked was a financial backer. The bank wouldn't bite on a big plan for a business with such a small turnover. I warned him he was barking up the wrong tree with my dad, who was old-fashioned about things like that. Money had to be earned and not just handed out whenever you fancied it and he was adamant that he wasn't going to remortgage the lodge to raise cash for anyone. The old arguments came trotting out about my dad not thinking Matthew was good enough for me and if Ciaran Jacob came knocking looking for a dig-out it would've been a different story – but of course Ciaran would've died before he would ask my dad for anything, just wouldn't have been his style.'

'So he left because of that?' Sadie asked, trying to gauge if her mother was telling her the full story.

'He seemed to get a huge chip on his shoulder about Ciaran and after that nothing I said made any difference. I could have begged Daddy for the money for him and I didn't do that. Just didn't want to get involved, which made him think I was disloyal, but he didn't seem to understand there were other people to whom I owed loyalty. My point was if the bank wouldn't give it maybe Daddy shouldn't give it either and that hurt Matthew's pride; he said on top of everything else I didn't believe in him. So you see I think he chose to believe you weren't his because he wanted to leave me and he wanted it to be my fault. After that he kept saying he couldn't forget what had happened between myself and Ciaran. If Daddy had given him the money he might have stayed I think but I don't know.' Gina exhaled a heavy sigh and fiddled with the car keys that dangled in the ignition. Keys to the lodge and the Lime Tree hung there too: all the places she spent her life.

'Did you love Matthew?' Sadie asked earnestly.

Gina coloured a little. She hated discussing her feelings as a rule and it felt plain odd to be talking about what had happened with Matthew after all this time. She had gained confidence from its concealment and such assuredness was ebbing away under her daughter's sharp scrutiny. 'I'm sure I did. I loved the safety of him. He was a good man. There were things that drove me mad of course about him when we lived together but I'm such a neat freak that wasn't surprising. Matthew preferred things more random and was always complaining when I insisted on tidying around him, but mostly we got on well enough. I loved what him being around meant for you. I felt I was able to give you back what I'd cheated you out of in the first place. I missed him when he was gone but as time went on I realized that I could survive alone and moving to Tobar Lodge was both the scariest and best thing I ever did. Do you understand? I know it's hard to because I can barely get my head around it myself and I have been living with it all these years.'

'Why all the letters at first and then nothing? I don't understand why he would keep in frantic contact telling you where he was living from year to year and then nothing at all. Unless Jessica only found some of the letters and there's more? Did something else happen?'

'No, it appears the nosy little wretch found everything. I looked through them when you were down at the lake with Ben this morning. From what I can see every single letter is there,' Gina said, imagining what she would do to Jessica if she got her hands on her. 'Matthew cut off all contact when Granddad died and left me the lodge. He just couldn't handle it, said it proved everything he'd ever believed: that Nicholas Miller was a stuck-up, snobby bastard who'd only hand over the cash when he was safely out of the picture, and that I was a coward who went along with him. Said he'd had the power to change our lives for the better years before and he had chosen not to do so.' An angry phone call late one night after her father had died but before Gina had left Melbourne Terrace for Tobar Lodge was the last she had heard from Matthew.

'Do you think he was right about Granddad?' Sadie asked, trying hard to take in all that she had been told.

'Maybe a little bit. As I say he could be snobby but I don't really blame Daddy. Tobar Lodge has been in the Miller family for generations. He had to sell off some of the farm to the Corrigans when he ran into problems paying back bank loans. I think until the last minute he thought he might turn the fortunes of the place around. That's why he did up the cottages and tried to get that business off the ground when anyone his age had been winding down for years. He didn't hold on to Tobar Lodge until the end to spite Matthew or any one of us, he held on to it because it was his life and he wanted to put right what had gone wrong while he was in charge. I think he felt it would mean more to you and me rather than anyone else because we lived in Tobarnaree and that's why he gave it to me. If Matthew had stayed with us there's no reason to think that his will wouldn't have been exactly the same but by then it was too late and too much had happened.'

Sadie felt the vibrating alert of her phone against the flesh of her stomach. She took it out and read Ben's message relating its content to her mother. 'He's wondering if all's quiet on the western front?'

'What are you going to tell him?'

'I'm going to tell him that we're going for an early lunch and I'll see him later when you've answered any other question that I might have roaming around in my head.'

'OK.' Gina allowed herself to be a little relieved that her daughter was still talking even though the conversation was likely to remain difficult for some time yet.

'Can I ask you something?' Sadie asked suddenly as they wandered the short distance along Strand Lane into the village.

'Fire away,' Gina replied, a little amused that her daughter should at last think to ask permission for a single fragment of the morning's formidable interrogation.

'Did you love Ciaran too?'

Gina did her best to put herself back in the mind of her teenage self so that she could explain her feelings to her daughter in a way that would make sense. 'I had a lovely time with Ciaran that neither of us planned. We didn't mean to hurt anyone. It saved me at a time when I thought I was going mad with sadness and confusion but it's impossible to love someone, Sadie, if you don't have a relationship with them. I'll always be fond of Ciaran and I think I allowed myself to have a crush on him for a little while afterward. But, no, I didn't love him.'

'You're a dark horse, Mam.'

'I'm just a girl who happens to be your mammy too.'

Sadie settled into a booth seat in the café across from the church; it had been smartened up since their previous visit. She left the ordering of food to her mother because that was their pattern, Gina slow to rescind the mother role even when they were out and about. Besides, sitting alone for a moment gave Sadie plenty of time to enjoy a few messages to and fro with Ben.

'Don't put vinegar on the chips, Mam, or I'll puke,' Sadie instructed when her mother brought the shared plate to the table to go with their toasted sandwiches, which were still in the making behind the glass-domed counter.

'I'll put a neat spray of vinegar on the handful of chips I'm going to eat so don't worry, I won't contaminate your share,' Gina replied, hardly knowing if she was hungry or not, though it seemed sensible to eat something.

Sadie's nose wrinkled in mock disgust. 'Just keep it away from mine.'

When her delayed hunger had been sated Sadie struck again with a question that tore into Gina's heart. 'Do you regret having me? Having a baby, I mean? There's plenty reason to really when you think about it. I mean you must be bitter about missing college and ending up in Tobarnaree without any real choice in the matter. I wouldn't hold it against you if you blame me for the way your life turned out.' She dipped a chunk of cold chip into the sketchy pool of ketchup on her plate before ramming it into her mouth – attempting nonchalance, as if whatever her mother's answer might be it could not faze her in the slightest way.

Gina thought for a moment before she spoke, knowing what

she said now would lie between them for ever. 'I didn't come on this earth ready to be a mother, Sadie. When I had you I didn't have the first clue what being a mother entailed. How could I? I was just somebody's treasured little girl who ended up crazily out of her depth. So I can't say that at times I didn't feel sorry for myself and maybe imagined how things might be different but I made choices and with choices come responsibility. What I gave myself credit for a long time ago is that I did my best and I count you as the best thing I've done. So, no, I don't regret having you because you're my life and there's nothing for which I would swap the experience of having you. Nothing at all.' She reached across the polished sheen of the wooden table, pushing the salt and pepper cellars out of her way, and wrapped the softness of her daughter's hand in the firmness of her own. Finally, the tears that Sadie had fought back the length of the journey from Tobarnaree appeared at the corners of her eyes despite her wilful efforts to blink them away.

When they arrived back late that afternoon from Aughasallagh Sadie asked to be let off at the lodge. Ben had texted her to say he was there clearing out the mess that Jessica had left in her room to save either of their mothers the thankless job. Gina watched through the open passenger window as her daughter disappeared around the gable end of the lodge, ducking inside the back door to dodge a sudden shower. Only when she had disappeared did Gina pull away.

She felt worn out by the day they had spent together but relieved that Sadie had been talkative on the way home. What Sadie had learned about her mother's life had clearly shaken her but Gina was hoping that it wasn't too optimistic to think that their relationship had sufficient strength to deal with the revelations. Gina had asked her daughter to promise that she wouldn't say anything to Rachel or Lottie. 'They don't know and that's the way I want it to stay, do you understand? It wouldn't achieve anything now except maybe upsetting Rachel when she doesn't deserve it and giving Lottie means for mischief which she really doesn't deserve.'

Sadie shrugged her shoulders and offered a lazy 'whatever'. It was a phrase that usually drove Gina to quiet distraction but now she welcomed the couldn't-care-less detachment it signalled.

Her daughter had wondered aloud about the possibility of tracking down Matthew after all the time that had passed and Gina offered to help her do that if that's what she wanted, while warning her that he could well have another family now who might know nothing about the life he had lived with them in Ireland, so she should proceed gently.

'I know that and maybe I won't look for him at all. I haven't decided yet,' Sadie retorted. Then, with a hint of humour that her relieved mother appreciated, she went on: 'Maybe he feels entitled to have his secrets but I guess you can't always count on secrets staying exactly where you leave them.'

'No, indeed you cannot,' Gina replied.

Gina had just put a mug of sweet tea to her lips when Ellen Carter bustled through the door of Beech Cottage, dripping with obsequious apologies for her daughter's transgression. 'She'd no right to go through your private things. I'm thoroughly ashamed of her and appalled that she would take such a liberty while in your house. You must be so cross.'

'Look, the harm done is hardly your fault, Ellen, but I'm glad that your daughter's taken it upon herself to go home. I've never had to evict someone from Tobar Lodge but I'd have relished getting your Jessica to pack her bags.'

'Well, you'll be rid of me very shortly too which you'll be glad about, I guess.'

'But you're staying until the end of the month?' Gina asked, confused and desperately wanting to be able to close the door and stretch out on the couch for half an hour to rest her exhausted body. Thoughts of sleep were hopeless, she knew, but she was certain she didn't have an iota left to give anyone after the shattering time she had endured.

'Oh, I can't possibly stay under the circumstances. Besides, I really should go home and see that Jessica is all right. I've rung her father but Jack being Jack he couldn't make a commitment that he would be there to keep more than a very casual eye on her and Jess needs stricter supervision than that as you can appreciate.'

Gina was unable to summon her normal good and gentle manners. She was exasperated and it showed. 'For God's sake, why should she get away with ruining your holiday on top of everything else? And is Ben going too? I'm in enough trouble with Sadie already. She'll never forgive me if Ben goes home earlier than planned.'

'Wild horses wouldn't drag Ben away from this place until his ticket expires. I wouldn't even suggest he come with me. He's been so sweet to me all day, couldn't do enough for me, beseeching me not to worry about his sister. But he's been watching his cell phone as if his life depended on it waiting for Sadie to say she was on her way back here.'

Gina relaxed a little, thinking at least one disaster had been averted. 'I wish you'd stay, Ellen, for your own sake but also for mine because to be brutally honest I don't want to have to refund you the money that you paid me for renting the lodge. I need it and you, if you don't mind me saying, need a break from your thankless daughter. So stay and finish your holiday. You deserve that at least.'

'My mind's made up, I'm afraid. I've just been online booking a ticket home. You're absolutely right, a bit of neglect might be exactly what Jessica needs but old habits die hard. I'm a fussy mother and there's not the slightest chance I'll change at this stage. I fly Aer Lingus out of Shannon on Sunday evening and I'll be home some unthinkable time when dawn is about to break. And please don't give the holiday rental fee a second thought. These things are always non-refundable. If you'll have me I'll be back next year – I'd like to stay in one of your cottages for a week or two. My needs and means will have shrunk significantly by then so were you to offer a discount I'd graciously accept.'

'No problem at all. Did the lodge live up to your high expectations?' Gina asked, relieved that the money wasn't going to be an issue because she had already mentally spent it all.

'Your home is lovely but without you and your daughter in it, it's merely a house. You need to go back to where you come from and so do I. Some of us take a little longer than others to work out where we'll finally call home and I've certainly taken my time.'

'Well, I'd love to see you back next year as long as you don't bring your daughter with you,' Gina said, trying not to be hurtful but making a non-negotiable point all the same.

Ellen flashed an indulgent smile. 'I've holidayed with my daughter for the last time in a while, I imagine. I'll probably be invited along for babysitting duties in a decade or two if I'm lucky. Next year I imagine I'll be travelling alone so save me a cottage, won't you? I'll email you with dates. I fancy being just me for a while. Just Ellen.'

Chapter Twenty

Rachel, against Ciaran's grumpy will it seemed to Lottie, had organized a get-together with Emmet and Jill in their cottage to discuss the difficulty of their shared business dealings over a glass of wine. When Lottie popped her head inside the door Orla and Billy were protesting loudly at having to go to bed early when it was still bright and there were so many games they could play outside. When Lottie offered to cancel her night out and mind the children in her cottage Rachel was having none of her kind intentions.

'One night of their holidays I need them to be in bed early: they can surely do that for me after everything I do for them. Tonight's important, so Orla and Billy, go to bed. *Now*.' At that point in Rachel's snappy sermon Lottie had held her hands up in surrender and reversed out of her sister's way, winking at her niece and nephew as they scampered to bed knowing that the game was up and their frazzled mother had won the night.

From the sulky look of Ciaran hunched over his laptop as if his life depended on ingesting the contents of its screen, it seemed to Lottie that he was taking his wife's interference in their finances badly. Lottie felt like telling him to smarten up and be grateful for Rachel's charitable understanding of his shite business sense, but not having time for a full thrash-out of the evidence she thought it prudent to hold her tongue.

Lottie didn't find things much better at Beech Cottage where Gina had settled in to all-picture-and-very-little-sound mode and Sadie it seemed had once again bunked off with Ben. No, nothing wrong as such. No idea why Jessica had gone home suddenly. 'But you must know,' Lottie said, unable to conceal her scepticism at the sparseness of her sister's account. 'Ben has to have told Sadie?'

'Maybe he did but Sadie and I don't tell each other everything. Jessica's gone. Ellen's following her on Sunday. End of story.' Gina's curt tone made it plain that she wasn't in the mood for discussing the Carters – or anything else for that matter.

Lottie watched her sister as she fussed with tourist board information leaflets that were strewn in great numbers on the kitchen table, making resolute efforts to appear heavily involved in an essential task. 'Well, in case anyone's wondering I'm going out for the night and there's my spin arriving now,' she said, gesturing to the dimmed headlights of Theo's jeep that had pulled to a sluggish halt outside the cottages.

'Out with Theo, is it?' Gina asked, willing to engage at last. She extended to her full tiptoe height in order to catch a glimpse of whoever had just driven in. 'Where are ye off to?'

'I couldn't possibly say, darling. Doesn't do to divulge every single detail as you well know,' Lottie delivered with considerable glee as she waltzed out the door and climbed into the passenger seat that Theo cleared roughly for her by landing its stray contents into the footwell. As they drove out the gate of Tobar Lodge, Lottie thought to herself that there was always a point in these summer weeks together when she realized she'd seen quite enough of her family and this evening's epiphany had been crystal clear. She looked forward to fresh company and even thought she might be missing Dublin and the Gaslight a little bit.

'I thought you were taking me out for dinner?' she quizzed tetchily when Theo's pick-up took the turn for the rough avenue up to his parents' old house and his dilapidated caravan instead of onwards to a smart restaurant in the city that she had fondly imagined and taken the time and trouble to dress for.

Theo waited until he had parked in front of the caravan before he answered. 'You're out here, aren't you?' He smiled at her. 'And I'll have you know I've gone to a bit of trouble to get this place ready for you. Having food delivered and everything.'

'Well, if you call sitting outside the prefab portaloo you like to call home *out* then I suppose technically speaking I am, yes, but I thought you meant *out out* when you suggested tonight.' Lottie regretted the effort she had made with her appearance. Still, how was Theo to know she would have been in her fleece pyjamas and furry slippers if she were in for the night at Rowan Cottage? It would do him no harm to think that she insisted on being so well presented always. She would enter into the spirit of the evening whatever that might entail because she needed to extend her sabbatical from her sisters for a little while longer.

When Theo returned from paying the delivery man Lottie couldn't resist a joust. 'Chinese from the takeaway on McCauley Street? New York's done fabulous things for you I have to say, Theo, turned you into a right smooth operator. Everyone from Tobarnaree could do with a stint there. Think what we might learn. How to order dish twenty-six from the Eastern Dragon's wipe-clean menu?' Lottie munched on a handful of prawn crackers from a bowl in the centre of the table.

Theo assured her that the food was excellent, having sampled it earlier in the week. 'Surely everyone loves a good chow mein,' he said as he handed her a foil carton and a fork before turning to the sink draining board from where he grabbed two bottles of beer from a cool box.

When they'd finished eating, and he had forced Lottie to agree that the food was perfectly adequate, Theo reached across and pulled his laptop from where it was perched on a shelf above her head. 'I've brought you here because I want to show you something.'

'Oh do tell,' Lottie said, clearing the empty foil trays to the worktop without ever having to leave her seat. A small but hardly redeeming advantage of living in a tin-can, she decided. 'What've you up your sleeve?'

'I want to hire you as a design consultant for my latest project.'

Lottie rapped on the caravan window and pointed at the farmhouse behind them. 'Look, I don't want to hurt your feelings all over again about that calamity out there but I'm not having a thing to do with it.'

Theo laughed and told her that she didn't have to worry; he and the builder had all that sorted out between them. 'I keep handing him cash and he keeps telling me it'll all be all right in the end. No, I've a bigger plan than all of that,' he said as he turned his laptop screen to her, 'and I think you might be able to help me.'

Lottie listened as he outlined a plan to buy the Lime Tree from his brother. Being familiar with Gina's account of working for him it didn't surprise her to hear that Louis had lost interest in the restaurant. It was all very well while business had been easily got in previous years but he had no interest in changing and reinvesting in order to survive when trade had fallen off. He'd wanted out long before Theo had cheered him enormously by telling him he wanted in.

'And what makes you think that you'd have the first clue how to run the Lime Tree? You know nothing about food, as you've demonstrated admirably tonight with your menu. Start with a few eggs from the hens I'd say, Theo. You're running before you can walk.'

'Thanks for the vote of confidence,' Theo said, his voice dripping with sarcasm but not a shred deterred. 'Firstly, it wouldn't be called the Lime Tree. Forget the place as you know it now. I'll gut the interior, open up the ceiling to double height and flood the ground floor with light. That building is gorgeous, not that you'd ever know the way it's set up now. I want Gina to run the food end of things because in all of Louis's whinging about the food business he's always said that Gina is a wonderful chef and I like the way she quietly gets on with things. She'd have free rein but I want excellence: local meats and cheeses, our own baking, soups and salads. The kitchen will have to be overhauled, of course, because the brother's been nothing short of miserly with equipment. I recognize some of the pots as my mother's. Good wholesome food at keen prices for local people. I mean, Louis hangs out the door waiting for tour buses to fall out of the sky while there's a town full of people that seem not to go near the Lime Tree from one end of the year to the next.'

Theo's enthusiasm was touching and Lottie felt mean bursting his bubble but someone was bound to and she felt it might as well be her. 'There's the tiny issue of a recession, darling. Hardly the time to kick off a great big plan? Downsizing's the buzzword around here and I think we flew in the concept from the States so it's one you should be familiar with. You know, cutting your cloth to suit your circumstances.'

Theo smiled and shook his head and she knew that she might as well have been talking to the wall. 'You see, that's where you're wrong. A good idea's a good idea no matter when you have it. People don't stop living just because there's less money swishing around. If anything they start needing to really live a bit more. This town deserves an excellent place to meet and eat that doesn't cost the earth. The Lime Tree as it stands *will* go to the wall but if we create something that people care about they will spend their money there.'

Lottie shrugged her shoulders and suddenly wondered where she came into Theo Corrigan's grand plan. As if he had read her mind Theo continued, his voice heady with excitement. 'Then I'm going to break out the back wall and convert the storage sheds across Tindal Lane into a gallery and that's where you come in, Lottie. I want a space for local artists and craftspeople to show and sell their work. There's nothing like it for miles around. I want to bring something amazing to Tobarnaree. Will you help me?'

Lottie popped up to the cool box and got them both another beer, taking her time opening them and chucking the bottle caps into the unfinished takeaway food before she turned around to face Theo. Gesturing around them at the caravan walls she asked gently, 'Not being nosy or anything but are you sure you've the means to pull off such a plan? You're not exactly living the magnate life at the moment. From this base your plan seems a touch delusional.'

'Look, I'd a good bit of property in New York, took the signals and got out at the right time so money won't be a problem.'

'Then why in the name of God do you live like this? Rent a house or rent a smart caravan if you've got the cash. They've new-fangled ones with doors that close over and everything.'

'Because I don't give a hoot about that sort of thing. I'll get the house here sorted eventually but my head is buzzing about Tindal Lane. So are you in or are you out?'

'Oh I'm in!' Lottie smiled, taking a generous slug of beer. 'For God's sake, if there's going to be an art gallery of any description in Tobarnaree I simply have to be involved but the Gaslight's my priority 'cause that's how I make my living and pay my bills.'

'Understood.' Theo clinked his beer bottle to hers. They spoke for hours, the beer making Lottie even more chatty than usual. Theo's enthusiasm was infectious and she began to see all sorts of possibilities for Tindal Lane that came tumbling out of her, with Theo telling her to steady on a little when she threatened to lose the run of herself. She shrieked when she checked the time on her phone: 'Sweet divine, it's twenty to three!'

'I've a number for a taxi company here somewhere 'cause I can't chance driving after a half-dozen beers. I'll try and find it,' Theo said, hardly knowing where to start or how the night had flown by.

'Dead right you can't drive but you can walk me home. It's all downhill from here to the lodge; we'll be there in twenty minutes.'

'Grand and don't worry about me climbing the hill back up and hitting the bed as the sun rises. Us Corrigans are made of stern stuff. I'll have to track down a torch or we'll fall into a ditch.'

'Who said anything about you coming home again?' Lottie said while she threw her jacket around her shoulders.

'Charlotte Miller, are you propositioning me?' Theo teased, watching her as she pulled her masses of curls out from under her collar.

'I'm certainly considering it but in the meantime I'm at least making the spare room in Rowan Cottage available. What do you say?' Lottie asked, feeling pleasantly reckless.

'Well, while you're considering your next move I'd be delighted to take up your kind offer. Will there be any chance of a nightcap?' Theo nudged her playfully while he struggled with the rusty lock of the caravan door.

'You never know your luck.' Lottie grabbed his hand in her own and headed for home.

'I think that went well,' Rachel ventured after Ciaran and herself had stood at their cottage door saying goodnight to Emmet and Jill Kinsella. They hadn't stayed long because even though everyone was doing their best the atmosphere had remained somewhat stilted.

'Yeah I suppose,' Ciaran said distractedly, 'though nothing concrete was hammered out.'

'For God's sake, Ciaran, will you take your head out of your arse and be a bit grateful? Emmet Kinsella has more or less offered to take over the mortgages on Ivory Square for at least two years and invest enough money into Jacob Design to keep it afloat. I'd call that something concrete,' Rachel snapped before grabbing the tea towel from the table and setting about clearing the wine glasses and coffee cups into the sink.

'You're right, Rachel, of course you're right. I just wish it all felt better. I know the Ivory Square mortgages are a noose around my neck but having Emmet involved in Jacob Design, in *my* practice, feels like swapping one problem for another. I hate the thought of being bailed out by him, that's all. Did you hear him saying that maybe De Courcey Row premises could be sacrificed for something more modest with a downsized staff? I mean where the hell does he get off telling me what's best for Jacob Design? He's a builder, for God's sake!' Ciaran said, draining his glass.

A builder with money we need, Rachel felt like sniping but she forced herself to say something a little more constructive. 'If he doesn't become involved you'll most likely be saying good-bye to De Courcey Row anyway. I know in an ideal world none of this would be happening but if you have to choose between having Emmet involved or losing the practice entirely surely the choice is clear.'

'Shitty choices both of them in my opinion,' Ciaran offered with considerable petulance before taking a slug from a poured glass of red that Jill had left untouched on the table.

'Some people have none at all so you'll just have to take it on the chin and count yourself lucky,' Rachel retorted. Managing her husband was sometimes more challenging than managing her son and she felt it unfair that it should be so. 'Come on, pour us some more wine and sit out the back with me. We can pretend we're somewhere exotic,' she invited before hustling him out the back door where a wooden table and bench were set up on a quadrant of stone slabs alongside a small covered barbeque.

'I've something else to tell you,' Ciaran announced after a few moments in the silence together. He paused, taking in her aghast expression that there could possibly be something else. 'I'm back on the fags.'

'Well, you may finish the packet you have and give them right back up again. You know I think it's a disgusting habit.'

'Agreed but can I smoke one now?'

'Go on, I suppose so, but you've chipped away big time at the allowances I make for you being under stress so it's time to shape up,' Rachel chided while observing him pull the nearly empty packet from his inside pocket. Ciaran cupped his hands around the cigarette and the lit match illuminated his face fully in the darkness. They agreed he would go back to Dublin on the following Monday and meet up with Emmet and see what could be worked out between them when they were both fully back in work mode. Rachel made him promise to return the following Friday no matter what the week held because the children needed to see him.

'I've ruined your and the kids' holiday with all this,' he said as he stubbed out his cigarette on the patio slab.

'Don't be silly. We're a family: if one of us is down then the other pitches in – that's what loving someone is all about,' Rachel said gently, reaching for his hand across the table. They both turned quickly when they heard Billy launch into a loud whine from the back-door step. Clutching his blue dog and with his pyjama bottoms pulled into a wrong-way-round twist he went into a longwinded explanation of how loudly Orla was snoring. 'I'm sure she couldn't be snoring *that* loudly,' Rachel ventured.

'She *is*, Mammy. Come and listen,' he said, turning back toward his bedroom, expecting her to follow him.

'I'll go,' Ciaran said, holding out his hand to stop Rachel from getting up, 'it's definitely my turn.'

'Thanks, love, and will you bring me out a jumper on the way back? It's bloody freezing here.'

EPILOGUE

Emmet came along the corridor quite startled to see Fionn's bedroom door ajar. He visited the room from time to time taking whatever comfort it could offer and he knew Jill did too but his heart thumped wildly at the thought of finding her there when they had, until now, made sure to go there only when the other was out of the house. He took a deep breath before putting his head around the door. The wardrobe doors were flung open and its contents were spread out in neat piles on the bed: jeans, T-shirts, jumpers and school uniforms lying there as if ready for someone to put them on.

'What are you doing, pet?' he asked gently. Jill spun her head around to face him from where she had sat on the bed looking out the window and by her face he knew she'd been crying. He walked over and plumped down near her on a spare spot on the navy checked duvet.

'There's just no point in holding on to everything, is there?' Jill asked, gesturing at the arranged piles behind them. 'They'll get all musty hanging there through the winter.'

'I guess so but remember the counsellor advised that we should take things gently and maybe clearing all this out is just too much too soon. There's no rush, you know. We can do it together when we're better able to face the job.'

'Oh I know and I've no intention of getting rid of all of it but some might be no harm. I got an email from St Declan's this morning to say that they are starting a uniform exchange programme so I can at least take his uniforms in there. Some child might get a little use out of them. I bought too many of everything and some of it's hardly been worn.'

'I can't believe the school's still sending you emails. I'll get on to them in the morning. A bit of sensitivity wouldn't go astray,' Emmet said but Jill was quick to douse his obvious anger.

'No don't, please. I know it might sound mad and probably is mad but I quite like getting the *Dear Parent* emails. Find it a bit comforting that someone somewhere still refers to me as a parent, even if that someone is a faceless central database in St Declan's Primary. Sad, isn't it?'

'Oh Jill, we are parents. Fionn *did* exist. He was ours.'

'I know, but I find it kind of hurtful that people seem afraid to mention their own children when they're with me as if I might break down in front of them. I went over to Shreve Court to visit Rachel today. Promised I'd keep in touch when we left Tobarnaree and her little fella climbed on to the worktop to scout the cupboard for biscuits. I could see from her face that she thought it would be upsetting to me to see him larking about but it wasn't. Fionn being gone upsets me. Nothing else comes close or ever will.'

'Have you had a chance to think about selling up here?' Emmet enquired, referring to the conversation they'd had a few nights before when they had forced each other and themselves out of the house for a meal that neither had any real appetite to eat. Selling up was the last thing Emmet wanted but he knew they should consider all options; the counsellor had said nothing should be declared out of bounds. He had surprised himself by how evangelical he had become about what the counsellor had to say in their weekly sessions with him. He valued the framework the sessions had afforded them and Jill's continual willingness to attend even though they often drove home in tears silently replaying what had come out of their mouths while in his rooms. Emmet held his breath wondering what Jill's decision might be and willing himself to be strong enough for any response.

After what seemed like an age Jill spoke. 'I never want to leave here.' Emmet allowed himself a sigh of relief and listened intently to what she still had to say. 'You'd think here's where I would be the most lonesome and I am but I panic a little when I'm out of the house and all I can think of is getting back here. This was Fionn's world and if I'm ever to find a piece of him that I can keep I'll surely find it here. Do you understand what I'm saying? Does it make any sense?' she asked earnestly, searching his face for an answer.

'You're the only thing that still makes sense to me,' Emmet said quietly, putting his arm around her shoulder and pulling her close. They stayed there for some time watching the tumult of the sea and mingling their memories of their little boy who not long ago had sat there too.

Tobar Lodge, September 2009

Gina scanned the inside of the car house for the canvas bag of boules she knew was buried deep somewhere at the back of one of the shelves. A middle-aged couple that had arrived at Sycamore Cottage just that morning had expressed an interest in playing the game on the freshly shorn run of grass down by the lake edge. *Whatever floats your boat*, Gina had thought silently to herself while reassuring them that given a while to search she could lay her hands on the set purchased by her father years before. There were golf clubs and tennis racquets listed in the cottages' pastime folder but there was usually little demand. Those sports-minded people that did come to stay were generally keen enough to favour their own equipment. To clear her route around the outhouse Gina stowed away her father's camping chair and the paraffin lamp where she could easily find them if Ben Carter were to visit the following summer as he had promised and wanted to use them again.

He had been gone over a month and although fearful that her daughter would be overcome with melancholy when he left, she had been surprised and heartened by Sadie's resilience. She was buoyed up of course by her giddy plans to visit him the following summer in Boston or for him to come back to Ireland. As they drove home from Shannon airport having left him to his flight she told Gina that they hadn't decided fully who would travel to whom. It would depend on how both their college exams went and what summer work they might be able to find. Sadie explained this ably as if she was utterly familiar with the new grown-up world of student life that she had yet to even taste. Gina prayed that if circumstances were to change their plans to meet again it would be partly Sadie's decision and not merely Ben's alone.

Sadie and Tara had taken off to Dublin to scrutinize places to live in October when they both would start different courses but at the same college. Lottie was charged with being their chaperone and host, a role she had taken to with gusto, and Gina relaxed knowing they couldn't be in better hands. She wanted her daughter to immerse herself in her new life in Dublin and allow Ben Carter to fade somewhat into the background while she adapted and found her feet. Gina imagined he would eventually marry a girl from some prominent family in Connecticut or Maine who skied well, could make his favourite sweet potato bake and whose clothes would pull across slender hips as if it was a challenge to find a size small enough. His handsome face would find a home in family portraits alongside someone maybe more suitable than a plump Irish teenager whose self-confidence he had bolstered for a short few weeks, helping to make her feel good about herself again. But she wouldn't say any of this to Sadie. She would let her girl find out the truth of this for herself because Gina knew that was the only way such things could ever make sense.

She tugged out what she thought might be the green canvas boules case and scraped her hand against a sharp nail jutting outward from the wall. She sucked on her bleeding finger in an effort to heal the sharp pain quickly. She was cursing her clumsy bad luck when she was startled by a man's voice calling to her. 'Gina? You in there? It's me, Ciaran.'

'What brings you here?' Gina asked, stumbling from the height where she had perched herself to search the upper shelves, dragging the heaviness and dust of the boules bag with her. The day was blustery and she hadn't heard his car pull in but behind him now she could see its black nose pitched in close to the lodge's back door.

'Oh, business. Theo Corrigan is going hell for leather on this Tindal Lane Gallery and Meeting House. Wants it ready to trade for Christmas so I got an urgent call to site last night. Builder querying something on the plans. Work's thin on the ground, as you know, so I just hopped in the car and came. If Orla didn't have school, Rachel and the kids might have come too but we don't like taking her out at short notice. Anyway, as I said this morning to Rachel, you might've seen quite enough of us for a while. I think together with the lousy weather we might well have put the kibosh on your whole summer.' He was trying to joke but there was a kernel of sincerity that she appreciated. Both weather and company had not been what she expected.

Gina laughed. 'Don't be so daft. I'll admit that I enjoyed the peace of the first few days when everything was back to normal but I soon missed you all. There's no appropriate distance with my siblings I think: too close and it borders on claustrophobic; too far away and I start to get all maudlin. Besides, with Lottie knee-deep in her plans for Tindal Lane, not to mention for Theo, I think I'll be seeing a lot more of her around here.'

'We didn't even get to have our barbeque this year – a pity, don't you think, seeing as last year's was such a success?' Ciaran quipped.

'Maybe next year,' Gina offered, 'but you can buy cheap burgers to burn this time!'

Gina invited him inside for tea and he said he could manage a quick one before he was due to meet up with Theo on the Tindal Lane site. In the kitchen Gina put the kettle on to boil while she found a plaster for her finger. She set out two mugs, milk and the sugar bowl. He took one spoon in tea, two in coffee and she had a head that memorized such things. She told him she was glad to hear that she wasn't the only one that Theo was tormenting about the progress of Tindal Lane. 'He seems to be in a dreadful hurry. I've already been to a trade auction with him where we bought masses of kitchen equipment for the restaurant and there's not a day goes by that he doesn't drop off another catalogue or a menu that I might like to look at. I hope to God that he gets the place up and running before whatever New York did to him wears off and he turns into the type of Corrigan I'm all too familiar with. I have to say I'm quite looking forward to my new job.'

'So you should be. You'll be brilliant and, much as it pains me to admit it, Lottie will probably be great too as long as the power doesn't go to her head. Rachel says she's almost offended, the only Miller girl not on Theo's star recruiting list for his big venture, but she assures me she'll get over it.' Ciaran reached into his inside pocket and pulled out an envelope, handing it across the kitchen counter to Gina. 'It's the money I owe you for our month in Tobar Rock. I promise it won't bounce this time.'

Gina shook her head as she handed him his mug of tea. 'You needn't think I'm taking that from you. Didn't you hear I've a new job? For once I'm going to be paid well.'

'Gina, please. Two months ago I would've given anything to be able to pay our way. Now I can, so take it. Please.' He held it out to her and Gina took it, folded the envelope and put it behind one of the dinner plates propped on a dresser shelf.

'OK. If you insist. I'm ever so glad it's all working out. You and Emmet have been able to come to some sort of arrangement, Rachel tells me.'

'Yeah, he's given me breathing space and I think – well, I think we'll be grand eventually. Jacob Design has had manners put on it and perhaps that's no bad thing. I've learned the hard way that a little less will do. Emmet's a good man: something I didn't give him credit for when everything was coming down around me and I was in a stupor of self-pity.'

'I hope he and Jill can work things out. They were in such a bad way while they were here. Rachel's told me she speaks to her a bit and that things are improving. It's good for Jill to have Rachel and Lottie in Dublin near her when they know the score.'

'Well, she thinks they're on the right track but it's a slow road, I'm sure. Emmet and I don't dwell on the personal when we talk. I like him but I don't know him and I think it's likely to stay that way. He doesn't give much away. Just keeps on working hard, not that that would tell you anything, I suppose.'

Ciaran enquired about Sadie and Gina told him that as they spoke she and Tara were combing places like Rathmines and

Phibsborough, examining flats that would suit their needs and come in under their strictly allotted budget.

'You'll miss her,' Ciaran offered gently, sensitive to her feelings and not wanting to upset her.

Gina agreed she would but added that mostly she was delighted Sadie was getting the chance to do precisely the course she wanted to do and that Tara was to be her partner in the adventure. 'She's thinking of tracking down Matthew, you know,' she said as lightly as she could manage, giving in to a compulsion to mention his name to Ciaran.

'I see,' he answered and after an uncomfortable pause added: 'Well, it probably wouldn't be that hard if she really wanted to, I suppose. How do you feel about her doing that? I mean he's been gone a long time and all on your own you've turned Sadie into the lovely girl she is. Hard to think where he comes in now when he just upped and left.'

'If finding him is what she wants I'll help her. She might have things to say to him and hear from him and I understand that.'

Ciaran nodded and with a look to the clock over the range motioned that it was time he was on his way. There was a lot yet to do before he could head for home.

As she walked him to his car, the boules bag tucked tightly under her arm ready to leave on the door step of Sycamore Cottage, Ciaran asked if she ever wondered how differently things might have worked out. 'You know, with Matthew and everything?'

And everything. So much echoed in those two brief words. It was the most he had ever said about the experience they had secretly shared and yet she knew exactly what he meant. Gina thought of all the different answers she might have given since the last time they'd stood so totally alone in the shadow of the lodge and she was glad he hadn't asked her until now. 'No, Ciaran, I don't. Whatever happened for whatever reason I know this is who I am and here's where I was meant to be.' When he was gone, his tyres crunching satisfyingly on the avenue gravel, she took a moment to go back to the car house to close over the wooden double-doors and secure the stiff bolt. There was much that could be cleared from there, but it was a job that could wait for another day.

Acknowledgements

Special thanks to my editor Lauren Hadden, whose gentle guidance has made *Come This Way Home* a better book. It's been a pleasure to work with you and I am grateful for your insight and constant good humour. I wish you every success and happiness in your new role. Eoin McHugh at Transworld Ireland is one of the calmest people I know and manages to make the publishing process seem relatively effortless and serene when it's probably neither. So thank you, Eoin, for your help and kindness. Thanks also to Katrina Whone, Kate Tolley and Jessica Broughton at Transworld Publishers for putting the book through the final stages of production. Everyone at Gill Hess has been incredibly professional and pleasant to deal with. Simon, Declan, Helen, Eamon and Nigel – huge thanks to you all for being so good at what you do.

I am lucky to be a member of two libraries in Ashbourne and Garristown. On one Saturday close to the deadline for this book I found myself writing some of the last chapters in Ashbourne library where I was offered kind encouragement, mugs of coffee and chocolate biscuits. Believe me, it's a potent combination! To the staff of both libraries I wish you heartfelt thanks.

Thanks also to the feisty women of my book club who are always ready to raise a glass or two in honour of a book. They are quite the cheerleading team. New York surely won't know what hit it.

Thanks to all the gang on our summer weeks at Shean Lodge in Mayo. The first round in Cleary's is mine this summer. And to the lodge itself, an inspiration where stories lurk in every corridor. If those walls could talk!

Thanks to friends and family who read early drafts and chapters and offered their feedback and comments, particularly Siobhan who always made me feel like I could finish this book on days when I felt sure I couldn't. I apologize for the sporadic bouts of whining into my coffee in the Seamus Ennis Centre. You're a bit of a gem, Flynn. Esther and Fiona were always ready with a pep talk or much-needed humour when the going was tough. Thanks, girls.

I owe love and gratitude to my parents, Mary and Michael Lyons, who taught me what home could be, and to Pat, Nora and Brendan for their good humour and loyal support. It means a lot. Joan Gough held the fort some afternoons and brought me lots of tea while I sat at the computer and made things up. I am sincerely grateful for your help.

My lovely girls Eva and Amy seem to be coping well with the disappointment that their mammy has written another book with absolutely no pictures. Thanks to you both for the endless supply of hugs and distractions. Thanks to Robert, our no-fuss new son, who came along and made us feel like he has always been here. I'll be hiding my laptop from you for a little while yet, Robert.

Huge thanks are due to Noel Gough, who kept me going when I was fit to give up with plenty of positive words of encouragement and more than the odd glass of wine to steel my resolve. I could not have written either book without your loving support and I am sorry for wrecking your head about what my characters might do next. Thanks for running the whole show while I scribbled like a mad woman upstairs. You are the very best.

Finally, I appreciate the enthusiasm and good will of the many booksellers who put books into the hands of readers every day, and thank you to each and every reader who told me how much they enjoyed *Barefoot Over Stones*. Hearing what you think makes every word worthwhile. Here's *Come This Way Home*. I do hope you like her.

Liz Lyons is a graduate of Trinity College Dublin. After graduation she spent ten years working in the Irish book trade. Born in Cork in 1970, she lives in Co. Meath with her husband, son and two daughters. *Come This Way Home* is her second novel.